I DID SOMETHING BAD

I DID SOMETHING BAD

PYAE MOE THET WAR

ST. MARTIN'S GRIFFIN
NEW YORK

First published in the United States by St. Martin's Griffin, an imprint of St. Martin's Publishing Group

I DID SOMETHING BAD. Copyright © 2024 by Moe Thet War. All rights reserved. Printed in the United States of America. For information, address St. Martin's Publishing Group, 120 Broadway, New York, NY 10271.

www.stmartins.com

Designed by Gabriel Guma

The Library of Congress Cataloging-in-Publication Data is available upon request.

ISBN 978-1-250-33051-2 (trade paperback)
ISBN 978-1-250-33052-9 (ebook)

Our books may be purchased in bulk for promotional, educational, or business use. Please contact your local bookseller or the Macmillan Corporate and Premium Sales Department at 1-800-221-7945, extension 5442, or by email at MacmillanSpecialMarkets@macmillan.com.

First Edition: 2024

10 9 8 7 6 5 4 3 2 1

For KHS, who has never let me down, not once

I DID SOMETHING BAD

One

W hat?"

I'm glad I haven't taken the sip of wine I was going for, because I would've definitely just spat it across the table cinematic-style. And spitting red wine on the editor in chief of *Vogue Singapore* who is conveniently wearing an all-white Gucci pantsuit is very low on the list of things I want to do today (or, you know, ever).

Clarissa Song's berry-red lips part once more as she repeats, "I want you to do the Tyler Tun cover story," with as much casualness as though she's just informed me of the way she had her eggs for breakfast this morning.

"The—" With slightly trembling hands, I *do* take a sip, but only because otherwise my dry mouth isn't going to form any words. Formulating a coherent response as I swallow, I place my glass back down beside my untouched Caesar salad and try to hide the fact that I can feel my heartbeat inside my ears. "You want *me*. For the. Tyler Tun. Cover story."

Clarissa nods, holding up her fork as she chews on *her* forkful of salad. At least one of us is able to eat right now. "Yes." She nods again and swallows. "We have an exclusive. He'll do the usual publicity tour closer to the movie release date, but while he's shooting on location here in Yangon, we're the only outlet who has access. Obviously, all the Asia offices fought over it, but you know me—" She puts another forkful of greens into her mouth, letting her wink finish the sentence. Because I do know her—*everyone* in the Asian media network knows her—and I know how the sentence ends: *I always get what I want.*

Which prompts me to ask the obvious with as much tactfulness as I can summon: "And you want . . . me? To . . . write it?"

"Well, obviously it'll be more than just *writing.*" She laughs. "He's in town for almost two months—"

"I thought shooting was only a month?" I had just read an article on this very topic a couple of days ago.

"Yes, but he's arriving a week earlier and staying behind for two weeks after filming's wrapped up. Wants to spend time with his mother's side of the family here. And he's all yours for the approximate two months."

I frown, wondering if it doesn't seem a *tiny* bit invasive to be shadowing someone whom *Rolling Stone* recently called "the busiest human being in the world" when he's specifically carved out personal time to spend with his family. But then again, I'm sure he would've said no if he weren't on board. It is Tyler Tun, after all.

Clarissa is still talking. "You'll have a company card. Charge whatever you'd like. Taxis. Food. Clothes if you feel like you need a new wardrobe. Flights if you need to follow him around the country. Trail him. You'll get him from nine A.M. 'til five P.M. or whenever he leaves set. Whichever is later. Except for Sundays. Nothing on Sundays."

"I—"

I am swiftly reminded that you don't cut off Clarissa Song. She continues like she didn't notice a thing. "It's a weird setup, I'll admit, but it's all in the contract. What I want you to focus on is *him*. I'm sure I don't need to explicitly clarify what a big deal this is. Learn his favorite breakfast. If he has a running playlist. If he does, who's his most-played artist? He has a private plane, but when he flies commercial, does he like the aisle or window seat? Is he a cat person? Dog person? Hamster person? Anything. Everything. Two months may seem like a lot, but you won't get any chances for follow-up questions. Learn"—she leans forward to emphasize—"*everything*. By the time this profile comes out, I want you to know Tyler Tun better than his own parents. I want you to know if America's favorite golden boy flosses every night, and if he does, I want you to know his favorite brand of floss."

I nod, and, because at this point Clarissa's finished half her salad—while I *think* I've had a cherry tomato?—I take a small bite off of my plate. I'm equal parts intrigued and terrified. I wonder if asking this next question will essentially be me shooting myself in the foot, but in the end, my curiosity wins out. "And . . . why me?"

Clarissa sits back, a small smirk curling one side of her lips. It's not a *mean* smirk, but more an *I thought you might ask that* smirk. "Because," she says, one perfectly microbladed eyebrow rising, her answer prepped and ready to go. "We needed the best of the best of the best. Not just the best, or the best of the best. The best. Of the best. Of the *best*."

But I've never done a celebrity profile before.

When Clarissa's eyes narrow and she says, "And yes, I know you've never done a celebrity profile before," I move slightly back. Did I say that out loud? No, I didn't. Did I? No. I didn't. "But every time we've worked together, you've arguably been the most professional journalist I've collaborated with, and I need someone who will be professional about this and not lose their mind over the fact that it's Tyler Tun," she says, and fear and flattery collide head-on inside my stomach. Because I'm not necessarily "losing my mind" over the fact that I'm being handed a Tyler Tun profile, but I'm only human, which means that I'm also not *not*.

I inhale. Professional. I am professional, and composed, and definitely listening to what Clarissa's still saying.

"Additionally, here's the thing about journalism, Khin. I used to work with Neil Gaiman, back when he was a journalist, and to paraphrase something he always said, in order to be a *good* journalist, you only have to fulfill two of three criteria: your writing is good, you file on time, you're fun to work with. If your work is good and you file on time, people won't mind if you're an utter asshole." Out of the corner of my eye, I catch the elderly couple at the next table shoot Clarissa a dirty look, but either Clarissa doesn't notice or she doesn't care (probably the latter). She continues, raising a second finger. "If your work is good and you're generally pleasant to work with, people will forgive you for missing deadlines. If you're pleasant to work with and you always meet your deadlines, people won't care if you're not *the* best writer in the game."

"I see. And which category do I fall into?"

"That's the thing. I had my assistant track down every editor you've ever worked with, and I personally rang each and every one of them."

"You did?" I don't know why I ask such an inane question, because of course she did.

"My reputation is on the line, Khin. I had staff writers and editors begging me to take them off of their previously assigned celebrity profiles so they could have this one. I said no, of course. But I also wasn't going to hand over this assignment to just anyone."

"And what did my editors say? Which category did I fall into?" I repeat. I mimic her smirk because I know that if there's one thing that impresses Clarissa Song, it's bold, unapologetic confidence. "Do I want to know?"

"You checked all three," she says, tilting her chin upward.

I'm taken aback by her answer but am also conscious not to let my surprise show. Instead, I return a smile that conveys something along the lines of *That's not surprising to hear, but thank you very much for the compliment.*

Clarissa pauses before she speaks again, her eyes scrutinizing my reaction. Most people would try to be subtle about it, but not Clarissa. Then again, I suppose if I'm going to be profiling one of the most famous actors in the world, she has to make sure I'm good under pressure. When she's seemingly satisfied with whatever it is she was testing me for (or with), she says, "I needed a journalist who checked all three. If even one editor had had one complaint, your name would've been crossed off the list. But you're always polite, always file ahead of time, and you have an astounding way with words."

There's something so finite and assertive in her tone that it zaps me out of my daze, like she's reached across the table and slapped me.

I have this job. Clarissa Song wouldn't have wasted her time traveling here if she didn't have something major (and official) to say. This isn't an interview, or her asking me to file a writing sample. I've got this job already. And I need to start acting like it. "Was it a long list?" I ask.

Judging by the grin that overtakes her face, my recovered boldness is what she was waiting for. "I'm not concerned with the rest of the list. I tossed it in the trash weeks ago." A beat. "You *are* taking this assignment." She doesn't pretend to phrase it as a question. I don't think it ever occurred to her that I might say no.

"When do I start?"

"He lands in two weeks. Private flight. Everyone's going to think he's flying in from Singapore that evening."

"But he's not."

Clarissa takes her time chewing another mouthful of salad, savoring the Caesar dressing, which I must concede is—as she noted when she ordered it on my behalf—*decadent* and the right balance of creamy and sweet. "No." She blots her lips with the napkin on her lap. "He'll be landing a full twelve hours earlier."

"Do you want me to email you my rates?"

A chuckle ripples out of her throat. "Your pay is already written in the contract, which has been sitting in your inbox since the moment you walked into this restaurant. But trust me, you won't need to negotiate," she says, and thrusts her hand into the space above our plate of shared potato wedges between us. "Are you in?"

I'm about to grasp her hand but pause just before my fingertips lift off of the table edge. "I want fifteen percent more." I say it before I can chicken out.

Clarissa's reaction is the closest I've ever seen her come to being ruffled. "You haven't seen the number."

"I make it a rule to always ask for more money." I shrug. "Nothing personal."

"And you want . . . fifteen percent more?"

"Yes."

"Than what's already in the contract."

"Yes."

One side of her lip quirks up. "I don't remember you being this bold last time we worked together."

I give another shrug. "I hadn't been doing this for six years last time we worked together. And also, *that* hadn't been a cover story."

Without so much as an apologetic hand raise, she starts laughing. *Oh fuck.* Was that too much? I suppose she could still rescind the offer if she—

"Khin Haymar, you are absolutely perfect for this job," she says. My relieved smile halts when she adds, "And I'm starting to think not just for *this* job."

"What do you mean?" I feel like I'm in the middle of a game I hadn't realized had started, like a media-themed, slightly less fatal version of *Squid Game*. And I somehow seem to be almost winning even though I don't know what the rules are, if there are any rules.

Clarissa's eyes gleam once more, as though she can see a hurtling train that I have no clue is about to hit me. "We might have an opening coming up."

"An opening?"

"A job opening."

I blink twice. "At *V*—"

"Yes." She nods. "One of our reporters *might* be transferring to Hong Kong soon. And I *might* already be looking at possible candidates to replace them. And if somebody—someone bold and tenacious and unyielding—if they were to get me a *good* story on a big Hollywood star, well, then I don't see how on earth anyone could object to me offering them the role."

I swallow. I'd come to this lunch expecting—well, I wasn't expecting anything specific, really (you learn quickly that Clarissa is full of surprises). But it had *not* been a Tyler Tun cover story *and* a (potential) role at *Vogue Singapore* within the span of ten minutes. There's a subtle spark in Clarissa's voice that makes me fidgety.

"When you say 'good story,' you mean . . . ?"

She leans closer and I mirror her. "Here's the thing," she says, enunciating each slow syllable, voice dropping as if the elderly couple next to us might be covert editors at a rival publication. "The rumor at the top of the food chain is that Tyler's gearing up for something big, that he's reading fewer scripts, turning down big modeling contracts. I want you to find out what's happening. Why did Tyler Tun *allegedly*"—she raises a brow, ever the cautious journalist—"turn down the most expensive spokesperson deal Rolex has ever offered? Is he getting married? Did he just have a secret baby? Has Marvel tapped him for a new Avengers movie? Is he, I don't know, pivoting to become a pop star? A thriller novelist? *Something* is going on, and I want to know what it is." She narrows her gaze down at the table, brain having kicked into overdrive. "This is the first time he and May Diamond are working together on a movie despite being best friends for years. Why *this* one? After all this time? They both shoot in similar genres, so why work together now? Is this them getting ready to announce they're dating? Engaged? Already eloped? Getting a joint reality show? Or is it a separate multi-year acting commitment? Has the studio behind Bond secured him? Daniel's made it clear that he's done, and it's no secret that Tyler's at the top of the short list. Personally, that's what *my* money's on.

"I mean, he has never, and I mean *never,* agreed to a profile this in-depth, to be shadowed for this long. It feels like . . . like he's delineating some sort of transition, marking a new chapter in his career. After this one, what is he moving on to?"

I'm not expecting her to abruptly look up at me straight on, so when she does, like it *wasn't* a rhetorical question, I cobble together a semi-confident "Let's try to find out?"

"Let's," Clarissa says with a dagger-sharp stare. She knows she's just dangled the shiniest, juiciest carrot in front of me. "So you're on board?"

My natural human instinct is to jump out of my seat and promise her that I'm the woman for the job, but then I remember that I'm probably still being tested to see how good I am under pressure. So, "I'm a big fan of Singapore," I say in a subtle acceptance of her challenge. "But I also still want that fifteen percent."

"Fifteen percent it is."

I grin as I finally shake her hand. I'm about to let go and dive into the rest of this salad, but she holds on to this handshake for just a beat longer than necessary.

And I clock them, even though they are the minutest of motions. A flicker of the eyes to my left hand resting on the table. A delicate pressing of her lips into a thin line, just for a millisecond. But when you've seen said motions enough times over the past couple of months, they become unmissable.

"It—" I begin.

"I heard the news. I'm sorry," she says, and to be honest, I'm thankful she doesn't make this awkward by pretending not to notice it. We both know that she knows Ben, too, so there's no point in dancing around this. "How long has it been?"

I reflexively glance down at my ring finger, as though it will show me—what? Something different from the small light-skinned band that has stared back at me for so long and yet still seems strange to me, like this hand should belong to someone else?

"It's been nearly two months since we signed the papers. We were already separated before that, though," I say. "It's not a big deal."

Her eyes widen with encouragement. "Exactly! Every smart woman has a starter husband, darling. Better to get it out of the way when you're young. Look at me." She gestures at herself with her fork. "Took me three failed marriages to get here, and I'd say it worked out pretty well."

I know it's meant to be a reassurance, but the phrase "failed marriage" makes me want to throw back up the two sliced cherry tomatoes I swallowed earlier.

"Thank you. We're okay. I wish Ben nothing but the best," I continue by rote.

My Professional Face must've cracked despite my best efforts, because Clarissa dials down her enthusiasm and gives me a silent nod. I know The Nod. I know it means *sorry I brought it up*. I know this because *everyone* is eventually sorry that they brought it up.

I clear my throat and raise my glass of wine, now realizing that this cover story is why Clarissa insisted on the most expensive bottle on the menu at the start of the meal. "To us," I say.

Clarissa shakes her head. Instead, when she clinks my glass, she says, "To *you*. Knock this out of the park like I know you can, Khin. Don't let me down. Tell our readers who Tyler Tun is."

———————

I know there are bigger things for me to focus on as I drive home, such as, say, getting assigned a *Vogue Singapore* cover story, but my brain cannot stop hyper-fixating on the words "failed" and "marriage." They keep ricocheting around in there while I say a passing hello to the doorman and walk into my still somewhat-new-to-me condo. I enter my twenty-first-floor unit with the spectacular view of Inya Lake, and as I awkwardly reach behind to unzip myself out of my Prabal Gurung dress, it's like the words are now bouncing off of the new furniture in my living room, from the cream couch to the marble dining table to my beautiful vintage Persian rug: Failed. Marriage.

I'm removing my watch to start my six-step skincare routine when it buzzes. It is, of course, the group chat; precisely, the "Bitch Bucket," as my best friends and I have named it.

Thidar
How was the meeting?
What did VOGUE SINGAPORE want from us??

Nay
And what are WE demanding from THEM in return?

Chuckling, I'm about to reply with a quick voice message when it happens again, ringing loud and clear to highlight the overwhelming quietness of this beautiful apartment and the giant bathroom with the rainfall shower in the corner: *Failed. Marriage.*

It's not that I'm under any delusions that my marriage is still capable of salvation. I know we tried everything—couples counseling, living separately for a month, going on our own "self-discovery" trips (me to Bali, him on some cross-country trek in Bhutan), more counseling— before we called it quits. Or, more specifically, before *Ben* called it quits and told me point-blank that he wanted a divorce because he didn't see a future for us anymore. I also know that a marriage that didn't even last a year is, by all means, a failure; it's nothing personal, just an objective fact. If I bought a new laptop and it combusted in my face as quickly and as spectacularly as my marriage did, I would march over to the store and tell them it was a piece of crap. And I meant what I said: I *do* wish Ben well.

I take a deep breath and begin rubbing my oil cleanser in small, tight concentric circles across both cheeks.

The last time I saw Ben was when we handed over the keys to our house—our *old* house—to its new owners. We were polite, like neighbors running into each other at the supermarket. *I'm okay. This is actually okay,* I remember thinking. And it *had* been okay, that is, until we parted with an awkward platonic handshake that in the moment had felt more appropriate than a hug, and I'd noticed that all ten of his fingers were fine. Ring tan–less. Admittedly, it could've been because his white skin had tanned faster and more evenly than my brown skin, but it'd still felt like the final twisting of a knife that was already six inches deep in the center of my heart. The final piece of proof that confirmed my worst, most embarrassing fears: that our marriage had meant significantly less to him, and that I was extremely easy to get over, so easy, in fact, that it was already as though we had never been married in the first place.

I shut my eyes and splash water onto my face, focusing on washing off the oil.

The thing about having been in a relationship with the same person in the same city for six-plus years is that the overlapping space in the Venn diagram of People We Know is almost a perfect circle. Even if I *didn't* want to know what Ben has been up to since we last spoke, I can't avoid it; a few weeks ago, I ran into one of our (many) mutual friends at a restaurant, and, against my will, was informed that Ben is thriving, and, in fact, had just scored a much-coveted gig to shoot the behind-the-scenes photos of some Netflix documentary on whale sharks in Triton Bay (which is located in West Papua in Indonesia, as my Chardonnay-fueled Google search that night informed me).

I am aware that despite it being a natural human reaction, it is also the pettiest trope in the book, that of Partner Who Was Unceremoniously Dumped (or, in my case, Divorced) and Wants to Show Their Ex that Their Life Is Even Better Now.

But here we are.

Because I will move mountains to get Clarissa her story, her big *scoop,* and she will offer me the full-time role on the spot, and that will be my literal plane ticket out of this miserable town, and by the time Ben and all of our friends see my name on the cover of *Vogue Singapore,* I'll have already moved on to my next assignment. Singapore will be good. Change will be good. And although I enjoy freelancing and have never had any trouble finding work, the stability that comes with a full-time reporter role will also be good. Maybe I'll be profiling Sandra Oh next. Or Viola Davis.

And "failed marriage" will be the last thing that anyone thinks when they see me.

Two

You've having dinner with who tonight?!" Nay screeches, and, because apparently nearly blowing out my eardrums isn't enough, throws one of my couch pillows at my face.

I jerk the round burgundy pillow back at her. "Why are you throwing things at me?!"

"Because," Thidar says, grabbing the pillow from Nay's lap and lobbing it at me again. "That is the appropriate response to finding out your friend is having dinner with Tyler fucking Tun and *didn't tell you until four hours prior*!"

"Okay, you two need to stop yelling," I say, putting an end to this game of hot potato by propping the pillow behind my back. "I signed an NDA. I'm not even supposed to tell you *now*," I say, deciding that it was also the right call not to tell them about the job offer on the table. I don't need the additional pressure, and while I generally don't believe in the concept of "jinxing," I want this too much that I'm going to play it safe on this one, just in case.

Nay whacks my shoulder. "Since when have NDAs applied to *us*?"

"I'm telling you now, aren't I?" I reach over for the water carafe on the coffee table and refill my glass.

"Are you also inviting us to dinner in an effort to say sorry?" Thidar asks with accusatory, narrowed eyes.

"Ha!" I snort.

The two of them exchange a quick glance. "Worth a try." Nay shrugs. "How're you feeling? Nervous?"

I don't typically get nervous over assignments. Excited, definitely. But not nervous. This one, though—this one makes my gut twist and turn in a way that it hasn't since my first year of being a journalist. "Actually, yes," I answer. "Mainly because it's different from anything else I've written, but you know what, I think it'll be a nice change. You guys know I love what I've worked on—"

"That piece on the Myanmar national women's soccer team still pops up on my feeds," Nay interrupts. "Also the one about the lesbian couple who couldn't find a local hospital who would help them with IVF."

"Ooooh yes!" Thidar says. "You are a *star*, Khin Haymar. I can't believe we get front-row seats to all your badass journalism."

I beam. "I love you guys," I say. "And I'm proud of both of those pieces, but I dunno, this *Vogue* thing is really exciting, even if I don't really know what I'm doing," I admit with a short laugh, because if I'm going to admit my nerves to anyone, it's going to be them.

Thidar's eyes light up. "Please, it's not like your name wouldn't fit right in on a *Vogue* cover. You're the best-dressed person I know! Your wardrobe basically looks like the fashion closet in *The Bold Type*. If the fashion closet were made up exclusively of secondhand pieces, obviously."

"'Secondhand' has such an un-chic vibe. Her clothes aren't

secondhand, they're vintage!" Nay points out. "And vintage is always trendy!"

"That's true," Thidar says. "But yeah, this will be good for you. It's something fresh. Something new. You deserve something good and fresh and new." I know where she's going before she and Nay even trade a look. Right as I expected, her voice tapers out into one that's more subdued. "Look, we absolutely do not have to go into detail on this, and especially not tonight, but, like, how're you doing? You know . . . aside from work, which, clearly, you are *killing* at?"

Her attempt at trying to cushion the Big Question with a compliment is sweet, but it doesn't override the fact that I know she wanted to ask, *How're you doing divorce- and generally love life–wise?* And what do I say apart from, *I am (still) divorced, and that is (also, still) that.* Why spend any time dwelling on it? Besides, no one wants to hear the actual answer, which is that divorce is messy, and in my case, embarrassing, and despite the fact that I write for a living and that I've had more than enough time to process all of this, I still cannot find quite the right words to explain how it feels when your husband tells you it is over, that there is no point, that the splinters of your once-love are too small and many to salvage.

"Oh, you know, the usual," I say, and flick my hair over my shoulder. "Spending my one wild and precious life being smart, hot, well-dressed. And humble."

There's a hurt in their smiles that I don't want to investigate more closely. Yes, it hurts to talk about divorce, hence why I don't do it.

"Well, we were thinking," Nay says. "You've been living here for a few months now." She gestures around at the space. "And we think it'd be good to officially mark this new chapter of your life with a housewarming." I grimace, but she holds up a hand before I can vocalize my protest. "And if you're too busy to do it yourself, which we totally get, then we would be more than happy to plan it. You just sit back, and we'll text you the when and where."

"Surely the *where* would be quite obvious," Thidar says, scrunching up her face.

Nay rolls her eyes. "Well, obviously. It was a *saying*."

They both turn to me expectantly, and when I don't reply immediately, their hurt smiles reappear. Even if I wanted a housewarming (which I don't, because I literally don't have the energy for a party right now), whom would I invite apart from them? Thidar's fiancé and Nay's latest Hinge fling? The slew of acquaintances who would only tell me about what projects Ben has most recently signed up for? "That is a very sweet offer, thank you," I reply. "But my schedule's going to be so packed that I really don't have time for a party right now."

Before they can make one final protest, I down my water, get to my feet, and head for the bedroom. Only when I reach my doorway do I swivel around and face them, crossing my arms. "So are you guys just going to sit there, or are you going to come help me decide what to wear tonight for my dinner with Tyler Tun?" I ask, and breathe a quiet sigh of relief when they erupt into squeals and sprint over, Nay smacking my ass as Thidar grabs my hand and drags me toward my walk-in wardrobe.

Two hours and approximately twenty outfits later, I usher them back out into the living room. "Why dinner? At a restaurant?" Thidar asks as she gathers up her things in her purse. "Aren't these profiles usually done in the celebrity's house? That's what I've always read."

I shrug. "He told my editor he wanted to settle down in his apartment before inviting anyone over."

"Oh my god!" Nay squeaks. "Does that mean you're eventually going to see the inside of Tyler Tun's apartment?!"

I roll my eyes and, one palm on each of their backs, start to move them toward the door. "*This* is why I didn't tell you earlier."

"Oh, wait, what purse are you taking?" Nay asks.

"The dark denim Kate Spade. With the wooden handle."

"Oooh, good choice." Nay nods. "And you moved all your stuff?"

"Yep. Wallet, portable battery, notebook, pen, Tide pen, tissues, hand sanitizer—"

"And the pepper spray and alarm?" she asks, referring to the presents they'd bought me after I got my first piece of hate mail years ago and made me swear, literal hand on heart, that I would carry them with me everywhere, *even if I one day take an assignment where I go underwater in a submarine* (they literally wrote an oath that I had to recite out loud).

"Yes, I—"

"Because men are men. And Chinatown at night can be sketchy. Are you driving?" Thidar asks.

"No, I'm getting a cab."

"Good." She nods. "Because you know it's not just carjackings these days. I heard a story the other day about a guy breaking into a car and hiding in the backseat until the woman got back and—"

"I said I was taking a cab, *Mom*."

Nay purses her lips to one side. "But you won't forget the alarm and spray, right?"

"I think," I say, reaching to open the door, then gripping their shoulders and forcing them out into the hallway, "that I will be just fine eating Chinese food with Tyler Tun."

"I—" Nay starts.

"But no, I won't forget the spray and alarm. Now can you please leave so I can shower and get dressed and not fuck up this job before I've even started?"

Three

Crow's-feet. Maybe it's shallow, but it's the first thing I notice about him: Tyler Tun has crow's-feet. I hadn't seen them in any of the TV appearances or magazine spreads I'd diligently studied in preparation for tonight, but there they are: deep and unmistakable.

Otherwise, and while I know it's trite to say he looks exactly like he does on-screen, he does. For a split second, my brain's neurons lag in their firing—a consequence of seeing a face that I've only caught in movie trailers and magazines and late-night social media scrolling now staring back at me from a few feet away: short, unruffled hair and full brows, both of which are just two shades darker than his dark brown eyes; jawline that you could use as a ruler; that famous million-dollar smile. He's *tall,* and despite the distance separating us, I have to slightly tilt my head backward to meet his eyes. He's also usually clean-shaven, but tonight he's got a five-o'clock shadow that makes him, well, hot. Not that I've ever thought he was unattractive, but it's taken me until this moment to realize that, actually, I find Tyler Tun quite hot.

I blink to clear my mind of *that*, and focus back on the present moment. He's still smiling politely, and it hits me that I've spent the past few seconds staring at him—although he doesn't seem the least bit disturbed, like this is something that happens all the time.

"Hi." I take his hand, and, apparently continuing tonight's trend, am caught off guard by how soft they are. It's probably written into all of his contracts that he has to stay moisturized to the point of feeling like a baby's butt at all times. Nobody wants a crusty Hollywood heartthrob. "I'm Khin."

"I'm Tyler. I hope you don't mind this place," he says as he leads us back to the small, metal folding table where he was sitting when I walked in. I memorize his outfit while he's still standing: white sneakers, gray chinos, plain black polo shirt with a subtly imprinted Burberry logo on the right chest. Clean, crisp, classic. Immaculate. Did his publicist pick it out?

He retakes his seat at the red plastic stool, and I plop down on the matching one opposite. Because the table is pushed up against the wall, there's only one more stool in the aisle, and, assuming that no one else is joining us, I put my purse down on it.

When I look around the narrow space, he continues in a somewhat apologetic tone, "This is my favorite restaurant in the city. I know it doesn't look impressive, but I've been craving their wonton soup for years."

"Was that the last time you were in Yangon?"

I notice a flicker of a knowing smile before he answers. "Yes." I open my mouth but he speaks first. "A little over one and a half years ago. I haven't been back since." He says it not only like he *knows* he was one step ahead of me and what I was going to ask next, but that he *prides* himself on it.

"I see, good to know," I say. I can't help but also think, *This is going to be more fun than I thought*; after all, there are few things in life I love more than taking someone down a peg, even—*especially*—if that someone is a bigwig Hollywood star who thinks I won't be able to see past the smoke and mirrors.

It doesn't take me long to clock that, despite the stool being a flimsy, backless piece of plastic, Tyler Tun doesn't slouch, his back instead a taut, straight vertical line. He steers the conversation, talking me through each of the menu items, throwing out recommendations when he arrives at a dish that he's particularly fond of. I nod, even though I'm already in interviewer mode, making mental notes of as much as I can. For instance, I also observe that he hasn't uttered a single "um" or "ah" this whole conversation—tics that I look out for to judge how a person *really* reacts to something I've said. He doesn't tap his foot or crack his neck or exhibit any of the other signs that people usually show when they're nervous about being alone with a stranger.

As I study him like a Nat Geo researcher studies an animal in the wild, it occurs to me that the reason Tyler Tun has managed to simultaneously maintain such a public professional life and private personal life isn't because past interviewers have been bad at *their* job—it's because he's extraordinary at his. The man is unreadable and presumably unshakable; in other words, a publicist's dream. Or, in other words, a challenge for me.

"How did you find this place?" I ask as I peruse the laminated A4 sheet of paper. I flip it over to find a blank page. I flip it back.

"It's been here for ages. The current owners' grandparents started it when they lived here."

"Aww, that's sweet. Did *your* grandparents bring your parents here when *they* were kids?"

I hadn't thought it a particularly inquisitive question, but he goes silent for a beat, then two. Sensing something, I flick my eyes up from my menu to his face. Nothing. Not a single crease in his smooth fore-head. I look at his hands next—once again, nothing; he's still holding on to the menu with the precise amount of tension that one holds on to any menu.

"No," he says. He looks over while I'm still staring at his hands, and, when we make eye contact, smiles. Feeling like a kid caught with her hand in the candy jar, all I can do is smile back. "My grandparents died before my parents moved out here," he explains.

Oh. Right. I knew that. The awkward silence makes sense, then. I'm tempted to say "Sorry," but from personal experience, I find it te-diously useless when someone apologizes for something that's already happened and is out of your control, because then you're obligated to say something like "It's fine!" or "It was a long time ago!" even if the former isn't entirely true and the latter is literally stating the obvious; so, I say nothing.

"Anyway," he says, shutting down that topic of conversation (which is understandable; I might be trying to get a scoop, but I don't want to make someone keep talking about their deceased family members). "It's been our family's go-to spot for as long as I can remember."

"Is that why they let you rent out the whole restaurant?"

He offers me a controlled smile. "You could say that."

As soon as he answers, I realize what a stupid question that was. Of course Tyler doesn't need to convince a restaurant owner to close the place for him for one night. Aside from the fact that he could af-ford to rent out an entire private island if he wanted to, the publicity that this place is going to get from posting a photo of him eating here will make them several months' worth of income in a matter of days.

Still, I am surprised that this is where he opted to have his first dinner in the city, especially with a journalist. When Clarissa texted me the address, I'd never heard of the place but had assumed it was some new hipster fusion eatery in Chinatown, probably on the first floor of a freshly renovated "colonial-style" building, somewhere where the lights are intentionally too dim, the prices aren't printed on the menu, and the other patrons are too cool to ask him for a selfie but not too cool to sneak photos from their respective tables. But when the taxi dropped me off in the alley, I'd walked past the shop three times before a nearby parked trishaw driver, taking pity on me and my heels, asked what I was searching for.

In my defense, the wooden accordion door had been shut, and it wasn't until I rang the somewhat-rusted doorbell hanging to the side that an old man popped out his head, asked my name, and ushered me inside.

I was worried that word might have leaked about Tyler's *actual* flight and the fact that he was already in town, that maybe paparazzi and sleuthing fans would be lined up around the block, Instagram streams open and ready to go—but *no one* outside would guess that the restaurant was open, let alone that Tyler Tun was satting on the other side of those splintered white wooden doors.

We both get the wonton soup. When our beers arrive, he lifts his in my direction.

"Shall we toast to officially signal the start?"

"The start of what?"

"The interview." He waves his bottle in a small circle. "This whole story. We're going to be seeing a lot of each other over the next two months, right? Feels fitting we start it off with a toast."

"R-right," I stammer, somewhat caught off guard by his "let's get 'em" attitude; for someone so private, he's awfully . . . friendly. After a few seconds, he shifts his bottle closer to me, and I realize he's waiting for me to clink mine against it.

As I (finally) raise my beer to his, I take a deep breath to shake off the nerves that have gripped me from out of nowhere. I need to get my shit together. I need to forget that he's Tyler Tun, whose last movie broke multiple cinema websites across the world when tickets were released. Or the fact that he's the only Asian man amongst the world's top ten highest-paid actors. Or the rumor that he was actually Shonda Rhimes's first choice for the Duke of Hastings, but it conflicted with another movie so he turned down the role, although that hasn't stopped Shonda from still trying to get him for future *Bridgerton* seasons. He's just . . . Tyler. And *I'm* interviewing *him*.

"Hey, speaking of the story, I did want to say something up front." He places his free palm down on the table, like he's literally laying something out for me. "If we're going to see each other six days a week for two months, I think we should be honest with each other. No . . . games. Maybe we could even be . . . friends?"

The word startles me. I can't tell if he's being sincere, or if this is one of his tricks for Disarming an Interviewer 101. "What a . . . novel approach," I say, careful not to make my confusion blatant. We're fifteen minutes into this meal, and I still can't get a thorough read on him. And that ticks me off. *Bad.* "Do you treat all of your interviewers like your friends?"

He smiles. "Depends on the interviewer." Before I can ask what that means, he adds, "But I've never had someone interview-slash-shadow me for quite this long before. So what do you say?" He lifts a shoulder. "Friends?"

Okay, I'll play along. I respond with a thoughtful nod. "That makes sense to me."

"Okay, so let's start."

"Start?"

"Getting to know each other. What was your dream job as a child?"

I blink, the question jolting me like an unexpected burst of static. I don't like talking about my personal life with strangers, period, but especially not with people I'm interviewing. "*I'm* the interviewer here, remember?" I try to deflect.

It doesn't work. "You can't expect me to be comfortable letting you shadow me for two whole months when I don't even know you," he says. "You've had a whole Wikipedia page at your disposal. All I have on you is your LinkedIn and a very sleek professional website."

I contemplate his point in silence until I have no choice but to acquiesce that it is a good point. Not because I'm necessarily worried about his comfort—I'm sure the rest of the world regularly bends over backward to make sure Tyler Tun is always comfortable—but because the more comfortable he is around me, the more he'll trust me, and the more he trusts me, the higher my chances are of getting *something* from him.

"Detective," I say. "I was *obsessed* with Nancy Drew." I don't ask him the same question because I already know he wanted to be a cruise ship captain.

He chuckles. "So was my sister."

"Does she still want to be a detective?"

"No, she wants to be a doctor. An ob-gyn." As soon as the words leave his mouth, he stills. The right side of his mouth jerks up, like a puppeteer has just pulled a stray string. Two seconds later, it falls back down, that perfectly symmetrical cover-story smile back in place.

Unfortunately for him, I can discern a tic from a mile away (it's why my friends no longer play poker with me, the cowards), and I settle a bit more into my seat. At least now I know what to look out for. But now I need to know *why* that happened.

"Your sister wants to be an ob-gyn? That's impressive," I say, trying to push this. I'm feeling around in the dark for something, and even though I don't know *what*, I'm almost certain there's something there, just paces away.

"It is," he says.

"I'm surprised she doesn't want to be an actress, too. You know,

given how well"—I make a spreading motion at him with my hands—
"*you've* done in Hollywood."

He shakes his head and laughs, but I notice that he hasn't put his
beer bottle down, perhaps using it as an anchor to keep his body language steady. I know from reading interviews that he's close with his
sister, so this could just be a case of him wanting to protect her from
being in the press. But also, it could be something else. *Is* she planning
on becoming an actress? Are the two of them filming something next?
I could see a studio wanting to keep a splashy announcement like that
sealed shut. "Trust me, Jess is determined to do the complete opposite of whatever I do. She's . . . how to describe her? Independent," he
says. Then, "What's your favorite movie?"

Despite my annoyance in the subject change, I reply coolly, "No
one has a favorite movie."

"But if you had to pick?"

I look up at the ceiling while I think. "*Legally Blonde.*"

"Huh."

"What?"

"I thought you'd name one of *my* movies. You know, to play to
my ego."

I can feel the smirk spread on my face. "Truthfully, I don't think
there's a big enough bat in the world to play to the ego of someone
who says something like *that*," I say, and he lets out a loud laugh. Not
a full torrent, but a big enough wave that my smirk opens into a grin.

"I can see it, though," he says, nodding now.

"What does *that* mean?" I challenge.

"I can see you and Elle getting along."

"Don't act like you've watched *Legally Blonde.*"

"What?" His two front teeth dig into his bottom lip as if stopping
a smile, and something zings down my spine. "Like it's hard?"

This time, *I* laugh, shocked by what happened inside my body just then and by his quoting *Legally Blonde.* Before I can ask him something more interesting and less obvious than *his* favorite movie (the first *Indiana Jones,* as he mentioned in his speech at the Oscars the year he presented Harrison Ford with a lifetime achievement award), the food arrives, delivered by the same uncle who let me in. "Thank you," Tyler says up at him with a respectful tilt of his head.

The uncle claps him on the shoulder. "I'll be upstairs. Let me know if you need anything," he says before retreating to the small staircase located at the very back of the restaurant and that, I'm assuming, leads to the second floor where the family lives.

"Are you seeing anyone?" Tyler asks with zero transition.

I halt, one shrimp wonton squished between my chopsticks, heart rate going from zero to a hundred. "What?"

Tyler picks up a wonton of his own and shrugs. "That's what everyone's always asking *me.* I'm sure you were going to ask me at some point, too," he says before putting the entire dumpling in his mouth and following up with a small, delicate slurp of the soup. "So I'm asking you first. Are you seeing anyone?"

"No," I say. "Are *you*?"

"Come on now, I thought you'd be subtler than that."

"That's not an answer. *Come on now,*" I mimic his patronizing tone. "I thought we were trying to be friends—"

"We are—"

"—and friends tell each other when they're seeing someone, don't they?"

His grin shows off his perfect teeth. "Fair enough. No, I'm not seeing anyone."

"Not on the apps?"

"Don't have time for a relationship right now."

"Ugh," I groan, rolling my eyes. "What a walking cliché."

"Do you call all of your interviewees a walking cliché?" he asks, eyes glinting as they scour my profile.

"To their face?" I look up at the ceiling as if trying to recall. "Only the ones that I also consider my friends."

He nods, then shakes his head as though he changed his mind mid-reaction.

"But," I point out. "You do know you can set the settings to make it clear that you're only in town for a few months and are looking for something short-term." That corner of his mouth that I'm now checking in on every few seconds pulls. Is he secretly dating someone here and he's trying to throw me off? "Wh—"

"And how would you know that?" he asks. "About the apps. Personal experience?"

"Unfortunately." I sigh. "It's a war zone out there."

"So I've heard."

"From whom?"

"May." His expression, which shifts to *I walked right into that one* in a blink, makes it clear that he didn't have time to double-think his answer.

"May Diamond?" I ask innocently.

All he does is chuckle and nod in answer. "Who's your celebrity crush?" he asks.

"Why? If it's someone you know, are you going to set us up on a date?"

Once again, his eyes shine with the reflection of the fluorescent lighting and a pinch of teasing. "Depends. Who is it?"

"Chris Pine. The most underrated of the Chrises."

"And the only one whose number I *don't* have," he says with an exaggerated sigh that, against my will, makes me giggle. Actually fucking *giggle* like he's the prettiest boy in school and I'm thrilled to be getting even a modicum of his time.

"Who's yours?" I ask.

"Jane Fonda."

"Tyler Tun," I say, raising a brow.

His eyes widen like I've uttered an obscenity. "What?"

"I didn't know you were into older women."

"It's Jane Fonda," he replies, unfazed. "Why did you take this job?"

We're playing ping-pong, him trying to get a point when he thinks my guard is lowered, me (obviously) not letting him.

"Easy," I say and take half a bite of a dumpling, being careful not to let the remaining stuffing fall out. "*Vogue* asked me to do a cover story."

"Is that it? Because it was *Vogue*?"

And because I wanted my ex-husband to hear that I was writing for Vogue *now.* "Yes," I say. "Why?"

He takes a sip of beer. "It's . . . different from your past work. Like that abortion clinic piece in *Time*."

I am not a fan of how often this man zigs just as I'm sure he's about to zag. I make a noise that sounds like I choked on some invisible beer, as though my body, along with my brain, cannot physically digest this new piece of information. He smiles. Point to Tyler. *Damn it.* "You read that?" I ask, regaining my composure.

"Like I said," he says with a chuckle. "You didn't think *you* were the only one who did research for this interview now, did you? It was a fantastic piece, too. Then again"—he lifts his chin at me—"I guess that's how they do it at Columbia Journalism School."

"Wow, name-dropping my college? You really went all in on my LinkedIn, huh? Are *you* the fourteen anonymous views I got last week?"

"You caught me." He lifts both hands in surrender. "I created fourteen separate accounts so that I could use the free premium trial fourteen times and keep viewing your profile anonymously."

I see my opportunity and slide right in. "I thought signing up to be the new James Bond came with at least enough money to cover a LinkedIn Premium subscription."

His hand, which was casually rubbing his chin, freezes. "Is that you asking if I'm going to be the new James Bond?" he asks. His tone doesn't fluctuate, but it *is* the slowest he's talked all night.

"Is that you confirming?" He opens his mouth, and I point my chopsticks at him. "Remember, you wouldn't lie to a friend now, would you?"

His mouth corner tics. I've got him. Except, instead of acting like you would when you're backed into a corner, he drops his chopsticks, folds his hands in front of his chest, and, forehead wrinkling with a joke that I didn't catch, says, "How about this? I promise you that *if* the time ever comes when I agree to be the new James Bond, my publicist will give you a thirty-minute head start before releasing the official statement."

I gape at him. Is he being serious? Is he confirming that he's going to be the next Bond? "And . . . why would you do that?"

"Because," he starts, then stops. Instead of continuing, his mouth splits into something halfway between a smirk and a full-on grin, his owlish eyes suddenly making me feel like the tables have turned and *I'm* backed into the corner. "Because I like to help out all my friends," he finally says.

"Well, how do I know you mean it? How do I know you'll keep your word? Or that you won't try to feed me false information?"

"Because what would I get out of doing that?" he points out. "Besides, you're too good of a journalist to fall for false information. Like I said earlier, that abortion piece was incredible. Why did you write it?"

My startled "What?" comes out squeakier than it would under normal circumstances, but he shrugs like he's surprised *I'm* surprised.

It irks me that he's still eating as though this is a normal conversation. One minute, he's quite possibly confirming the biggest entertainment scoop of the decade, and the next, he's circled back to my piece on the abortion clinic. "Why did you write a piece about the city's only underground abortion clinic in a country where abortion is illegal?" he asks.

Despite wanting to steer us back into Bond territory, I restrain myself. I'm playing the long game here. Annoying and pushing him at this one dinner won't bode well for me over the next two months. I need him to lower his defenses, not feel aggravated.

"Why does it matter?" I ask. "It's my job."

"Because it takes guts. You could do your job in a lot of other ways that don't involve potentially prosecutable activities," he says, a solemnity overtaking his features, the confident smile from earlier loosening. His eating also slows down. "Weren't you worried you'd get interrogated by the authorities? Or worse?"

I shake my head, refusing to break his gaze, unsure whether it's because I don't want to or because I can't. "Eh, a few eyebrows were raised in my direction, but I don't scare easily. And in the end, the pros far outweighed any possible cons," I answer. "I've had a lot of women contact me after reading that piece. That alone makes it worth it."

"And you connect them to the clinic?"

"Used to. Now I forward their details to a friend who runs a women's shelter."

"So the clinic is still running? Because that piece came out a while ago."

"It is."

After another long stretch of quiet, he simply nods.

There's something about his fascination with this story that's nagging at me. Sure, it was my latest big byline and also the biggest byline I've had to date, but he's pressing on it awfully hard. Is he doing research? Maybe for his next film, or some type of documentary he's doing voice-over work for? Something to do with abortion policies in

American politics? A political endorsement? Wanting to focus on the current conversation, I file the note away in my "possible Tyler Tun scoops" folder.

"My turn. I have a question," I say.

He nods, and when he leans the closest toward me that he has all night, I am *not* expecting the scent of pinewood that floods my nostrils. I don't know what I thought he'd smell like, but a pine forest was not it. I don't even have a particular affinity for pine trees (or anything remotely nature-related), but this man smells *good*. I can't stop myself from taking another deep inhale, and this time, am able to better parse the various notes: fresh, crisp, but with a grounded center that's rounded out by a nearly imperceptible sweetness, like someone sprinkled in a dash of concentrated lychee extract at the last minute.

"Yes?" he asks after a few distracted seconds on my part.

Get it the fuck together, Khin. And stop smelling *him, Jesus Christ.*

"Why did you agree to this?" I ask.

There's that stray puppeteer half smile again. "What do you mean?"

"This." I move my head around in a circle. "Me trailing you for two months. You're notoriously private—"

"Oh, am I?"

"Yes." He's not the only one who can cut people off. "So why did you agree to this? You rarely even walk the red carpet these days."

His features pull as though this is brand-new information to him. "The truth is," he says through a short chuckle, "you have my publicist to thank for that."

I don't buy it. "You agreed to let a stranger follow you around for two months because your publicist bullied you into it?"

"I wouldn't say 'bullied,'" he counters. "But Bolu can be very persuasive."

"Why this movie? Compared to all the other ones."

"This one is important to me. It's . . . different. Special."

I perk up. "Special how?"

"Come on, Khin, we're both Myanmar. Don't make me go through the *representation* spiel. You're too astute of a writer to need me to explicitly lay out what's riding on this movie." And then, ping-pong serve landing in front of me out of nowhere, he continues, "Tell me a secret."

"What?"

He goes quiet although we both know I heard him correctly. It's not the fact that he's surveying me in silence that's getting under my skin, but it's how he's doing it. I don't know how to describe it, but the steadiness in the way his eyes are tracing my face makes me feel like he's just discovered something about myself that even *I* don't know.

He's not trying to *be friends*. This man is trying to even the playing field.

"A secret. Tell me a secret," he repeats. "And not something like *I once shoplifted a Snickers bar*—"

"Have *you* ever shoplifted a Snickers bar?" His expression droops for a second and I gasp. "Tyler Tun! Do the authorities know?"

This time, his laugh is unrestrained, deep but joyous, just like in the movies. "Damn, I should've worked on my poker face. I gotta be honest, I didn't come to this dinner thinking I'd be questioned about my sordid past."

"I'm *really* good at my job," I say with a proud, knowing smile.

"I can tell," he says, still grinning. "But now you know a secret of mine. So it's your turn. Tell me one. Tell me something that you would rather sell your soul to the devil than have someone find out."

"Okay, now we're just—"

"Khin."

I don't know why I stop breathing at the sound of him saying my name, voice all low and anchored. What am I, a lusty teenager? "Why?" I ask, buying myself time.

"Because I need to know that I can trust you."

"So you can blackmail me if you don't like the profile?"

He shakes his head. "Please don't take this the wrong way, but I don't actually read the stories. Never do."

"Why not?"

"Khin," he repeats, and there goes my breath again, hitching on an invisible jagged edge. "You're stalling. Tell me a secret. I need to know that I can trust you."

Vogue. That's what's on the line here. If I give him this one thing, and he feels like he can trust me, and he lets his guard down, and I find out something that makes Clarissa happy, I will get a full-time position at *Vogue.* "I'm recently divorced."

His eyes jump from my face to my finger and back to my eyes. "Not a secret."

I feel like an animal caught in a snare that only gets tighter the more I squirm.

Vogue. Singapore.

And then I realize—*he* can't fact-check *my* life. Interviewing 101: be relatable.

"It's . . . making it hard for me to be happy about my sister's engagement," I say, trying my best to sound like I feel an overwhelming sense of guilt for ever saying this out loud; picturing Nay's and Thidar's faces kind of helps because hey, I do *technically* have sisters—we're just not related by blood. "I keep telling myself that it's ninety-five percent happiness and five percent bitterness, but if I'm being honest, it's probably more seventy–thirty."

"You have a sister?" he asks, taken aback by this information. "You didn't mention it earlier."

"You . . . didn't ask. And I try not to bring up my personal life in interviews." It's the best lie I can come up with on the spot.

He's studying my face like that again, like at this point, he could pick it out blindfolded just by tracing my features with his hands. *Don't let him get inside your head*, I remind myself.

"I understand. Are you close with your sister? Newfound romantic bitterness aside?" he finally asks as his careful expression breaks into a soft smile.

I feel simultaneous bursts of relief and triumph. Bull's. Eye. I wasn't expecting to do this tonight, but it's worked. His shoulders lower a few degrees, and my sense of smugness rises. I just gained the upper hand in this relationship, and he doesn't even know it.

"Yeah." I nod. "Apart from, you know, the usual petty sibling nonsense."

His smile widens. "I get that."

His head is tilted to the side, and he looks the most relaxed and guard-down he's been all evening. On instinct, I seize the opening. "Now, what about you? Snickers heist aside. Do you have a secret that you'd—how did you put it? Rather sell your soul to the devil than have anyone find out?"

My eye catches on his Adam's apple bobbing as he swallows. Obviously, he has secrets. All celebrities have secrets. Every *human* has secrets. But it's the way he pulls back, sits up, and resumes eating before the half-teasing "Just the usual" has fully left his lips that snaps me to attention.

"How about one of your upcoming roles?" I press.

"Like what?"

"You tell me. Can you reveal anything that's currently in the pipeline? Anything that *doesn't* rhyme with Dames Lond?"

He smiles, but turns his attention away, like one of his facial muscles might reveal something if this goes on for too long. "Nothing confirmed," he says.

"Do you want to do another indie film, like *Beginning, Middle, End*?

Or are you continuing down the more conventional rom-com route for a while? Are you and May planning on shooting anything else?"

"Maybe," he says with a caution that the question doesn't warrant.

"Maybe?" I echo.

He looks back up at me, a surge in confidence lifting his features. "May and I need to see if we get through *this* movie first without killing each other. It's one thing to be best friends"—he lifts his bottle to his lips—"it's another to be best friends *and* coworkers."

"You're telling me," I challenge, "that, should it arise once more, you would actively turn down the opportunity to work on a movie with May Diamond?"

"Truth be told, May can be a brat," he says, then pauses. "But you didn't hear it from me," he adds with a wink and a teasing lilt that only best friends have a right to.

I know when I'm hitting a dead end. It's fine, I'll find a way to circle back to this somehow. For now, I'll try a different approach.

"What's your favorite role you've ever played?"

He takes his time chewing and swallowing another wonton. "It changes regularly but right now, probably . . . *I Won't Tell If You Won't.*"

My forehead creases in surprise. It was, if I remember correctly, his second-ever movie, the one right before *Renegade* made him a household name; if you stopped someone on the street and asked them to name five Tyler Tun movies, *I Won't Tell If You Won't* probably wouldn't make anyone's list. I was expecting him to say *Lost and Found* because what kid who grew up watching WWE doesn't dream about starring alongside The Rock, or *Call It What You Want* because what human being doesn't dream about making out with Emma Watson in the middle of the Palace of Versailles, or, the most obvious one—Dylan McClane (aka John McClane's nephew) in last year's *Die Hard* reboot.

"Why?" I ask.

His eyes wander around the table, as though he's searching for the answer in a script that someone might have secretly taped onto the side of the chili oil pot. "It was—" he starts, and pauses. I have a feeling that it's not a case of him not having an answer, but that he's trying to put it into a nice, tidy package before presenting it to me. "Because I was experienced enough to not be too anxious to enjoy it, but also not famous enough to be too anxious to enjoy it." He laughs at my puzzled expression. "That sounded much sager in my head, I gotta be honest. Basically, I was a kid, and it felt like this acting thing *might* work out and also it might not, so I was having fun on set every day like it was the last time I'd ever get to do one of these because, well, back then, it might have been."

I smile at his earnestness. "Do you miss it? Before all the hubbub and lights?"

"Do I miss the measly paychecks? Believe it or not, not really." He laughs. "I kind of enjoy perks like being a homeowner. Truly lives up to the hype."

I hold my smile, but I'm not letting him get away with distracting me with humor. "I mean, do you miss . . ." I try to frame it so it doesn't sound so sentimental. "I guess, do you miss those days when acting, this whole job, didn't come with all the pressure and obligations it does now? Without all the publicity tours and the multiple international premieres and brand endorsements and shit?"

"What, do I miss acting just for the sake of acting?"

I wouldn't have put it that way, but the way he said it, with a rueful smile and a tone that bordered on wistfulness—it makes me curious.

I nod.

He tries to avoid my gaze again, but this time, I lean over to the side and prop my chin on my fist. Realizing what I'm doing, he releases a low chuckle like *Okay, fine, you caught me.*

"Sometimes," he answers, and without either of us meaning to, we're locked in a stare-down. One of the first big journalism rules

I learned was to not jump into the silence; if you let it linger long enough, eventually the other person will speak first, and you'd be surprised what people will blurt out to fill the quiet. After a long period of this, he blinks first. "But hey, no such thing as a dream job under capitalism, right? I guess to sort of answer your earlier question, I'm trying to make sure whatever roles I take from now on, they're *fun*. A feeble attempt at recapturing the magic, I suppose. I know people write off genres like rom-coms because they're *fun* and aren't the titles you see on the ballots when awards season comes around, or the ones that get the three-minute standing ovations at Cannes, but I don't see what's wrong with wanting to make people laugh, to bring joy to the fans. If I have fun while I'm filming, and they have fun while they're watching, then surely *that's* what we should all be aiming for, right?" he says, and finishes the last bite.

"Right," I say, allowing the silence to resettle as I turn his words over in my head.

What would be more "fun" for a young actor than getting to be the next James Bond? What would bring more joy to fans than finding out that Tyler Tun and May Diamond are, in fact, best friends turned lovers?

Although I still can't see even the outline of this vague thing I'm searching for, I would bet my entire wardrobe that there *is* a thing here.

My gut has never failed me. Not ever. Some people's do once or twice, but not mine. It's why I'm so good at what I do. And right now, it's telling me that Clarissa was right: Tyler Tun is hiding something. Something really big. Something that might very well be big enough to get me a job at *Vogue*.

Four

The movie is a rom-com about two private bodyguards, Nanda and Mra, who work for the same security company but loathe each other's guts. Despite their history, they both end up being assigned to protect the crown princess of a fictional European country while she's on vacation in Myanmar. But on her first night in Yangon, the princess escapes her protection detail, gets kidnapped, and it's obviously up to Nanda and Mra to find her. They track her down across the globe, and as they rush to save her before political chaos erupts, they get close, realize their hatred for one another is actually misplaced passion, have sex in the bathroom of their company's private jet, et cetera, et cetera.

I have to admit, it sounds (as Tyler noted) like a *fun* movie. Obviously, it's also cool because it's the first romantic comedy backed by a major Hollywood studio that's directed by a Myanmar director *and* stars two Myanmar actors *and* is (partly) shot on location here. But all that aside, even though I haven't read the script, the synopsis alone makes me want to watch it.

At 3 P.M., we're in the backseat of Tyler's assigned car on the way to the first day of shooting, which is apparently supposed to go late. I've never been on a movie set so I don't know if this is normal, and while I'm not *thrilled* at the idea of hanging out with the mosquitoes and bugs in the park until midnight or whatever "late" is, my curiosity and that familiar journalistic rush override my disdain for all insect life. Additionally, if I don't get the *Vogue* job, then I'm probably never again going to get the chance to be this close to a movie set, let alone a movie this big.

Today's scene will take place in Kandawgyi Park. This is the inciting event where, in the middle of a night market, the princess gives Nanda and Mra the slip. Tyler gave me a peek at the storyboards, and it looks like rows of vendor stalls with white canopies will cover approximately a third of the grounds, complete with fairy lights and hundreds of extras—a near one-eighty from the usually lush but sparsely populated grounds. When I asked what was going to be the hardest part of this scene, his sincere answer of "trying not to trip while I repeatedly run through a park on command" made me smile.

"So why was this one of the scenes you wanted to shoot in Yangon?" I ask as I consult my notes. "Surely you could've replicated it closer to home back in the US, say, in Central Park? All you need is literally a park."

He nods, vaguely distracted by something on his phone. "True; but parks are different, even within a single country, but especially across continents. The main differences are the flora and fauna. The trees and animals that you'll find in Central Park are completely different from what you're going to find here."

"Will that matter to most viewers, though? Unless you're a professional botanist and/or ornithologist, will you even notice?"

"It matters to us. To me," he replies, and although he says it with a smile that (I think) is meant to assure me that he wasn't being mean, I am nonetheless left feeling the most professionally ignorant I've felt in a while. "We're actually going to do all of the scenes that require Myanmar extras here, mainly because, unsurprisingly, it's *much* easier to find the correct attire and props here than in LA. Turns out American costume departments, as lavish as they can be, don't exactly stock an array of hta meins and taikpons."

After taking another five to recover from *that* internal embarrassment, I mentally rummage through my list of questions from the other night. "Tell me why you picked this movie."

"What do you mean?" Tyler asks, his eyes shifting sideways toward me.

"You have your pick of projects. This must've thrown a wrench in your schedule, having to come out to Myanmar to shoot and all." After studying him, and keeping Clarissa's theories in mind, I venture casually, "I thought you were going to be the new Rolex spokesperson just in time for their holiday campaign, so shouldn't you already be shooting ads for that?"

His chest puffs slightly as he chuckles. "Is that so?"

"That's what the internet says."

"And you believe everything the internet says?"

"Would the internet ever lie to you?"

He leans his head back as he laughs. "I signed up to do this movie for many reasons, but will you be disappointed if I say that the main one is because I wanted to work with May?"

"Have you wanted to work with May for a long time?" I'm tempted to ask if there's ever been something more between them, but I also know that tons of people before me have asked them some variation of the same question and that his answer has always been a firm "no."

If there *is* something going on between them now, I need to get it out of him another way.

"Kind of." He nods. "I was approached first, but as soon as we did the chemistry read together, I told the producers that this movie needed *both* of us. I know it's not a particularly juicy or deep answer, but that's kinda it. I wanted to make this really fun movie with my best friend in our hometown."

It's such a simple answer that I don't *entirely* buy it. He was abrupt in shutting down the May conversation the other night, but he seems to be more open to it today. "How'd you two become friends?" I ask.

"Hollywood connections. Met at a party. The usual."

"And—"

"No, we didn't hook up that night. We haven't ever hooked up."

I frown at his assumption, a little offended that he thinks I would ask such a tactless question. "That's not what I was going to ask at all."

"Oh?" he asks, caution tinting his voice. "What *were* you going to ask?"

"I was going to ask," I sharpen my tone to reiterate my irritation at his presumptuousness that I'd be so obvious about it. What am I, a novice celebrity gossip blogger? "What made *her* different from everyone else? Surely you've met thousands of people at thousands of parties. What was the connection there? Was it just that you're both Myanmar?"

He's angled his body to face me directly now, but I'm not fazed. I can almost see his brain taking its time crafting the perfect answer, aware that anything and everything he says can be used against him. For a second, I can't help but feel tired on his behalf, for always having to think three steps ahead before you speak.

Finally, he puts his phone facedown on his lap. "The first time I was ever invited to a big-shot Hollywood party—and this was ages

ago, probably a decade by now—it was the *Vanity Fair* Oscars party. I
don't know *how* my publicist scored me an invite considering I wasn't
even invited to the actual Oscars, but somehow she did. And this was
before *Renegade*, before *Campfire* and even *P.S. Forever*." He pauses, and
I try to picture what that Tyler Tun must've been like, before all the
madness and the lights and glamor and award show invitations, let
alone the permanent front-row seats. "As you can probably imagine, I
was nervous as all fuck that night. I knew I had to socialize and min-
gle, get people to remember my face and my name, but I was terrified.
I walked in, grabbed a drink, and then walked over to a corner and
just . . . *stood*."

"You . . . stood? For how long?"

"It felt like hours, but then I checked my watch and it'd been six
minutes. Anyway." He cracks his neck. "Eventually, just as I'm wondering if maybe I should, I dunno, go get drunk in the bathroom first
so that maybe I'll be a little braver and actually talk to people, May
walks over to me and says, 'Hi, I'm May.'"

"Had you met her before?"

He shakes his head. "Nope. But obviously I knew who she was.
My little sister was obsessed with her on the Disney Channel, and
Kiss Her had come out just a few months prior, so *everyone* wanted to
talk to her. At one point, I could see a literal line forming behind her.
But she never turned around, and instead she kept talking to me, a
nobody who could've easily been mistaken for an overdressed server.
And then we both found out that we were Myanmar, and that wasn't
the whole or even the *main* reason we clicked so well, but it *was* kinda
the final puzzle piece. Half an hour later, and to the horror of her
publicist, we ditched the party and got a taxi to a McDonald's an hour
away, and we sat in a corner booth for hours. We demolished six Big
Macs and four bags of fries between us."

I don't realize that I'm grinning until my cheeks start to ache.

"Sounds like a good night," I say. The way he recounts it, I feel like I somehow lived the memory myself.

He nods, his own grin expanding like he's right back there, too. "It was one of the best nights of my life. And that's just who she's been for me since then. I'm sure you've heard about how Hollywood is ruthless and this industry will spit you out once you're a second past your prime and all that, and unfortunately it's all true. But I never—" At this point, he turns the other way and looks out the window, and for a second, I'm worried he's stopping and self-censoring again. But then he says, voice steady like this is the surest thing in the world, "I never have to worry if she won't stay. Because I know ninety-nine percent of the people who are currently cheering me on will jump ship the moment something goes wrong. But not May. Because she's the kind of person who excuses herself from a conversation with Madonna to go say hi to the new kid who's standing all alone in the corner. *That's* who she is."

In the moment, I'm stunned, trying to process this much honesty all at once. It feels like such a raw, earnest story that I can't even think of any follow-up questions, because the way he's said it is just perfect.

My bubble of awe is popped, however, when he throws me a sly sideways smile and reminds me exactly what our setup is by adding, in a tone whose smugness is not lost on me, "And you can absolutely quote me on that."

As we near the vicinity of the park, it's clear that word has gotten out. The car crawls toward the entrance while what looks like Yangon's entire female population aged between thirteen and thirty-three (and a few outliers on either end) swarm the area. I know they can't see inside the tinted windows, but part of me feels tempted to tell Tyler to duck in case, I dunno, a freshly divorced middle-aged auntie tries to push herself through the glass.

We make it past the gates without hitting anyone, but cars aren't allowed inside the park grounds, not even for Tyler Tun, so we park in the front parking lot, just a few feet of grass and a half-crumbling brick wall separating us from what I can only describe as mayhem wearing shirts plastered with Tyler's face and holding up signs with messages like I'D LIKE TO TY YOU UP IN MY BED and YOU LIGHT A CAMPFIRE IN MY PANTS and a very succinct TYLER LET'S FUCK.

"I'm going to go say a quick hi," Tyler says to Tun ("Nice name!" he'd also joked), his PA who greeted us at the car.

"Oh, no, I don't think—" The poor kid, who is probably no older than twenty-one and for whom this is clearly the most important job he's had to date, tries to say. (*I don't think you should go into the throng of screeching women, at least one of whom is waving a Sharpie and starting to remove her shirt* was probably what he was going for.)

"Just five minutes, promise," Tyler says, clapping Tun on one shoulder.

As soon as he rounds the car and starts walking toward the crowd, it's like an invisible hand turns the sound dial up to a thousand. Tun and I exchange looks that say, *You're seeing this, too, right?* And then, when three different bras are flung over the wall, *Do you think he'll make it out alive?*

But he does, and once Tyler is ushered away, the guards get to dispersing the crowd. I don't know how they do it, but in less than half an hour, I can't spot a single fan outside the gates. I imagine the threat of legal action and/or (worse), confiscation of phones, was used more than once.

Speaking of phones, absolutely no recording of any kind is allowed, which means I have to do things old-school. I scribble down as many notes as I can while mumbling a quick "Hi!" to everyone Tyler is (and consequently I am) introduced to as we make our way around. As I predicted, he's polite beyond belief, saying yes to every single photo and autograph request from whoever asks, even the park janitorial staff. But every time he gets a break from introductions, I can tell he's looking for something. Or someone.

Another thing I learn about Tyler: he prefers having his hair and makeup done in his private trailer so he can run lines with someone if he needs to; so that's where *I* sit and scrawl furiously while he, script in hand, alternates between quietly running lines by himself and conversing with his stylists. Finally, Tun knocks and pops his head in. "Ready?" he asks. When Tyler nods, he says into his headset, "Tyler's heading for set."

"You excited?" he asks me as he holds the door open.

"Actually, yeah," I say, smiling. The converging realizations that I'm about to watch the first few scenes of the new Tyler Tun movie and that I'm covering it for *Vogue* start to sink in, and every nerve in my body begins to thrum with nervous electricity.

We've only advanced a couple of feet, though, when a voice calls out, "Who let the riffraff in here?! Security!"

Tyler, his small hair and makeup army, and I all swivel to see May Diamond—the chicest bodyguard I've ever seen (fictional or not) in her black skinny jeans, cropped gray mock-neck top, hair in a low ponytail—full-on sprinting in our direction, a giant grin on her own perfectly made-up face.

Before I can react, Tyler takes one large step forward, open arms locking tight as soon as May's body launches into his. "Hi, asshole," he says into her ear.

It's one of those moments that almost feels too intimate for an outsider to witness, especially in such a public setting. For a split second, I'm tempted to put my notebook away and pretend I never saw this. But then I remember what Clarissa had said about how maybe this is the lead-up to the reveal of a secret relationship between May and Tyler, and, coupled with his vague answer earlier about why he chose *this* movie, I inconspicuously jot down my notes so I can revisit this moment later. How their eyes glint with something familiar, like ships spotting the warm beacon of the lighthouse. How, in spite of the raucous mob running and yelling into headsets around us, you can see their bodies relax, palpably feel them shift things around to welcome each other into their space. I think of how comfortable he'd looked earlier when he was talking about May, and I thought I'd gotten it at the time, but now I *really* get it.

And out of nowhere, a memory: Thidar and Nay letting themselves into my house at 6 A.M. the morning after Ben had packed a suitcase and walked out, three iced lattes and five boxes of tissues in hand, dressed in pajamas because they'd known that we weren't going to get out of bed that day, crawling under the covers on either side of me and holding me while I cried and cried like it was the end of the world. Because that day, that was exactly what it'd felt like, and if I had to face the end of the world, then there was no one else I wanted by my side.

I'm thankfully yanked out of my own brain by May's voice saying, "Hi! I'm May!" with her arm already stretched out.

"H-hi," I stammer as I take her hand, a small inner voice unable to stop itself from quietly squealing, *Holy shit, you're touching May Diamond*. "I'm Khin."

"She's the one doing the profile," Tyler says at the same time that May says, "You're the one who wrote that piece on the abortion clinic, right?"

I blink once, then another two times.

"The one in *Time*?" she prompts.

"Yes," I answer, apparently having forgotten my own article that I wrote earlier this year and that has already been nominated for two Society of Publishers in Asia awards.

May jerks her head at Tyler. "Ty's the one who sent it to me. I forwarded it to everyone I know." She takes one step forward, and her mouth curves into a small, sweet smile. "I bet it wasn't easy to get all of those stories on record," she says. "Thank you for what you do. Journalism is important, necessary work."

I've had people, especially women and particularly Myanmar women, reach out to me with some variant of the same sentiment over the past several months, but I did not expect May freaking Diamond to be one of them.

"Thank you," I parrot back at last.

May gives a nod before turning her attention back to Tyler. "You ready?" she asks, linking their elbows together.

"Am now," he says.

———

That was approximately five hours ago. It is now nearing midnight, and I am exhausted and perspiring like we've been shooting on location with the location being the sun. My arms and ankles are covered in red, blotchy mosquito bites, and we still have about two more hours left. And apparently this is one of the shorter shoots. I'm surprised that May and Tyler are still as cheery and nice as they were when we first arrived, because truthfully, I now get all those stories about actors banning people on set from talking to them. *I* would like to ban anyone from talking to me if I could. I already miss being able to hear myself think.

When a thirty-minute break is announced—the longest we've had all night—I start toward the wooden walkway that surrounds the lake, not caring where my feet take me as long as it's away from all of *this*. A few other crew members also disperse in different directions, as well as a group of three extras who're passing around a lighter, unlit cigarettes in their mouths as they stride toward the parking lot. A few paces ahead, one guy is headed in the same direction as me for the walkway, his face scrunched up as he concentrates on his phone screen.

I take out my own phone as I walk, and as predicted, the group chat has been going nuts this whole time, even though Nay and Thidar both know that I don't answer when I'm on assignment. The texts are basically different all-caps iterations of DO YOU KNOW HOW MANY PEOPLE'S INSTAGRAM LIVES YOU'RE IN!!! and HAVE YOU SEEN HIM SHIRTLESS YET? and IF THERE IS AN AFTERPARTY TO-NIGHT AND YOU DO NOT INVITE US, WE WILL NEVER EVER EVER FORGIVE YOU.

Trust me, nobody here has the mental, physical, or emotional capacity for an afterparty, I type before I realize that there's no signal in this section of the park. I look around to see if anyone else is having the same problem, but there *isn't* anyone around. I actually can't hear anybody anymore either, not even the majority of the cast and crew who were still hanging around the set; all I can see of said set through the trees and across the grass are the white canopy tops, and that's only because they're lit by the string lights. I didn't mean to get *this* far away from it all, but then again, I have been told (read: reprimanded by my friends) more than once that my regular walking pace is most people's power-walking pace, so.

I'm lifting my hand in a feeble attempt to find a single bar when I feel the hairs on my neck stand up a millisecond before I hear the cough. It's deep and drawn out, and my body takes in a huge gulp of air and doesn't exhale.

When I turn, the man from earlier has done a one-eighty and is now approaching me, phone gone, hands tucked into each of his pockets. Under the sparse, dingy yellow lamps, I can tell that he's white, dressed in jeans, a black T-shirt, and a baseball cap, and, most important, looks not insignificantly taller and stronger than me. My brain's first automatic command to my body is to find my pepper spray and alarm—which are sitting attached to my bag in Tyler's trailer. All I have on me is my phone, which is a glorified rose-gold brick right now. My eyes subtly scan around for anything I can use as a weapon—a rock, a large branch, pebbles to throw in his eyes—but there's nothing. All there is is darkness and the silent lake and me and a stranger and this narrow walkway.

"Hi there," the man says in what sounds like an Australian or possibly a New Zealand accent.

"Hey," I say, making my voice as unperturbed as possible, my unfounded optimism positing that he's just a friendly (and socially awkward) crew member trying to make conversation. After all, it's too dark for me to see if there's a set-regulated lanyard tucked under his shirt.

"Khin, right? You're working on the movie? The one with those two big stars?" He jerks his head toward the loud, bright set, which now looks and sounds like it's on another continent.

I nod, now certain that he does *not* work on the movie. How long has he been hanging around the set if he knows my name? How did no one notice him?

"Yeah," I say. "I should actually be heading back."

"Cool," is all he says.

I don't want to turn my back to him, but I also can't leave without turning away. "What's the movie about?" he asks, still strolling toward me at a steady pace.

How could I be so stupid to leave my entire bag behind? I thought the whole park had been sealed off to outsiders, but he must've snuck in through another entrance and loitered in the background. Was he just waiting for *any* of the women to wander off? Why the fuck had *I* strayed so far?

"Oh, just your standard rom-com," I say with a light chuckle. My left foot takes one cautious step backward, every brain cell screaming, *Get the fuck out of here right the fuck now.*

"I like rom-coms." With two, three, *four* steps, the guy is much closer than I thought he could or would be in just two seconds. "They always cast such . . . *pretty* gals."

I feel the boulder sink in one heavy motion, right from the top of my throat to the bottom of my gut. Any previous foolish notions I'd had about misjudging this guy have evaporated into the thick humidity. I want to cry. I know what happens next.

"My crew is waiting." I'm still trying to remain calm, breezy, not let my spine-warping fear show.

"They can wait a little longer, can't they . . ." And then he does it. He takes one final step and he's so close I can smell the alcohol on him, so searing and pungent I gag, see the stubble on his chin, feel his disgusting warm breath on my forehead. ". . . *sweetheart?*"

My brain switches off the moment his hand grips my left shoulder. When I feel the tightness of his hold, I *know* that he's not going to let me go, not unless I make him. I attempt to scream but he thrusts his free fist into my mouth. On reflex, I bite down into his salty palm.

"Fucking journalist bitch," he growls. Tears trail down my cheeks as he sandwiches me between him and the rail and starts grinding against me.

Something. I have to do *something.* I scratch his face with my right hand, and as my free hand falls to my side, right as I'm thinking that I should just let him do what he wants, because then at least maybe I'll get out of this alive, I feel it: the long, thin bulge of my pen in my front pants pocket.

Without thinking, I pull out the pen and, in one smooth motion that six years of using this exact pen has trained my thumb and forefinger to do, twist the cool silver top, and stab the newly protruded tip into his ear.

"What the fuck!" he screams, letting me go completely. His eyes bulge to the side of his head where the pen is still hanging from his ear. Blood trickles down his cheek and onto his shirt. "You crazy Asian bitch! I'm going to—"

When he lunges for me, I kneel. And when I see him wobble forward, hands trying to grasp at air before clutching his chest, I summon the strength of every single barre class I've ever gotten up at 6 A.M. to attend, wrap my arms around his calves, and lift him up and over the rail and toward the lake eight feet below like one of those mothers lifting a tractor off of their child.

But the sense of relief that I'm anticipating doesn't drop, and it takes me several beats to realize that it's because he hasn't either. Despite the blood pounding in my ears, I'm aware that I don't hear the splash I was anticipating. Still stunned, I'm trying to figure out what the fuck is happening when, through the railings, I see violent movement in the dark, something thrashing in the air. It doesn't occur to me that the movement is his legs flailing about because the fucker has managed to hang on to the rail—this doesn't occur to me, that is, until he grips my wrist with one sweaty palm, the act making me lurch forward, and I can see the full scene. I try to shake him off, but he digs his fingers under my watch to use it as a sort of hook. His eyes are huge, but not in a pleading *Please save me, I'm sorry* way, more in a *You crazy Asian bitch, if I'm going down, you're coming with me* way.

"Let me go!" I scream. His whole weight is pulling me lower, and although I'm already digging in my heels, I have to use my free hand to grip the rail. I want to reach over and bite his hand, but I'm worried he'll use it as an opportunity to grab my hair and take me down with him that way.

My throat burns. I'm fighting too hard to spare a moment to shout for help. Thidar's and Nay's faces flash through my mind. Then my parents. Even Ben. Even Tyler.

"Khin," comes Tyler's low voice as my brain goes haywire. I blink, but before I can make out how my imagination came up with *that*, there's a heavy enclosing pressure around my waist, and a third hand comes out of nowhere and smacks the guy's fingers with a large rock. He lets go and I stumble forward, but the pressure around my center tightens and stops me from falling over, too.

There is a thud before there is a splash.

I squint into the dark. With only some dim lamplight at my disposal, I can just make out the small trickle of blood already spreading out in the water.

I wait for him to scream. To splash around. To call me a fucking bitch again, but he just floats there, facedown.

My mouth makes a gasping motion, but there's no sound.

Oh no. Oh no oh no oh no oh no. I watch in mounting horror as the half of my pen that was jutting out from his ear floats out and sinks into the murky lake water. My *favorite* pen. My favorite pen . . . that has my fingerprints on it. Suddenly, every *Law & Order: SVU* episode I've ever watched (and I've watched all of them) starts replaying on fast-forward in my brain. DNA. My DNA will be under his nails. Oh my god. Maybe there'll be a strand of hair stuck in his shirt fibers. Oh dear god, a single strand of hair is going to be my downfall. Sure, I can say that it was self-defense, but that part comes later, after live footage of me being cuffed and escorted out of my building has aired on every news channel. Somewhere out there is a no-nonsense Myanmar Olivia Benson who is going to find that hair and meticulously bag it and track—

"Khin."

For a brief, hallucinatory moment, I wonder if that's him talking. If maybe I'm staring at someone else's body in the water, and the guy is actually still standing right beside me.

But it's not him. The pressure around my torso eases, and Tyler rounds and steps in front of me, almost shielding me from the scene in the water.

Tyler. Tyler's here. Tyler . . . saw what just happened.

"He was going to hurt me," I whisper.

The words have to be dredged out but as soon as they are, I race to the rail, lean forward, and retch, my body hurling vomit like it's physically trying to repel any traces of the past few minutes. My knees go weak and I have to grab the top wooden bar, but still I can't stop crying and throwing up at the same time.

"I've got you," says Tyler's voice.

He reaches out, probably to hold back my hair which has come out of its ponytail, but the instant his fingers touch my back, I whirl around and scream, "Don't touch me!"

He lifts his hand and steps back. "Sorry, I'm sorry."

"He was going to hurt me," I repeat.

Tyler nods. "I know." He swallows. "I saw it. I . . . saw everything."

Right. My brain tries to fill in the blanks, the pieces *I* didn't see: Tyler grabbing a rock, running over, grabbing me to keep me from falling over, hitting that guy's hand so he'd let go.

My shocked laughter vibrates in the air as my last functioning brain cells try their best to process the information at hand. "Tyler . . . I think we killed someone," I say as my mind thinks, *How is this a sentence I'm actually saying?*

He leans over the railing and stares at the corpse, his eyes gradually widening until they're as gawking as possible, and then he rubs at them as if trying to scrub away the sight he's just taken in. "Okay, let's not panic," he says, voice dropping. "We need to figure out what to do next. Let's go back to the set, and we can call the authorities and explain to them what happened."

"Which is what?" I ask, wiping my chin with the back of my hand. His head tips approximately twenty degrees to the left.

"What do you mean? The truth. That it was self-defense."

I know what he's saying is the legally correct thing to do, but my brain's already in crisis management mode, and I'm trying to come at this from the perspective of a complete stranger. "Do we have proof?" I ask out loud.

Tyler's head re-straightens, but there's a deep *V* between his brows. "What do you mean, *do we have proof*? I . . . saw it. You can tell them what happened before I showed up, and then I can pick it up from there."

A tiny, almost-muted splash makes us both jump. My body locks up, but Tyler peeks back over his shoulder, sighs with relief, and shakes his head at me. "I think it was fish," he says. "The b—" I wince at just the start of the word, and he catches himself. "*It* isn't moving. But as I was saying, look, we'll explain that it was self-defense."

I nod my head up and down slowly, then shake it side to side, the weight of the puzzle I'm trying to mentally solve bogging it down. "I don't have proof of what happened before you showed up." I make a wide, sweeping gesture with one hand. "There are no cameras. No one else was around. You only caught the last, what, three minutes? You can't testify to what happened before that."

"I—"

"I'm a journalist, Tyler," I say.

"What? What the hell does that mean?"

"It means I know the importance of evidence!" I yell in a sandpaper voice. "And right now, we don't have any. *I* don't have any." As I slot in the last piece of the puzzle, I know what we have to do. Or more precisely, what we have to *not* do. "We can't call the authorities," I say.

Tyler blinks and moves back like I've suggested we retrieve the body, chop it up, and invite everyone over for a barbecue. "Why *wouldn't* we call the authorities? That's literally what you do when you witness a murder!"

"When you *witness* a murder," I say, emphasizing each word. My annoyance breaks my trance, and briefly, I wish I had another pen so I could stab *him*, too, just a little bit. "We didn't witness a murder. We *committed* one."

The fact that he's as unperturbed and calm as ever makes me feel something akin to anger. "It was self-defense," he says. "We can explain that that was self-defense. Everyone will understand. I'll back you up on that."

"It doesn't work like that." I give a dark laugh, blinking more rapidly as I shake my head in disbelief. Is he *really* this ignorant and isolated in his little Hollywood bubble? "Tyler, we killed a man. A *white* man. We both know what happens to Brown people who kill *white* people. Anywhere in the world. Even in this country."

"It was self-defense," he repeats, although his tone is more strained. I can't believe what he's suggesting, just like he can't believe what I'm suggesting.

For the sole reason that he stopped me from potentially (almost definitely) getting killed tonight, I *don't* roll my eyes and switch over to a patronizing tone like I'm explaining basic math to a child. Instead, through gritted teeth, I say, "It won't *matter*. Whatever country that scumbag is from, their embassy will demand someone pay for this. And guess what? One of us doesn't have an army of the best lawyers money can buy on speed dial. One of us didn't have dinner at the fucking White House last Christmas."

"We'll *both* get lawyers," he starts, and for a second, I want to laugh at his naïveté. Call it collateral damage from the job, but I've covered one too many stories where the discrepancy between how a society's laws should work and how they actually work was several dark, twisted miles apart.

We're running out of time but what he's saying is beyond the realm of possibility. My knees cave and I fall back down on my ass.

"It's not just about the lawyers! Nobody can touch someone like you! People will bend over backwards to make sure nothing happens to you," I say, raking my hand through my hair and gripping the roots so I can have *something* to hold on to in lieu of patience and general sanity. How is he not getting this? How do I *make* him get this? "You're *you*. And I'm . . . not." If I were in a better state of mind, I'd be able to phrase it more eloquently, but then again, that *is* the crux of it.

Sitting down in front of me, Tyler ducks his head so he can see my face. "Khin," he says softly even while I teeter on the edge of hyper-ventilation. "So, what? We don't tell anyone? Ever?"

"No, never. We can't," I say, and the way his face crumples makes it clear that he was certain that that wouldn't be my answer. "Look." Despite the hysteria pumping through me at full force, I take a deep breath, because I have to calm down, because I *have to* get him to see this from my point of view. This only works if we're both on the same page. "Say, somehow, we *do* ultimately get acquitted. But this trial will go on for months, probably over a year. And during that time, our faces will be everywhere. Our lives will never be the same. My career will be over. And there'll be a serious dent in yours, too. Starting with this movie, for example." I point over his shoulder in the direction of the set. "This movie will be shut down *immediately*."

There's that mouth twitch, and I know I've got him. It's that moment in the middle of tug-of-war when you manage to pull the rope an inch closer to your side and you catch the flash of panic in the other person's eyes.

I keep pulling.

"This has been in the works for *years*. This would ruin more than just the two of us. Think of what this will do to May. The studio, the rest of the cast and crew." I remember him going out of his way to greet everyone on set, and I press on that. "How will we explain this to all of *them*? And the fans? Movies like this don't get green-lit every day, I know you know that."

Say what you will about Tyler Tun, but the man is dedicated to his job. Or maybe to May. Or his fans. Regardless, it's working in my favor.

"Okay," he says at last with an air of defeat, like he's run through every single scenario in his head, and he has to conclude that I'm right every time. "We need a plan, then." He presses his lips into a tight line; another forms between his brows as he thinks. "I'm just taking a stab here—"

"Heh."

"Wh—" He lets out a groan. "Okay, that wasn't intentional."

"Still funny."

He smiles. "You don't happen to know how long it takes for a body to sink, do you? I'd google it, but no cell service. Also, we probably shouldn't have that kind of thing in our search history."

"Actually." I sniffle. "Soon. It'll start sinking soon."

With a quick, dry laugh, he asks, "Do I want to know how you know that?"

I return a meek smile. "I watch a lot of *SVU*." I swallow and continue, "But it'll resurface quickly. Maybe a few days. Bodies stay submerged longer in cold water, but because of the heat, this one won't stay under for too long."

Tyler nods. "But this is a public park. Hundreds of people come here every day. By the time it resurfaces, it'll be impossible to track down anyone. The water will wash away any DNA. The fish will probably start nibbling, too."

"The humidity will help speed up decomposition," I add.

"Good. That's good."

I stare at him, unsure whether I'm about to burst into tears or if I've already emotionally shut down. I'm beginning to shiver even though my cheeks feel like they're on fire.

"What?" he asks.

"How do I know I can trust you?" I blurt out.

There's that line between his brows again. He scoots an inch closer, although still making sure to leave plenty of space between the two of us. "Because *I* trust *you*," he says.

"Why?"

"Because you—" And then he catches himself. He tries to play it off as though he's trying to come up with an answer, as though he didn't already have one that, for whatever reason, he thought twice about telling me. A backup explanation doesn't come as quickly as he'd like; I think the shock and adrenaline are slowing him down, too.

"Because I what?" I prompt.

"Because *you* have to trust me, too, right? That's how this works, right? We just . . . have to trust the other. We . . . we have to. We both have things to lose."

I want to tell him that that's not nearly a good enough reason. Minutes ago, he wanted to call the police. He still could, at any moment, and I'm aware that I have to keep a close eye on him going forward.

But also . . . he's right. We just . . . *have* to. I have my career (not to mention the rest of my life), and, to an extent, so does he. He wouldn't be destroyed the way I would, but I bet a lot of things would be taken off the table. Bond, for example.

I freeze when I remember something, a last burst of cognizance. "My pen. It's still lodged in his ear."

We both look over at the water. "It's gone," he says resolutely. "And considering that it's a single pen in a large body of water, the odds are good that it's never going to turn up."

"But *if* it does—" I can't even finish the sentence, but I don't have to.

"*If* it does," Tyler says, picking it up. "It's still going to be one of hundreds, possibly thousands, of random objects that are in that lake. It's almost definitely going to fall out of his ear, and whoever finds it will just toss it back in. They can't match a random person with a random pen that was found in a public park. There's nobody else around. It's just you and me."

Just you and me. He says it so effortlessly, like it doesn't occur to him that we now possess the ability to blow up each other's lives in a matter of seconds if we want to. But I guess mutually assured destruction is one of the most airtight ways to keep secrets.

Five

When I get home, I throw up two more times: once while I'm brushing my teeth, and the second during my hour-long scalding shower.

While at the park, we took the long way back to the parking lot so as to avoid the main set area. Tyler asked Tun to grab my stuff while he walked me straight to the car.

"What are you going to say when people ask?" I mumbled, brain still not working, feet stepping in the same spots that his were in front of me, like a baby deer literally following in its mother's footsteps.

"That you weren't feeling well so I made you go home."

"Food poisoning," I said. "No one ever wants to know more about food poisoning. Or say a heavy period. Like, World War Three blood-bath level," I added. Neither of us laughed.

After I got my bag and made sure everything was inside, and Yan, the studio-assigned driver, had started the car and was ready to leave,

I mustered up my most grateful smile. "Thank you," I said to Tyler. I could still smell and taste the tangy bile on my tongue and was *not* looking forward to my next encounter with a mirror.

He nodded and, right as he was stepping back and about to shut the door, moved forward, reinserting himself between the door and me. In silent synchronism, we looked to make sure the driver's door and window were both closed, *and* the partition between the front and backseats fully rolled up before saying anything.

"Do you . . . need me to come with you?" Tyler asked, scanning my face.

Even in my state, I snorted out a laugh. "Tyler, this is your first day of shooting."

He shrugged. "May and I agreed that we each get one diva moment on this movie. I could storm off. You know how volatile actors are."

"I'm okay," I said. A blatant lie, but he let me have it. "I just need to shower and sleep it off. Shooting is at the lot tomorrow, right? For the scene with that diplomats' party thing? Two P.M. call time?"

His frown deepened, and I watched him almost reach out for my shoulder before catching himself and settling his hand atop the car door. "You can't work tomorrow."

"Yes, I can."

"Khin—"

"I just need to sleep it off," I repeated, aware that I sounded like a single-minded toddler. "And it'll look suspicious if I don't show up tomorrow."

After a long silence during which I'd refused to be the first to break eye contact, he at last sighed and nodded. "I'll come pick you up," he said. "We can . . . sort out a story."

"Okay," I said.

"Okay," he repeated. "I'll see you at one thirty."

I take a Xanax right before I change into a pair of cream silk pajamas—my favorite, although unlike in the past, they don't improve my mood—and then I crawl into bed, pull the covers up right under my chin, and prepare to drift off.

Except I can't close my eyes. Because every time I close my eyes, I'm there again. And again. And again and again and again. It won't stop.

At 5 A.M., I do my laundry. By seven, I'm re-color-coordinating the pile of clothes in my wardrobe that Nay and Thidar had flung around while trying to choose my First Dinner With Tyler outfit, Saweetie's "Best Friend" blasting in the background. I know that night was less than a week ago, but it feels like a memory from a distant life. Like someone else's life. Someone who did not commit first-degree murder.

So this is how it's going to be, I think as I grab a stray purple Kate Spade dress from between the pinks and hang it in its correct section. *There's going to be a before and an after.* When people talk about defining moments that split your life into two distinct segments, *this* is what they're talking about.

I have another coffee, take another shower, have a small sandwich while still in my pajamas, then decide on my outfit for the day: dark blue jeans and my favorite black vintage Prada halter-neck top. If I'm going to feel numb, I might as well look hot while doing it.

Except—I can't be feeling numb. I can't go through the rest of today on this precipice of a panic attack. I want to talk to someone. Not Tyler because I can't afford to freak him out (even more). The first names that I want to reach for are Thidar and Nay. Nay wakes up earlier because she likes to have a run before going into the office for another day of Important Publicist Things, but I can't bring myself to go further than stare at her name in my call log. For one, I don't want to bring them into my mess. And two, as I recall the way they were worried about me just last week, worried about things that, objectively, are much less important and urgent than my committing a murder, I can only imagine what this news will do to them. I can already picture them whisper-arguing while I'm out of the room, telling each other, *We should've checked on her more*, and *See, I told you she was barely hanging on*. In spite of them being my best friends in the whole world, the thought of having them see me like this, at my absolute, definitive rock bottom, ignites a searing shame.

I have a habit of checking my email as often and as thoughtlessly as most people check their Instagram feed, so I open my phone and refresh my inbox—and right at the top is an email from Clarissa from five minutes ago.

From: csong@vogue.sg
To: khinh@gmail.com
Subject: Checking in

Hope yesterday went well. Let me know if you need anything on my end. Can still send you that company card if you need one.

Remember—write me a good story. I want to be *astounded*.

C

As much as I want to forget last night, I take a deep breath and force myself to remember *why* I was in the park in the first place. The shoot. The film. Tyler. The article.

There's also the rest of my fucking life.

What happened has already happened, Tyler and I have both agreed we can't tell anyone about this, and now I have to put it behind me. I *have* to. I can't spend every single night of the rest of my life in an insomniac daze, unable to do something as simple as make myself a breakfast that's more substantial than a slice of cheese between two pieces of bread.

Unsure of where exactly one starts when embarking on The Journey to Get Your Life Back on Track After Killing Someone, I gravitate toward what I'm most familiar with: work.

The night after that dinner with Clarissa, as the start of my research, I'd stayed up to gather as many celebrity profiles as I could find by entertainment writers I admired. Now, opening my laptop, I swipe to the browser window that has approximately ten tabs still open. Caity Weaver on Cardi B for *GQ*. Jia Tolentino on Selena Gomez for *Vogue*. Allison P. Davis on Meghan Markle for *The Cut*. Ashley C. Ford on Serena Williams for *Allure*. All of E. Alex Jung's profiles in *Vulture*.

I start with the Selena article, and keep a blank document open to compile a list of questions and observations to be mindful of for my own story. But despite being a fairly quick reader (at least, pre-murder), sentences keep blurring as I reach the end, and I have to return to the beginning, only to realize I've lost focus again by the time I read the last word. Fifteen minutes later, and I've read the first—I scroll back to the top of the page to double-check—one and a half paragraphs. Even better is the fact that I've absorbed approximately 10 percent of it.

My frustration begins to fuse together with my exhaustion and anxiety, and it takes me another fifteen minutes to finish that second paragraph.

A break. I need a ten-minute power nap to recoup.

I put the laptop down on the floor, pull my throw blanket tighter around me, and flip so I'm facing into my cushions. As I rest my burning eyes, I congratulate past-Khin for splurging on the larger, more expensive couch.

The next thing I'm aware of is my phone vibrating from where it's fallen underneath my chin. It's Tyler.

"Hey," he says. "I texted you to say I'm downstairs but you didn't respond. If you're still asleep, I—"

The clock at the top of the screen says 1:45 P.M. Fuck fuck fuck. "No!" I say, jumping up and running into the bathroom for a quick pee while simultaneously putting my hair up into a tight ballerina bun. "Be right there, give me five," I say, and use my elbow to end the call.

"Afternoon," Tyler says when I enter the backseat exactly five minutes later.

"Good afternoon," I say with my biggest, brightest, it-*is*-a-good-afternoon smile. "How'd you sleep?"

"Good," he says.

"Good." I nod.

"You?"

"Yep," I say. It's not even the right answer, but I can't be bothered to amend it, and he lets it go.

The rest of the ride is undiluted silence, the kind that suddenly makes you aware of your own breathing pattern. Although Yan is in the driver's seat just a few feet away, the black opaque rolled-up partition makes it feel like Tyler and I are blocked out from the rest of the world. I know we should be using this alone time to get our stories straight as planned, but he's giving me the grace of waiting for me to bring it up first, and as hard as I try, I can't bring myself to even think about last night without wanting to vomit again. *It's okay*, I reason. We'll talk about it during one of the breaks.

"Ready?" I ask as we pull into the lot.

Reminding myself that my job is still on the line here, I envision myself taking everything from the Before and shoving it into a large, airtight, opaque container. Weirdly, it works. I can already feel that part of my brain shutting down, the lights dimming to complete darkness.

"Khin," he says while Yan parks the car. "We should talk—"

"Tyler!" The door swings open and Yasmin, the director, is standing there, a small army of people with headsets around their necks and clipboards in their hands on standby right behind her. I only had a brief chat with her yesterday, but I like Yasmin. She's a few years older than me, talks quickly and efficiently like someone who doesn't have the time for small talk, and although she has a string of highly acclaimed indie flicks under her belt, this is her first big blockbuster. "Afternoon! Hi, Khin!" she says, leaning over to wave at me.

"Hey, Yasmin," I say, hopping out of my own door that Yan is holding open. I take the two seconds while I round the back of the car to gather myself.

But my conviction that I can get through today in a composed, professional manner is shot to pieces when Yasmin says, "Tyler, we have . . . a situation." Her eyes dance over to me toward the end of the sentence to imply that I, too, am included in this "we."

"What's up?" Tyler asks.

Yasmin sucks in her cheeks. "There's . . . police. Inside." She nods back at the set which, from the outside, looks like an unassuming giant container amidst the colony of trailers. Crew members carrying long ladders and large circular reflectors enter and exit the container through one semipermanently open door. Extras pulling up the hems of their hta meins and pa soes are shuffling about, presumably not running so that they don't sweat through their long-sleeved tops; I'm assuming they're going to be in the background of one of the first scenes of the day, which is a lavish dinner soirée at the house of Princess of Fictional Country's Ambassador.

I stare at them, all these human beings doing their jobs and going about their day, but the longer I stare—and I can't *stop* staring, in fact

I'm incapable of doing anything else, even blinking—the more those individuals blur into one multicolored kaleidoscopic haze. One of my last few functioning brain cells is aware that I'm having the kind of out-of-body experience that I've only ever heard people talk about. *My chest shouldn't feel this tight,* I think. Do I want to cry? Sit down? Run away? I don't know. I don't know how to do . . . anything.

The police are here. And they must be here because the body's turned up; it's the sole logical explanation. But *how?* In less than twelve hours?

"Oh?" Tyler's voice flicks some sort of switch, and, albeit with great effort, I turn both my head and attention toward him. "Is there a permit problem?" he asks, eyebrows raising in surprise.

"Not . . . exactly." Yasmin draws out every word. "Apparently there was . . . a situation . . . last night. In . . . the park."

As though someone's called "Action!" Tyler looks baffled, brows furrowing, chin tilting slightly to the side. I, on the other hand, can feel the backs of my thighs start to sweat inside my jeans. "Let me guess." He rolls his eyes. "Noise complaint from the neighbors."

Yasmin gives a short, nervous laugh. "No, no noise complaint. More like . . . a body."

Okay, now the undersides of my boobs are sweating.

Tyler, however, frowns more, never one to break character. "A body?" he asks. "What do you mean a . . . body?"

Yasmin makes meaningless gestures in the air with her hands. "This morning, some people were fishing in the lake and it would appear that they discovered . . . a body. Like . . . a human body."

"Oh my god, that's awful," he says, jaw dropping.

"Yes, terrible. They're still trying to figure out who it is. Poor man didn't have any ID on him. All they know is that he's a foreigner. A white man in his forties, probably."

"Holy shit! And you said the police were *here?*"

"Mm-hmm," Yasmin says, the apprehension returning in her voice.

"Do they think one of us saw something?"

"Not . . . exactly," she says in the same protracted tone as earlier. "Basically—" She coughs, like the rest of the sentence is lodged in her throat. "The coroner put the time of death between midnight and seven A.M. The body was discovered around eight." When she says, "The water damage is making the investigation difficult," my knees almost buckle in relief. That small, sweet moment is quickly snatched away by her next words: "They think he was murdered."

My gut gives out like I'm free-falling off of the world's highest roller coaster.

"They don't think it was an accident? Maybe he was drunk and fell over?" Tyler offers.

Yasmin shakes her head. "They're saying it's murder because they found scratch marks on his face. And bruises as well, although that might have been from hitting himself on the bridge as he fell over. But there was also some sort of injury in one of his ears. Looks like he might've been stabbed there, although we're waiting on the official autopsy report to confirm this."

"Damn." Tyler exhales, tugging a palm down his face. "Okay, do they think one of the cameras caught something? Because we didn't start shooting until six. We can hand over the footage if—"

"Tyler." Yasmin says his name like a mother preparing a child for devastating news. "We closed off the park at noon."

Tyler takes a second, his eyes darting around as he processes the information. "But *this* guy got in."

"Yes, and they checked all the park security footage and saw him sneaking in past the entrance on the other side when the guard on duty went to the bathroom—"

"So it's possible that someone else—"

"He was the only person who entered via that entrance all day. They've gone through all the footage on all of the cameras except . . ."

Tyler shakes his head. "Except what?"

"Except the ones that *we* had them turn off. On *our* side of the park. And the only people who were allowed in through our entrance was *our* people. We had five guards there."

"I'm . . . not following," he says, not fidgeting in the slightest. If I didn't know firsthand that Tyler knew what he knew, *I* would believe his performance, and the knowledge that I would be just as gullible as Yasmin is now if he ever decided to lie to *my* face doesn't sit well—but I can't contend with that fear right this moment.

"Tyler—" Yasmin sighs again. I feel a surge of pity for this poor woman who just wanted to shoot a rom-com with two of Hollywood's biggest stars, and is now having to inform one of said stars what he and I already know: somebody got murdered last night, and the police know the culprit was—is—part of the movie crew. "They think it's someone from the set."

"That's absurd!" Tyler says with a bark of laughter. "*Loads* of other people were there! The park cleaning staff—"

"All left through the other entrance, and every single one of them was gone before the man entered the park. The cameras accounted for all of them. The only people in the park at the time were us."

"So what are you saying?" Tyler asks with another half laugh, like surely there's a miscommunication here. "The police are here to, what, arrest us?"

In a feeble attempt to blend in, I mimic Tyler's laugh, although mine peters out in a sharp downturn. Thankfully, Yasmin joins in, snorting as though it's the most ridiculous thing she's ever heard, more ridiculous than the idea that she might be working with a potential murderer. "Oh god, no!" she says. "Please, I would have our legal team here so fast they wouldn't know what hit them. But they do want to talk to us. And in terms of the movie, this does throw a wrench into our shooting schedule. We're trying to iron everything out ASAP, but our on-location shoots are called off for the foreseeable future. We're going to be in this lot"—without looking, she points behind her—"until we've been given the all-clear. Legal doesn't want to take any chances. The police will talk to you two in a couple of hours if that's okay?"

I swear my heart outright stops beating. "The two of us?" Tyler asks.

"They asked me for a timeline of as much as I could remember from yesterday, and I mentioned that Khin had left early and that you escorted her out. I think they just want to double-check with you both that you didn't see anything as you were making your way back to the car."

In the most casual fashion, Tyler shrugs and shoves his hands into his pockets like he's heard everything that Yasmin has said, but doesn't see how any of it affects him in any way whatsoever. "Okay," he says. "I can talk, as long as it's between takes."

"I—"

"I think this is an absurd accusation, especially because everyone was so exhausted last night we barely had enough time to use the bathroom, let alone go murder a man, but I get that they're doing their job. But similarly"—he waves over at the people striding around the lot—"*we* have jobs to do, too. There are a lot of hardworking people on this set who were here long before we were, and will have to stay behind for hours after we leave. And unless the police are going to personally pay for their overtime, I'm not going to make this team work even longer hours than they already are. And if they have a problem with that, then *I* can call Legal."

There's a pause during which I worry that Yasmin is going to snap at him or, for some reason, turn to me and ask if I saw anything.

I suddenly become aware of my posture, specifically, how quiet and hunched over I am, like I'm cowering with guilt, so I straighten my back, and—because who better to take cues from than a professional actor—put my hands in my own pockets like I'm chill, casual, innocent, just a woman hanging out while those in charge clear up this small, unfortunate hiccup.

At last, Yasmin nods and spins on her heels. "Send hair and makeup to his trailer. Is May ready?" she asks one of the staff who begins talking into their headset.

I seem to have loaded lead into my sneakers when I got dressed, because my feet will not move. I don't notice Tyler hanging back until he shifts close enough to me and, now that everyone else is already scrambling back toward the main area, places a hand on the small of my back.

"It's okay," he whispers, and gives me the gentlest of nudges. It works. My feet remember how to walk.

"How?" I ask.

"We'll figure it out."

"How?" It's a demand more than an ask this time.

I look up at him, but his gaze is trained forward, still resolute in its ignorance. "Not here," is all he says.

Six

════

nd . . . done!" Moh Moh, the makeup artist, announces with a triumphant smile after rubbing the makeup sponge across Tyler's cheekbones one final time.

Tyler, still in his chair and facing the mirror, flashes a smile. "Thanks, gang," he says. And then, "Hey, do you guys mind stepping out? I need five minutes with Khin." When they exchange repressed smirks, he inclines his chin at my reflection and adds, "Your editor still wants to talk to us today, right?"

Once Tyler tightens his smile at my dazed reflection, I understand. "Yes!" I check my watch. "In fact, Clarissa should be calling any minute."

"Right," he says, standing and turning to face everyone. "We'll be out as soon as we're done." Addressing Tun, he adds, "Please make sure no one disturbs us," and the kid nods with such determination that I'm surprised he doesn't add a little salute.

When they're gone, Tyler locks the door and joins me on the other end of the couch.

The panic attack that I've been staving off since my shower this morning punches me right in the face. "Tyler," I say, voice already trembling. I will *not* survive a police interrogation. "What are we going to do?"

"It's going to be okay," he says, so calmly that it almost hypnotizes me into believing him. "The fact that they're interviewing everyone means that they don't have any suspects."

"But we can't let someone else take the fall for this."

He shakes his head. "Of course not. No one is going to take the fall for this. And no one is going to find out what happened."

I hug my knees to my chest, fear tightening and twisting my nerves. "I killed a man. Oh my god, I really killed a man. *We* killed a man. But everyone knows I went home early. I was the only one who left." My eyes start to widen, which is weird, considering my lungs are rapidly constricting. "I'm the only viable suspect."

He slides closer to me and puts a hand on my elbow. "Even if that is true, as long as neither of us breaks, they don't have anything concrete. But Khin." His warm, soft fingers curl around my skin and, to my surprise, the gesture grounds me, preventing me from floating away completely. "You need to trust me, remember?"

I blink, really registering him for what feels like the first time today. "Trust you?" I echo, my body coiling tighter, so tight that it feels as if I'm going to snap clean in the middle.

He seems confused by my question, but nods nonetheless. "I'm not going to tell anyone. You have my word."

I stare at him, sentences starting and finishing in my head.

"Khin?" Tyler tips his head, trying to get a better read on me.

The filter between my brain and mouth collapses. "We just met. I don't know anything about you. You don't know anything about me. We're strangers! We could betray each other at any second!" I close then open my mouth. When a sob leaps out, I shutter my face with my palms. "I don't want to go to jail," I whisper.

"Khin," he says, and tries to interlace his fingers through mine, but immediately I startle backward. "Sorry," he says, raising his hands.

I swallow. "What if they break one of us?"

"They won't."

"How can you be so sure?"

"Because we're in this together." And, as though he knows that by *What if they break one of us,* I meant to say, *What if they break you,* he adds, "I have things on the line, too, remember?"

My heart is pounding so hard, I'm worried a blood vessel is going to pop somewhere. "But—"

"I won't break. I promise. You *have* to believe me, Khin." His upper body straightens as he inhales. "The only way we'll get through this is if we trust each other. Now I trust you completely. But I . . . " He pauses. "I need you to do the same with me, too."

I study his face and body for the smallest tic, anything to indicate that he's lying—but I get nothing. Either he's *very* good under pressure, or he's telling the truth. Or he's someone who acts for a living and is transferring those skills over to his private life; there's also that possibility. After all, I just watched him lie to Yasmin. He's had no trouble playing it cool as a small team of artists cocoons him and does his hair and makeup, whereas I still want to scream anytime someone so much as brushes their arm against mine. If it weren't for my panic attack, he'd already be on set right now, shooting scenes and hanging out with May.

But I also know he's right. As much as I detest leaving my fate in someone else's hands, we won't get through this unless I trust him, even if it's only the minimum amount required. All I can do is trust him *and* be wary of him—*that'll be fun,* I think with a silent, rueful scoff.

To his surprise, in one swift and wordless motion, I stand up, walk toward the mirror, and brace myself on the vanity counter. My eyes are red-rimmed and my hair is a flat mess, although I do pat myself on the back for having the foresight to skip the mascara today. I undo my bun and shake out my hair. "He was going to rape me and then he was going to kill me. It was self-defense," I say to my reflection.

Tyler nods. "It *was.*"

Straightening my posture, I start fixing my hair into a new neat bun. I'm scared and sleep-deprived and a little angry and, overall, exhausted, but I need to rally. *Yesterday was the worst day of your life,* I remind my reflection as I comb my fingers through my strands. *You lived through the worst day of your life, and you're still here.* "We need a plan," I say with newfound determination. "Starting with the pen. That pen is still out there, and I need to go back to that park and find it before they do."

Tyler gets to his feet. "When—"

Several consecutive loud thuds on the door make us both jump.

"Yeah?" Tyler calls out.

"I'm really sorry to disturb you," Tun's voice answers, muffled by the door. "But they're asking if you're ready. May's done with her scene."

"Okay! Be out in a minute!" Tyler turns to me, briefly surprised to find me facing him now.

We don't have time to come up with a plan right this second. I walk forward until I'm near enough to smell his fresh pine scent. I tilt my head up, noting that he is probably the tallest Asian person I know, before trying to find one last indication that he's lying to me.

"Can I really trust you?" I finally ask when I don't see anything, although it feels a lot like peering into a dark cave from the entrance and going, *From this vantage point, I can't see anything that could potentially kill me, so surely it* must *be safe.*

"I promise," he says.

---

f at any point during filming it hits Tyler that he's now an accomplice to an actual crime, he doesn't show it. At all.

I watch him nail his lines, cry on command, laugh at May's character's jokes. *That's weird, right?* I want to pull someone aside and whisper. *That he's still this good at his job despite, you know,* everything?

But of course I can't do that, so instead I stand in the shadows and decide that, hey, if Tyler's doing his job, then that means it's time for me to do mine, too. I reopen that plastic container from earlier and shove all this new information—the police, the investigation, Tyler saying with complete seriousness, *I promise*—into it and shut it once more. Flipping through my notebook, I land on my list of questions from earlier and—

"Boo!" A male voice in my ear makes me jump and I let out a small yelp, to everybody's immediate and obvious disapproval. "Sorry!" I squeak, holding up a hand in apology.

When Yasmin commands, "Alright, let's start again from the top," people descend onto the set and begin rearranging the room in which Nanda and Mra had been having an intense argument that will eventually lead to their first hookup.

"Wha—" I hiss as I turn to the source of the voice, and stop, shock replacing my anger. "Jason!" I gasp.

"A little birdie told me you were here," Jason says and wraps his lanky arms around me.

In a stiff motion like I'm hugging *that* uncle at a family gathering, I put my arms around his waist for two seconds before letting go. "No one told me *you* were here!" I sputter. "What *are* you doing here?"

"My job." When I respond with a frown, Jason rolls his eyes and motions over at May, who's running lines with her PA. "What, did you think *any* common makeup artist could blend neon blue and orange eyeshadow that seamlessly?"

I *had* been thinking earlier that May's makeup looked incredible. "Wait. I didn't see you yesterday."

He waves a hand. "My flight from Mandalay got canceled and the next one out was this morning."

"Oh," I say. Jason looks like he's waiting for me to say something a little . . . *more*. "I . . . see."

His jaw works, and he squints at me as though double-checking that he has the right person. "You okay?" His initial enthusiasm has tapered. "You don't look so good."

Fuck. I throw my free hand in the air. "Sorry, this whole thing," I gesture around us, "is still so bizarre to me, and my editor emailed me early this morning, so I'm . . . feeling the pressure."

Jason's face lights up with an *Ah* expression. "That's *totally* understandable, but—"

I don't know how long Tyler's been standing beside us, but when he says, "Hey," Jason and I both whip our heads at the same time.

Tyler looks at me and then at Jason before extending a hand. "Hi, I don't think we met yesterday? I'm Tyler."

I know that as one of the region's most sought-after makeup artists, Jason typically does not get starstruck. *Typically*. But at Tyler's hand reaching out for his, he lets out a giggle, reddens at the sound that he just made, straightens himself and tries to smile, and, after several awkwardly long seconds, takes Tyler's hand. "I'm J-Jason," he says, tripping over his own name in the last moment. "I'm May's head makeup artist."

"Hi," Tyler says. With a half shrug in my direction, he asks, "You two know each other?"

Jason and I exchange *a look*. "I'm . . ." His smile stiffens. "Ben's brother."

"Ben?" Tyler asks.

Jason gives me another look to ask if he should take this one as well. "Ben is my ex," I say, and add for context, "Husband. My ex-husband."

"Ah." Tyler nods.

"Yep," I say.

"I know this one *pretty* well." Jason nudges my shoulder with his. "I miss you! It feels like it's been ages since we last saw each other."

It's *my* turn to draw my smile into something civil. "I missed you, too." A part of me means it, but this is the first time I've seen Jason since he helped Ben pack up his stuff, and I really don't want to be doing this here right now. I'm never a fan of putting my personal life on display for people to gawk at and probe, but I'm *especially* not into doing it in front of a film crew, each of whom undoubtedly knows someone who knows someone who knows about my and Ben's divorce. Funny how cities are always big, except for when you need them to be.

"She'd even tag along to our shoots sometimes," Jason continues, addressing Tyler.

"Shoots?" Tyler raises a brow.

"Ben was a photographer. *Is*. He's a photographer," I explain.

"Sorry, I thought you knew," Jason says, oblivious to my dagger eyes. "My brother and I often overlap on shoots. And it'd always be a blast whenever Khin showed up. We always talked about doing a story together, the three of us, and then—" When he looks back at me this time, I know there's nothing subtle about the way I'm flashing my teeth via my most menacing smile (but a smile nonetheless!).

"I mean—" he starts.

"Jason!" May calls out. She's holding a coffee flask in her hands.

"Do you mind redoing my lipstick? Sorry, this latte was speaking to me."

"Coming!" Jason yells and sprints over.

Before I can make any small talk, Tyler takes a half step closer. "They want to talk to us," he murmurs.

"What?"

"The police. They want to talk to us after this scene," he says, body language cloaked in normalcy, like we're chitchatting while crew members re-angle the paintings on the walls. "Immediately after."

"You have to stall them. Throw a tantrum."

"Over what?"

"I dunno, actor stuff!" I hiss. "Maybe you don't like your outfit."

A sound comes out of his chest but it's muffled by him pressing his lips shut. I think it was meant to be a laugh but it translates into a low rumble. "You don't think it'll be suspicious if I *stall* the police? Police who are asking to speak to people about a murder investigation?"

"You're the star of the show," I say, contorting my mouth into a taut smile. "If you can get an assortment of sorbets stocked in your trailer, I'm sure you can figure this out. What *is* that about, by the way?"

"How do you know about the sorbets?"

"I checked out your rider."

"You mean you snooped."

"I'm a journalist."

"Snoop."

He's technically right, but I'm not admitting that. "You're missing the point," I mutter, and crack my neck. "You need to stall so that we can coordinate our stories. Or else they might hear a discrepancy and get suspicious and press and one of us will crack."

Out of the corner of my eye—because for some reason, we're

still not looking at each other—I see his shoulders shake lightly with a silent laugh. "Khin, I lie for a living, remember? *I'm* not going to crack," he says. My eyes trail up to his face which, at last, turns to me. "Are *you*?"

I scrunch up my own face in offense. "I wouldn't crack if my life depended on it."

He lifts a brow. "Didn't you just have a meltdown in my trailer?" His tone is teasing, and instead of being mean or accusatory, the question comes out like a friendly jab, like the kind Thidar or Nay would give me.

"Nope, you must have the wrong person," I reply with a sneer. His soft smile wrinkles the corners of his eyes, and in a short glitch, my heart goes light and jittery in my chest. "Why the sorbets?" I counter, breaking eye contact and peering over at May, whose hair team is spritzing her with three different sprays.

"I'm trying to go vegan."

"What?"

Tyler shrugs. "Better for the environment."

"But a *vegan* James Bond?" I gasp-whisper. "PETA is going to have a *field day* with that. They're going to have a giant billboard of you cuddling bunnies in the middle of Times Square!"

"PETA is a racist and misogynistic organization and my team knows I will never work with them," Tyler responds. After a beat, his eyes slide over to meet mine. "I would say you can quote me on that, but I should probably clear it with Bolu first. Just in case she needs to get a head start on the PR."

"Too bad, pal," I say, pursing my lips to the side. "No take-backs."

He laughs, and for a split second, the sound grates over my skin in a simultaneously delicious and uncomfortable way. And then the next second, I'm slapping myself with an invisible ruler because that is *so* unethical and also because I've remembered why Tyler came over in the first place.

"I—" I start.

He seems to remember, too, because, expression sobering, he mutters, "Take off an earring."

"What?"

"Your earrings. They look expensive."

"They *are*. They were my thirtieth birthday present to myself. I got them at this little boutique in Florence."

"Good. Now take one off. Quickly."

"But—"

"Khin, *trust me*."

"I—"

"Once that last pillow is fluffed," he inconspicuously points his chin toward the set, where people are starting to scamper off and May's strolling back to her mark, "we're screwed. Lose one earring. Now."

I tilt my head down so that my hair falls over my left ear. Then, pretending like I'm scratching the back of my neck, I remove the backing from my rose-gold-encased sapphire earring and drop it in the back pocket of my purse.

"Good," Tyler says. "Now gasp *really* loudly. Like you've just found out *SVU*'s been canceled."

Unintentionally, I *do* gasp really loudly. I also jerk back and my face contorts with horror. "How dare—"

"What's wrong?" Tyler asks, also loudly. He shifts to face me, and tucking his chin in so that his expression is hidden from view from the rest of the now-silent cast and crew, flicks his eyes at my left ear.

Oh, I mouth. "My earring!" I gasp, and feel around my lobe. "I lost my earring!"

"The family heirloom?" Tyler asks. His eyes are frantic as they start darting around at the floor.

"Huh?"

"The sapphire ones, right?" I'm lost, but Tyler's act doesn't falter, not even once. He looks up and widens his eyes. "The *irreplaceable* ones that your grandmother left you in her will? The ones that *hold a lot of sentiment?*"

"Oh!" Right. Yes. "Yes!" I say and, for some reason, drop to my knees like someone's kicked them from behind. The move is so sudden that Tyler grabs my shoulder, looking genuinely concerned.

"You good?"

"Everything okay?" Yasmin has walked over, and so have May and Jason. Wonderful.

"I lost an earring," I say, now half crawling in a circle around their feet, only giving them the view of the back of my head. My face is fixed firmly downward because the second they see it, they're going to know something's up. "It's a round sapphire set in rose gold."

"It was her grandmother's," I hear Tyler explain. "Who . . . inherited it from *her* mother."

I crouch lower, like I'm physically carrying the ever-increasing weight of our lies on my literal back.

"Oh no!" May gasps. "Everyone, we're looking for an earring! Be careful, we don't want to accidentally step on it! Get on your knees!"

And then, to my absolute, utter, inconceivable horror, *everybody* drops to their knees and starts crawling around. Including Yasmin and May. May Diamond, the first non-Angel to close the Victoria's Secret fashion show, the newest face of Burberry, the fifth highest-paid actress in the world, is on her hands and knees, scouring the dirty floors of this massive set for an invisible heirloom earring that I inherited from my dead grandmother. I hear people whispering all around me. One person starts to yell "I fou—" only for someone else to say, "That's a piece of gum, stupid!" My head hangs lower, and I don't know if it's with shame or because I *definitely* cannot let anyone see my flaming cheeks right now.

"Tyler!" I hear May yell. "Why are you standing? Start looking! *What* is wrong with men?!"

"Maybe you dropped it in the car," Tyler says. It takes me a couple of seconds to realize he's talking to me.

I look up to find Tyler's eyes staring so fixedly at me I'm surprised he didn't burn holes into the back of my head. "Yes! Good idea!" I scramble to my feet.

"Good call," May says. I catch Yasmin pause and open her mouth to say something but May announces, "We'll keep looking here," and crawls a few feet away. Yasmin smiles, sighs, and crawls in the opposite direction.

"What the hell was that?" I whisper-yell when we've marched far enough away from the set.

"That," Tyler whisper-yells back, "was me saving our asses. Now we need to think of a story."

"We? I feel like *you* should be the one to think of a story since you're so good at it, Mr. It Was a Family Heirloom."

He presses the button on the keys that Yan had handed over on our way out. Once the car beeps twice, he opens one of the back doors while I angrily jerk the other open. We lean in from opposite sides, torsos hovering above the backseat.

"I didn't think *the expensive earrings you treated yourself to at a small boutique in Florence* were going to warrant us pausing the entire shoot," he says through gritted perfect teeth that I bet never needed braces. "Do you *know* how much a single delayed minute costs?"

"Do *you*?"

"Of course I do! It's my *job*!"

"Since when?!" I'm trying my hardest not to yell, but the burn of shame on my face is being replaced by one of growing annoyance. "All you have to do is show up and read the script and look pretty!"

Tyler's creased forehead softens. That rogue smile tugs one corner of his lips upward. "You think I look pretty?" he asks, and bites the inside of his cheeks like he's trying to hold back a cheeky comment.

"Uggggh!" I put a fist to my mouth. "Are you serious right now? May is right! What *is* wrong with men?! Focus! What's our story?"

He holds up a hand. "You're right, sorry." A part of me feels bad when the creases on his forehead return. "Obviously Yasmin's mentioned that you left early last night, so the police will probably focus on that."

"What did you say? Food poisoning or period?"

"Period. We all ate at craft services, so it didn't make sense that you were the only one who got food poisoning."

I nod. "Smart. Okay, so my period got really bad. I took a walk to get some fresh air but when that didn't work, I came and told you—"

"—because you needed my help covering for you if your editor asked how the shoot went—"

"—and I said I was feeling woozy, which is why you walked me to the car."

"Did we see or hear anything?" Tyler asks.

I chew on my bottom lip as I consider it. "Would it be suspicious if we didn't? But would we open ourselves up to questioning if we say we did?"

I don't realize I've switched to thinking aloud until his cautious voice answers, "We thought we heard something as we were making our way to the car, but the set was so noisy anyway so we disregarded it. Maybe we saw the man, but people were also taking cigarette breaks, so even if we did, he didn't catch our attention."

A queasy sensation begins to sprawl across my gut. I know I should be thankful that he's taking the lead, that while I'm losing my mind,

Tyler is composed and has come up with what sounds like an actually plausible story. But it's the way he came up with it—so easily, so quickly—that's making me want to turn and run. I just watched him lie to his best friend and not even blink. All that his calm confidence is doing right now is giving me more proof that I shouldn't trust him.

"You okay?" Tyler asks, head tipping to the side. "Does that . . . sound good to you?"

I nod because what else am I supposed to do? "Yes," I say. "It does. It sounds *great*."

Seven

'll go second," Tyler says as we stride back to the set, both earrings secured on my lobes. "To talk to the authorities. This scene is only going to need one more take," he says with unwavering speed and composure. "I'm guessing they only have one interrogation room because it is *very* hard to get any privacy on a movie set. They probably made them set up in prop storage. But that means we're going to have to take turns, and when they ask, you volunteer to go first."

"Why?"

He doesn't answer immediately. When I look over, there's a faint smile on his lips. "What?" he asks when he catches me looking at him.

"You're *smirking*," I say.

He lifts a brow. "Am I?"

"What is it? Why are you going second? Do you have some master plan to listen in on my conversation? Have you planted a bug in my earring? If I turn on you, are you going—"

"Are you always like this?"

I do a double take. "Like what?"

"So . . ." He squints up at the sky. "Antagonistic."

"Antagonistic?"

"Distrustful."

That makes me pause. I swallow the lump in my throat before it can solidify. "And you're not?"

"I meant what I said earlier. I trust you," he says, gaze dropping back down to mine, that faint smile returning.

"Tell me why you were smirking then."

He sighs and rumples his hair, seemingly forgetting that he still has a movie to shoot. "You *are* a journalist, aren't you? *Always* on."

"I—"

"I was smirking because I was imagining your face if I told you why I think I should go second."

My interest is piqued. "Tyler," I say, more out of annoyance than anything.

But he halts as though I've said something much more damning than his name. When his body rotates to face me, I'm conscious of how close we're standing, how the sunlight is making him look like he's walking around with an Instagram filter slapped on. "Yes, Khin?" he asks, voice angelic.

I school my face into as stern of an expression as I can pull off. "Why do you want to go second?"

"Because from *past experience*—" He sighs and rolls his eyes. "People tend to be . . . excited. To talk to me. Clamoring, even."

I snort. "God, you really think you're the shit, don't you?"

He rolls his eyes again. "See, I knew you'd react like that. But if we're lucky, the police will rush through *your* questioning so that they can . . . talk to . . ." He trails off with a shrug.

I bark out a laugh. "Oh my god, you *do* think you're the shit!"

With a third and final eye roll, he pivots and resumes walking. "Please, just . . . do it," he says.

"Why does it matter if they rush through my questioning?"

He slows down his pace and stretches out the last few feet between us and the main entrance. "Because it would appear that one of us is *slightly* better at being under pressure than the other."

Offended, I stop walking and scoff. "I'm having an *off day*—"

"And that's okay," he says, stopping, too. "But it means it's better if I take the lead." My scowl deepens and he adds with a chuckle, "Just for today. And then you can fight me on my *next* suggestion, whatever the hell it may be."

He turns out to be right. Other than the questions that we'd prepared for—"It was the second day," I'd explained, and although I wasn't sure how much the two male detectives knew about the second day of your period, I'd hope that two adult men would know enough—they didn't ask me much else. Of course, that could very well be because they didn't have much to go off of (yet): no ID, no motive, not even a definitive time or cause of death. But it *could* also have had something to do with one of them asking, "How many selfies did Chief say we could each have again? Five?" before I'd even left the makeshift interrogation room (which was, yes, prop storage).

We had fallen *way* behind by the time Tyler was done with his interview, and, cursing under her breath, Yasmin rushed everyone through the rest of the schedule.

In a way, it was nice that the past six hours had been nonstop chaos. I didn't have time to catch up with Tyler, who, as one of the stars and executive producers, had had exactly two ten-minute toilet breaks.

And, as though the pressure of a police investigation weren't enough, my inbox had also been graced with yet another email from Clarissa, this one informing me that she was in NYC and had just had lunch with "Radhika and Samira" (after a hasty Google search, I've assumed she's referring to Radhika Jones and Samira Nasr, the current US editors in chief of *Vanity Fair* and *Harper's Bazaar,* respectively) both of whom had been "salivating with envy" at the story, yet "a little surprised" that she'd assigned the piece to a "new" freelancer, but she had assured them that there was nothing "new" about the way I worked. Translation: *This is your regularly scheduled reminder that my ass is on the line here, so do not fuck this up.* The silver lining was that she didn't mention anything about the police, which must mean she doesn't know. The fewer people that know, the fewer lies I need to juggle, the better. It was also the kick I needed to remember that I'm not going to get a do-over on this story. I don't get the same day of shooting twice, so I'd lowered my head, shut out the noise, and focused like the impeccable journalist I was—*am.*

And for the rest of the (very long) day, it felt like that was the only reason we were there: Tyler, to film this movie, and me, to write about it. No murder, no elaborate matching cover stories, no nothing.

And now, I'm slouched against the front of his trailer while waiting for him to change out of his costume when I see May leaving her trailer. She's also changed back into the black linen romper in which she arrived this morning. I wave in a "catch you tomorrow" gesture, but, upon seeing me, she grins, puts up her hand, and bounces over.

"Hey! Where's Ty?" she asks.

I nod at the vehicle behind me. "Still changing. Great shoot today, by the way!" I say, only then realizing that I don't quite know all the technical filming terms yet. "You were fantastic! And that scene where you cut up your dress to crawl through the vents! You got it in one take!"

She laughs as she pulls her hair up into a high ponytail with a chic black velvet scrunchie. "That was a fun bit. Speaking of fun, today was a long one. Wanna join us for drinks?"

"Oh, were you guys going to—"

Just then, the trailer door opens, and Tyler steps down. He does a short double take at the sight of May. "I thought you'd be gone by now," he says, joining us so we're standing in a small triangle.

"I was inviting Khin to drinks with us!" May beams.

Tyler's brows pinch. "We were getting drinks?"

"Ty, it's like you read my mind!" May's bottom lip juts out, and she slings one arm around his shoulder. "I'd *love* to get drinks with you! And I bet Khin would love to join us, too. We can go back to mine! I'll make you an old-fashioned. Ty loves my old-fashioneds," she explains to me. "What's your favorite drink? My bartending skills are my secret superpower."

"I—" I start, but don't know how to finish. On the one hand, I would love to get drinks with May Diamond (and god knows I need a strong one tonight). On the other, I need to regroup with Tyler vis-à-vis the investigation.

Under her arm, Tyler's shoulders shake with a short chuckle. "Can we take a rain check?"

May's face scrunches into a pout, and when Tyler doesn't relent after a beat, tweaks into a half-confused, half-annoyed expression. "Come oooon, I want to catch up after these wild first two days! A potential murder *and* a police investigation to kick off this movie? We need to talk about how we're going to get rid of these bad vibes. Maybe we can go burn some sage."

"I'm just exhausted today," Tyler says with an apologetic shrug. "You know how I am with jet lag. I'm sorry. Next week? I promise I'll get so wasted, I'll fall asleep in the middle of the hallway again."

May retrieves her arm and folds it over the other into a stubborn

X, lips now pursed to one side. "Fine," she mutters. "Khin? Wanna have a girls' night?"

"Sorry." I grimace. "I need to type up my notes."

May rolls her eyes and gives a dramatic sigh. "Fine, fine, you people go home and be responsible and *sleep* and *type up notes.* I'll see you both tomorrow," she says and flashes us a lackluster peace sign before whirling away.

"I *really* like her," I say under a stifled laugh.

When I look over, Tyler's smiling and shaking his head at her receding figure. "Me too," he says.

We don't quite make the quick getaway I was hoping for. Tyler's accosted a couple of times to sign some more autographs, record a few more "Happy birthday" and "Happy anniversary" videos, and (of course) he obliges.

Half an hour later, though, we're alone in the car and on the way back to my place, and the reality of our predicament swallows me whole once more.

"I think I did okay back there. You?" His voice slices through my jumble of thoughts.

"What?" I ask, blinking.

"The police. They didn't ask me anything difficult. Just routine stuff. How about you?"

"Good. I think I did pretty okay, too," I say, and he nods.

I don't know where we go from here. I do know that more information is going to come out eventually. Maybe it already has. Maybe while Tyler and May were securing the diplomats' residence for the eighth time, somebody has figured out who that man is. Maybe they've found and cracked his phone, and now they're triangulating cell tower histories of every crew member and—oh man, I *do* need to cool it with the *SVU.*

"You know what's weird?" My question pierces the quietness.

From his position where his back is sunk deep into the seat, shoulders actually slouched for the first time since we met, Tyler turns his head. Even with a full face of makeup, he looks *exhausted*. It's the mouth, I realize. People are always going on about how the eyes are the windows to the soul, but with Tyler, his mouth gives everything away. Right now, it's sagging at the corners, lips chapped after hours of wiping and reapplying light lipstick. "What?" he asks.

"Wh-what?" I say. I'd gotten distracted with tracing the shape of his cupid's bow.

"What's weird?"

I make a vague gesture with my hands. "How did no one else see him? I thought at least one other person would've mentioned that they remembered him lurking around or something, but everyone seems to be completely taken by surprise. Which is *bizarre* because how did that guy hang around without a single person noticing him? I mean, *you* shook hands with every single person on set and yet even *you* didn't see him? I know it was getting dark and it's a huge set and everyone had first-day nerves—"

Tyler sits up. "What do you mean *how did he hang around*? You *saw* him on set? Before the . . . incident?"

"No. But he knew my name and what I did, so—"

"What do you mean he knew your name?"

"He . . . said my name." I frown down at the section of leather separating us. I don't want to think about that night, but I need to get this right. "Yes." I nod, flinching internally as the asshole's rasp rings through my brain. "He called me Khin. And he called me a . . . journalist bitch."

Tyler's voice drops low. "And you're sure you'd never met him before?"

"Never," I confirm, to him and to myself.

"Khin." I watch him inhale but not exhale. Instead, he starts rubbing the back of his neck. "I think we—"

Thud thud thud. We both jump in our seats at the knocks on the black glass partition in front of us. "Yes?" Tyler asks.

"Sorry to bother you," Yan says as he lowers a few inches of glass. I notice for the first time that the car has slowed down. Like, *really* slowed down to the point where we might as well be parked. "But we have a situa—"

Our collective attention snaps to the screams that cut through the (supposedly) soundproof glass windows. We're in front of the entrance to my apartment. Which is swarming with teenage girls like this is a zombie movie and they're the zombies and this building is housing every single human left on this earth.

"What the—" I start.

"Fuck," Tyler mutters. I'm not prepared for the fear in his eyes when he looks back at me. Fear and . . . something else. Something like . . . guilt? He confirms it when he says, "I'm so sorry. Someone must've trailed me here this morning. I didn't mean . . ."

I don't know how to respond to a situation like this (I never thought I would have to). But Tyler looks so miserable with guilt that I wave it off like it's no big deal that my building looks like it's the site of a one-night-only One Direction reunion.

"It's not your fault. I'm more worried about *you*," I say, giving him my most empathetic smile. "They're going to leave once they realize you don't actually live here. But what about what might be happening at yours? Do you have enough security? Wait—" I say, realizing something for the first time. "Why *don't* you have security? You do back in the States."

Tyler gives a small shrug. "I didn't want my family to feel weird when we went out. The staff in my building have all been informed on how to deal with this, but generally speaking, I didn't think it'd ever get this bad."

"You're Tyler Tun," I say.

He shrugs again like that means nothing to him. "Do *you* want security, though? Because I can—"

I shake my head frantically. Have a stranger trail me and be up in my business at all times? NDA or not, no thank you, sir. "I don't think we should be actively hiring people to follow us around," I murmur with a pointed raise of my brows.

"Oh. Right."

"Sir?" Yan pipes up. "What, um . . . should we do?"

"We can leave," I offer, ignoring the thrumming ache in my calves and my heels, a result of being on my feet for the better part of nine hours. "I can grab dinner at a restaurant and get a taxi back later."

The truth is, I had planned on driving to the park after Tyler dropped me off to try to find my pen in the area around the lake. I know crawling around a park this late at night with a phone flashlight is not the smartest idea (especially given what transpired approximately twenty-four hours ago), but this is the only free time I have. Otherwise I'll have to wait until my day off, which is four days away, and what if someone else finds the pen before Sunday?

"Absolutely not." Tyler's firm reply drags me back into the present. "Someone could've spotted you this morning and recognize you at the restaurant. Do you . . ." He searches my face. "Want to come back to mine? Just until this goes away. Yan can call the building staff to see what's happening," he adds. "Like you said, at some point, they're going to figure out I don't live here and they'll leave."

"Oh, I don't—" I clear my throat. "I don't think that would be . . . appropriate. Journalism ethics, appearances in case someone spots me, you know? It's quite late already, and if someone happens to see me entering your place, then they might assume . . ."

"Shit, of course," he says hurriedly. "Sorry, I wasn't thinking. Um." He looks around the car. "Is there anywhere else you can shelter in place for a few hours? With someone you trust?"

I could argue again for the restaurant, but the protective crease between his brows tells me either he's leaving me at a friend's house, or we're going to shelter in place in this car until this crowd disperses.

Two addresses spring to my mind, and, making a split-second decision, I choose the geographically closer of two evils. You home? I text after giving Yan directions.

My phone buzzes a minute later. About to make dinner. What's up? Look presentable is all I write back.

Eight

told you!" Thidar squeaks at her fiancé, Patrick, once I open the car door and before one foot has even hit the asphalt. Then, in what I'm assuming is meant to be a whisper, she asks, "Is he inside?" Unfortunately, her voice is still in squeak territory, so it absolutely is *not* a whisper.

"I—" I begin.

I hear the other door behind me open. When I turn, I just catch it closing. I turn back to Thidar and Patrick, who are standing outside their front door in pajamas—with their dog, Pizza, watching through one of the living room windows—right as Thidar's jaw drops.

"I thought it'd be rude if I didn't say hi. Hi, I'm Tyler." Tyler strides over and offers his hand. Patrick takes it because, thankfully, he still remembers how to function like a normal human being.

Thidar, on the other hand, is clawing at her chest like the alien from *Alien* is trying to burst out from her ribs. "Hi," she squeaks out. "Oh my god, hi."

Tyler chuckles. "Hi," he says.

"I'm Patrick," Patrick says, and nods over at my friend, who looks so stricken it's like her soul has left this corporeal plane. "This is my fiancée, Thidar."

"Hi," Thidar says with a smile so wide I can see every single one of her teeth. "I'm Thidar."

"Wonderful, we all know each other's names now," I say, hopping out of the car. "Tyler needs to get home. I'm leaving after dinner. And *you*," I grip both of Thidar's shoulders, "are going back inside and not embarrassing me any more than you already have." Thidar digs in her heels, refusing to budge. "T," I groan. "Please don't—"

"Do you like lasagna?" she asks.

"You *know* I do."

Patrick coughs. "I . . . don't think she's talking to you," he says with a dry laugh.

At that, I look up and find my best friend grinning at Tyler. Tyler looks at me, then back at Thidar, then, hesitantly, nods. "I love lasagna."

"Do you wanna come have some?" she asks, not missing a beat. "We make the pasta from scratch."

"I—"

"We use seven cheeses."

"Wow," Tyler says, impressed. "Most people stick to four."

"Pfft." Thidar whacks an invisible fly. "Amateur hour. Unless you have dinner plans," she adds quickly. "I heard you want to visit family while you're here?" Great. I *love* having friends who have zero clue what an NDA means, or at the very least, have zero respect for them and their potential legal consequences. "If your parents are waiting at home to eat with you, then we understand."

"I . . . I'm not living at home," Tyler says, smile flickering. "Just in case paparazzi got out of hand. I have my own place."

Thidar frowns. "You were going to eat alone tonight? Absolutely not! That's a sad image."

"You know," I sputter, a little offended. "It can be *freeing* to eat alone. Empowering, even. Who wants to do extra dishes?" I say, but Thidar's not listening.

Instead, she struts over to the driver's seat and knocks on the glass. "Yes?" Yan asks, lowering the window.

"Hi, Uncle," she says with a wave. "Tyler's going to stay for dinner. We'll drive him home."

Yan stretches his neck out to look at Tyler. Patrick and I both also look at Tyler. Tyler looks at *me* with an expression that even an infant could decipher as *What do I do?* The idea of Tyler having dinner with my friends is far too close and chummy for my liking, but what am I going to do? Knowingly let the man have dinner alone after a nine-hour shoot? Not to mention the wrath that I'll have to face from Thidar.

At my shrug, Tyler shoots Yan a smile. "I'll see you tomorrow morning. Seven?"

Yan nods. "Of course, sir. Have a good night, you two."

And then he's driving off and the gate is closing behind the car. And now I'm standing in front of my best friend's house. With Tyler Tun by my side.

"You know you're dead to me," I mutter as we enter the house. Patrick leads Tyler upstairs so he can get a full tour before they bring out the food.

"My, my," Thidar says as she arranges another place setting. "What's got you so hostile? I simply invited my best friend and her new friend to dinner. Sharing is caring!"

"You know if I don't kill you, then Nay surely will."

Thidar waves a fork in the air. "Nay's out at that new karaoke bar. I saw her Insta stories." Lowering her voice, she squeaks out,

"I cannot believe we're having dinner with Tyler Tun! Can we take photos? Pleeease let me ask for a selfie. Or is that too cheesy? Oh, who cares! How many chances are we going to get to have dinner with *Tyler Tun*? Also, is he somehow even more handsome in person?"

"He just came back from set," I say with an indifferent shrug. "You should see him in the morning when his voice is still weird and gravelly. Celebrities, they're just like us! See if you still think the same when he's bare-faced and he's got coffee breath which he hides with these mints that he always carries in his pockets and—" I look up to find Thidar smiling. It's not her earlier grin, but a smile like she's holding in a secret. "What?" I ask.

"Nothing."

"*What?*" I insist.

"*Nothing*," she repeats.

I round the table and am about to shake her by the shoulders when she grabs a nearby knife and points it at me. "Don't you—" She starts to laugh, but cuts herself off when she sees my reaction. My head is rotated sideways, my shoulders hunched, both my hands protecting my face as I squeeze my eyes shut. "Hey, I wasn't actually going to stab you," she says. When I turn back, she's lowering the knife, her expression marked with concern.

"Sorry," I say, and try to laugh at myself. "I'm . . . *really* tired."

I can tell she wants to buy it, but doesn't entirely. "You sure? You okay?" I nod. "Like, in general?" she presses.

No, I say in my head. *No, I murdered a man in the middle of the night and I might go to jail and I can't remember how it feels to be able to sleep for more than three consecutive hours.*

The three of us have been best friends since we were five, and I have never kept a secret from them. More than one of our exes has accused us of being codependent, but we prefer to refer to it as Collective Only Child Syndrome. They are my emergency contacts, my *first* in any scenario—the first people I text for an outfit check, the first people I called when I got engaged, the first people I saw after Ben left me, the first names that pop to mind whenever I need a plus-one for an event. But currently, standing here in Thidar's dining room, it feels like I'm staring at her from across a chasm that only I can see; from *her* vantage point, I'm a little preoccupied, but no more than usual when I'm on a big assignment.

"Please, don't act like I'd actually be scared of you. I know you can't take me," I say, and throw in a light punch to her arm.

Her giggle is sweet and gentle, just like her whole personality, and the sound both makes me smile and reaffirms my decision that I can't drag her into my mess. I know she'd go to the ends of the earth and back for me, but I also know the toll it would take on her big, soft heart.

"Watch out, hot lasagna coming through!" Patrick announces just then.

He enters with a wine bottle in one hand and an opener in the other. Behind him is Tyler, wearing the pale pink oven mitts to carry the matching pink Le Creuset baking dish that I'd bought for their engagement gift. When he places the dish down in the middle of the table, it smells so good that I can't help but bend over and take a deep sniff. The cheese is still slightly boiling on the surface, but the edges are already nice and crispy.

"I admit, this looks *delicious*," I practically moan. I push the curtain of hair that's fallen over my face behind my ear, and give a small start when I find Tyler looking at me with an indecipherable expression, lips parted and eyes soft at the edges where some makeup has wiped away—probably his own doing—and those deep grooves are starting to show.

"What?" I ask, a little embarrassed when it comes out breathy.

"Nothing," he says, and shifts his gaze downward while he removes the oven mitts.

"Why'd you only bring three glasses?" Thidar asks as Patrick pours the red.

"I have an early start time," Tyler answers for him. "I'll stick to water. Thank you, though."

I groan and swipe the last glass before Patrick can pour into it. "That means *I* have an early start time, too," I say. "Water it is for me, then."

Thidar cuts out a piece of lasagna for herself before passing the utensils to me. While I focus on removing a nice large corner piece, she asks, "So Tyler, what's next on the agenda for you? After this movie."

From the corner of my eye, I can see him smiling politely. *Thinking* before he answers. I stay quiet. Maybe he'll be less guarded if his brain forgets that I'm in the room. "I'm weighing my options," he says.

"But you must have an *idea*," Thidar presses on my behalf. "Is it the Bond movie? Or the new season of *Bridgerton*? You can tell us. We won't tell anyone. Your secret will be safe with us. And Pizza," she adds, nodding toward the living room where Pizza is sleeping in his crate.

Tyler laughs. "I wish I could tell you. But I'm trying to do this new thing where I don't plan too far ahead. You never know what life might throw at you, right? What's the point of stressing yourself out with all these plans when you could, say, slip getting out of the bathtub and die?"

Thidar nods with a contemplative look. "Or choke on a piece of lasagna."

Tyler tilts his glass at her. "Exactly."

The sound of Pizza playing with a squeaky toy catches our collective attention, and, uncomfortable with all this talk about death, I casually call out, "You okay in there, Piz?"

For a second, Pizza stops playing with his toy to let out a quick but loud affirmative bark, and we all laugh. "How long have you had him?" Tyler asks.

"A little over a year," Patrick answers. "He was a stray on this street. We moved in and he immediately zeroed in on Thidar—"

"I'm a vet—" Thidar offers.

"—and she was feeding him twice a day and giving him all his shots. One day, she brought him home to give him a bath—"

"—he'd jumped into a giant mud puddle!"

Patrick chuckles. "I know, sweetheart. And she asked him if he'd like to *stay for dinner*—"

"It was dinnertime!" Thidar says defensively.

When Patrick leans over and kisses her cheek, my heart feels like that scene in *The Grinch* where it grows three times larger. I peek over at Tyler, who's also smiling at them, and I have a hunch he's feeling the same thing I'm feeling. "I know, sweetheart," Patrick repeats. "And then he just . . . never left," he says, shooting a smile in the vicinity of the living room.

"Was it hard? To adopt a stray? Did he have trouble adjusting?" Tyler asks.

Thidar shakes her head. "Not really. Maybe a bit at first, but it helped that we have a large yard. Why, are you thinking of adopting?"

"I'm—" Tyler begins, but doesn't finish. Instantly, my journalist senses start to tingle. "*May*, actually, is thinking of adopting," he says after a short beat, which only makes me more suspicious. "Bringing them back to California with her when we go back." Why did he catch himself there? What's the big deal with May adopting a dog? Unless . . . He tries to cover himself—literally—with his glass, but before he can hide it, I see the mouth quirk. Unless he *and* May are thinking of adopting a dog? *Together?*

Thidar nods and continues, "You definitely need to put in more work at the beginning, so I'd recommend making sure you really have the time before you commit to it. And the patience. But once you do, it's the best thing in the world. I'll give you my number! Pass it on to May, and tell her to call me if she ever wants to really do this."

"Thanks, she'll appreciate that," Tyler replies. Unbeknownst to the other two, I could almost swear that his gaze shifts over to me for a nanosecond, that his spine straightens against the back of the chair before he grins down at his lasagna and says, "This is probably the best lasagna I've ever had, by the way. Mind sharing your recipe?"

Thidar lifts her glass at Patrick. "Your time to shine, babe."

Patrick clears his throat and wiggles his shoulders like he's been preparing for this moment his whole life. "Well, the secret is in the sauce. . . ."

At the end of dinner, Tyler insists that he'll clear the table, load the dishwasher, *and* hand-wash the baking dish.

"He's *perfect*," Thidar whispers. Patrick has popped over to the living room to answer some last-minute work emails. I give a shrug that neither confirms nor denies the statement. "Khin, come *on*," she insists. "This is major Take Me Home to Mom vibes."

I snort. "He's polite."

"He's handling the dishwasher *and* he knew you have to wash a Le Creuset by hand. Could he *be* any hotter?" she asks, to which I respond with a drawn-out eye roll. "What's it like?" she continues. "Being on a movie set. Is it as exciting as you envisioned?"

"Honestly? It's kind of . . . boring."

"Boring?" Thidar's voice deflates with disbelief. "You're on the set of Tyler Tun and May Diamond's latest movie and it's boring?"

"Well, for instance, they were shooting this night market scene, and I watched them order the same strawberry smoothie *ten times*. I can literally recite their lines word for word. Watch: May goes, 'Hmm, I'm thirsty. Do I want a smoothie?' And Tyler goes, 'Drinking on the job? My, my, I wonder what HQ will have to say about that,' and May says, 'I wonder what HQ will have to say about my fist—'" I catch myself at Thidar's bemused expression. "You get the point," I explain. "It's either boring or tiring. Usually both. There's no time for us to have any substantial conversations. I'm either waiting or rushing. *He's* constantly running lines or shooting scenes or talking to the writers or getting an outfit refitted or any of the million other things that leave *me* exhausted by the end of the day, and all *I* have to do is watch him." I have to give Tyler and May credit—acting is a thousand times harder than I could've imagined.

"Huh, who would've thunk," Thidar says.

After both men have finished their respective tasks, Patrick and Thidar take Pizza out on his night walk. "We need to finish our earlier conversation," Tyler says. We're in the living room and facing one another on the armchairs that bracket the large sofa at a slight angle.

"What conversation?" I ask, rearranging my curled-up legs.

"About how the guy knew your name."

I stiffen as it comes rushing back. "It doesn't matter," I say, aware it's a lie. Of course it matters.

I'm conscious how scheming this sounds and how big of a lying hypocrite it makes me, but, as with my park plan, I want to hold on to a piece of information that Tyler doesn't have, just in case he tries to turn the tables on me. I don't have the same resources as him, but it won't hurt to have an extra trick in my back pocket.

"What do you mean it doesn't matter?" He puts his glass down on the coffee table and leans in, forearms resting on his thighs. "This guy knew who you were. He could've been targeting you."

"Or," I speak slowly, buying time to assemble a story, "he *was* hanging around on the set, heard some people mention my name and the word 'journalist,' and realized that the only woman running around and watching you while writing in a notebook must be the aforementioned journalist named Khin."

"No," he says, not even pausing. "You know that's too simple of a story. It wasn't merely as opportunistic as that—"

"Tyler," I cut him off brusquely. "Has it occurred to you that I *don't* want to relive the most traumatic night of my life? He's dead," I say, shushing my voice even though we're still the only ones in the house. "Why does it matter who he was? What am I going to do, see if he has children? Track them down and apologize for leaving them fatherless?"

The back door opens, and Thidar's laughter travels through the corridor. "Drop it. I don't want to think about this anymore," I hiss in one breath. Despite his frown, Tyler raises his hands in acceptance.

Patrick drives us both back, Thidar staying behind because she had two exhausting surgeries today and she wants an early night. We drop Tyler off first just in case somebody catches a glimpse of him in the car when I hop out at my place.

"I'll pick you up at seven thirty?" Tyler asks, hand on the door handle.

"You don't have to do that," I say. "I know where the lot is now. I can get a taxi."

His forehead creases. "I'll see you at seven thirty," he says. Before I can respond, he opens the passenger door and ends the conversation. "Thanks again, man," he says, clapping a hand on Patrick's shoulder.

"Anytime," Patrick replies from the driver's seat.

We sit in silence as he makes a U-turn and heads toward my place. I check the time, even though I knew hours ago that it was far too late for my park plan. "Nice guy," Patrick says, breaking the quiet. "Like, an *actually* nice guy. My agency works with a lot of celebrities and he would be a dream client."

I catch his eye in the rearview mirror. "Guess so."

"You don't like him."

I startle in my seat. "What? Why would I bring someone I didn't like to my best friend's house?"

"Okay." He tilts his head with a thoughtful air. "But you don't . . . trust him?"

I consider it, then sigh. "He's an actor," I admit, deciding that it's not like Patrick's going to go and relay this information back to Tyler. "I . . . don't trust actors. They act for a living. And he knows I'm writing a story on him. Of course he's going to be on his best golden-boy behavior."

He gives a short chuckle. "Guess I can't argue with that."

Back at mine, I change out of my clothes, go through my skincare routine, and put on a pair of fresh pajamas, but I don't head for bed. Instead, I march into the guest room that doubles as my home office, pull down the whiteboard that's hanging above my desk, and wipe clean the notes from my past few assignments.

I'm about to write TYLER TUN in all caps at the top, but decide against it on the off chance that someone wanders in here at some point—I don't know how or when. It's not like I'm throwing a rager anytime soon—and sees this. Instead, I write GOLDEN BOY.

In one spot, in a smaller font, I write ABORTION STORY, remembering his obsession with my article at our first dinner.

In another spot, I write POSSIBLY ADOPTING DOG???

In a third, BOND? followed by FUN ROLES.

In a fourth, BRIDGERTON?

In a fifth, NOT MAKING ANY PLANS.

And, just so I have all my bases covered, RELATIONSHIP WITH MAY?

because at this point, I'm taking everything he's told me with a grain of salt. MOVIE PREMIERE REVEAL? I scrawl.

I hang the board back on the wall and step back so I can take it all in at once. There is *something* here. Tyler is hiding *something*, and it has to do with at least *one* of these things. Maybe all of them? I don't know.

My mind races back to that night in the park, when I'd asked him why he trusted me so blindly, and he was going to give me an answer—the *real* answer—and then he didn't.

My concentration shifts back to the board in front of me.

Tyler Tun, what were you going to let slip?

I don't immediately go to sleep once I'm under the covers either; I know I should, but I can't help it. Ben used to joke that he needed a seat belt to keep up with the speed of my mind. On my laptop, I open Yangon's unofficial yellow pages—Facebook, obviously—and start looking into the guy I murdered (my murderee?).

Or I try to.

Methodically, I first go through all of my immediate friends and make sure that he's not in any of their profile photos. Once that's been checked off, I browse all the variations of the public "Australian expats in Myanmar" and "New Zealand expats in Myanmar," as well as the wider "expats living in Myanmar" and "Yangon expats" Facebook groups (what *is* it with white people who insist on calling themselves "expats"?) I can find and zoom in on the member photos, but at one point, all the middle-aged white men start to look the same.

I'm aware that this is a "careful what you go Facebook-trawling for" situation, but I want to know if I can find him. After all, *this* is why I became a journalist in the first place—because as dark and disturbing as the things I find at the bottom of the well might be, I still want to dive in and hit that bottom. And while I understand that finding out who this man was and how he knew my name won't undo his murder, I still want to know. Because he knew *my* name and job. Additionally, if there *is* some connection between us that I've overlooked and that the police discover, that's a pretty damning way to link this all back to me.

I turn to plan B: my friend Kira, who is Australian, and more specifically, who works at the Australian Embassy as their head of public relations. Given the overlap in our jobs, we've gotten to know each other well; I was even the one who encouraged her to go up and talk to her now-boyfriend Charlie at the bar a few years ago.

On her profile, I open her friends list of—I gulp—1,062 people, zoom my browser screen up to 200 percent, start scrolling very, very slowly, and open up any middle-aged white man's profile in a new tab. Half an hour later, I have . . . nothing.

I shut my laptop and put it away on my console. My brain hurts, my eyes are stinging, my fingers are stiff, the ache in my feet has returned with full force. And before I can stop myself, a desperate and worn-out voice in my head murmurs, *I don't know what to do.* And then, *I wish I had help.*

Because I do. I really, really, *really* do.

Nine

"You seem jumpy," Tyler says. I'd noticed that he'd been observing me since we wrapped up, but he hasn't made a comment until we're near my place. "Everything okay?"

I couldn't go to the park on the night we had dinner at Thidar's, or again the next night (last night) because shooting ran late, but by my calculations, today, I can get home, change, and arrive at the park right around golden hour. Which is perfect, because the place will be flooded with couples and families who have come to watch the sunset, and if anyone asks why I'm combing through every random object that's washed up in the dirt by the water, I can just say I lost an earring (again, apparently).

"Excited to get home before sunset," I chirp.

He chuckles. "I hear that."

I say my usual quick "Thank you, see you tomorrow!" and try not to be so obvious about my hurry as I stride to the elevator. Sprinting into my bedroom, I change into a more plain-looking, blend-right-in outfit of denim shorts and black cropped T-shirt, a pair of round black oversized sunglasses, and my least favorite black sneakers that I don't mind getting dirty, and take the elevator back down. I don't want to drive in case the police are still scanning the park's security cameras and notice my plate, but, of course, because as is the law of the land whenever you are in a hurry (or, perhaps, because it is rush hour), none of the apps can find me a ride. I cancel my current request and try one more time, but before it goes through, a text appears at the top.

Nay

Drinks tonight? I have had A WEEK so far

Followed by:

Thidar

Can do!

How about you, big-time vogue girl?

And, because they have best-friend telepathy and can sense what I'm about to text even before I start typing:

Nay

Please please??? We really miss you!

Dying for updates!!

For a second, the stinging pierces me as I realize how much I miss them, too—this is the longest I've ever gone without seeing them in person while living in the same city—but it only lasts for a second, because my ride app suddenly displays a pop-up confirming that, yep, still no rides.

Sorry, busy tonight! Will catch up soon, promise!!! I reply with three kissing-face emojis.

Cursing, I do things the Neanderthal way and sprint out onto the main road, and stick out my arm and neck to aggressively locate a free cab.

Attention laser-focused on spotting an empty backseat, I yelp when someone says my name a few millimeters away from my ear. I hadn't heard his footsteps on account of the usual rush-hour ruckus, and I do a double take when I wheel around and find Tyler standing very, *very* close to me, head bent down, a cap *just* shielding his face. Anyone who walks by us and looks over for more than two seconds will recognize him.

"What the fuck!" I whisper.

"Sorry, didn't mean to scare you," he says, retreating.

Without thinking, I grab his shoulder and pull him back toward me. Under my grip, his biceps tighten and push back against my hand. "That, and what the fuck are you doing standing on the side of the road in the daytime? Do you want to cause a pileup?" I ask, gesturing at the multiple rows of cars that are at a standstill, bored drivers and passengers alternating between scrolling on their phone and gazing out the window.

"What are *you* doing hailing a taxi? Where are you going?"

His tone makes me roll my eyes, which in turn makes him narrow his gaze. "Sorry, did I forget to fill in the sign-out sheet?" I ask.

His eyes drop, clocking my outfit change. "You changed," he says.

"I sweated through my clothes. They were disgusting."

"You looked good to me," he says, and, stupidly, frustratingly, I feel my face redden like I'm a teenager and my biggest crush has just tossed an unexpected compliment in my direction.

"Why are you still here?" I demand.

"Flat tire," he says, jerking a thumb behind him but holding my gaze. "Yan was just finishing changing it."

"Then you should go back and get home so *he* can go home, too."

"Where are you going?"

I purse my lips. "None of your business."

He studies me in silence. "You're right," he finally says, except instead of walking away, his mouth loops upward with an air of righteousness. A dare. "But let me give you a free ride. Save the cab fare."

I blow out a sharp blast of air through my nostrils and promise myself that I will *not* let him get under my skin, at least not more so than he's already burrowed. "I can afford a taxi. Have a good evening. See you tomorrow."

He steps in closer, so close that the brim of his cap brushes against my forehead and tilts marginally upward so that it's shielding both of our faces. I'm a champion at staring contests, but I've never had one this up close with somebody. I can see every faint line and acne scar on his face, the spots he missed with his makeup wipes, every single hair that makes up his thick brows. That scent, still a tender crispness that simultaneously contradicts its own tough woodsiness.

"Khin," he says, voice gravelly. Does he somehow know that *that's* how he keeps making my brain glitch? "Where are you going?"

"A date," I lie, and am surprised when his face muscles twitch. For the first time, he looks away.

But then he looks back at me, recomposed, smirk as vengefully arrogant as ever. "You're lying." His eyes motion down at my outfit. "You'd be dressed considerably better for a date. Scuffed black sneakers? Come on, this isn't even you trying."

I glare, angry that he's spoiled my lie so quickly, and also startled by how spot-on he is. "Has anyone told you you're insufferable?" I ask, moving back and out of the shadow of his cap.

"Just this absolutely antagonistic journalist I recently met," he says, readjusting it downward.

Despite myself, my mouth twitches with a smile that I don't pull back in time. Tyler's face softens, and he scans my outfit once more. When his eyes draw back up to mine, he sighs and shakes his head, jaw clenching. "Park?"

I bite my bottom lip, neither confirming nor denying.

"You *are* aware that it's a commonly known fact that perpetrators can't help but return to the scene of the crime. You're smarter than to become a walking cliché, aren't you?"

"Only if you get caught, and look at me"—I motion at myself from head to toe—"I'm as inconspicuous as they come. Besides, it's the city's biggest park. It's not illegal to go hang out in the park. Maybe I wanted to clear my head after a long day at work."

"Huh, now that you mention it, that *does* sound like a good idea. Come on, I'll join you," he says, tilting his head back at the car where Yan is waiting on the sidewalk, and with the air of a parent giving in to the demands of an unrelenting child.

I want to laugh in his face. "You can't go to the park at sunset," I say, because someone needs to state the obvious here. "You'll be mobbed. Remember what I just said about not getting caught as long as I remain inconspicuous?"

He contemplates it for a beat. "I'll wait in the car."

"Yan will know something's up. I have to go alone. I don't need a handler."

"That'd be a little bit more convincing if the last time I left you to stray alone in a park, it *hadn't* ended in murder," he huffs. "You're not going alone. It's about the pen, isn't it? What is it about this pen that's got you so worried anyway?"

The full truth is that the pen is monogrammed with my initials, which, while not exactly as damning as DNA evidence—thank God my initials aren't as idiosyncratic as, say, XXZ—*is* still pretty damning. But Tyler's already in macho protective mode, and I have the sense that if he finds out that piece of information, he's going to go into overdrive and probably insist he come help me find it himself, which is something I do not have the patience to contend with right now.

"You're not coming. I'm not taking any risks," I say. "This isn't up for debate."

He folds his arms. "You're right. It's not." Our sixth-grade staring contest resumes. After many seconds of this, he says, still unblinking, "What if we told Yan to go home? We can still take the car."

I chew my lip as I think. "What if they run the license plate on the security cameras?"

"Then I simply wanted to unwind in the park tonight. You know, *clear my head after a long day at work*. That's not a crime."

"What if Yan tells someone we took the car? Surely he'll suspect something's up."

Tyler hitches a shoulder. "But he won't know *what*. Chances are, he'll think we're secretly fucking."

"Why would he think that?" I ask, surprised by the statement as well as the blasé manner in which he says it, because *I* personally am having a physical reaction to hearing him say that last word. *Fucking*. Heat ziplines down my spine as I hear it again in my head. Tyler Tun's front teeth grazing his bottom lip right before he says the word "fucking" to my face—

"Because that's what anyone thinks when I go off alone with a woman," he states plainly. "It's why everyone's convinced May and I are dating. It's why *People* once printed a photo of me with a 'mystery woman' who was my cousin."

"You don't mind that he'll think we're secretly fucking?" I ask, keeping a close eye on his reaction, my ears simultaneously straining to catch his reply over the sound of my heart, which has leapfrogged into my throat and is thudding at ten times its usual rate.

The fact that his cap is obscuring half of his face makes it difficult for me to read him, but his mouth presses into a tight line, as though he doesn't want to accidentally say the first thing he's just thought. "Better that than him thinking we're hiding a murder. Come on, Khin, it's the best plan we've got. The windows are tinted so no one will see me while I wait inside. Afterward, we'll take the car back to mine and leave it in the parking garage there, and you can get a cab home. And I'm sure Yan can be . . . persuaded to be discreet."

Hell of a lot more work than if I just got a cab there and back, I think with indignation. "Only if I drive," I say in a final attempt to maintain a morsel of control over the situation.

"Antagonistic," he mumbles, and, not giving me a chance to reply, adds, "Forgot to pack my license anyway. It's still sitting in a drawer back at my LA house."

I don't like this. At all. Seized with displeasure bordering on anger, I stand there, meaning to glare furiously at the back of his head—but then my eyes drop and involuntarily note how hot his back muscles look when they flex under the fabric of this lavender cotton tee that's sticking to his skin thanks to the heat, and then proceed to drop even lower, tracing the curvature of his spine downward until I am, as they say, *checking him out.* I sheepishly look around to see if anyone just caught me staring intently at Tyler Tun's ass, but it's still just him and Yan, and if Yan saw, well, he's a master at being discreet.

As I adjust the rearview mirrors and driver's seat to my height, I see Tyler and Yan talking on the sidewalk. Tyler reaches into his pocket for his wallet, takes out what looks like *all* of the cash he carries, and discreetly slides it into Yan's pocket with one hand while clapping him on the shoulder with the other. So *that's* how Tyler Tun "persuades" people to do what he wants.

In my defense, I don't bring it up lest I further cement my *antagonistic* reputation.

A few minutes into the so-far silent drive, though, Tyler asks—without a shred of self-consciousness, mind you—"Is that going into the article?"

"What?"

"That Tyler Tun regularly bribes people into doing his bidding."

My grip on the wheel tightens on reflex, as if my body is jumping into defense mode. "I—"

"If it makes a difference, I was going to give him a bonus tomorrow night once he dropped me off and signed off for the week anyway. That's why I had that much cash on me already. His kid broke his foot last week, and they're swamped with hospital bills."

"Oh," I say, snarky remark catching on a jagged shard of guilt. On the one hand, that is, obviously, an unequivocally compassionate gesture. On the other, what are the chances he's telling me this to protect his image? America's altruistic sweetheart. "I . . . wasn't even really paying that much attention," I say.

I catch his smirk out of the side of my eye. "Liar. Then how come you were watching me? I saw you." He always sounds like he's taunting me, like he knows me well enough that he can see through everything I do and say.

"How would you know I was watching you unless you were watching *me*?" I shoot back.

We're at a red light so I can look over. His face twitches, and he works his jaw before replying, "Guess we're just always watching each other." Suddenly, the air thrums with an immediate and intangible metaphysical energy.

I can't think of a single witty reply, so I say nothing.

———

Two hours later, I jump back into the driver's seat, knees and palms specked with dirt, neck and forehead and armpits and underboobs smothered in sweat.

"What?" I snap when I discover Tyler trying to suppress a grin. I reach over and direct the air con shutters to my face.

"Was it a good date?"

I give him a cordial smile. "Obviously. All of my good dates end with me panting and covered in sweat."

My comment catches him off guard. He hacks a cough into the water bottle he was drinking from, and I smile for real this time.

He opens his mouth, but his phone vibrating on his lap catches our attention. Before I can do the polite thing and look away, I see May's name.

"Everything okay?" I ask. He nods and immediately texts back, his pinched brows telling me he's lying, or at least not being entirely honest. "Want me to drive you to hers?"

He looks up in a half daze. "Who?"

"May," I say, gesturing at his phone.

"Oh. Nah, she tried to round me up for drinks again, but I'm exhausted. Took a rain check."

His phone vibrates again. And again. And once more.

"You sure?" I ask, not needing to look anymore.

He chuckles as he reads her replies. "Yes," he tells me as he types. "She's just annoyed because this is my fourth rain check. *Excluding* that first time on set when we *both* turned her down. Apparently, she's been keeping track. Anyway." He slides his phone into his pocket. "Did you find the pen?"

I shake my head, wiping my face with multiple tissues. "I don't know if that's good or bad news. I *was* thorough, though."

"I can see that," he says, peeping down at my shorts and sneakers, which have brought in a small sandbox's worth of sand and pebbles into the immaculate SUV. I make a mental note to profusely apologize to Yan.

After leaving, we ride without talking for a few more minutes before, with no preamble, Tyler shifts his body to face mine. "Why did you do that?" he asks.

I fidget in my seat, not expecting the serious alteration in his tone. "Do what? Run that yellow light?"

"Try to sneak around my back. Why didn't you tell me you were planning on going to the park?"

For the first time since we met, he sounds angry—what, is he pissed off that I might've found something without his knowledge and the ball might be in *my* court for once? "Because I knew *you* couldn't join me in the park," I reply, keeping my own cool. "Besides, it's not like I was going to poke around a sketchy alley on the city outskirts. It's a public park. I was fine."

"Why are you so deathly allergic to asking for help?" I don't have to look at him to know that he's tempering his irritation. "Or is it just *my* help you detest for some reason?"

"I wanted to keep you out of trouble," I say, focusing on the road. "Let you have plausible deniability." It's not *entirely* a lie.

My peripheral vision catches his half smile making an appearance, if only for a second. When he speaks, he sounds calmer. Still frustrated, but as though he's working on it. "You can't go do things like this on your own, Khin. What would we have done if the police had caught you on the park cameras tonight, and I hadn't known where you actually were, and when they asked me, I tried to give you an alibi and said you'd come over to mine or that we'd gone out to dinner? We would've been caught red-handed."

"I hadn't considered that," I admit. "I just . . . I work better on my own, okay? I'm a freelancer."

He palms his face. "Well, you're not on your own anymore. Not as long as I'm around. We can't have secrets, not between you and me. How many times do I need to tell you that you can trust me before you actually believe it?"

I scrunch up my nose. "How does eight hundred and three sound?"

His laughter rumbles through his chest. "And *I'm* the insufferable one," he mutters before turning away from me, but not before I catch the shadow of a full smile; that itself is enough to make me cognizant of a gooey feeling in my chest, like someone accidentally knocked over and shattered a jar of honey.

His words replay in my head as I sit in the backseat of the taxi taking me home. *We can't have secrets, not between you and me.*

Not between you and me.

You and me.

You. Me.

Before I know it's happening, I'm smiling at the idea that there is a "you and me" here. Not just a "him" and a "me"—as in, two entities who often come into each other's orbits but nonetheless remain wholly distinct—but that we're bound now. Together.

You *and* me.

Tyler *and* me.

Ten

Excited to get some time away from me?" I ask as the lot security barrier lifts and the car exits the area. It's a few days later since our park rendezvous—Saturday, to be specific, which also means tomorrow I get to stay in, order pizza, and binge old *SVU* episodes to my heart's content. No movie. No murder. No Tyler. Ideally, I won't leave my apartment for a full twenty-four hours.

"Huh?"

"Tomorrow's Sunday," I remind him. "No work, plus you get rid of me. No antagonistic journalist hounding you all day long. Win-win."

"Of course," he says, with a laugh that lags behind for a second and a half. "I have brunch with my parents. You know I haven't seen them once since filming began?"

"Oh?"

"It's terrible, I'm a terrible son." He laughs again and scrubs his chin with his palm. "We're going to some dim sum place that my sister insisted on. It'll be my first time meeting her new *boyfriend*." He cracks his neck and chances a glance at me, one that I catch and in which his discomfort could not be more blatant.

"Tyler Tun," I say, picking up on his emphasis on the word "boy-friend." "Don't tell me you're the macho protective older brother type."

He lets out a chuckle. "I try not to be. But it's hard. She's my little sister. But my parents say he's great, so that's a good start. And some of my aunts and uncles are in town from Mandalay so they'll be there tomorrow, too."

"Wow," I say, smiling at the image. "Big crowd."

"Yep. How about you?"

"Hmm?"

He lifts his chin at me. "My day off means it's your day off, too. What's on the agenda for you? Seeing your folks?"

"Oh," I say, redirecting my attention anywhere but his face. How do I say, *My big plan tomorrow is to become one with my couch*, without sounding like a total loser? "My parents actually live in Hong Kong," I say. Feeling like I've looked away for long enough, I glance back only to find him still waiting for an explanation, which I *really* don't want to get into, but this is what I get for prying. "They do a lot of overseas work," I say, realizing I sound like a walking cliché, but there's a rea-son clichés became clichés, right?

My parents and I don't have a strained relationship or anything like that, but we've also never been particularly close. It's not like they skipped out on my wedding, but I also didn't turn to them for emo-tional support throughout my divorce.

"Do you miss them?" Tyler asks.

I don't want to get into the boring details, but considering how close he is with his family, I can see why this would be an important topic in his eyes. "Sometimes," I admit. "But we're at a point in our lives where there really isn't that much overlap."

"Gotcha," he says with a short nod, getting the memo this time. Then, right as I'm about to exhale, he says, "Khin." What is it about the way he says my name, an otherwise incredibly common and average name, that makes my lungs forget how to function? "Are you . . . seeing people tomorrow?"

I huff in offense. "Of course I'm seeing people." I'm seeing the pizza delivery guy. And probably the doorman when I go down to check my mail. "What, you think my whole world revolves around you and the cast and crew of this set?" Even as I ask it, I'm doing a mental rundown of the last time I saw someone who wasn't associated with this movie. Apart from my doorman and that dinner with Patrick and Thidar, I'm drawing a blank. No, that can't be right. I *must* have interacted with other people. In my defense, I'd normally make plans with Nay and Thidar on my day off, but Nay is out of town for the weekend and Thidar and Patrick are hosting his parents who are visiting from Chicago.

"Khin," Tyler repeats, a teasing lilt to his tone that I don't like because it feels a lot like he's laughing at me.

"What?" I snap.

"Do you . . . wanna come to brunch?"

I blink and scrunch up my nose, making a sound that's supposed to sound like *Huh?*

He shrugs with an aura of casualness that I can't fathom, as though he's just asked to reconfirm our pickup time on Monday and not if I want to have brunch with his parents. "If you're not doing anything tomorrow and you like dim sum, you should come to brunch."

"Why?" I ask, my confusion making the word sound more offended than I intended.

That corner of his mouth twitches and gives him away. He wasn't expecting that. When was the last time anyone, especially a woman, turned down an offer to have brunch with him? In fact, he almost looks disappointed.

"What, do you have another date in the park?" he asks, recovering in a blink. "Is this the same guy, or a different but similarly invisible man?"

I scoff but can feel the heat zing to my cheeks. "Both. Trying to assemble an orgy."

"In the park."

"Hey, it's my day off. A girl's gotta de-stress somehow."

His Mona Lisa–esque expression unfurls into a real smile, which, against my will, makes *me* smile. "Come to brunch with me," he repeats.

As I revel in the fact that I've won this round of banter, my brain hitches on that "with me." I make it unhitch itself.

"Why?" I repeat.

"You want the truth?"

I tip my chin inward. "I would know instantly if you gave me anything else. My bullshit meter is impeccable."

His eyes glint with amusement. When he talks, though, his voice is low. "Fine, the truth is, while I know you've put the fact that this guy was very possibly stalking you behind you, it's still bugging me. I can't stop thinking about it, about what would've happened to—" He shakes his head as if halting himself from going down a dark, familiar route. "And I know it's our one day off and god knows we could both use it, but I don't want to spend my day off worrying that you're dead in a ditch somewhere, so"—my gaze cuts to the way his forearm muscles flex as he rubs the back of his neck—"can you please do me a favor and come to brunch with me? Just for a few hours."

"Tyler, you worry about me?" I say, feigning sentimentality. Although, if I'm being honest, I *am* slightly touched. Just slightly. He seems to be gauging whether I'm asking a serious question or not.

Feeling nice, I let him off the hook. "Or are you trying to get an invite to my park orgy?" I ask. "You know, tit for tat. It *is* RSVP only, though. We keep it discreet."

There's that mouth twitch once more, and this time, it's out of control. "You're asking if I'm trading brunch with my parents for a park orgy with you?"

"Are you?"

"Will there be refreshments?"

"Not included, I'm afraid. Too many logistics as it is. But you can bring your own booze with no additional corkage fees!"

"Damn," he says with a heavy sigh. "I'm afraid I'll sit this one out, then. Brunch, on the other hand, *does* include drinks. For free."

Despite this gratifying back-and-forth, I'd already made up my mind as soon as Tyler asked the question: Nope, thanks but no thanks. Because why would I agree to have Sunday brunch with Tyler Tun and his family? I am overworked and exhausted and I miss my couch. Besides, what would Clarissa say if word got out that I had a meal with his parents and aunts and uncles who flew in from out of town?

I'm about to point out as much when I stop and think. *Actually*, she'd probably think that was a prime opportunity to find out more about him. Who is he when he's not on set? Who is he around his parents?

Find out his favorite dim sum dish, I hear Clarissa clairvoyantly insisting.

"You're not worried your mom will spill some huge family secret about you that'll make its way into *Vogue*?" I ask, half teasing, half not.

He shakes his head, fingers raking through dark brown hair that doesn't have to be done up for the next thirty-six hours. It's starting to get floppy in front, and I wonder when his last haircut was. "Obviously, I'll prep her beforehand," he replies. "Besides, I'd like you to meet Jess. I think you guys will get along."

"Oh yeah? Why's that?" I ask, wondering how much time he's spent thinking about me and his sister hanging out together (and why).

"Because considering the amount of time and energy the two of you put into it, it would appear that you both are pursuing doctorate degrees in how to antagonize me. So, you know, there's at least *one* common interest. I'm sure you'll find others, too."

Despite myself, fresh, delighted laughter bursts out of me, and he grins back. "But . . . what if people see us?" I ask, a new, more crucial reason to turn down his offer occurring to me. "What if the police find out? Won't it look like we're colluding outside of work hours?"

He pauses, and resolves it with a chuckle. "It's just brunch, Khin. It'll look like we're two coworkers having brunch on the weekend."

I'm too anxious to be entirely convinced, but on the other hand, this could be a potential gold mine for my story. "And you're . . . really okay with this?" I ask to double-check.

"Yeah. It'll be fun."

This isn't right. Something is off. I am aware that it feels ridiculous-bordering-on-paranoid to say that this feels like a trap, but it feels like a trap. Or a trick. How could the biggest movie star in the world *not* be wary about inviting a journalist to brunch with his family? And on his one day off? This feels like the type of damage-control setup your publicist arranges because someone just leaked a secret voice recording of you going off on a racist tirade.

Maybe he is worried about you, I fleetingly think.

Or more likely, another voice perks up, *he wants to keep a close eye on you so he can keep making sure he knows everything you know.*

That has to be it. He doesn't want a repeat of the park incident. What was it that he'd said? *Guess we're always watching each other.* If he wants to watch over me this badly, then I'm at least going to twist this to my advantage.

"May will also be there," he adds. "If that . . . I dunno, makes a difference either way?"

It does, actually. I haven't gotten a chance to get to know May outside of work, and I wanted part of the profile to include her reflections on their friendship. Maybe I can tease out some of that tomorrow.

"Text me the details," I say.

Y ou don't think they'll think it's weird that we drove over together?" I mumble as I back into a parking spot in the basement garage of The Dumpling Dealer. It's one of the oldest (and best) dim sum restaurants in the city, but it recently moved to a new location with more space. Despite its new, more central and trendy-ish location, however, the menu has more or less stayed the same since my childhood, and my stomach is already craving their crystal shrimp dumplings.

"I can't exactly get a cab now, can I?" he replies over the *beep beep beep* of the car's backup camera. "Besides, carpooling is good for the environment."

"Didn't you fly here on a private jet?"

"All the more reason for me to play my part in saving the earth."

"How about May?" I ask while I use my rearview mirror to reapply my lip gloss. "Why didn't you carpool with her?" I put the gloss back in my purse and rearrange my curtain bangs.

"Because she's a terrible backseat driver, and, more importantly, she was at her sister's house on the other side of town. I would've used more gas going to get her first," he replies. I'm giving my bangs one final touch-up when I detect him looking at me. He's chewing his bottom lip; when I worry my lip like that, I'm trying to hold myself back from saying something that I'll most likely regret later.

"What?" I ask.

"You . . . look good," he says with a nod. When he adds, "Your hair looks good, too. And that . . . lip. Color," I feel the tips of my ears begin to heat up. He's flirting. It's nice to be reminded that I am an attractive woman with whom attractive men want to flirt. Hey, maybe I'll even give the apps another go once all of this is over.

I run my hands through my hair and smile to signal a silent thank-you. "By the way," I start, curiosity getting the better of me. "How did you . . . describe me? To your parents."

One brow arches before he answers. "I said you were the rudest, most persistent, least charming journalist I'd ever met in my whole career. Left out antagonistic, though."

I scoff and, as a reflex, whack his shoulder. I do *not* linger on the tingle in my fingertips that spreads and makes my whole right hand go a tiny bit wobbly before I can retrieve it. "First off, I am *brimming* with charm—"

"Is that why you just physically assaulted me?"

"That was not assault."

"What do you call it then?"

I purse my lips to the side, trying my best not to focus on the sudden sparks of static that seem to be fizzing in and out around us, like tiny fireflies that disappear the second you look at them. "Physical banter." As soon as I say the word "physical," I feel my crotch clench.

I expect him to laugh or lob back something clever, but Tyler goes quiet and simply *stares*. In my peripheral vision, I note the previously upturned corners of his mouth fall, and a muscle in his jaw jerks. I want to look away, but I also don't—god, this man is hot—and I want him to look away first but also . . . I don't.

And now I'm aware of how dark and secluded this corner of the parking garage is, how *well* those chinos fit him, how *easy* it would be to—"Do your parents *know* I'm a journalist?" I ask abruptly, because nothing kills the beginnings of an erection like talking about your parents.

Tyler startles as though I've snapped him out of a trance, but if he *was* preoccupied by something, he eases back into the conversation with zero hiccups. "Yes," he says.

"And they didn't mind?" I ask, stepping out.

"No," he says, coming around the front of the car. He waits as I re-tuck my pink scalloped camisole into my jeans. "I told them you were also a friend, and my mom jumped in and said I should invite you and I told her that I already had."

"You know, moms *love* me. It's my shining yet effortless charm, *despite* what some people think," I say and start for the elevator. When Tyler pulls his baseball cap farther down, I give a small chuckle. He looks over like, *What?*, and I point at the plain black cap. "I thought the whole incognito sunglasses-and-baseball-cap disguise was a highly inaccurate trope."

Smirking, he's about to say something, but gets distracted and snaps his fingers. "Oh, one thing I forgot to mention. We have a seating chart."

I stop, one foot in front of the other. "A seating chart?" I echo.

Two couples pass us and Tyler turns and takes one large step in my direction, lowering his head even farther down, toward me. *Pine trees.* It hits me, and that tingle from earlier returns, stronger now and spreading farther and faster, right down to my toes. *You smell like a weekend away*, I think without quite knowing what I even mean by that, but it's my brain's knee-jerk response.

"An *informal* seating chart," Tyler answers.

Without meaning to, my lungs take in a deep inhale of his minty breath, and before I can help it, I'm thinking, *Have you ever let a date smell your morning breath?* And then my gut doubles over with mortification because why am I thinking of Tyler Tun's morning breath?

I hope I sound breezy and *not* like someone who's thinking of morning breath as I ask, "Is this a quirky family thing?"

At the elevator, he presses the button four times in rapid succession, and breathes out an audible sigh of relief once when it opens, and again when it closes without anyone else joining us. "It's a my-father-insisted-that-getting-a-private-room-would-diminish-the-authentic-chaos-of-the-dim-sum-experience-so-we-need-to-be-strategic-about-seats thing," he grumbles.

I jerk backward once I process his words. "Tyler!" I yell a bit. "Don't tell me that we're eating in the main—"

Ding.

You know it's a good dim sum place when you can hear and smell it before you see it. The cacophony of chopsticks clanging on porcelain plates, kids squealing as they run around, impatient adults calling out to get the servers' attention, the aroma of stacks of freshly baked, steamed, and poached foods—all simultaneously hit our senses. Tyler grimaces as he pulls his cap so low I wonder if I should hold his hand so I can guide him to the table—for safety reasons, obviously.

Before we reach the front desk, though, a female voice calls out, "There you are!" For a moment, I'm convinced someone's already recognized him, and panic, unsure what the protocol is for getting a celebrity out of a restaurant unscathed. But by the time I've turned in Tyler's direction, he's hunched over, a pair of someone else's hands placed on his back.

"Hi, a may," Tyler says into his mom's ear before placing a kiss on her cheek. When they part, he takes a small step back and gestures at me. "This is Khin. Khin, this is my mom, Su."

"Hi, Auntie." I smile. I let out an inadvertent *oomph* when my upper torso lurches forward three seconds before my feet can catch up, and I find myself in the middle of a tight hug from Su. She's tall, about Tyler's height, so my face meets her collarbone, but, unlike him, she's round and very, *very* smiley.

"We're *so* glad to meet you," she says. "We love meeting Tyler's friends! May's already here! Your shoes are *gorgeous*, sweetheart," she says, and we both look down at my black floral Gucci pumps.

I wonder if she's had five cups of coffee or if this is all her sans caffeine. "Thank you!" I say loudly so she can hear me.

"Are you into fashion?"

"I—" I stammer. I'm trying to compose myself but the noise and screaming children aren't helping; neither is the fact that Su is still gripping my arms. I settle on a straightforward "I like fashion."

"Oh great!" she says, squeezing me. "You'll *love* my older sister. She's a tailor!"

Her enthusiasm takes the corners of my courteous smile and effortlessly stretches it out into a genuine grin. Despite being parents, my parents aren't really "children people," and growing up, I always had the suspicion that having to pay attention to one biological child was more than enough hassle for them, so I never really invited friends over to my house. I knew my mom and dad would pretend to care only to forget their name ten seconds later, and even at a young age, I knew that was a small but acute heartbreak that I didn't want to bear, the idea that I could try and try to integrate them into other parts of my life, but they simply didn't have the time and energy to *want* to on their end.

Su, though, seems like the kind of mom who happily chaperoned field trips and took great pride in embarrassing her teenage children with an incessant stream of hugs and kisses out in public, and who whipped up homemade snacks for every sleepover while being aware of each of Tyler's friends' dietary allergies and restrictions. The kind of mom who *wants* to be a mom, to her children but also to any child, including, right now, me.

"Hey, where's . . ." I turn to Tyler just in time to catch him glancing at me before redirecting his full attention to Su. "Jess?"

"Didn't you see the family group chat this morning? She left for Bangkok."

Tyler's shoulders tense, and the side of his mouth pulls; I'm sure to anyone else, it'd be interpreted as a subtle half smile, but I know what it is. Something's up. "She left for Bangkok? Are you serious?" he says, the words stilted like someone made a last-minute change in the script and thrust it to him while the cameras were still rolling. "So she's not here?"

"Her boyfriend surprised her last night with concert tickets to . . . what's that artist she likes?" Su, releasing me at last, swats the suddenly uneasy air. "Oliver? Something Roberts? Oliver Roberts? No, you know her. Very purple. Olive? Starts with an *R*? Olive Roadkill?" She *tsks* with frustration. "The young girl with the long hair with a lot of teenage angst "

"Olivia Rodrigo?" Tyler and I both offer at the same time. Su nods, face brightening with recognition.

"Did you seriously just say *Olive Roadkill*?" Tyler asks. I have to stifle a laugh at that.

Su rolls her eyes. "You knew who I meant! Anyway, Jess texted the chat. I'd assumed you'd read it."

Tyler's deep sigh is more annoyed than I'd expect. "I'm about seventy texts behind in there. You all have *a lot* to say."

"You know how our family is."

"Yeah, apparently the kind that cancels last minute without even following up," he mutters, then, catching my eye, slaps his (clearly fake) movie-star smile back on. "Shall we eat?" he says, and drapes one long arm around his mom's shoulder.

With his head down, we pass the front desk where there are several families who committed the frankly rookie error of not making a reservation and are now mingling to the side in the hopes that they'll be squeezed in between preexisting reservations. Inside, and although it's a huge space in comparison to your average restaurant, the place is packed, and I almost trip over a toddler on two separate occasions. The large round tables are laid out in four parallel lines, with *just* enough space between the backs of chairs for one slightly-larger-than-average person to squeeze through. To be honest, though, now that we're here, the havoc works in Tyler's favor. Unless you really zoom in on him—and everyone is too busy to be zooming in on any one person, the staff included—he passes as someone who makes you go, *Huh, that guy kind of looks familiar.*

Our table is located in the far back of the restaurant, wedged in the right corner. "Speaking of, Khin!" May says, jumping to her feet when we arrive. She's wearing a matching purple knit short-sleeved top and midi skirt set, and a white bucket hat that both looks chic and executes the job of keeping half her face hidden. "I was just telling everyone how incredible you are to work with!" She pulls me in for a hug while making sure never to face the rest of the restaurant, and then reaches for Tyler. "And you, Jesus, it's like you've been intentionally avoiding me outside of the lot," she mumbles. Tyler and I make eye contact, our lips simultaneously pressing into a taut line, although no one else notices.

It turns out that when Tyler said there would be a seating chart, he meant he and May would sit with their backs to the restaurant while the rest of us slightly scooted our chairs closer together so that there were no gaps for a server or wandering fan to pop their head in. I'm directly opposite him, facing the restaurant, about two millimeters of space between the back of my chair and the wall, and a straight, clear view of my subject(s). Perfect.

I meet his father, two aunts, three uncles, and two cousins, all of whom are shockingly down-to-earth for members of Tyler Tun's family. It's not that I thought they'd be stuck up, per se, but I know Ty-

ler's net worth, and I can imagine he's bought his parents a nice present or two over the years—I was picturing at least a non-flashy Rolex
on his dad's wrist, or an Hermès bag hanging behind his mother's seat.
But instead, Alex (his dad) is sporting a regular stainless steel silver
watch, and Su's bag is a plain navy Longchamp tote with a few scuff
marks. And the only reason people throw stray peeks our way is when
Alex and Su lean in for an innocuous kiss, although it takes me a few
minutes to realize that not only is Alex the only white person in this
restaurant, but the two of them are also the only interracial couple
here. Despite the general increase in the city's immigrant population
over the last decade, you don't really find them (especially if they're
white and middle-class) frequenting restaurants like these that are
older and don't do marketing the way the new, say, fusion bistros do,
and where the menus are entirely in Myanmar (and in this case, also
Mandarin). I'm somewhat embarrassed to admit that I had assumed
Alex didn't know any Myanmar language, but he's fluent. And then I
remember what Tyler said about their old apartment in Chinatown,
and about how it was his father who wanted to eat dim sum the right
way. Alex was probably a regular at this restaurant's old location, too,
has probably known about this place longer than *I* have; something
about him refusing to forego the "authentic dim sum experience"
even for his movie-star son makes my heart squeeze. At this table,
Tyler is just Tyler. I'm not the kind of person to be sentimental at the
sight of other families' obvious tight-knittedness, but the portrait of
this family together sparks a small flame inside me.

Unable to whip out my phone and write my notes due to social protocol, I stay quiet and try to observe as much of the scene as I can, taking mental Polaroid pictures of every single one of Tyler's interactions.
Click: the way he sucks in his cheeks after taking the first bite of his
favorite dim sum dish, har gow, which is apparently his one "weakness" in regards to his new vegan lifestyle. *Click*: his shy, embarrassed

expression when his aunt pulls his face flush to hers for a surprise selfie. *Click*: the roar of his inadvertent laugh when his mom recounts a story about an address mix-up that led to his sister's weed brownie delivery arriving at their house to the ignorance of their father who just so happened to be peckish that day after a particularly long morning jog. *Click*: his sneaky, relaxed smile as he watches his parents mock-bicker.

"Khin, I have to say—" His cousin Aye's voice seizes all of our attention, but not before Tyler finds me looking at him and . . . smiles. Before I can even be embarrassed, Aye says, "We were all so excited to hear you were joining us today."

"Oh?" I am . . . confused? Surprised? Flattered? All three, possibly. "Why's that?"

"Auntie and Uncle told us that Tyler can't stop talking about you. Which, by the way"—she points her chopsticks across the table at him—"I don't understand why you haven't mentioned her in the cousin chat. I thought we were friends."

In an effort to clear up my ongoing confused-surprised-flattered state, I look at Tyler for answers—and find him cheeks flushed and widening his eyes at Aye as he tries to communicate something through Cousin Telepathy.

"Khin is *the best*," May answers on his behalf (sort of), but her tone and the shoulder nudge she gives him feels less like she's saving him and more like teasing. "She's probably the best journalist I've ever encountered. Very dedicated to her work, including this profile. She and Tyler are practically inseparable on set."

Now it's my turn to have heat stretch out across my face. Despite my spaghetti-strap top, I can feel my elbows start to sweat. Everyone's eyes are ping-ponging between me and Tyler, and in spite of my instincts, I make sure not to look at him.

"Two months isn't a lot of time to shadow someone—" I hear him start to say.

"Interesting," his other cousin, Paing, interrupts. "Because remember when the *New York Times* wanted just half a day with you and you said you could spare an hour, max?"

Aye snorts beside me. Perhaps against my better judgment, I sweep a swift gaze across the table. I don't need Cousin Telepathy to read the blatant embarrassment (and anger) on Tyler's face as he glares at Paing, who is smiling back with an innocent *What?* expression. Everyone else is trying to hide their unbridled glee by looking down or away. Everyone except for May. When my eyes land on May, she's already watching me. She gives me a warm smile, but doesn't break eye contact. She is, I realize after a few seconds, pulling a me. That is to say, she's observing me, gauging how I'm reacting to all of this. Does she . . . does she know? No, she can't know. But her quip about Tyler and I being inseparable definitely hints that she suspects something—I'm just not certain how farfetched (or not) her suspicions are.

"I have to go to the bathroom!" My announcement comes down like a sledgehammer, but hey, at least it breaks the uncomfortable tension. "Sorry." I grimace. "I . . ." I scramble around at the table before my eyes land on my glass of watermelon juice. "I had *a lot* of watermelon juice," I say.

"Oh, I feel you, thamee," Su quips. "Once, I made the mistake of eating half a watermelon for breakfast before a road trip, and it ended up taking us three times as long to get there!"

I nod enthusiastically, like I've never heard a truer statement in my life. "Yeah, and I have a *really* small bladder. My doctor was concerned at my last checkup." I want to suck the words back in as soon as they've left my mouth. It's not even true! As far as I know, I have a normal-sized bladder.

"Oh!" Su says, taken aback but not wanting to appear rude. "You should go then, thamee. Don't want a UTI!"

I give a weak laugh, not believing that I'm talking about UTIs with Tyler Tun's mother. "No, I don't!"

I push my chair back against the wall and stand up. To my right, Alex does the same and everyone to *his* right follows suit, the last person being Tyler. It's a tight squeeze thanks to our proximity to the corner, and as I awkwardly wiggle my way out between these near-complete strangers and a table stacked with bamboo trays of dim sum, I try to recall why I said I had to go to the bathroom right now even though I could've probably held it in for another hour?

Oh right, because Tyler shot me a single smile and the feral part of me that hasn't had sex in six months wanted to jump up and crawl across the table and undress him then and there. Tyler, who—

"Tyler!" Su yells, but it's too late.

Two kids playing a game of tag run right into him, and I watch him fold, knees buckling. He tries to grab his mother's outstretched hand but misses. I extend my arm to catch him as he stumbles in my direction. He manages to grip my *shoulders*, only for us both to tumble backward and rest horizontally on the maroon carpeted floor, Tyler right on top of me. I catch sight of the cap hurtling in the air above his head while the sunglasses that he had hung on his shirt's neckline slide under the table.

"Fuck," he whispers a nanosecond before somebody screeches and screams, "It's Tyler Tun!"

I freeze as murmurs of "Is that Tyler Tun?" and "Holy shit, that's Tyler Tun!" become louder and less murmur-like around us until they're an overlapping chatter, like birds squawking in the jungle over two shiny pieces of fruit (*we* are the fruit).

"We have to go," Tyler says through gritted teeth. Before I can nod, he's already scrambling to his feet and stretching out for me.

"May—" I whisper, but Tyler squeezes my arm before I can look for her.

"Don't look at her," he says sharply. "They're looking at us. If you look at her, they'll look at her, too."

"Okay," I say. In fact, I don't look anywhere but the floor as I clutch his hand and try to get up without one of my boobs popping out in front of the entire restaurant. "My shoe," I mutter when, once upright, I realize I'm tipping to the left.

"Here!" Tyler's aunt Nilar (the tailor) says, grabbing the shoe which had flown under her chair. Tyler takes it and gives it to me, and, holding on to his shoulder, I hop on one foot to put it on.

"Here's your bag," Alex says, and they fling my purse around the table before one of Tyler's uncles hands it to me.

"Ready?" Tyler asks.

I nod. Only then do I look up—and my whole being spasms with regret when I come face-to-face with a sea of cell phones that boasts the steadiness and intensity of a SWAT team's lasers. They're all pointed right at us, and they stay trained on us as we run out of the dining area and toward the fire escape stairs, Tyler leading the way, my feet following his, our hands clasped as though we're hanging from a cliff and either we both survive, or neither does.

Eleven

"Tyler Tun's Darling's Dim Sum Debut,'" Clarissa says through the phone, enunciating each *s* and *d*. "'Dim Sum and Chill.' 'Tyler Tun's Dim Sum Dine and Dash, but Who Is His Accomplice?'"

We didn't dine and dash, I retort in my head. Out loud, though, all I say is, "Clarissa, I can explain."

"Please," Clarissa says, and I can picture her unamused countenance as she swipes the headline tabs closed. Headlines that everybody I know—and their mother and second cousins—have been texting me since before my alarm went off. My phone log is a list of red: missed calls from my parents, Nay, Thidar, even Patrick (although I have a feeling this was Thidar trying to be sneaky). I hadn't picked up a single one. Because I was busy getting ready for a 9 A.M. call time, because I am a professional, a journalist who is still on the job. Or at least, I *hope* I'm still on the job. Judging by Clarissa's tone and the fact that she didn't even respond with a "hello" when I'd picked up with my most effusive "Morning, Clarissa!" I might actually not have this specific job for much longer.

"We were having lunch—"

"With his family," Clarissa clarifies for the record.

"Yes," I state coolly.

"On a Sunday."

"He invited me."

A pause. "Khin. You know I'm not into bullshitting, so I'm going to come out and ask it. Are you and Tyler dating?"

"What? No!" I yell. Beside me, Tyler, who had otherwise directed his intense focus out the window since the start of this call, rolls his shoulders. The quiet back here is biting, so I have no doubt he can hear every word on the other line.

"Are you fucking?"

A mortified scoff escapes me. "No, Clarissa, we're not."

"Then why the hell—" She pauses, as though she's also trying to temper her reaction. "Did a hundred cameras catch Tyler literally lying on top of you on the floor?"

"Clarissa, he *tripped*." My tone is right on the edge of snappy, but the more I think about this, the more ridiculous this line of questioning is. "Has nobody seen a person trip before?"

This time, she's the one to scoff. "Nobody's seen Tyler Tun trip *on top* of a woman before, I can tell you that."

"Clarissa, come on, those tabloids are chasing clicks." Remembering that she is technically my boss here and has the ability to kick me off the job faster than I can say "Action," I force myself to take a deep breath and hold it for three seconds before I speak again. "I know it doesn't look good. But what happened was he tripped and I tried to catch him and then we both fell over. That's literally it. I'm not dating Tyler. I don't *want* to date Tyler." To my left, I catch Tyler give another shoulder roll, but I can't focus on him right now. "Clarissa," I say. "You gave me this job because of my professionalism and because I am good at what I do. Why on earth would I jeopardize the biggest assignment of my career?"

I *think* I can hear a rhythmic tapping from her end, as though she's clacking her nails against a laptop or tabletop as she considers my answer. "Khin—" She doesn't say my name so much as she sighs it. "I have a board to answer to. We can't be giving our biggest cover story to a journalist who might have a . . . personal bias. HR alone will be a nightmare, and I don't even want to think of how much overtime PR is going to have to put in. And on a personal level, *I* will not be accused of being unprofessional and handing this story to you simply because you are Tyler Tun's girl—"

I can see it slipping through my fingers like oil-coated grains of sand: this assignment, *Vogue Singapore,* my fresh start in a new city, my new post-divorce plan. "Clarissa, this is sexist bullshit."

"Oh?" she asks, staggered into silence.

"People already assume that every time a woman interviews a male subject, we're secretly hoping that they'll ask us out. Screw the board! Why do *we* have to pay because a group of old men can't stop hyper-sexualizing every single movement that a young woman makes? Since when did 'tripping in the middle of a restaurant' become a valid reason to fire someone?" Did I just tell her to screw the board of *Vogue?* I push myself back into the leather seat, wishing I could melt into it and out of existence.

"Tell her we'll release a statement."

I fling open my eyes and turn toward Tyler. His stern frown is aimed not at me, but at my phone. "What?" I whisper, covering the mic with one hand.

"Tell her we'll release a statement," he repeats. "If the board fires you after *that—*"

"Khin—" Clarissa's voice takes on an even firmer texture. "Is he there with you right now? Has he been listening to our conversation this whole time?"

Widening my eyes, I make a shushing motion with one finger at Tyler, and then to really drive the point home, also make a zipping motion across my lips. "No," I lie. The absolute *last* thing I need right now is a statement from Tyler, because it would simply be more proof to Clarissa that I'm getting some sort of special treatment because I'm his girlfriend. "We're on the way to the set, but he's talking on his phone. He's . . . talking to *his* publicist about all of this. He's telling her what I'm telling you, that it was an unfortunate series of accidents. But that's all it was. An accident."

This time, the sound of her nails rapping is undeniable. "Fine," she says at last, but the tension on the line hasn't decreased a millimeter. "But Khin, don't let this happen again."

I nod frantically even though I know she can't see it. "It won't," I confirm. "I'm grateful for this job, Clarissa, you know that."

"Good." For some reason, I can see her giving me a curt nod. "That's also good to know because you're working next Sunday."

"Of course!" I say. At this point, she could've said, *Make me the sole benefactor of your will,* and I would've started texting my lawyer immediately.

"It's for the photo shoot. Sunday was the only day Tyler was available. We've rented a studio. I think it'll help you to start framing the story if you see what direction we're taking the photos."

"Absolutely," I say.

"I'll email you the details. We'll speak soon," she says, and hangs up as briskly as she started the conversation.

"Ready?" Tyler asks. "Or do you need a moment?"

"Huh?" I respond. My whole body is jittering, and I feel like I've lost my spot in the space-time continuum.

I look out when he nods toward the window. We're at the lot already, although how long we've been parked here I have no clue.

"I *can* get my team to release a statement," he says quietly. I turn back to him to make sure I heard correctly, and find him looking at me with complete seriousness.

"No, that's okay, let's just let this die out," I hear myself saying politely.

Internally, though, my veins are pulsating. How can he be this ignorant? I was seconds away from losing this job and very possibly having my entire professional reputation tarnished as the girl who slept her way to getting this assignment—all because he wanted me to come to that stupid brunch to show me that he is the perfect son and brother. And that is, of course, on top of the fact that my coming to brunch also allowed him to keep tabs on me even outside of work.

"We should get going," I grumble, and, ignoring the way his smile fades, open the door.

"Tyler!" Yasmin's voice greets us before I've even come around to the other side of the car. My features freeze and tighten into something painful once she is in my line of sight, and I see who's behind her. "You remember Detectives Zeyar and Htet, right?"

"Of course." Tyler, still his usual collected self, gives them an acknowledging nod. "You were here last week. Can we help you, Detectives?"

Blood is thrumming in my ears. They saw us on Saturday. They were still keeping an eye on the park—like Tyler said, some culprits just can't help but return to the scene of the crime—and someone clocked me. Then they ran all the plates in the parking lot, and saw that one of them was registered to the car service that everyone on this movie uses. Tyler and I are *both* going down.

"We'd like to talk to you again, Khin," Detective Zeyar says. I look up and realize they're not looking at me and Tyler. Just me. His tone becomes blatantly accusatory as he adds, "You failed to mention to us that you've had a run-in with the police before."

"I . . . didn't see how that was relevant to this case," I say, trying to coax my body language into relaxed territory even though my escalating anger and anxiety are making me anything but. From a glass-half-full perspective, though, it doesn't sound like they know about us revisiting the park.

"Well, from what we hear," Detective Htet says, stepping in my direction. I brace myself to stop from flinching back. "You're a bit of a troublemaker."

Troublemaker? I open my mouth, ready to spit out something like, *Now, now, your misogyny is showing,* but then remember where I am, remember that Tyler and Yasmin and several crew members are also present. "Why don't we let them"—I nod at Tyler—"get started with the shoot? I don't want to be holding anyone up."

Detective Zeyar opens his mouth but it's Tyler's voice that I hear first. "Do we need to call our legal team?"

"That depends," Detective Zeyar replies to him, and I can tell that whatever he was going to say to *me* wasn't nearly as polite. "In our experience, though, it's only the guilty ones that require legal representation."

"Or the smart ones that ask for it," Tyler says with an innocent head tilt.

Both detectives exchange a look. "Of course Khin is entitled to legal counsel if she wants. But we just have a few follow-up questions. We don't think it'll be necessary."

I know the responsible course of action here is to insist I'll wait for a lawyer, but I'm too fixated on the disgusting, smug sneers on these men's faces to remember to be scared. "It's okay," I say, fixing my own dauntless smile. "I'm happy to cooperate. I'll come find you when I'm done."

"Khin—" Tyler begins.

"Go. I don't want to be the reason you guys run late today."

"Right this way," Detective Htet says, and turns to lead me toward their pathetic makeshift interrogation room, his colleague sandwiching me from behind like I'm some perp who might flee at any second.

"So the thing is," Detective Zeyar says once we're sitting at the wobbly wooden table in the storage room, the two of them huddled together on one side because that's the only way they can both face and (I suppose) intimidate me. I hold back an eye roll as I watch them consciously make an effort not to rub shoulders because, of course, that's too much physical contact for their macho (and most likely homophobic) personas. "A funny thing happened yesterday. A few of us were gathered at my place to watch the football game in the evening when my teenage daughter ran into the living room in tears. Do you know why?"

I shake my head.

"It turns out, Tyler Tun has a girlfriend now. And when I asked who it was, she showed me an Instagram video of Tyler on top of a woman. Now, of course, I'm sure you're aware that that woman was you."

"That was a misunderstanding. Tyler and I aren't dating. We're colleagues."

"Right," he says, his tone making it clear that he does not believe me. "I did remember you, though, and imagine my surprise when my buddy Zaw jabbed a finger at the screen and said, 'I know her,' even though he's been nowhere near this case."

I swallow. "Oh?"

At this point, Detective Htet leans in. "You see, it turns out he was part of an investigation that was looking into an article you wrote earlier this year? About an—" I know the pause is deliberate. I *know* what the article is about, and *he* knows I know. "Abortion clinic?"

I draw up the corners of my smile. "That investigation was closed. And like I said earlier, I'm not quite sure how *that* is relevant to our current—"

"Do you hate men, Khin?"

I give a small jump in my seat. "What?" I ask, and curse myself when both of them smirk at having caught me by surprise.

"It's a simple question," Detective Zeyar says with a nonchalant shrug. "Do you hate men?"

"I don't see how that's an appropriate question."

"Oh, my bad," Detective Zeyar says, shaking his head. "I forgot to tell you why we are here, because you're right. We didn't have a reason to come back simply because you were part of an earlier closed investigation and because you might or might not be dating Tyler—"

"I'm not."

"Right," he says, and I swear under my breath that if he says *Right* one more time in this conversation, I am going to choke him with the neon purple feather boa that's draped around the mannequin behind him. He takes out his phone from his jacket pocket, unlocks it, and rotates it around to me, obviously having planned this big reveal hours ago.

"What's this?" I ask with a bored sigh. "I don't—" I stop once I take in what's on the screen. In a daze, I grab the phone with both hands, zooming in and out of the photo.

"There's more," Detective Htet's voice says. "Swipe to the left."

And I do. And he's right. There *is* more. *So* much more.

They're photos of me. In front of my current apartment building. In front of my old house. At the park with Ben. At my favorite café, hunched over my laptop, wireless headphones atop my head. Inspecting a mug at a farmer's market with Thidar and Nay. There's a picture of me walking Pizza. Another of me and Ben leaving a restaurant after a double date with Thidar and Patrick.

The last dozen or so are of me getting out of a taxi in Chinatown on the first night I met Tyler.

When I put the phone down on the table, my hands are trembling.

"What—" I breathe, trying to speak through the rush of blood to my head. "What is this?" *Who took these?*

"*That*," Detective Zeyar says as he retrieves and pockets his phone, "was what we found on the dead man's phone. It washed up a few days later. We assumed it was useless due to all the water damage, but it turns out our tech department recently got quite the equipment upgrade. They also got us an identity."

"Oh?" is all I can say as I try to stave off the panic attack, unsure which part of this conversation I'm panicking in response to.

Detective Htet nods. "Yes. His name is Jared Kirkwood. He's an Australian citizen who's lived here for eight years. Does that name ring a bell?"

I shake my head so hard I almost give myself whiplash. "I've never heard that name."

"Interesting," he says, furrowing his brows as though he's doing some quick mental math. "But then . . . how come his camera roll is nothing but photos of you? We went through the whole thing. There are no pictures of his friends, food, holidays, nothing. It's all . . . you. To be frank, it's like he got a whole new phone *just* for you."

Despite the thudding in my ears, I retrieve enough cognizance to repeat, "I . . . don't know this man."

"But he knows you."

"But *I* don't know *him*."

"Are you sure?" Detective Zeyar steeples his fingers and leans in. "All these photos, and you don't know him at all? Maybe you ran into him somewhere? Went on a date with him at one point? Help us out here, Khin."

At last, a voice inside my brain manages to cut through the jumble of confusion and panic that's swirling around. "Lawyer," I say, remembering Tyler's words.

"Now, Khin, we're just having a chat here," Detective Zeyar continues, his saccharine tone making this situation ten times worse. "But if you lawyer up, well, you can see why we might start to get suspicious."

I steel my spine and swallow, pushing my despair and bile back down. If I'm going to buckle and vomit—either words, or the bagel I had for breakfast—it will *not* be in front of their ugly faces. "And I don't appreciate you harassing me about a man who has clearly been stalking me," I reply with a glare.

He sighs like I'm a child who won't listen to reason. "Look, sweetheart, just because we're doing our job doesn't mean we're *harassing—*" The "sweetheart" was bad, but when he rolls his eyes on "harassing," like I'm now a child who throws the word "harassing" around without really knowing what it means, the anger from earlier resurfaces.

"I'm not answering any more questions until I have a lawyer present."

"Kh—"

"Lawyer."

They release me without any more questions, but not without a final subdued "You've made things very difficult for yourself."

———

Tyler's in the middle of a scene when I slip onto set. I grab an empty chair in the back, take out my notebook and open it on my lap so it looks like everything's peachy and I'm working as always.

Obviously I have to resume looking into that man. Good news is, now I have an actual lead. I press the tip of my pen into the center of the page as I think it through. What was his name again? Jared Kirkwood. Australian. I write it down in the back of my notebook before I forget.

I have to find out who this Jared Kirkwood is, for two reasons. One, this random man whom I have never encountered apart from those ten minutes in the park was most definitely targeting me, and I want to know why. And second, I need to see how close the police are to finding me out; I need to track down the same leads that they're inevitably going to, and, *somehow*, be sly about asking about Jared and why he might've been stalking a random woman.

The obvious course of action here would be to call Kira, but what would I ask her? *Hey, did Charlie propose yet? Oh, and while I've got you, and not to be all "do all Australians know one another," but* do *you happen to know a Jared Kirkwood who's been following and taking photos of me for the past several months?* But if I do that, I might as well also take a red Sharpie and write "Suspect Number One" on my own forehead.

Tyler was right—this wasn't a moment of opportunity; this man was *stalking* me. A chill spreads across my arms as that last realization really settles: this stranger was following me around for literal months and I never knew. What was he going to do in that park? Did he come there that night to kill me? How long had he been waiting out there? My stomach starts churning like I had a big meal before getting on a roller coaster, but I'm at the top of the tracks now, and whether I like it or not, the ride has started.

———

S o are you going to tell me?" Tyler asks as soon as the car divider rolls up.

"Tell you what?"

"Khin, what's going on?"

I give him a few innocent blinks. "Oh, the interrogation? It was fine," I say with a dismissive shrug. "I *did* tell them I wanted a lawyer if they want to talk to me again, though. I already told Yasmin."

Silently, he surveys me in that way I don't like, that way from the first night as though, against my will, I've got my entire history etched all over my body and clothes for him to take his sweet time reading. "What did they mean when they said you'd had a previous run-in with the police?"

I wave a hand. "Don't worry about that. You're not a real journalist until you've had at least one brush with the cops."

"Khin," he says, voice going protective. "What happened?"

"Nothing happened. They just had a few questions."

"About?"

My face twitches, and I don't hide the fact that I'm gritting my teeth to hold myself back from exploding. "My personal history is none of your business," I reply politely.

He flinches, eyes quickly darting to the soundproof car divider to make sure it's still up. "It is when it involves me. And the authorities. Look, I'm only asking because I wanna be able to keep an eye out for you. And I can't do that unless we're on the same page."

"Oh really? Is *that* why?" I scoff.

"What does *that* mean?" Tyler asks, and the fact that he's still keeping up this façade is what pushes me over the edge. I know you're supposed to keep your enemies closer, but why am I still acting civil and playing ignorant toward a man who keeps putting on this performance to my face?

It means that I'm aware you're asking about my interview so you can gather more dirt to use against me if you get backed into a corner and want to cut a deal, I want to yell. *So that if it comes to it, your team can point out that you are a law-abiding citizen with not so much as a traffic ticket to your name, whereas I actively write full-page features on illegal abortion clinics.*

"It means that I'm not stupid, Tyler," I snap, not caring an iota about professionalism anymore. "That night, you only agreed that we shouldn't call the cops when I pointed out the repercussions it'd have for *you,* because that's all *you've* ever cared about from the start. Which is, you know, fair. We all have our own priorities."

"That's not—"

"I said it's *fine*. But don't keep reiterating this nonsense about caring about me. You're keeping me close because I am the only person in the world who knows something that could damage your otherwise faultless reputation." And then, at the point of no return, it comes out like word vomit: "I also know you're keeping something from me. You've been keeping a secret from me since the first night we met, so don't keep blindly repeating that I need to trust you when we both know that I have a very good reason *not* to."

His mouth opens but no sound comes out. He's more than startled. *Hurt.* But I am so furious right now that I can't even curtail my tears as I continue.

"I don't need you to come up with any more lies that I'm coerced into playing along with. If my editor heard the police had interrogated just *me*, which, by the way, would not have happened if I hadn't been at that damn brunch in the first place, not even a press release from you would save my ass. From now on, you do your job and I do mine, and I'll clean up my own messes *myself*. We're not a team. Let's at least do each other the courtesy of admitting that we're only looking out for ourselves. Regardless of what your big secret that you're keeping from me is, and don't you dare try to tell me that I'm imagining things because I know I'm not, stop trying to convince me that I should tell you everything when you won't do the same with me. At least show me that modicum of respect."

I snatch a tissue from the box in front of us and blow my nose. To his credit, he waits until I'm done dabbing my eyes and have somewhat recomposed myself before saying softly, "I'm sorry. I—" He cuts himself off. "I'm really sorry," he repeats.

I shake my head, sapped. Of everything. "Stay out of my business. Please. I'll take care of this on my own from now on."

Twelve

I know who Jared Kirkwood is. Okay, I don't know his full identity down to what size shoe he wears, but I *have* found his Facebook and Instagram profiles (both public because of course he's sloppy) and from what I've pieced together, I have a pretty good idea of who he was. Like the detectives said, he moved here from Sydney eight years ago. He's a self-employed financial advisor who works remotely, which explains why no colleagues reported him as missing. According to the most recent photos of his apartment views, he lives downtown. And—this is the part that's tripping me up—he has a girlfriend. Not just someone he started seeing, but a girlfriend of approximately two years. Her name is Dipar, she's Myanmar, looks to be a few years older than me. They live together and even have a dog. Her profile isn't public, but judging by her tagged photos, she's alive and still lives in Yangon.

So why didn't *she* file a missing person report?

I'm tempted to send her a follow request, but what if the police have contacted her first already and then they see my name on her phone? *That* would be a tricky situation to explain, even with the best lawyers that money could buy sitting beside me.

I know I could ask Nay or Thidar to do it (have we done it in the past after being unceremoniously dumped by a guy and wondered if it was because there was someone new in the picture? Who's to say, really?), but I haven't talked to them since dim sum–gate apart from a short I'm fine. It was a misunderstanding. No we're not dating. I'll call you guys as soon as I'm free." And the next text I send in the group chat can't be Can one of you guys add this completely random woman that we share zero mutual friends with but not ask me why? Besides, I'm still adamant about not pulling them into this.

After combing through the profiles of Jared's followers whose photos Dipar has been tagged in over the last five months—and, yes, aware of the hypocrisy of my cyberstalking *my* stalker's (potential) girlfriend—I've determined that she's going to be at the Nagar's Breath bar tomorrow night. If this were a regular assignment, I'd get there early to grab a prime seat that was centrally positioned enough that I could watch the entrance, the bar, and the toilets, but far enough away that I remained inconspicuous. But there's Tyler's shoot.

We're starting at 11 A.M. until "tbd," according to Clarissa's email. I haven't heard of this photographer—which is apparently the point. Keeping in mind that the whole cast and crew are Myanmar, Clarissa has tapped an up-and-coming Myanmar photographer called Thuzar Thant for this spread; the shoot is also taking place at her house, the second floor of which is her studio. Unconventional, but I'm intrigued.

Tyler, on his part, has respected my wishes all week. We don't carpool anymore; I'm wary of cab drivers being bribed into sneaking photos of the set and of lurking paparazzi snapping photos of my license plate, so I've rented a car. And although, admittedly, I hadn't realized quite how much I'd enjoyed our morning chats in the car, those forty-ish minutes of only the two of us in a soundproof limo backseat before we had to face the racket of a movie set, this new arrangement is for the best. His trailer is still my first stop when I arrive at the lot, but the extent of our greetings stops at a mutual, genial "Good morning." Which is good. Preferable, even. Like I instructed, he's doing his job and I'm doing mine.

Except, the rest of the week has also been a complete waste of time in terms of getting a scoop, and when you are working with a very limited amount of time (I triple-checked this morning, and this draft is due in under six weeks), half a week is *a lot*. At this point, I might as well already email Clarissa something along the lines of: *Sorry, but it looks like I'm not going to be able to get any kind of scoop on Tyler because he's keeping his distance because I, in a moment of unfettered fury, explicitly told him to.*

I realize there's a somewhat easy solution here: I apologize. Say, *Hey, Tyler, I'm sorry about the other day. I'm generally in a bad headspace these days and I took it out on you when I didn't mean to (even though I absolutely did). Let's be friends again?* and pick up where I left off vis-à-vis gaining his trust. While my pride would rather I jump into shark-infested waters than apologize to Tyler, I know this is what must be done. It's the only way out. I suck it up, make niceties, become "friends" (ugh) again, get my scoop, file the story, get that job, and then before I know it, I'll be shoving my entire wardrobe into two (okay, maybe four) suitcases.

Vogue. I can suck it up and be buddies with Tyler Tun if it means a job at *Vogue*.

On Sunday, I'm out the door by ten, and to pump myself up because it hits me that I'm casually on my way to a *Vogue* photo shoot, I put on a loop of Reyanna Maria's "So Pretty," Beyoncé's "Run the World (Girls)," Fifth Harmony's "That's My Girl," and Lizzo's "Like a Girl." I might be a one-woman team, but being a one-woman team is nothing new to me, and I'm not going to get overwhelmed now. As soon as this shoot is over, I'm going to haul ass over to Nagar's Breath and sort out the rest of this mess.

Thuzar must either come from money or have recently won the lottery, because how else does an "up-and-coming" photographer afford a house with a front yard this size? It definitely screams "artist": terra-cotta bricks starkly contrasted by neon-yellow shutters, mismatched wooden animal sculptures lining the concrete pathway, and tall metal gates whose imposition is undermined by their aquamarine-and-neon-yellow-flowers design. Not my taste at all, but I'm always a fan of someone who knows exactly what they like. Does it fit in with the neighboring white mansions and black gates? No. Does it seem like it cares? Also no.

I give my lips a final touch-up in the car mirror before I step out. Maybe I can find a way to apologize to Tyler without actually apologizing, for the sake of my article. Maybe something neutral like *Hey, are we cool?* without explicitly mentioning what it is I'd like us to be cool in regards to.

Despite its size, the pathway is already filled with cars, and I wedge myself into the last remaining space as the automatic gate doors rumble back shut. I press the doorbell—gold and shaped like a twinkling star with two long triangles jutting out from north and south, and two smaller triangles on either side—and a couple of seconds later, the door opens and I'm greeted by—

"Jason?" I ask, retreating backward.

If his bulging eyes and the pink tinge on his cheeks are any indication, Jason wasn't expecting to answer the door to me, either. "Khin!" he says with a tad too much enthusiasm that snaps me to attention. "I . . . thought we were doing only photos today. What . . . are you doing here?"

"My editor wanted me to sit in on the shoot so I could have an idea of how to frame the story. What are *you* doing here?"

"I—"

"Khin?"

Every nerve in my body goes numb while the blood zings straight to my head. The result is an inability to blink, let alone speak. Is this what people experience when they get shot? Like you technically know what's happened, but for a few seconds that extend for several eternities, you can't feel anything, including the bullet inside of you?

It's Ben's voice (again) that snaps me out of that liminal state. "Khin?" he repeats.

"Ben?" I ask, probably looking like I've seen a ghost. He looks generally the same, still a solid foot taller than me, medium-length-ish hair still pomaded up and out of his face. The only noticeable new addition is his tan, although I guess spending several months on a beach in Indonesia will do that to you.

"I didn't know you'd—"

"What are you doing here?"

"This—" Ben looks at Jason, who returns a panicked smile. "This is my . . . girlfriend's house," he finally says without looking at me.

I can feel the bullet now. I can feel the searing heat burrowing deeper inside my chest, feel my blood pooling and boiling in places it shouldn't. Unsure where to look, my eyes wander around the foyer, up at the staircase with side glass panes, before skipping over each of the several dozen photographs that cover the walls. Ben always wanted to have walls plastered with photography, but I never saw the appeal of black-and-white portraits of strangers' backs or the inside of a volcano as it explodes. Sure, they make great screen savers, but why would I want to stare into the volcanic abyss while sipping my morning coffee?

"Khin?" Every time my name leaves Ben's lips, my insides have a small seizure. "I can leave if—"

I don't *mean* to sound like a member of Alvin and the Chipmunks, but that's what happens as I squeak, "What? That's ridiculous!"

"Are you—" Ben eyes me like he's getting ready to catch me in case I faint. "Sure?"

"Of course!" I roll my eyes in a *please* manner. "This is your girl-friend's house! Who I'm *so* excited to meet!" I say, now thankful that I chose the jeans that make my ass look nice and perky.

"Okay then." Ben nods. "Shall we?" He starts up the stairs with the speed of someone who has taken this route hundreds, if not thou-sands, of times before.

Thuzar is short, even shorter than me. It's the first thing I notice about her, because despite her size, her presence is undeniable. Face framed by large, round, neon-pink-rimmed glasses, she's marching around and talking to people, camera in one hand, the other free to gesticulate as she speaks, and I can tell even from over here that she knows how to toe the line between reminding everyone who's in charge and not being a dick. Her smile expands into a grin when she walks over to us.

"Hi," she says with a quick wave. "I'm Thuzar. I'm the photog-rapher."

"Hey, I'm—" I pause, not sure how serious the two of them are, and consequently, how much she knows about Ben's personal history. "Khin."

The small *O* that forms on Thuzar's lips tells me instantly that she knows. She glances up at Ben, who returns an acute, confirming nod. To my shock, she doesn't snap into some weird or tense mode. Instead, she opens her arms, exclaiming, "Oh my god, Khin! I've heard so much about you!"

"Really?" I ask, frowning.

"Yes! Ben has shared *so* many of your articles with me! You know," she says, raising her brows at Ben, who rolls his eyes like he knows exactly which story she's about to tell, "the day after our first date, he texted me one. Of your articles, I mean. And he was going on and on—"

"Okay," Ben says, opening his palm in the air. "First off, I texted you because the article was relevant to our conversation the day before. And I wasn't going *on and on*—"

"—and at first I was like, *Oh great, this guy is clearly hung up on his ex.* But then I opened the link and started reading and then I was like, *Ah shit, I'd be bragging about her, too.* It was your interview with that writer who was the first to translate bell hooks's *All About Love* into Myanmar. And then I was like, *Well, fuck, this Khin is so cool.* And I've been a huge fan of your work ever since! I'm so glad you're here! Ben didn't tell me he invited you, though. Not that that's a problem, but I would've prepared myself to tone down my fangirling beforehand if I'd known."

Not knowing how else to process the avalanche of information that she's just thrown in my face, I give a weak laugh. "Ben didn't invite me," I say. "I'm writing this story."

Thuzar's mouth hangs open. "Shut. Up. *You're* doing the Tyler Tun profile? Holy shit!" She throws her hands in the air. "This is huge! Oh my god, now I'm *really* feeling the pressure. Because obviously *you're* going to write a bad-ass profile and what if the photos don't measure up? Ben!" Her jaw hardens. "No more messing around. We have to be serious about this."

"We *were* se—"

"We're starting in fifteen!" Thuzar yells back at the room, and her command ramps up the noise and movement and overall mood. "*So* great to meet you, Khin," she adds with a smile. "I've gotta go switch out a couple of mood boards, but I hope you have fun today!" And then she leaves, and despite his legs being twice as long as hers, Ben visibly struggles to keep up.

I'm still watching the two of them when a voice whispers behind me, "Hey." When I jump and turn, Tyler has his hands raised. "Sorry." He grimaces. "I was trying *not* to startle you."

"You're good," I say, the feral, objectifying part of me that he always seems to briefly bring out noting that he looks incredible. He's wearing a light cream shirt under a bubblegum-pink suit, white-with-beige-accents sneakers finishing off the outfit. His vibe is that of someone who will bring the perfect gift to your parents' anniversary party, but also give you the best orgasm of your life when you get home.

Wow, Khin, what a weirdly specific vibe to have on hand.

"You know Thuzar?" Tyler asks.

I follow his gaze to the corner where Thuzar's setting up for the first shots. "Apparently," I say.

"Oh?"

I sigh and jerk a thumb over my shoulder. "You see the white guy helping her out?"

"Yeah, her boyfriend-slash-assistant. Ben." His brows jump when I laugh. "What's so funny?"

"Ben, before he was Thuzar's boyfriend-slash-assistant was . . ." I chuckle, both at myself and at the situation. "My husband."

Tyler's eyes hop back and forth between me and Ben, gradually enlarging as my words settle in. "Oh," he says at last. "He's—"

"Yep."

"Did you know he was—"

"Going to be here? Dating someone new? No and no."

"Are you—"

I hold up a hand. "I'm fine. We separated over six months ago. Thuzar seems good for him. I mean, look at them." I turn around and tilt my head to where Ben is holding up two different lenses as Thuzar studies them. "They . . . make sense. She's an *artiste*. Look at her with her funky artiste glasses and flowy artiste overalls. He can now talk about apertures and ISOs with someone who'll actually get it."

"We're starting in two minutes!" Thuzar calls out as she grabs the lens in Ben's left hand.

"That's my cue," Tyler says. I flash him two thumbs-up and expect him to start walking, but he doesn't move. "I just wanna say, Khin," he begins—and yep, right on cue, my heart does that stupid twisty thing at the sound of him saying my name; apparently, it missed the memo that Tyler and I are no longer friends, but more in a somewhat cold war situation. "As someone who dated Annie Leibovitz's niece for a year—"

My jaw drops. "You dated Annie Leibovitz's niece for a year?"

One corner of his lip turns upward, just so slightly. "—*Artistes* might be what some people are looking for, but it's not exactly in my top criteria when it comes to dating. It's not in a lot of people's, actually."

Maybe I'm looking for an ego boost, or maybe I'm realizing that this is the longest conversation we've had in a week and I've missed talking to him more than I let myself admit, because against every iota of logic, I hear myself reply, "What *is* in your top criteria?," aware that I am, by all accounts, trying to flirt.

"Overalls are overrated," he says, brown eyes flickering down at something behind me, something that makes his smile quirk a tiny bit wider before adding, "I've always been more of a classic blue-jeans kind of guy." And then he moves past me like he doesn't clock my stunned reaction.

It doesn't bode well for me that, as the situation dictates, I have to stare at Tyler for the next three hours. Things, thoughts, *scenes* are playing out in my head, and I don't know how to make them stop. I want to be in front of him, near him, touching him. I begin inserting myself into each shot—and the longer I stare at him, the more my deep, primal (and not to mention, embarrassing) want grows. In my head, I walk over and take his hand to show him a new pose. I imagine Tyler staring down *at me* as he undoes his jacket buttons. Tyler winking *at me*, one hand casually ruffling his hair. Tyler grinning into a stand-alone lighted makeup mirror *at my reflection*. In that last setup, imaginary Khin then approaches him from behind, one hand reaching around to untuck his shirt as she tiptoes and whispers into his ear—

"Got it! Let's take a breather! Good work, everyone!"

As soon as Thuzar calls for a break, I'm the first to speed-walk out of the room, down the stairs, and out into the blazing sun. Maybe the external heat will temper my internal heat and I'll reestablish equilibrium. Maybe it'll burn these—

"Khin—"

"What?" I ask, recognizing Ben's voice before he's in front of me.

"We need to talk." He motions at me to follow him to the small walkway on one side of the house.

"What?" I repeat, eyes narrowed, defenses raised, a new, different flush replacing the previous one.

"Jason told me the police came to talk to you."

I scoff. "Jason needs to remember that he signed an NDA."

"Khin, for Christ's sake—"

"And second, they came to talk to *everyone*."

Ben is unfazed. "What about on Monday?"

I feel my nostrils flare. The last thing I need is for yet another person to start digging around and me having to fend them off, *especially* when that person is my ex-husband. "Jason needs to shut the hell up. That's none of your business. It's not *Jason's* business either."

"He was worried about you." He pauses, eyes flattening as they monitor my expression. "*I'm* worried about you. If you're in trouble—"

"I've got a handle on it," I snap, my arms folding into a fortified *X*. "Besides, why do you even care?"

He recoils like I bent down, grabbed a handful of pebbles, and threw them in his face. "What do you mean, *why do I care*? I'm always going to care about you."

"We're divorced, remember? A divorce that *you* asked for."

A humorless laugh drifts out of him. "You think I've stopped caring about you because we're divorced? Because I *asked* for a divorce?"

"That's usually what happens when your husband of less than a year asks for a divorce minutes before literally walking out of the house you shared with a suitcase that he came home early that day to pack!" Feeling the first prickles, I lift one hand to swipe at my eyes before folding it back in front of me.

He shakes his head down at the pavement, as though I'm giving him the most absurd speech he's ever heard. "Is that why you've been angry at me this whole time? Because *I* was the one to say the words 'I want a divorce' even though *you* had been thinking it yourself for a long—"

"I—"

"—and don't you dare say that you weren't because you were still my wife and I knew you better than anyone in the world, which is how I also knew that you were too proud to walk away even though we were both miserable! We fell out of love. It *happens*. I loved you, Khin, and believe me, getting divorced was the last thing I wanted to do. But we were forcing a relationship that was already in the grave." Every word lands precisely where he meant for it to. Before I can recover, he asks, "Does this have something to do with the abortion article?"

Goose bumps needle my arms and chest, but I don't flinch. "What the hell would you know about the article? We weren't even married anymore when it came out, remember?"

"Oh, I remember," he says, rolling his eyes, and then, catching himself, looks back at me with a remorseful expression. "Sorry," he says.

I shake my head. "No, you have something to say. Don't be sorry. Say it."

"Come on, you're doing that thing—"

"*Thing?* What thing?"

"That thing where you pick a fight so that you can distract someone from, god forbid, trying to help you! That thing where you find something to distract *yourself* with so that you don't have to admit that something is wrong! We might be divorced, but I still remember how you can be."

"What the fuck does that mean?" I ask, and he grimaces in a way that reads, *Don't make me say it.* "Say it," I order. "What exactly do you remember?"

He swallows, regains control of himself. "I saw you, Khin. I remember that the more our relationship fell apart, the more you threw yourself into that article. Into work in general, and—"

"I will not apologize for being good at my job," I cut in. Ex-husband or not, no one gets to guilt-trip me with some backward misogynistic nonsense about being the Uptight Career Wife. "I was working on something important."

"I know," he says, voice not rising in tone or hardness to match me. "And I was *so* proud of you for that. I always will be. But I remember Nay and Thidar trying to reach out to you, and you kept plastering on a smile and saying, *It's fine, we're fine, I'm busy with work anyway,* even though our marriage was crumbling. Look, there were fundamental issues in our relationship that we couldn't work through. But just because we were getting divorced, it didn't mean I wanted us to be on opposing teams. I still wanted to be on your team. I still *want* to be on your team. So, please?" His eyebrows raise imperceptibly as he asks, "Please, will you tell me what's going on?"

The anger is so overwhelming that a primal part of me wants to scream in his face. He doesn't get to do this. He doesn't get to pull the plug on our marriage and then act like he's the concerned good guy and I'm the workaholic ex-wife.

"If you care so fucking much about being on my team—" I take in a deep breath, but it's not enough. There's not enough oxygen in the world to bring me back to equilibrium. "Then why did you quit on us?"

"Because we weren't in love anymore!" he snaps, and even though there's nothing but open space around us, it feels like it echoes off of every rock and blade of glass. "You really wanted to spend the rest of your life with someone you didn't love anymore?"

We stand there, eyes cloudy, chests trembling. I don't know what to say, instead wondering how the hell it got to this. The life we used to have feels unfathomable now, like a wistful fairy tale that I read about in a book when I was a kid. Because now here we are, having a screaming match outside his girlfriend's house.

He takes a deep inhale and I do the same in an attempt to dilute the adrenaline coursing through me.

"I only want to help—" he starts.

"I don't *need* your help—"

"Fucking hell, can you please not act like this?"

I scoff. "Like *what*?"

"Like you're too good, too smart, too *together* to accept anyone's help, when, hey, news flash, those of us who know you also know when you're lying to our faces. That's what you did then, and I cannot believe that you're still doing it now."

My jaw drops, and Ben visibly reacts, which at least tells me that he didn't *mean* for it to cut as deep as it did. "Well then," I try to stay even-tempered, but I'm unable to pack the surge of tears and hurt back in anymore. "Guess it's a good thing you found a new partner who *always* accepts your help, even when it comes to something as trivial as picking out a fucking camera lens."

Ben opens his mouth and I prepare myself for him to throw

another log on the blaze, but the next sound that I hear comes from behind me, and is a register too low to be his.

"Everything okay?"

In a half-assed combination of blinking rapidly and rubbing at my eyes with the palms of my hands, I say without looking back, "We're good."

Except my voice cracks, and I don't have to see him to sense Tyler move to stand beside me. "Khin?" he asks.

"I said I'm fine," I snap, head facing down and away from him.

After a long pause during which I assume he and Ben exchange silent *looks,* he lets out a long sigh. I'm expecting him to remind us where we are, or tell me that I should take a walk to cool off, but instead, he asks softly, "Oh no, did they cancel *SVU*?"

A disgusting, snotty laugh leaps out of me and I *have* to face him because how else am I going to make sure my punch lands on his arm as I reply, "Don't you dare even joke about that."

His eyes do a quick sweep of my face, but his expression isn't reactive whatsoever. I, on the other hand, am two hiccupping sobs away from having a breakdown on my ex-husband's new girlfriend's impeccable lawn. I take a deep breath, square my shoulders, and lift my chin. "Just for the record," I say, hating and consequently ignoring how wobbly my voice is. "I am generally an independent, self-sufficient, incredibly put-together woman. You just . . . have terrible timing."

He looks like he's pulling back a smile. "Did Reese Witherspoon back out of *Legally Blonde 3*?"

Despite myself, I gasp, and Tyler laughs, and I let out a wet laugh of my own. "You know," I say with a glare. "One day, you're going to speak one of these terrible misfortunes into existence and I will personally hunt you down."

"Oh yeah?" One brow raises in challenge. "And then what?"

"I'll tell PETA you would *looove* to sign a five-year spokesperson contract with them."

He widens his eyes in horror. "You wouldn't."

"Try me."

"Are you threatening me?"

"Maybe I am, and maybe I'm not." I shrug. "As long as Reese doesn't back out of *Legally Blonde 3*, you don't have anything to worry about."

He shakes his head. "What have I gotten myself into?" he asks, smile no longer restrained, and the sight makes my spine sizzle.

Our bodies both stiffen when Ben's voice says from the side, "I'm gonna go back inside."

Ben. Somehow, *shockingly*, I had forgotten about Ben. The last ten minutes come rushing back to me as though someone's turned the volume from zero to a hundred in one flick. Wordlessly, Ben leaves, but Tyler doesn't.

"So." Tyler gives an awkward half shrug. "Do you wanna . . . talk?"

I blink, although my tears are still presenting him to me as a tall semi-blurry figure. "About what?"

"Anything?" he says, although it comes out like a question, as though he doesn't know what we need to talk about either. "Whatever you want. We can talk about why you were fighting with your ex, or about how you think this shoot is going, or your opinion on the Carly Rae album that came out yesterday? Anything. Do you want to just . . . talk?"

I know I should say yes—if there ever was an opportunity to call a truce and get back on track, this is it—but I . . . can't. I want to rally, but after my shouting match with Ben, I don't have the energy to walk back into that house and be present for the rest of the shoot, let alone don a smile and slide into Cheery Interviewer mode.

Besides, for some inexplicable reason, I get the sense that Tyler would see right through me if I even tried to fake it.

I shake my head, my chest squeezing when I notice the corners of his mouth droop. "I'm sorry I brought my personal issues to work and interrupted your shoot. I know we both agreed to stick to being professional, and I'm sorry I didn't keep up my end of the bargain."

"Kh—"

"It won't happen again," I say, and march toward my car without waiting for him to respond.

———

I know that I cry all the way home, and that I am *still* crying right now, bundled up on the couch with *SVU* playing on the TV. What I don't know is whether the tears are because I'm jealous of Ben, or because I am furious with him for reminding me of this investigation during the few precious hours today when I was determined *not* to think about it. Or because this is the episode where Barba leaves and that final decision of his breaks my heart every time; I'm getting to the good sad part where he's in the hospital room when my doorbell rings.

I scramble for my remote and press pause, hoping that if I stay still long enough, Nay and Thidar will leave. There's another ring—which I expected, and to which I also don't respond because they're not going to break me with this amateur shit. A third ring, then a fourth. When there's no fifth, I peer over at the door, stretching out my ear to listen for the sound of receding footsteps, but I don't hear any.

Instead, what I *do* hear is the buzz of my phone on my lap.

It's a text from Tyler: I know you're in there. You really need to lower your TV volume or else you're going to blow out your eardrums

I snort but don't reply.

Another buzz. I should not be able to recognize Mariska Hargitay's voice from down the hallway

Begrudgingly, I yank the door open to find Tyler—not model Tyler, but your friendly neighborhood Tyler, who's changed into jeans and a plain black T-shirt. Disregarding how good he looks thanks to his outfit's deceptive minimalism, I growl, "How *dare* you trespass onto my place of residence and critique my TV-watching habits. How did you even get up here?"

His expression turns sheepish. Guilty. "I filmed a video wishing your doorman's daughter a happy birthday and he swiped his keycard for the elevator."

Great, even my doorman has fallen victim to Tyler Tun's charm. "You should go," I say, knowing he won't go, but still feeling compelled to insist.

"Ten minutes," he says, using his palms to indicate the number. "Please."

I rub the back of my neck, wincing a little at the giant knot between my shoulder blades. "Whatever it is that you have to say—"

"You're right. I *have* been keeping a secret from you. The other week, I invited you to dim sum because my sister wanted to meet you. Or, well, she wanted to see you. Again."

"What?"

He nods at the sliver of space between the door and the wall. "Ten minutes."

"Speak," I order as I sit back down on the couch and burrito-wrap myself back under the blanket. Tyler rolls in his lips like he's restraining a smile while he takes in my giant pink faux fur throw, but doesn't say anything.

"God, I rehearsed this so many times in the car ride over," he says, propping one elbow on the back of my couch so he can face me. "I have a whole level of newfound respect for writers. This speech shit is ha—"

"Congratulations, you now have nine minutes. Now why did your sister want to meet me? Or"—What was it that he'd said? —"See me?"

He gives a dry chuckle. "You know her."

"What? Jess?" He nods. I look down at the coffee table as I try to process this. Once I'm certain that he must have me (or his own sister) mixed up with someone else, I shake my head. "No, I don't."

"Yes, you do," he says, sounding as sure as I've ever heard him.

"Tyler, I don't know a Jess—"

"She had an abortion."

I sit up, the motion pushing the blanket down and off my shoulders. "What?"

Tyler nods once to indicate that I heard correctly. "A few months ago, my seventeen-year-old baby sister had to get an abortion because some old creep she hooked up with in a club bathroom knocked her up," he says. His jaw hardens, teeth grinding silently. "And when she told him, he told her he was married, and gave her an unmarked bottle of pills from who the fuck knows where. And I only found out because she called me in tears, because she wanted an abortion but she didn't want to take the pills, which, thank fuck she was still rational enough to come to that realization, but there was also no way she could tell our parents. And it was the middle of the school year, so I couldn't just suddenly fly her out without making them suspicious. Which is—"

When his shoulders raise and drop, they slouch farther down than I've ever seen them, like it took him a while, but he's finally gotten rid of the weight of the world. "Which is how I came across your article. Because all I could do while I was in LA was google 'abortion clinics Yangon.' And there was your article." He closes his eyes while he recites the title. "'Meet the Underground Clinic Performing Life-Saving

Abortions in Myanmar.' It was the first search result. And I swear I nearly cried. And then I emailed you."

"No, you didn't," I say, because I would've remembered this.

"Yes. I did. I said my name was Nita, and that I was a seventeen-year-old high school student in Yangon. Basically, I pretended to be Jess, but under a different name. I needed to make sure you were legit. And you responded almost immediately. And you were so compassionate and patient and just . . . *kind*." He pauses, gauging my reaction for something. "You know . . . you *have* met her. In person."

"What?" I shake my head. At no point in this conversation have I been able to predict what he was going to say next. "I've met your sister?"

"She's my height but with a more athletic build," he confirms, nodding. "When you met her, I think she had bangs and the tips of her hair were blue. Very chatty. Although she might not have been on that particular day."

Oh shit. He's *not* making this up. Because I remember that girl.

"That was your sister?" I ask. It had been less than a month after the article came out, when I was still handling incoming emails by myself. I had insisted on meeting the email sender in person to make sure it wasn't some undercover cop trying to bust the clinic.

"Yes. And she told me everything. How you paid for lunch, that you let her pick the music when you drove her to the clinic the next day, that your husband called and you told him you were in the middle of a really important meeting, and that you told her that the fact that she didn't *want* a child was enough reason to get an abortion. She said she felt so embarrassed and scared, but you never once made her feel judged. That's pretty much the main reason she wants to go to med school and become an ob-gyn now. She wants to be specifically trained in abortion procedures.

"The plan *was* for her to tell you herself at brunch, but—" He rolls his eyes. "Apparently, it's not every day that Olivia Rodrigo is in Bangkok. Or that your boyfriend manages to score pit tickets. Teenagers," he grumbles with a bemused shake of his head.

"Tyler—" I exhale. I would say I feel like I missed a step, but it feels more like I missed three steps. I slam into a wall of guilt as I remember what I'd yelled about the "real" reason he'd invited me to brunch, and how I had been so goddamn certain that he'd wanted me to meet Jess purely to promote his image.

"And I actually . . . have another secret," he says. He doesn't look away, as though he wants me to know that he's telling the full truth. "I told *Vogue* that I wanted *you* to write this story."

"What?!" Now it feels like I've missed the whole staircase and am plummeting through the air. "Tyler, what the hell are you talking about?"

He shrugs like he couldn't have put it clearer. "When my publicist told me about *Vogue*, I said I would only do it if I got to choose the reporter. Not just because I didn't want some random white reporter who only asked me questions about 'representation' and had never spent a week in Yangon, but because I wanted to meet the person who was there for my sister on the scariest day of her life. And because you sounded like a damn good journalist who actually *cared* about her subjects and wasn't just hunting for clickbait."

His words wash over me in a dizzying way. "*You're* the reason I got this job?"

He shakes his head, expression toughening. "No, absolutely not. Yes, I said I wanted you, but they didn't give in immediately. But I insisted, and at last, Clarissa said that she'd look into your recent work. She must've seen what I did, because she emailed me back a week later to say she'd set up a lunch with you."

"This doesn't—" This doesn't make sense. None of it makes sense. "Why didn't you just, I dunno, send me a thank-you email?"

He surprises me with a laugh. "Because that felt a *bit* underwhelming given the situation. Believe me, I wanted to find a way to thank you immediately, but . . ." One corner of his mouth quirks like he's holding back a joke.

"But what?"

He scans my face before answering, a spark of humor re-injected into his voice. "But Jess said you didn't exactly seem like the kind of person who'd be, and I quote, *swayed by a stupid pair of movie premiere tickets or an invite to Cannes like you do with all of the girls.* I wanted to thank you in a way that would matter. To *you.* When we signed with *Vogue,* I knew this was it."

"You were . . ." My brain's neurons fail to fire once more. "This whole time?"

"Khin." The way he states my name with such conviction is what breaks me out of my spiral. "I know what it's like to be really good at what you do, to *know* that you're good at what you do, only to have to wait and wait around for someone else to give you just one big break. I didn't keep the murder a secret solely because I wanted to protect the movie. Yes, cards on the table, you'd made a fair point about how this would impact everyone else on the team, including May and Yasmin—but that wasn't the whole reason. I changed my mind because you pointed out that *your* career would be over, and I realized it would overwrite all of the amazing past work you've already done. You don't deserve to have your whole career, your entire life, derailed because of one prick. You *are* good at what you do, Khin Haymar," he says with a small smile. I'm tempted to cocoon myself in the blanket again, if only to cover up the goose bumps that have sprouted down my arms. "It didn't make sense to throw that all away over the actions of one asshole."

"You're . . . telling the truth?" I ask, even though I know he is.

I can read you, I realize. This isn't the secret that Clarissa is hunting for, but he's being honest, to the bone. And the way in which he's allowed himself to be so vulnerable makes me feel like . . . like maybe, just *maybe*, I can let myself do the same, too.

He nods. "I'm sorry I kept all of that from you. I wanted to tell you, but there was never a good time."

"Why are you telling me all of this now?"

He studies me. "Because you were right. I couldn't keep insisting you should trust me when I was keeping secrets from you. Although, it does kind of hurt that I'm not as good of an actor as everyone keeps telling me I am."

My laugh is broken and messy, but he doesn't seem to mind. In fact, it makes *him* laugh.

"Do you want to know why those cops wanted to talk to just me on Monday?" I ask with a miserable smile. For once, the voice in my head that's always on the offensive doesn't chime in.

He nods. "If you want to tell me."

"As shocking as it might be to hear, after that article came out, the authorities weren't exactly *thrilled* about the fact that an underground abortion clinic had gotten such publicity. My divorce was nearly final by then, but we hadn't sold our house yet and they came by while Ben was there. Twice. Of course, they couldn't exactly charge me with anything, and there was no way I was going to reveal any of my sources, but it . . . wasn't easy for a while there." I look down at my hands, pausing to catch my breath. "At one point, Ben suggested I leave town for a bit. Until things kind of died down. But I didn't."

"Because you don't scare easy." I look up from my hands to find Tyler smiling, and it's small but genuine and gorgeous and I feel the most naked I ever have in front of him, but it's not scary, not even a little. And maybe *that* should scare me, but it . . . doesn't.

"No, I certainly do not," I say, returning his smile. "But *that's* why those cops wanted to get me alone. Apparently the target on my back never really went away."

For a couple of seconds, he stares at me with an intent that I can't decipher. Right as I'm about to ask, he gives a slow nod. "Oh."

"Oh?"

"Oh, as in, *oh*, I get it now." At my quizzical expression, he gives a small shrug. "Why you didn't want to go to the cops in the first place. I mean, I know you told me a few *eyebrows were raised*—"

"Yeah, I might've downplayed it a bit," I admit through a grimace, noting that he can quote me word for word from our first conversation. I don't have time to explore the small radiator between my ribs that that observation kick-starts before he continues talking.

"I understand now, though. I'm sorry I was so . . . what's the correct word here?" He turns and squints out the window, as though the correct word will float by. "Ignorant," he decides, and turns back to me. "Thoughtless? Both, really. I'm sorry I was pushing you so much."

"Thank you," I say.

"But . . . there's no connection here. With the, um, incident—" He pauses, and for two seconds, our guilt stretches our faces to the point where you don't need to be a body language expert to know what the hell we're talking about. "What does you writing that article have to do with this murder? Why are they zeroing in on you?"

"Well," I say, understanding for the first time that he's never been working against me, not once; the shame I feel makes me want to look away, but instead, in a gesture of truce, I give him the two things he's been pleading for this whole time: my trust, and the whole truth. "Funny story. *I* have a small secret, too."

I tell him about my most recent interrogation and about the photos, and his demeanor unravels with every new detail. By the time I've caught him up on Dipar's girls' night out at Nagar's Breath, he's shifted so much that his knee is pressed against mine, one of his palms splayed firmly across my lower thigh. And for the first time since I've moved into this apartment, it feels . . . relaxing. Good. *Safe.* Like a place where I don't have to pretend, where I can fall apart.

"Let's go," Tyler says, checking his watch.

"Go . . . where?"

"The bar. What's the name? Nagar's Breath?"

I nod. "But—"

"We can take your car. I'll drive."

"Tyler." I laugh. "First of all, *you* can't go to a bar here. You wouldn't last twenty minutes! And I would prefer not to have a front-row seat to Tyler Tun getting ripped apart limb by limb. I don't need to be in the center of yet *another* police investigation, thank you very much. Still trying to deal with the first one, remember?"

"I—"

I stop him with an open palm. "And to be honest, I'm not even *entirely* certain that talking to her will help me out. Maybe she knows why her boyfriend had been stalking me? I'm going off of a hunch here."

"I think you've proven that your hunches are spot-on," he cuts in with a playful smile.

"Well, if anyone knows why he did it," I say, wanting to ignore but also reveling in the way he's looking at me, "it *would* be his girlfriend of two years. But what if someone snaps a photo of us and she's also in it? Won't that look suspicious to the police if they see it somewhere online?"

"Probably," he admits. "But for one, it's my experience that club lighting makes for notoriously grainy photos, and two, that's only if we get caught. We'll be careful, and seeing as how she's our only lead right now, I think it's a risk worth taking."

Of course I agree with him; it's why *I* was going to risk going there on my own in the first place. "I need to get her alone," I say, revealing the rest of my plan. "But she's not going to just follow me because I ask nicely. It's the first rule of girls' night out: nobody leaves alone."

After a beat of quiet reflection, Tyler says, "But . . . what about with a guy? Assuming everyone in the group had vetted him before-hand? Surely another rule of girls' night out is 'no cockblocking.'"

I snort and move back, propping myself on my elbows. My top rolls up, and as his eyes fall onto the section of my stomach that's now exposed, warmth unfurls across my skin. "I mean, yeah, if he's been properly vetted," I say, snapping both of us back to attention. "But it can't be just *any* man."

The corner of his mouth curves like, *Don't make me say it.*

"What?" I ask.

"What if," he says, pursing his lips as though he's musing it over, "it was someone who was *potentially* in talks to be the next James Bond?"

Thirteen

I gave Tyler exactly sixteen minutes. If he's not out when my timer beeps, I'm going into Nagar's Breath and dragging him out by his Hermès belt buckle if I have to.

I leap forward when my phone vibrates in the dashboard holster, in case it's Tyler texting that he's been cornered by a horde of fans and he needs me to come help him squeeze out of the bathroom window.

It's not, though. Instead, it's a text from an international number that starts with +65—Singapore's country code—and that contains four words: How was the shoot? My first thought is, *How did Clarissa get my number?* But my second thought is, *Of course Clarissa has my number.* Before I can reply, another four-word question that makes my gut flip upside down and inside out: How is the article?

With shaky hands and a clearly extensive vocabulary, I type back Great!, then, wanting to add a bit more, send another text clarifying On both ends!

Three dots appear, then three words—Good to hear—that, in her very Clarissa way, indicate that the conversation is over just as instantaneously as it began. And although now would be an excellent time to have a panic attack about my definitely *not* great article with the definitely nonexistent Tyler Tun–career-related scoop, I have to prioritize.

Swiping back to the timer, I see that I'm down to one minute and forty-five seconds and am about to shove the phone in my purse when one of the back doors opens. I turn from my position in the driver's seat just as Dipar is sliding in, Tyler ducking and shutting the door behind him.

"Hi," I say, twisting and leaning over into the space between the driver and passenger seats.

Dipar's flirtatious smile freezes as she looks at me, then at Tyler, and back at me. Making a one-eighty, her mouth droops, pupils dilating as it dawns on her that she's most likely *not* going to have a one-night stand with Tyler Tun tonight.

"We're not kidnapping you!" I blurt out, only to realize that that sounds like what a kidnapper would say.

"Cool. I'm . . . gonna go," she says, trying to escape without making any sudden movements. She gives the other door a tug, and jolts in her seat when she finds that it's locked.

"We can explain—" Tyler starts.

Dipar flattens her back against the door, not knowing whether to focus on me or Tyler. "Who are you?" she asks me. "What do you want?" she asks Tyler. Then, "I don't do threesomes!"

"We just want to talk!" I jump in. "No threesomes! Not that I'm kink-shaming. I think threesomes are a perfectly legitimate means through which to explore new territories in your sex life—"

"Khin," Tyler says, bringing me back.

I shake my head and start over. "My name's Khin. I have a few questions about Jared. We're not murderers or kidnappers, I promise."

"Then why did you trick me into getting into this car and lock the doors?"

I wince in the face of a perfectly reasonable question to which I do *not* have an equally reasonable answer. "I know how this is going to sound," I say with a light chuckle that I hope will ease her worries. Instead, her face twists some more. "We needed to get you alone."

"Oh my god," she groans. "This is how I die, isn't it? I have a dog at home! His name is Kauk Swe. My sister hates him because he farts in her face, but can you tell her my last dying wish was that she loves him as her own—"

I fling up a hand to interrupt. "You live with your sister?"

Dipar nods. "Yeah. But not in a mansion if that's what you're thinking. It's a one-bedroom in Yankin; I sleep on the couch!"

Tyler and I trade a *Huh?* expression. "What about . . . Jared?" he asks.

Dipar swallows. "What about him?"

I shift in closer to make sure I don't mishear her. "You don't live with him?"

"What?" She seems as confused as we are. "Why would I be living with him?"

"Because he's your boyfriend?"

"We broke up months ago," she says, squinting at me. Something hits her, and she immediately looks scared once more. "Wait, how do you know about me and Jared? I've never met you in my life." Turning to Tyler, she asks, voice raising several octaves, "How do *you* know about Jared? What is going on?"

I raise both hands to reassure her that we're not going to hurt her. "You haven't seen him recently?"

"No, I haven't."

"So you don't know Jared's dead?"

"What?!" Her body visibly tenses. "Jared's dead?!"

Tyler tilts his head at me with a look that reads, *You really couldn't have been more tactful about that?* "Sorry," I say with a grimace. "I assumed you knew."

But I don't know if Dipar even hears me, because she's staring down at her lap, motionless.

"I'm sorry for your loss," Tyler begins in a low, cautious tone. "Are you . . . were you guys in touch recently?"

Dipar lifts her head, her eyes clouding over with an indistinguishable darkness that pierces the sheen of tears. "No." She exhales. "I . . . cut him off. Completely."

"What does that mean?" I ask.

She gives an unthinking shrug. "It means that—" She pauses, swallows, and looks out the tinted windows. We go silent while a group of drunk teenagers stumbles past on the sidewalk. Once their voices fade out, Dipar continues, "Jared wasn't a good man. Or even a good human being." She turns to us, head slightly tipping like there are so many things in her mind she's weighing whether or not to say aloud. "I don't know why you guys are looking into him, but let me guess, it's not good news," she says, and even though she says "you guys," she's looking directly at me.

I shake my head. "He was—"

"I don't want to know," she interrupts. "I left him because I was tired of being collateral damage. I'm not happy that he's dead, but I'm not going to be mourning him either. I can't help you out with whatever it is that he dragged you into, but I hope you find peace soon. *I* have. Now can I please go?"

She sounds like someone who's been through a lot. Enough, even. I'm about to admit defeat and unlock her door when Tyler's gentle voice asks, "Can you direct us to someone who might have seen him recently? We . . . have some questions."

The sound of Dipar's inhale and slow exhale is amplified tenfold by the car's silence. "There's a bar across the street from our old place," she says, eyeing us, probably wondering if she's making a mistake by telling us this much. "It's called Devil's Lounge. I'll warn you, it's dark and sleazy and almost exclusively filled with old white men. One of Jared's favorite things to do was rack up a tab there. So if you do go, you should tell them that they're not going to be paid anytime soon."

"Thank you," Tyler says.

A mild "Good luck" is the last thing she mumbles before exiting.

It's nearing midnight when we pull up in front of Tyler's building. "Thanks for coming." I shoot him a smile. "I'll go to Devil's Lounge tomorrow and see what I can find," I say, not expecting the frown that overshadows his face.

"What?" I ask.

"Khin." He laughs through my name. "You have to stop."

"Stop what?" I reply, pulling back.

"Stop trying to get rid of me," he says matter-of-factly. "I'm helping you until we solve this. I'm seeing this to the end."

I let out a "Ha!" into the dark. "And what if it ends with me going to prison?"

"You're *not* going to prison."

"What if I do?"

"Then—" In one fluid motion, he unbuckles his seat belt, the fabric emitting a soft *whoosh* as it slides across and up his torso until he's free to lean forward. One elbow rests on the center console, and his hand lowers onto my thigh. "—I'm going to watch the entirety of the 2005 American serial drama *Prison Break* starring Wentworth Miller so I can take notes and come up with a foolproof way to, as the title states, break you out of prison."

I burst out laughing, and a smile spills and seeps into every corner and crevice of his mouth and *god* if the sight doesn't ignite a flurry of embers in my gut. *You are a good man*, I think.

"Tyler, I don't want you risking your job over my mess. It's okay. I'm a freelancer, remember?" I say, hoping I'm not letting on that my insides are nowhere near as solid as my tone. "I'm used to going out on my own. Your assistance is appreciated, but I can get out of messes myself."

He shakes his head, and, to my horror and misfortune, gives my thigh a light squeeze. I say "horror and misfortune" because it feels like he's squeezed *other* parts of me, and I know I need him to leave this car within the next five minutes or I cannot be held responsible for the actions I'm about to commit. Currently, my center of gravity is the spot where his palm is (still) connected to my thigh, the heat between our skin alleviated only by the blue satin of my skirt. If this were anyone else, I'd say this was intentional, a *move* in a dark car. But it can't be, because *we* cannot be; we are professionals, perhaps friends, but definitely not a "we," not in this sense. If nothing else, there is a professional brick wall of a *Vogue* article standing between us, even though, truth be told, I enjoy peeking over that wall every now and again, just to see what I'm missing out on.

"Unfortunately, you're stuck with me now," he says. "Like Elle and Emmett. But, you know, less white."

"Oh, Tyler." I extend my bottom lip as though I pity his delusional thinking. "You're not nearly smart enough to be the Emmett to my Elle. You can be Bruiser, though."

This time *he* laughs in surprise, and I just *know* that my smile is bordering on psychopathic.

"Wow, that's what I've been demoted to? A chihuahua?" He cocks his head. "You *do* know I graduated from Yale's drama school."

"Look, buddy, either you're Bruiser or you don't get a role in the movie."

"Well, Bruiser is Elle's best teammate and she takes him everywhere, so," he says, winking and hopping out of the car without waiting for my reply, which is just as well, because it would've been something absurd and embarrassing along the lines of, *Is* that *what we are? Teammates?*

———

The next morning, I spot the car before the lot gate is even fully raised. I do a quick visual sweep, and, not seeing anyone I should be looking out for, power walk to Tyler's trailer.

"Morning!" I chirp as I enter.

Tyler catches my eye in the mirror, script in one hand. "Morning!" he says, and whirls around. "You arrived just in time. We're starting early."

His team excuses themselves as they slip past me and out the door I just walked through. By the way he's pretending to fumble with his shirt while sliding me the occasional deliberate stare, it's obvious we're both trying to find a moment alone to talk about the cop car currently parked outside. However, by the way Tun is holding the door open and muttering into his headset, I know *he's* fully intent on delivering Tyler to set ASAP.

We step out, May and her team exiting the trailer opposite at the same time. We've only taken a few paces when a voice that makes my eyes reflexively squeeze shut calls out my name.

"Detectives!" I say as the two men catch up. "Morning."

"Morning!" Detective Htet grins, and my stomach roils not just because he is, generally speaking, the personification of the word "slimy," but because there's a glee in his eyes that can't be good news for me.

"We're about to start shooting," Tyler says.

But neither of them move. "This'll just take a moment," Detective Zeyar tells him before turning to me. "Khin, you take notes in a notebook, right? With a pen?"

I don't catch my startle in time. "A what?"

"Your notes." He nods over at my tote bag. "I noticed that you carry a pen and notebook with you all the time, right?"

The roiling in my stomach is out of control, like a boiled pot that's overflowing, water and foam spilling and sizzling all over everything, everywhere. "Why?" I ask.

He shrugs. "We're trying to figure out where a piece of evidence came from."

"What kind of evidence?"

There's a crinkling sound as he reaches inside his front pants pocket to withdraw a small clear ziplock bag. A bag that contains what is one hundred percent, undoubtedly, unmistakably, my pen. To be specific, my Cartier pen that I had bought for myself after one full year of freelancing full-time. It had cost nearly $400, but I've used it every day since—at least, until it fell into Kandawgyi Lake with a middle-aged white man attached to one end. Even through the wrinkled plastic, I instantly recognize the sleek blue-steel lacquered body with the silver palladium finish.

I would feign ignorance and ask why they think this pen has anything to do with me, but I don't, because I know the answer. It's capitalized in the classic Cartier CG font and was a complimentary service, and I was spending four hundred American dollars on a pen so why the hell *wouldn't* I have gotten it monogrammed?

But of course, Tyler doesn't know this, so he shakes his head and asks, confused, "May I ask why you're questioning Khin about this? It's a pen. Everyone on set has a pen."

Detective Zeyar's smile remains cool—a lion confident in the knowledge that their prey is trapped. "That's true," he says with a small nod. Then, lifting the bag, he pinches the pen between his thumb and forefinger and brings it closer to Tyler. "But *this* one has 'KH' engraved on the clip," he says with a cutting stare in my direction.

This is how I come undone, isn't it? I think as Tyler squints at where the detective is pointing with his thumb. *Over a pen.* The headline is going to be a stupid play on "pen," isn't it? Something like "Crime and Pen-ishment" or "The Pen *Is* Mightier than the Sword."

"Where did you find this?" Tyler asks. He's still trying to sound exasperated, but his tone doesn't have quite the same bite anymore.

"My colleagues and I returned to where the body had initially been discovered, and somehow our team had missed this the first time around. Probably because two-thirds of it was submerged in the sand, or the crime lab had initially dismissed it as some random lost pen." Then, "Khin," Detective Zeyar says, bringing the pen to me in what feels like slow motion. I work to keep my facial expressions neutral even though he's reading me with a magnifying glass. "Is this your pen? KH. Those are your ini—"

"*Holy shit!*" May's screech makes everyone literally jump. "You found my pen!"

What? I think.

"What?" both the detectives ask.

May bounces over and opens her palm, gesturing at the ziplock bag. "May I?" she asks sweetly. As though in a trance, Detective Zeyar hands it over.

Her grin expands as she turns the pen back and forth in her hand.

"I thought I'd lost it! Thank you *so* much, Detectives!" she says, beaming at the two of them.

Detective Htet shakes his head and points to the bag. "This is *your* pen?"

Snapping out of his temporary hypnotic state and realizing that he's literally just handed over evidence, Detective Zeyar reaches to retrieve the bag. However, May either doesn't notice or pretends not to, and instead passes it over to her assistant, Kyi Kyi, who is now clutching it to her chest as though she would protect it with her life if it came to it.

May flicks her hair behind one shoulder. "Yes! I lost it on the first day of filming. I was taking a walk around the lake before we started shooting, you know, to work off the nerves. And the purse I was using that day is expensive and pretty but definitely *not* practical," she says, rolling her eyes. "My phone rang and as I was digging around inside, a bunch of stuff fell out. I thought I'd gathered everything, but I didn't realize until I got home that night that I'd lost my pen. It must've rolled off the boardwalk and into the water." She throws her hands up in the air in glee. "But you guys found it! It's a miracle!"

Detective Zeyar gives a short *Heh*, but his attempt at a smile fails miserably. He looks at the pen, at May's grinning face, at my own face which is doing who knows what at this point, then back at May. "But KH—" he stammers, and scratches his head, bewildered. "That stands for . . ." He trails off, his gaze on me silently finishing the sentence.

Except it doesn't, because May says, "For *Kiss Her*! I got this pen to celebrate my first Oscar nomination."

The detectives aren't pretending to play it cool anymore; I don't think they can. They're just standing there, mouths open, two invisible thought bubbles that scream, *What the fuck is happening?* hanging over their heads.

"So it . . . Khin . . ." Detective Htet frowns over at me, then, admitting defeat, asks point-blank, his earlier coyness nowhere to be found, "'KH' doesn't stand for 'Khin Haymar'? That's not *your* pen?"

I think before I answer. Technically, I haven't told them a lie up to this point. I've definitely fudged the truth and omitted some facts, but I haven't lied. "I—" I start, then clear my throat, buying some more time while I try to remember what the typical sentence is for lying to an officer of the law.

"Detectives." May's laugh interrupts us. "This is a *four-hundred-dollar* pen. I don't know any freelance journalists who make enough disposable income to waste four hundred dollars on a pen. No offense, Khin," she says to me with an apologetic smile.

I shake my head. "None taken," I say. I turn back to the two men who I can tell are torn between wanting to interrogate me further, and not wanting to offend May Diamond. And also, she has a point. Who else but an actress who paid twenty million dollars for her latest house in a single cash transfer would be ridiculous enough to drop four hundred dollars on a singular pen?

With clear trepidation, Detective Htet says, "Still, you . . . can't take the pen back."

May's smile drops. "Why not?"

"Because it's . . . evidence?" His voice goes up at the end so that it sounds entirely like a question and not a blatant fact.

"But it's my pen," May says. This has dragged on long enough that she's no longer cheery, America's sweetheart May Diamond, but a formerly purring cat now flashing her fangs. "Am I a suspect in the case? Because my lawyers weren't informed of that."

"No!" You can see the sweat stains forming under his arms in real time. "You're not, we've cleared you."

"So why can't I have my pen back?"

"Because—"

"If *I'm* not a suspect, and this is *my* pen, which it *is* as we've established, then it isn't evidence, right?"

"Right," Detective Htet agrees. He licks his lips like his tongue is physically scrambling for words. Any string of words that *won't* result in May's team of lawyers calling his boss and demanding to know why the hell he didn't give back her most beloved pen. Without warning, he redirects his attention to me. "Khin, we need your fingerprints."

"Why?" May and I ask in unison.

"Because—" He's not looking at May. Coward. "We lifted fingerprints off of that pen, and if—"

"This is *ridiculous*," May states. Her tone is biting, bordering on threatening. "Detective, I can guarantee you that there are *hundreds* of fingerprints on this pen, because lots of people have used it, as is the nature. Of. A. Pen. *My* fingerprints will be on it." She points at Tyler. "*His* fingerprints will be on it. Any wandering child who picked it up at the park and then tossed it back into the sand's fingerprints will be on it. What, are you going to fingerprint the entire city? This entire crew? Every single person I've ever worked with throughout my career?"

The detectives' jaws hang very, very low.

"We've established that this is my pen and that I was nowhere near the scene of the crime, and I have a long shooting schedule ahead of me, and this much sun exposure is already making me start to sweat off my makeup, so can we *please* get on with our day?"

In one final attempt at maintaining a shred of procedure, Detective Zeyar asks once more, "You're . . . sure this is *your* pen?"

At that, Tyler leans forward. "If I may," he says, "*I* can confirm that's May's pen. In fact, it's her favorite autograph pen."

"It's all in the tip," May explains. She straightens and, shaking out her scowl, addresses her and Tyler's small entourages. "What a great omen! I knew today was going to be a good one. Let's bring this energy to set!" She shoots the detectives one final showstopping smile and repeats, "Thank you again soooo much," before turning and marching off to work.

Despite our collectively perceptible *what the fuck just happened* mentality, we all scurry on behind her. Kyi Kyi has the ziplock bag pressed up against her chest, her clipboard shielding it from anyone who might dare try to take it.

"Four *hundred* dollars?" I hear Detective Zeyar say behind us. "That's, what, seven hundred thousand kyats? On a *pen*?"

"Actors are weird," Detective Htet mutters.

Tyler whips out his phone and concentrates on reading something, his gait slowing until he's fallen into step beside me. "We might have a problem," he mumbles.

"What the hell was that?" I whisper out of the side of my mouth. "Does—" I hesitate, not knowing if I *want* to know the answer to my next question. "Does May really have a Cartier pen with 'KH' engraved on it?"

Because I mean . . . it's not a wholly implausible possibility. KH. *Kiss Her.* It *had* been the movie to shoot her career into the stratosphere. And she does sign a lot of autographs, so—

"May knows."

My brain malfunctions. Forgetting about being covert, I swing my head in his direction. "Huh?" I ask, realizing I'd already half convinced myself that I had gotten lucky and May and I had just *happened* to have the exact same pen that we'd both lost in the exact same lake on the exact same day. (Okay, when I frame it like that, I hear how delusional it sounds.)

Tyler tucks his phone into his pocket and gives me a breezy smile as he repeats, "May. Knows."

And just like my precious four-hundred-dollar pen on that godforsaken night, my stomach plummets down, down, down.

Fourteen

May, I can—"

"How long have you known?" Tyler asks.

Hours later, we're in May's trailer, the two of them supposedly running lines while the crew sets up for the final scene of the day, a formal ball, which is why I'm now watching May Diamond in a backless mauve ball gown and Tyler Tun in a black tuxedo partaking in a silent duel of the gazes.

Finally, May pulls her knees up under her layers of tulle and rolls her eyes. "Does it matter?" she asks, her know-it-all smirk confirming Tyler's suspicions.

"Yes," Tyler says, plopping himself down on the other end of the couch.

Which leaves me the makeup chair. I swivel it around, and the squeak interrupts their staring showdown. "Sorry."

"Did you really think you could keep a secret from me?" May's eyes narrow once more at Tyler.

Tyler's brows lift in response to her tone. "Where'd we mess up?"

"*We?*" May's own brows waggle in a suggestive manner as she shoots me a glance. "I knew something was up when Tyler walked you back to the car because you were *having a bad period day*. To be honest, I thought you guys had had a quickie in some dark corner of the park, especially because he could *not* stop talking about you after the dinner you guys had. And after you left the set, he kept checking his phone and—" Tyler opens his mouth, but she holds up a hand before he can even get half a syllable out. "Please, I know you were checking to see if she'd texted. I'm your best friend, I know the look on your face when you're waiting for a girl to text."

My throat constricts and emits a weird gulping sound. Tyler is silent, but when I look over, shades of pink are starting to appear on his cheeks. "May," he says, shifting in his seat.

May rolls her eyes again. "But then on that Monday when the police came to question everyone, you were fucking up every take. And while Khin was being interrogated, all you kept asking was if she was done yet. And then earlier—" She passes me an amused look. "When you went deathly pale when they brought out the pen, it all clicked. You could never be an actress by the way, Khin. No offense."

"Heh," is all I can say.

"This isn't a game, May," Tyler says, surprising me with his terseness.

But May doesn't seem the least bit bothered. "No, it's not. Now I need to know what the plan is."

"Plan?" Tyler scoffs. "There *is* no plan. You're going to stay quiet while we take care of this."

"*We?*" May repeats once more, this time definitely giving me a pointed look. "If *I* can figure it out, do you really think *no one else* will find out? You're welcome for earlier, by the way. There goes my diva pass."

"We didn't ask for your help," Tyler retorts. "And that was so stupid earlier. What if someone had called you out? Like your assistant?"

"Oh, I'm sorry." May sits up and lifts her shoulders as if to say, *Come at me.* "Should I have let your girlfriend incriminate herself with her pen?"

"I'm not—" I try to cut in.

"This has nothing to do with you," Tyler tells her, either not hearing the *g*-word, or ignoring it altogether.

May bites down on her bottom lip, eyes flattening into cutting slits. "Look, asshole, you can either loop me in and let me help you, or I start tracking your every move and meddle to my heart's content."

Tyler throws up his hands. "Why are you doing this?!"

"Because I'm not letting my best friend go to jail!" May counters without missing a beat. "Are you telling me that if *I* was caught up in a murder, *you* wouldn't help me get away with it?"

"You—"

"Answer the question."

He presses his eyelids shut with a thumb and forefinger. "Of course I would," he finally says.

He opens his eyes and as the two of them hold their gaze, my mind races right back to that first night of shooting where I saw then what I'm seeing now, what I recognize because I have it myself with Nay and Thidar: a soft, deep love that could stretch and bend across thousands of miles without ever once ripping. Many people assume friendship love isn't as fulfilling, as unconditional, as overwhelming as romantic love; those people are so, so wrong.

"Of course you would," May repeats with a nod. An *I'm not leaving you* nod. A *we're a team* nod. "Now—" She turns to me. "Where are we on lawyers? Do you need—"

"No lawyers," Tyler answers.

"Why no lawyers?" She tosses a frown in his direction. "What happens if people find out?"

"People aren't going to find out."

This time, with a pointed eyebrow raise, she asks, "And what if they do? We need a backup. If someone finds out, what happens to Khin? What happens to . . ." The silence cloaks the air like thick netting, but she doesn't need to finish the sentence. *What happens to you?*

"They're *not*," Tyler counters with an air of finality. "You wanted to know what the plan was? Well, that's it. The plan is that nobody finds out."

Despite his harsh tone, May doesn't parry. Instead, she stares, and stares—and stares for several more seconds. It occurs to me that she's waiting for him to change his mind, waiting for him to be sure that this is what *he* wants to do before she agrees to follow him to the ends of the earth. At last, when she's certain *he's* certain, she nods. "Okay, then," she says, confirming my theory. "How are we doing that?"

Tyler looks like he's ready to try to push her away again, but I can tell by now that May Diamond and I are cut from the same cloth—that look she has in her eyes right now is the exact same look I get when I've decided I want something. "We're going to a bar tonight," I say. Tyler glares at me, but I respond with a defiant lift of my chin.

"Well, well." May settles back and gets comfortable in her triumph. "Thank you, Khin. I would *love* to join you guys." Someone gives the door several loud raps from the outside. "Catch me up in the car? I'm assuming we'll take yours?"

We've been parked about a block away from Devil's Lounge for a solid twenty minutes while trying to come up with a plan. Except, in the words of the inimitable Phoebe Buffay, we don't even have a "pla."

"Let me flirt with the bartender!" May grumbles, head bobbing in the center space between me and Tyler.

Tyler looks over at me for backup. "Flirting with the bartender isn't the solution to everything."

"No, but it could work in this case. We could go undercover—"

"Undercover?!" Tyler gives his hair a violent, impatient rake. "We're not going undercover! Way to lean into the melodramatic actor stereotype."

"Oh so, what? We walk in there and," May puffs out her chest and says in a low, mocking tone, "you introduce yourself as Tyler Tun and ask if anyone will give us any information about this Jared in exchange for a ticket to the movie premiere?"

"You are so in—"

I halt one hand in front of each of their faces. "Stop! *I* have a plan." I turn to May. "Any bartender you flirt with is only going to be trying to get into your pants. And it's going to look way too suspicious when people hear that May Diamond was asking around about a specific person who they're undoubtedly going to later find out is already dead." Then to Tyler. "But *you* can't just waltz in either. Actually, neither of you can."

After a pause, Tyler scowls as he realizes what I'm implying. "Khin, I'm not letting you walk into that seedy bar alone."

Protectiveness isn't always a turn-on for me, but I kinda like it on him. "Tyler," I say, cocking him a half smile. "You don't think I've walked into seedy bars alone before?"

May props an elbow on my headrest. "It's annoying, right? There he goes again, thinking that we women aren't capable of handling ourselves. God forbid we enter a bar on our—"

"It's not the women going to bars alone that's the problem," Tyler says. "It's the *men*."

His gaze lands on me and there's a dark flash that I hadn't expected. And then it makes sense. Of course. What happened with his sister.

"Hey," I say. He looks like he's starting to drift off to an unpleasant place. I rest my palm on his shoulder and give it a light squeeze.

As though it works, as though I've managed to ground him just as he was starting to lose himself, his expression softens, eyes refocusing on me. "Hey," he says.

"I'll be okay. And you'll be right here, listening through the phone."

I hold his gaze, hoping that each of my silent reassurances gets through.

Nothing is going to happen to me.

This is totally different from what happened with Jess.

I'm not scared because I know you two have my back. Especially *you*.

"Okay," he says, his halfhearted nod telling me that he's anything but. "But the second something seems off—"

I return a firm nod. "I promise."

I didn't mention to Tyler that I'm not really a dive-bar person because I didn't want him to have another reason to freak out, but . . . I am *not* a dive-bar person. They're dark with sticky floors and countertops, and just generally give me the creeps. Nonetheless, I take a seat in the middle of the counter, placing my purse on the stool beside me and my phone on the countertop. I've already clocked four white men—two at one far end of the counter, and two in one of the side booths near the entrance—and all of them are not subtle about their interest in me as I settle myself.

It's a quiet Monday night. The bartender excuses herself from a conversation with the men at the end and comes over. "Hi there," she says.

"Hi," I chirp.

"What'll it be?"

"Gin and tonic, please."

"Huh," she replies, looking like she's trying to hold back from saying something.

With a tentative smile, I ask, "Is . . . everything okay?"

"Sorry," she says with a short laugh. "I just . . . have never had someone under forty order a gin and tonic."

Despite my phone volume being on zero, I swear I heard Tyler snort. "You sound *just* like my friends," I say with a jovial eye roll. "But with the week I've had, it *feels* like I've aged ten years. I'm Kh—" I catch myself in time. "Carina."

"Julie," she says with a nod. She places a glass on the counter and starts mixing. "Wanna talk about it? Let me guess—men?"

I prop my chin atop a fist. "Isn't it always? I met him on this dating app, and we had a *great* first date. Like, I kept worrying that the butterflies were going to pummel their way out of my stomach."

"Awww." Julie pauses to place a palm over her chest. "That's cute!"

"Right?" I say with a one-shoulder shrug. "And we had an incredible night together, and were texting nonstop until a few days ago when he just—" I give her a *what the fuck* grimace. "Ghosted me."

Julie lets out the deep sigh of someone who's heard this story a hundred times. "Men," she repeats.

"You wanna know the worst part?" I ask sheepishly.

"Hit me."

"I . . . kinda went down a social media wormhole and saw that he was a regular—" My eyes dart from side to side. "Here. So I kinda came tonight hoping that maybe . . . I'd see him? Ugh, I know, it's pathetic."

Julie puts the drink down in front of me. "It's not pathetic. What's his name?"

I take a slow sip, pretending to mull over whether or not I should tell her. Finally, I say, "Jared."

"Jared?" I look up, and Julie's whole face is scrunched up. "Australian? Dark brown hair? White? *That* Jared?" she asks, but her reaction makes it clear that what she *really* wants to ask is, *That's the Jared you were gushing about?*

I nod. "He doesn't have a girlfriend or anything, right?"

"He did, but I hear they broke up a while ago. Maybe about a month? Two?"

So Dipar was telling the truth. "And you . . . haven't seen him with anyone else? Heard him *talk* about anyone? Sorry, I know I sound nosy," I hastily add. "I just . . . *really* liked him."

"Huh," is all Julie says, working overtime to be polite.

"Have you seen him?" I ask. "Recently?"

I can tell she's really trying to school her face, but it's like her face doesn't know how *not* to look disgusted when talking about Jared. "No, sorry," she says. She doesn't sound sorry. "Last I saw him was about two weeks ago? Maybe two and a half? I *do* remember that it was also a Monday. I try to take the Monday night shifts because they're quiet," she explains and gestures around at the venue. "But lucky me, I got to serve Jared that night."

She gives a surprised start when I snap up in my seat. Two weeks ago. A Monday. That was the night— "Oh my god," I blurt. Her head rears back at my attitude shift. "That was . . . the night after our date," I say. "How was he that night?"

Julie frowns at the ceiling, face screwed up in concentration. "His particular crusade that night seemed to be how"—she forms air quotes—"*all women are bitches, and all bitches need to be trained.*"

I sputter. "Oh. Wow. Shit. Really?"

"Like I said," she says with a wry smile. "Lucky me got to serve him all night. He got weird right at the end, too."

"Weird? Weird . . . how?"

"Well, it *was* otherwise a slow night, so I was checking my Instagram, and one of my friends was livestreaming from in front of the park where they were shooting that Tyler Tun and May Diamond movie—" Bile threatens to rise up my throat, but I force myself to seem unperturbed. "Out of nowhere, Jared perks up from his seat and asks what I was watching, so I told him, and then he demanded I show him. He was fairly drunk by this point so I didn't want to argue, and I tilted the screen toward him, just for a few seconds. I didn't think he would be interested in a livestream of Tyler Tun getting out of his car, but I don't know how that guy's brain works. And then it was like he got this rush of energy, and he downed his drink and left. Without paying, obviously. I don't know what the fuck happened, but hey, I was glad he was gone."

He saw me. He was wasted and angry and he saw me on that livestream and despite his inebriated state, he got lucky and managed to sneak into the park from the other side. That's what happened.

After a pause, she adds, "You know, Carina, sometimes . . . you should *let* people walk out of your life."

I cock my head. "What do you mean?"

She wipes her hands on her apron and leans forward. Her shock has been replaced with concern, and she's giving me more "big sister" vibes than "bartender." The lines in her forehead constrict as she says, "You seem like a good person. And Jared, frankly, is *not.*" After shooting a quick glance at the men at the end, she lowers her voice to the point where I have to bend closer to hear her. "He doesn't have any friends. Not even the other men who use this place as Yangon's unofficial White Men's Lounge want to be associated with him. Which says a lot. He comes in here already drunk and leaves even more drunk. My boss lets him have a tab because it's easier than fighting him to pay for his fucking drinks. I've heard rumors that he's also a shit gambler and owes more than a couple of people more than just a few thousand kyats. Basically, and I know how it'll sound"—her eyes drop—"I wouldn't be surprised if somebody refused to take his bullshit anymore and he's lying dead in a ditch right now."

———————

T his is good news, right?" May says in the car. Although her place is farther out, we're dropping Tyler off first because he has a meeting with his publicist and manager in approximately twenty minutes.

"What do you mean?" I ask.

"Well, according to what Julie said, it sounds like half the city wanted him dead. That is a *huge* suspect pool."

"But I'm the only one who was the star of his camera roll," I remind her.

"But they can't arrest you based solely on *that*."

"Because cops are notorious for being just," Tyler mumbles. "Apart from Detective Olivia Benson, obviously."

I look over to make sure I heard his little quip right. It's a good thing we're waiting at a stoplight because otherwise his teasing half smile would've quite possibly led to a small crash, and the last thing I need right now is to crash a car that has Tyler Tun and May Diamond in it. "Obviously," I say, and his smile grows into a full grin.

"Soooo what's plan B?"

At the sound of May's voice, Tyler and I break eye contact and whirl our heads to face the windshield. "I don't know," I say. "I've already talked to the two people anyone is most likely to spill their secrets to: their partner, and their bartender. What am I supposed to do, track down his therapist? But—" I mutter through a frustrated exhale. "I'll try to see if I can find any other leads."

When we near his place, Tyler directs me farther down the road to the side street that leads to his building's back entrance. "What's this meeting about, by the way?" May asks.

"Oh, the usual. Just movie stuff," Tyler says, keeping his eyes ahead so he can point out the turn before we miss it.

Suddenly, I'm not giving the road the full attention a responsible driver should. I don't need to see either of their faces to feel the agitation that's crept in and is dissipating in the air around us, like a stealth gas leak.

"Movie stuff? What *movie stuff*?" May scoffs. "*I'm* interested in movie stuff."

Suddenly, *I'm* interested in movie stuff, too. Just because the focus tonight is murder doesn't mean I can't also be doing some (quiet) research for my article; after all, it hits me that this is the first "normal" off-set time that I've ever been alone with May and Tyler, the first time I've seen them interact when no one else is around. What is Tyler Tun and May Diamond's relationship when no one's looking?

"I—hey!" Despite being startled by Tyler's yell, I maintain control of the car. When I glance over, May has Tyler's phone in her hand—I'm guessing his "Hey!" was in response to her swiping it from his lap—and is unlocking it. "Give that back!" he presses, but May retreats to the far corner of the backseat where his seat belt prevents him from reaching her.

"Tyler," she says. Her reflection in the rearview mirror is squinting at his phone, then over at him, then back at the phone as she scrolls up and down. "You said it was just Bolu and Christian. There are, like, thirty people on this call."

"I said Bolu and Christian would be the only ones from my *team*," he says, still trying to swipe for his phone like a dog at the end of its leash.

"I don't know half of these names! What is this meeting about?"

"Studio stuff," Tyler exhales. "It's going to be long and boring. I can give you the minute-by-minute details tomorrow if you want, but I'd like to get in a quick shower beforehand, so can I *please* have my phone back?"

Now that we're parked by the entrance, I no longer have driving as an excuse to busy myself. And while a part of me is, for obvious reasons, very intrigued by this series of events, another part is aware that this feels more akin to a private conversation between the two of them.

"Promise?" May asks at last.

"Sure," Tyler says.

At that, May hops out from the backseat, gives him a hug good night, and takes the passenger seat.

"Hey," I say as she types her address into my phone's Maps app. "I'm sorry again that we got you tangled in all this."

"Pfft." She waves a hand. "Like I said, no way in hell I was going to let my best friend try to figure out a murder on his own. Or I guess he's more trying to *get away* with murder?" She slips on her seat belt. "You know what I mean."

"You're a really good friend," I say, reversing the car and rolling toward the exit.

"Hey, Khin?" she says, then pauses.

"Mm-hmm?"

"This profile of him you're writing."

"Yeah?" I ask casually, even though it occurs to me that since she's the one who brought it up first, this time alone with May is a potential gold mine for said profile.

"You're—" She hesitates again. I'm waiting for a break in the stream of cars so I can join the far lane, and can't look over to gauge her expression. "You're going to be *fair*, right?"

I see my chance and curve onto the road. "What do you mean?"

"I know you have a job to do, but . . . don't take advantage of him? Please? He—" I glance over into her unexpected silence, and find a sweet yet unsure smile spreading on her glossy pink lips. This is the first time I've ever seen May . . . nervous? Tense? "He's really enjoying spending time with you. I can't remember the last time he let his guard down like this with, well, anyone. Especially someone who also happens to be a journalist. It's been a long, long time since I saw him like this again, all . . . soft."

I frown, not enjoying how the line *He's really enjoying spending time with you* has given me immediate heart palpitations. "Soft?" I ask, ignoring the first part of what she said.

She nods. "Ty has the biggest, purest heart of anyone I know. It's this soft, golden thing that he used to wear on his sleeve. You know he used to be one of those people that strikes up conversations with strangers on planes?"

I make a mock gagging sound. "Ew."

"Right?" She laughs. "But now he . . . keeps it in a glass case because all the world keeps trying to do is crush it. Like he's a circus animal and if they prod enough times or at the right angle, they'll find something that makes him not soft, not kind, not *him*. I've seen way too many reporters try to catch him out, trick him into saying something potentially career-ruining, all so they can, what, say that Tyler Tun isn't as wonderful as everyone thinks? I want to tell him to stop being so guarded and distrustful all the time, but I can't when I see how everyone treats him. So Khin, please don't . . . do that, okay? Please be fair? Kind, even?" she asks.

I know I should, at the very least, pretend to be on board even if I don't think what May's asking for is completely fair. I'm obviously not going to print his *real* big secret about his sister, but that doesn't mean I can't print any other confessions he relays to me. Especially ones that relate back to his career, like, say, if I managed to get out of him what his big meeting tonight was about. His family aside, everything else he tells *me*, a *journalist*, is fair game . . . right?

"I . . . I will," I reply, and force the corners of my lip upward, relying on the darkness to hinder her ability to see through my coerced expression.

"Thank you," she says, but I can still discern something in her tone that tells me she doesn't believe me wholly. Then again, like she said, I suppose that's par for the course in their line of work: How close is anyone in their inner circle to being offered the right sum to expose a secret? "Anyway, moving on." She laughs to brush off the tension that has sunk into the creases of the leather seats. "Are you seeing anyone?"

It's an innocuous question, one that acquaintances have asked me while we're waiting for drinks at the bar, but coming from May's mouth, it's both shocking and, for a vague reason, feels loaded. "No, I—" I swallow. "I don't know if Tyler told you, but I recently got divorced. I'm trying to take some time away, focus on myself, focus on new projects, you know, all that usual 'wellness'"—I make air quotes with one hand—"stuff before I start dating again. Which I will, eventually. But right now, no."

"I see." The two words are slow, intentionally so. I peek over again, and again, there's that sly smile on her glossy lips.

"What?" I ask with a timid laugh that I hadn't planned.

"Nothing!" she says, but her voice not so much projects as it dances across the center console. It's the voice she puts on during talk shows, the bright, cheery May Diamond that men, women, and nonbinary individuals alike would inexplicably bend over backward to please. It's the voice that, paired with her gleaming smile, makes people go, *Well, we don't usually allow this, but let me see what I can do.*

"You know," she starts with an almost singsong inflection. "Tyler's been taking a break from dating as well, but I'm pretty sure he's looking to start again. Eventually. Maybe even soon."

If we were talking about literally any other guy, I would say with complete certainty that she's trying to wingwoman me on her friend's behalf right now. But we're talking about Tyler. Tyler, who was last seen in Sicily with Zoë fucking Kravitz. Not because I don't think I'm on his level, but because I am not on Zoë Kravitz's level (nobody is).

Instantly, my brain sparks with an idea. "But he dates a lot, doesn't he? Or at least, he used to?" I ask, making great effort not to slip into what my friends call my "journalist voice."

"He'll go *on* dates, but that's only because he doesn't want people to think he's a recluse loner."

"People?"

"Industry people. The people who do the hiring," she says with a rueful scoff. "He—*we*," she clarifies, "need to stay relevant in people's minds. That's why I do so many modeling campaigns, go out all the time. But Ty doesn't like those, and he doesn't like parties, which is another way that people stay relevant. It's not like one of those fake Hollywood dating PR stunts," she reassures me hurriedly. "He *does* like the people he goes on these dates with, but it's never serious. He never, say, started watching *Law & Order* because it was Zendaya's favorite show."

This time, I have no doubt what she's doing, and May knows I know. I am usually the cat in the game of cat and mouse, but right now, she's got my blushing mouse ass cornered.

It is suddenly scorching in here. I glance at the air con to see if it's still on. Yep, it sure is. "Oh," I say, and it sounds like I barely managed to scrape it out of my throat. "I have to ask, just to hear straight from the source," I force myself to say even though I'm now wondering if my voice has always sounded this stilted. "Have you two ever dated?"

"No," she replies instantly.

"Have you . . . wanted to? At least on your end?"

May chuckles to herself. "Of course I have. Have you met the guy?" Her honesty catches me by surprise. "Did you ever tell him?"

"No."

"Why not?" I ask. My journalistic senses kick in, sirens start blaring *scoop* in my head. The world would've gone *nuts* at the news of Tyler and May as a couple. Would *still* go nuts.

"For a while, it was your run-of-the-mill cowardice. *What if I lose him as a friend,* blah blah, same old shit. But after a while, I realized he had things he needed to sort out," she says in a pragmatic way, as though this is a line of thought she's spent a long time threading together and ironing out. "I know it makes perfect sense on paper. We're best friends, there's no one I trust more in the world. Dating Tyler, having him as my partner in every context including a romantic one—it would make things so much easier."

She keeps talking, but in my head, it's transitioned to that scene in a movie where the background music gets turned down. For several worrying seconds, I forget that I am a journalist, or that I have no actual stake in this game. To be honest, I even forget that I'm driving (which I rectify by recalibrating my attention to the road immediately).

It takes me another beat to put an overarching name to the series of chain reactions that's flooded my system: jealousy. I am jealous at the idea of May and Tyler dating. Of the fact that they *make perfect sense on paper*; she's correct, but factual accuracy doesn't do anything to abate my queasiness.

There is nothing I can do to deny it: I am jealous at the idea of Tyler dating May. I turn the epiphany over and over, trying to come at it from all angles, trying to see it through as many different perspectives as possible like it's a prism and surely it must be distorted.

And then another, more excruciating thought flies through my brain cells before I can close the gates: I am jealous at the idea of Tyler dating *anybody.*

The epiphanies fall like dominoes in my brain.

Because I do not want to simply "start dating" again.

Because there is only one person I actively want to date.

"But we never have, I promise." May's voice cuts through the warm, heavy haze that's blanketed all of my senses.

"Wh-why not?" I ask, because I need to know. Why would anyone choose to not date Tyler Tun?

"Because Tyler doesn't know what he wants in a partner, and as much as I love him, I want to be with someone who does know what they want from a relationship. Someone decisive and who, if it comes down to it, knows where his priorities lie."

Pulling up at a light, I cock my head in her direction with a generally confused expression.

"Okay, so you know how everyone is juggling a lot of balls, and sometimes you gotta drop some plastic balls to save the glass ones?" she asks.

I nod.

"But with Tyler, *everything* is a glass ball. You know he personally campaigned for *two* years to get this movie made?"

I gape at her. "What? *This* one?"

"Yep. He attended pitch meetings and sat down with the writers afterward to see how they could implement the feedback into the script. He'd fly twelve-hour round trips while he was in the middle of shooting other movies or doing press tours because he wanted to be present for in-person meetings," she says. "No studio wanted to fund this film. A rom-com starring two Myanmar people, set in Yangon? But Tyler and Yasmin refused to give up. I've been trying to get him to chill, but of course, he's already thinking ahead to publicity time. He and I are both listed as executive producers, but he deserves the title a thousand times more than I do. And this big call he's got tonight? It's probably about his next movie, or the one after that, or even the one after that. Knowing him, he's got his next six films already lined up. Do you know he drinks three coffees every morning?"

I don't notice that the light has turned green until a succession of loud, angry honks jolts me. "Every morning?" I ask. I guess that explains all the mints.

"Yep. He wakes up, has one coffee, runs three to seven miles depending on how much time he has, showers, has another coffee, replies to his emails because he has a self-imposed forty-eight-hour response time, and then has one last one before he heads out the door. Every. Morning."

I'm trying to do the mental math of how long all of that takes. How early does Tyler wake up on the mornings that he has an 8 A.M. call time? Guilt warps my insides as I realize how late he's been staying out with me in the evenings.

"He is *exhausted*," May continues. "But if he's not busy working, he's busy looking after everyone else. The first big paycheck he got, he used it to build his parents their dream house. He was so excited to hang out with them more while he was here, but after what happened at that dim sum place"—she shoots me a quick look to let me know that she's not blaming me, but stating facts—"now he's terrified that people will start hounding them. I know his mom and dad keep trying to tell him they don't care as long as they get to see him, but he keeps rescheduling meals with them."

I glance over at my phone to make sure I'm still on the right path. I have no idea how I've been driving for the past ten minutes. Shout-out to muscle memory. "And the same is . . . true when it comes to dating? This juggling act he's got going on?"

May chuckles, as though this whole time she was waiting for me to circle back to this question. "Yes, unfortunately. It's so fucking cli-chéd, but he doesn't let anyone get close because he doesn't want to be distracted and accidentally drop a glass ball. But ever since his career kicked off, he hasn't taken the time to figure out his identity outside of it. As though he's scared that if he takes even one break, all of it will disappear in a flash. I love him to death, but he's one of those people who, if you take away his job, doesn't know who he is. Or what he wants. And like I said, I want a partner who knows what he wants."

And there we go, yet another item to add to the list of Reasons Why Crushing on Tyler Is a Preposterous Idea that I Cannot Believe

I Am Even Entertaining—because that is exactly who *I* am: someone who knows what she wants. If I were to (after drinking a bottle and a half of wine, obviously) ask him out, it wouldn't be for a one-night stand. No, I already know that if I were to admit out loud that I wanted Tyler Tun, I would want to dive headfirst into the deep end. The problem is, *he* would hesitate on the ledge.

Everything May's saying—has said—is helping cushion the blow of my recent epiphany (although now I'm wondering if I am the last person in this world who has realized that they want Tyler Tun in that sense? Probably). After all, she knows him better than anyone in the world, and if even *she's* aware that being with Tyler can only end badly, then *I'm* certainly not ready to offer up my heart like that. My brain rewinds to another thing she's said in this conversation, about how hard Tyler's worked to get this movie made. Because *that's* what he's here for, and in spite of the ever-growing guilt that I hadn't anticipated when I first got this assignment, it helps me refocus and remember what *I'm* here for. We're both simply doing our jobs. This time we're spending together is just that small sliver in the middle of the Venn diagram where we temporarily overlap.

"What about you?" she asks. "Do you know what you're looking for?"

"No," I say, the lie pricking my tongue.

———

That night, I enter my office—noting guiltily that this is the first time in weeks that I've opened this door—and write on the whiteboard, not at all a note for my assignment but a giant, block-lettered reminder to myself for if and when I come close to having a lapse in judgment: DOESN'T KNOW WHAT HE WANTS. NOT FOR YOU.

Fifteen

Sooo how's the story going? Got anything juicy for me yet? We're a little over four weeks away!" Clarissa reminds me, like the little blue entry on my iCal hasn't been counting down for me every day, murder cover-up be damned.

Snapping to attention, I smile up at my car's speakers like Clarissa's is the voice of God, which, in certain circles—mine included—she kind of is. "It's going great! I've got . . . stuff!"

"Great to hear!" Clarissa replies. "Oh, and as an FYI, we've secured Sandra Oh for our April cover. I was chatting with her yesterday, and Sandra mentioned that she'd ideally like an Asian woman writer for the story, and I might have told her that I already have a stellar person lined up."

An inelegant hacking sound bolts out of me. "Sandra Oh?" I ask up at God-slash-Clarissa. "*The* Sandra Oh? *Killing Eve* Sandra Oh?"

"Yes, Khin." Clarissa laughs. "This is *Vogue*, sweetheart. We go big. But of course, this is all contingent on you delivering on *this* story."

I nod with such ferocity that the people in the next car start to look at me like they're wondering if I'm having a seizure and they should call an ambulance. I hold up a palm to reassure them I'm not dying. Not physically, at least. "Clarissa," I say, straightening my shoulders. "I'm already putting together the outfit I'll be wearing when I meet Sandra for the first time."

Clarissa's laugh rings out through the car once more. "I'll speak to you soon, Khin. Looking forward to reading this . . ." There's a twinkling lilt in her voice. ". . . *stuff*."

I crank Ariana Grande's "7 rings" on full blast. Sandra Oh. I nail this one story, and I will be months away from sitting down with Dr. Cristina Yang herself. The mental image is enough to make me squeal.

In an unjust, maudlin moment, right as I think, *When was the last time you wanted anything this badly?*, I pull onto the lot and Tyler's figure is the first thing my eyes hook onto, like lightning to a metal rod. A tall, handsome rod who's standing in his usual parking spot, arms folded and leaning against the back of the car while chatting to Yan. *Be fair—* May's voice jumps out like she's a ghost haunting my passenger seat.

I park several spots away so I can take my time collecting my bag and my thoughts. Clarissa wants something juicy? How about the line *At one point, even May Diamond confesses to me that she used to be in love with Tyler?* But I can't print that . . . can I?

I let out a small groan and drop my forehead against the wheel. This is ridiculous. Why am I feeling guilty? I'm a journalist. Everyone here knows that that is my job. My duty, even. And May and Tyler are both professionals; if they'd wanted something to be off the record, then they know to specify that beforehand, *and* they know that I don't necessarily have to agree. I have every right to write that May told me she used to be in love with Tyler. Or about his three morning coffees or—

Rap rap rap. I jump up and a sharp pain grips into the back of my scalp, literally—my claw clip is squished between my head and the headrest, making the claws dig into my skin. Tyler mouths a *sorry* and steps back so I can open the door.

"You good?" he asks.

"Mm-hmm," I say, smoothing down my shirt. "Any word from Yasmin today? About the . . . you know . . ." Tyler stares at me with a blank expression. Is he being serious? I make sure the coast is clear before I mumble, "M-U-R-D-E-R?"

"Ohhh," he says, snapping his fingers. "N-O."

"Are you choosing violence today?" I ask with a scowl that dissolves the second his crow's-feet wrinkle with laughter.

"Sorry," he says, his blatantly unapologetic voice speckled with amusement.

For a few moments, we stand there, doing nothing but grinning at each other. But then in my head, I hear Clarissa saying, *Sandra Oh,* which is an excellent reminder that I have a story that's due in a little over a month, and so far I have enough information for approximately two paragraphs (and that's if I am very generous with my employment of adverbs).

"Hey," I say, thinking up the plan on the spot. "Do you mind if I come over tonight?"

"T-tonight? My place?" he stammers, and briefly, I remember May last night. *I'm pretty sure he's looking to start dating again.*

"Yeah. For the story," I clarify, both for him and myself. Because this is not a date and I am not doing this to, god forbid, *flirt* with him. This is for work. "We've been so busy taking care of my, you know—"

"You mean the M-U-R-D-E-R—"

"Yes," I respond with a glare. "But I *do* still need to file a story by the time you leave. I'd like to do a standard sit-down Q and A. If that's alright with you."

"You want to come to my place? Tonight?"

"It'll only be a few hours. And now that everyone knows you're in town, I can't think of anywhere else where we'll have privacy. And we can order in dinner, obviously, since we need to eat." I'm acutely aware that I've started blabbering, but I can't make it stop. "But it's strictly work, so it's not like we're crossing any ethical lines, even though it's at your place. Because it's work."

Amusement pulling at his features, Tyler nods, and I pretend not to notice the way he rolls his shoulders back, like suddenly there's an intense buildup of tension. "Sure," he says. "Let's get Thai for dinner?"

The second he switches on the lights, I do a double take at how homey Tyler's apartment is. I'd expected something sleek and minimalistic, with very little furniture, something out of a condo showroom photo—so essentially, *my* place—but this looks like someone lives here.

The large brown leather L-shaped couch looks soft and worn-in with lots of faint white scratches, like it's been witness to hundreds, if not thousands, of movie marathons and late-night gaming sessions (if the PS5 beneath it is anything to go by). There's a stack of books with bookmarks haphazardly sticking out on one side of the coffee table. Over in the kitchen, there is an array of mugs of various sizes and colors and shapes hanging from a mug tower—a far cry from my perfectly identical IKEA yellow four-piece set. A faded cream-colored apron adorned with bright yellow padauk flowers hangs on a hook next to the stove.

"This used to be my cousin Thiri's place. When she put it up for sale, I was too nostalgic to let a stranger buy it," Tyler says, removing his shoes. "She's the oldest cousin, so she was the first of us to get her own apartment. We thought she was *so cool*, and we couldn't believe we could hang out here after school without any grown-ups around."

My smile shows up involuntarily. "Was it hard to leave your family behind? When you left for the States?"

He heads for the kitchen and fills up two mugs with water. "Definitely. It was the most difficult part. And I couldn't come home until I got a work visa. Man, I missed them so much. But hey—" He turns, startling a bit to find me standing behind him, but recomposes himself as he hands over the mug. "Now I get to fly them out to anywhere in the world, which kind of makes *me* the cool cousin these days."

"Oh, so *I* have to speed-drink my matcha latte before my straw dissolves into papier-mâché while *you're* picking out which private jet you want to fly your family out on?" I ask, lifting a reprimanding brow.

"They've never flown private," he counters.

"But *you* do."

"Is this going into the story?" He makes a horizontal swiping gesture with one palm. "Tyler Tun: THE WORST THING TO HAPPEN TO THE ENVIRONMENT SINCE FAST FASHION."

I've never noticed before how his smile expands whenever he makes me laugh, but it does, and this newfound information melts my insides.

I place the mug down on the nearby island with a smidge too much force.

He tilts over and his eyes widen with genuine worry. "Woah, be careful, that's my favorite mug."

I direct my attention to the mug in question. It's matte black, with an image of a gold Oscar statue, and the words "And the Oscar goes to . . ." written in gold, curly script on one side. I rotate it and find a photo of kid Tyler in sunglasses on the other side.

A wild laugh vaults out of me at the sight, and when I turn back to him, Tyler's silently laughing, too. "Jess bought it for me after I landed my first feature role," he explains. "It's the one thing I bring with me whenever I travel."

"Awww," I say with full sincerity, unable to recall whatever snarky comment I was going to make. I can't tell what's more endearing: the story, or his sheepish embarrassment. "And you let *me* drink from your favorite mug? Even though you've seen how lethal I can be with an everyday object?"

It's a dark joke that could go either way, but Tyler's shoulders shake with audible laughter this time, and before I can stop myself, I remember what May said and imagine himself laughing like this with a stranger on a plane, loudly and wholeheartedly, no baseball cap, no sunglasses, no lowered voice.

"Shall we place our order?" he asks, taking out his phone.

"Yes," I say. I pick up the mug again, this time with both hands.

———

The food arrives and we've just laid all the boxes out on the table when my phone buzzes. "It's my building's front desk," I say and pick up, hoping there hasn't been some freak accident like the ceiling falling in or my fridge glitching and defrosting. Wouldn't that be my luck, though?

"Hi, a ma," Yarzar, my doorman, says, his tone already telling me that it's not great news.

"Hey, Yarzar. Everything okay?"

A slight pause. "I . . . have two detectives here."

Despite the warm air in the room, a chill spirals through me. "Detectives?" I look at Tyler, who's also stiffened.

"Yes." The wariness in Yarzar's voice tells me that they're standing in front of him. "They're asking me to let you into your apartment, but I told them I needed your explicit permission."

I feel like I'm going to faint. I try to stroll in order to jolt my brain into working, but only manage one awkward backward step. "Do they have a warrant?"

"No, a ma."

I shut my eyes and let out a silent sigh of relief. "Then tell them we don't have to show them anything."

"I—excuse me?" There's a muffled conversation and Yarzar returns. "They're asking to speak to you."

The hand gripping the phone is shaking, and I grasp my wrist with my other hand. I look at Tyler again, who moves closer and gives me a slow nod. *Stay calm*, he mouths.

"That's fine," I say, keeping my voice nonchalant. "Please put them on."

"Hi, Khin," Detective Zeyar says. I hadn't realized I'd memorized his voice, but I have, and it's just as revolting over the phone as it is in person.

"Hi, Detective. What's this about you wanting to search my apartment without a warrant? And without our lawyers knowing? And at this hour?"

"Woah there, sweetheart, slow down." He laughs like I'm blowing this out of proportion. "We know how hard you always work," he says, voice coated with condescension that makes me clench my jaw, "so we wanted to make sure you'd be home. Don't know how late movie shoots run. And this isn't really a search, more like . . . a conversation. We kept thinking about that pen—"

"Which was May's—"

"Right. But just like we missed it the first time around, maybe there's something you missed from that night, too. Maybe you *have* seen this man before and forgot? Like I said, we just wanted to have a small chat. Nothing that needs lawyers involved."

Tyler looks like he wants to reach into the phone and strangle the prick. "Are you going to go to May's and Tyler's homes, too? And Yasmin's?" I ask, hoping the edge in my voice covers up my fear.

His quiet "What?" tells me he wasn't expecting me to be so confrontational.

"Well, if you're going to come to *my* apartment, surely you're going to go to all of theirs and question them, too. Especially May. It was *her* pen, after all."

His hesitant throat clearing gives me a boost of confidence, which I snatch and stretch for the duration of this conversation. "Well . . . we were . . ."

"Or are you honing in on me because I'm not American?" I ask, making a point to sound civil so they have no way to accuse me of *overreacting* or being *uncooperative*. "You thought you could bully and intimidate me, even though you have no evidence or just cause, because I'm not American and you don't have to answer to an embassy if you barge into my apartment without a warrant?"

"That's—"

"I know my rights, Detective." I pause to see if they'll throw back any arguments. They don't. "Didn't you say you had a daughter? It's late. Why don't you go home and tuck her into bed? You guys work *so hard*," I amp up the saccharinity. "You should at least get to go home in time to kiss your children good night."

After a few silent seconds, all he says is, "Good night, Khin," and hangs up.

I check the phone to make sure the call is over before I put it down beside my plate. I look over to find Tyler still glaring at it. "Those motherfuckers, trying to corner you when they *knew* we wouldn't be around," he says through gritted teeth. Making sudden eye contact with me, his brown pupils flash and he says, "Tell me if they ever try to pull something like that again, and I will have Legal call—"

"No!" I say quickly. "Don't tell Legal. Or Yasmin or even May. I don't want to have to build on the lies."

"But they—"

"Tyler." I put a hand on his shoulder. He looks down, but doesn't react. "I got this."

He looks at my hand again, then back at me.

"What?" I ask.

"You're literally trembling," he says.

At that, I snatch my hand back and interlace my fingers in front of me. "I've got—"

"If you say 'you've got this' one more time . . . " he says, eyes narrowing before he blows out an impatient puff of air. "How many times do I need to tell you? You can trust me. You don't have to do this on your own. You're *not* doing this on your own. *I've* got *you*."

I don't quite know how the sequence of events unfolds, but the next thing I *do* know is that I'm sobbing, palms pressed onto Tyler's chest, face folded into the crook of his neck, while his hands rub small circles on my back. "I'm so scared," I say, a sob interjected between each word. "I'm so tired and scared and stressed and I don't know how much longer I can do this. Any of this."

Despite me bracing for it, he doesn't try to shush me, or tell me everything will be okay. Instead, he leans down and simply whispers, "I know."

"I—" *Hiccup.* "I miss—" *Hiccup.* "Normal. I miss my old, normal life. Before all of this."

"I know," he repeats. "It's . . . a lot. And I know you're exhausted, but I need you to push on for just a little bit longer." My face sinks deeper into him, wet tears sticking my cheeks to his shirt. "They don't have anything. They're just trying to scare us."

"Well, it's working!" I cry.

His chest moves with a short snort. "Hey now," he says, sounding like he's smiling. "You don't scare easily, remember?"

I let out an inadvertent snort of my own. "That I absolutely do not. Clearly."

I sniffle and pull back at last, ignoring the horrid snot stain I've left on his shirt. I blink away the tears and look up at him. He is smiling, soft and sweet, and for some reason, that's what finally prompts me to exhale.

"We can do this," he repeats. "We'll see this through together."

"Together," I say, realizing that I mean it. In this moment, it feels like he's carrying the both of us on his back, and I don't mind it at all. I don't mind that I just fell apart in his arms, or that he's seen me at my worst, time and time again. I don't have to be always-have-it-together Khin around him.

He stays, it dawns on me. He is the kind of person who, once he's committed to something—a movie, or a secret, or another human being, like May or his family or myself—*stays*. I might've started out (warily) collaborating with him because I had no choice, but right now, I can't think of anyone else I'd rather have by my side, anyone else I'd rather trust with my whole life.

"I'm going to go change," he says, glancing down at the snot stain. Thankfully, he looks more amused than repulsed. "And then how about we get some food in us and start the interview?"

I pull out a chair, and before he's even closed his bedroom door, I know: I'm not printing his secret. I *can't* be. I still want the *Vogue* role, of course I do, and maybe (albeit unlikely) it'll be the case that my article will be good enough that Clarissa will still offer it to me even though I don't get her her exclusive. I'd like to think that my feelings for him have nothing to do with my decision—although I am self-aware enough to admit that that's not *entirely* true—the main reason is that after all that Tyler and I have been through, after all he's done with and for me, I can't expose what he did for his sister, or anything else he's told me as a friend. A friend that he trusts. He deserves better than that. *I* am better than that.

"What're you so deep in thought over?" Tyler's voice startles me, and I look over to see him emerging from his bedroom in sweatpants and a new T-shirt. Filters removed, I wonder if this is what he wears to bed.

You.

You, you, you.

"About how I'm going to find out exactly which convenience store you shoplifted that Snickers bar from," I say, propping my chin on my fist.

Do you cut your sandwiches into triangles or rectangles?"

"I've been asked a lot of questions in my day," Tyler says, thinking while he finishes chewing. "But that's a new one."

"It separates the sociopaths from the non-sociopaths."

"Triangles," he says after a considering pause.

I smile. "Non-sociopath it is. Shame. The other one would've made for a better story."

"Sorry to disappoint."

"Favorite song."

"Easy. 'The Best' by Tina Turner," he says.

I swallow my pad Thai and ask, "Why?"

Tyler shrugs. "Reasons." He reaches out for a spoonful of the vegan green curry from one of the takeaway boxes laid out on the dining table.

"Such as?" I ask.

"It was my parents' first-dance song," he says after he swallows. "And they would randomly start singing it to each other all the time. I thought—" He stops himself, head dropping down like he was an inch away from saying something mortifying.

"What?" I prod with a gentle laugh. "You thought what?"

He coughs. "I . . . used to think that that was how people confessed their love to each other. Cut to me in fourth grade, walking up to Susie, the cutest, smartest girl in my class—"

My hand flings up to my mouth but the gasp still seeps out from between my fingers. "Stop, you didn't—"

"I sure did," he says. "I walked right up to her, looked her in the eye, and told her she was simply the best and better than all the rest. Recited the whole thing like it was spoken-word poetry. Which, if I may say so, was pretty impressive. *You* try being nine and memorizing an entire song."

"Sounds like you were ready to memorize whole *scripts* at nine."

He laughs. "Guess so."

"Did it . . . work out?"

"Huh?"

"With Susie."

"Oh," he says, before letting out a long exhale. "No, she gave her coveted Valentine to Aung Myo. The prick," he adds under his breath.

"Tyler!" I exclaim. "You can't call a nine-year-old a prick."

"Why? Who's going to tell?" His gaze jumps to my phone, which is facedown, but still recording. "Oh, right, you, probably."

"I could probably be bribed into staying quiet if you let me have the last spring roll," I say, already steadying the container with one hand while spearing my fork into the roll.

"The price I pay to keep my image intact. You journalists just keep getting more and more unreasonable these days," he mutters through a smile.

"Have you"—I swallow—"serenaded any other girls with the melodies of Ms. Turner lately?"

I meant it as a joke, but the moment his eyes hitch onto mine, nothing seems funny, especially not the way my stomach is threatening to toss everything I've consumed back upward. I forget that I'm supposed to wait for an answer. "Hey," I say, aware my voice has dropped to a pitch that some might label "husky."

"Hey," he says in an equally husky timbre.

"I have a question."

"You have many."

I ask the question that I can't stop thinking about, because it feels like time has stopped for us, and whatever his answer is and whatever happens next, it won't matter anyway outside of this apartment. "Is it true that you wanna start dating again?"

His Adam's apple bobs, but otherwise, his face remains unmoving. Because of the sheer size of the table, we'd decided to sit adjacent to each other instead of opposite, and I don't know when his knees first made contact with my thigh but now that I know it, I can't *un*know it. When he speaks, his words are steady, but not in a forced way. "I am going to murder May," he says. "Any tips?"

He might not be blushing, but I know for a fact that *I* am. Moreover, this surge of bodily heat is no longer limited to just my cheeks. "So, what, we just go around murdering people now?" I ask, although by the roughness of my voice, I might as well have admitted, *I am ten seconds away from jumping you.*

"An Asian Bonnie and Clyde. But, you know, with the stakes raised."

"They'll make movies about us," I say, widening my eyes for full dramatic effect.

Tyler's hand slowly approaches my face until his thumb makes a quick, firm brushing motion on one corner of my mouth. "Sauce, Bonnie," he says, and, knowing exactly what he's doing, and not to mention my simultaneous horror and euphoria, sucks off the neon orange blotch on his skin.

"Who," I run my dry tongue over my lips, "would play me?"

His eyes glint. "Scarlett Johansson, obviously."

The force of my unanticipated laughter propels me forward. "Stop!" I cry.

Above my keeled head, Tyler's voice says sagely, "Color-blind casting, baby."

I lift my head to find that my nose is placed at a precise downward forty-five-degree angle an inch away from his own. The scent of green curry and pine trees on anyone else wouldn't be even remotely appealing, but on Tyler, it smells warm and delicious, in an excruciatingly alluring way. "You didn't answer my question," I say. My voice sounds like it's been put through a sieve.

When he speaks, his own voice isn't faring much better. "Can you repeat it? I got distracted for a second. Brain glitch. You know, the usual."

"Brain glitch? The usual?" I repeat as though I'm teasing him when the reality is that I'm trying to recall what my initial question was myself.

"Well, yeah," he says, a subtle, confused line appearing between his brows. "I mean, it's . . . you. My brain does that a lot around you. Really, Khin, as a journalist, I thought you'd be perceptive enough to notice that."

You are not real, I think, aware that my mouth is hanging open but unable to regain enough control of my motor cortex to shut my jaw muscles. "You can't—" I start, but it peters out. He can't what? But I *want* him to.

"What if—"

We jump at the sound of a phone buzzing on the table. It's his. He frowns at the unsaved number.

"Do you . . . want me to get it?" I ask, realizing that unknown numbers for him are probably way more of a safety hazard than they are for me.

"Oh no, I'm sure it's—no, you don't—"

I take his phone and open the speaker. "Hello?"

"Hi," an elderly woman tentatively answers in Myanmar. "I'm looking for Tyler?"

I look over at Tyler, whose face has transformed, a cold, opaque sheen having dropped across it in the past three seconds. He catches my eye and gives a short shake of his head.

I nod, not needing to know anything else. "You've got the wrong number," I say.

"This isn't Tyler's phone? Tyler . . ." The woman hesitates but ultimately finishes, "Tun?"

I give a loud laugh. "Auntie," I say. "I would know if this was Tyler Tun's phone. Sorry, I'm afraid you have the wrong number. Have a good night!" I hang up before she can speak again. "Do you," I tilt the phone still in my hand, "want me to block her?"

Tyler seems surprised at my suggestion. Still, wordlessly, he nods.

We swivel back around to resume our prior forward-facing positions. I feel like it'd be imposing of me to stay, but also like it'd be wrong to leave. I start counting the seconds in my head. If he doesn't talk after a minute, I'll take that as a hint that he wants to be alone.

One, two, three, four, five, six—oh my god, since when did sixty become such a high number to count to—*seven, eight, ni*—

"What's *your* favorite song?"

I keep my eyes trained on my plate. "'Treacherous.' By Taylor Swift."

"Why?"

"Because it . . . sounds like falling in love."

"I see."

"Have you listened to it?"

He shakes his head. "Afraid not."

"Heathen," I reply, and he chuckles before falling silent once more.

Just as I'm wondering whether I should reset the counter or pick up where I left off, Tyler clears his throat and says simply, "I'm sorry."

"For what?"

"For . . . ruining our night. With that call."

I shift my head to find him staring at the empty spring roll container, eyes blank but glistening.

"Hey," I say. I adjust my body to face him, one palm settling on his knee.

When, instead of jostling, he places his own palm atop the back of my hand, every single one of my nerves responds to the pull of his touch.

"You didn't ruin the night. If anything, I'd say *my* call ruined the night. I *think* murder investigation trumps random old woman." His mouth stretches and opens, but no laugh comes out. "But I can go—" I start, already stopping the recording and going to put my phone away.

"That was my grandmother," he says.

There's a muffled *thud* as the phone slips out of my hand and back onto the table. "I thought your grandma was dead," I reply without thinking.

Wordlessly, he squeezes his eyes shut, and the action pushes the tears over the edge and down his cheeks. He grabs a tissue with the hand that was under his chin, the other still firm on mine, like he needs it to keep himself grounded lest he floats away.

"No, my grandmother is alive," he says, and blows his nose. "Both of them are, actually. So are both of my grandfathers."

I frown, because he's wrong. I know he's wrong. He doesn't often mention his grandparents, but he was the one who reminded me at our first meeting that his grandparents were dead. "But you—"

"My dad's parents were outraged that he was marrying a Myanmar woman. Or, really, someone who wasn't white. And my mom's parents were the same about her marrying someone who wasn't Myanmar. You know—" He chuckles before dabbing his eyes again with the tissue. "Sometimes I think it's *such* a shame they never met because I think they would've gotten along. Just four bigots meeting up for afternoon tea."

At my snort, Tyler shifts to face me. "I'm so sorry!" I say, horrified. "That wasn't funny. Well, no, it *was*, but the situation isn't. I don't think racism is funny. Just for the record."

"Glad we cleared *that* up," he says with a small laugh.

I'm babbling, which I only do when I'm either a) extremely nervous, or b) extremely caught off guard; in this case, it's the latter. I recall us at that first dinner, me asking if it was his grandparents who had taken his parents to that Chinatown restaurant, Tyler flinching, guard going up. He *had* been hiding something about his personal life: hurt. The kind of hurt that no amount of time passed can ever quite erase. Hurt over what would've been the first, honest answer to jump to his brain: *No, because my grandparents wanted nothing to do with our family.* An answer that he hadn't told any journalist until now. Until me.

My embarrassment is replaced with a new heat when his fingers glide into the spaces between mine and his fingertips curl down into my palm.

"Can I . . . ask you something?" I drop my gaze to our laced hands.

His thumb starts making circles atop the knuckle of my own. "Don't you always?"

"Why have you been telling people your grandparents are dead?"

"Because as far as I'm concerned, anyone who only wants to have a relationship with me and my parents because I'm now rich and successful *is* dead to me. You know my mom's parents kicked her out of the house when they found out she was engaged?"

The confession yanks my jaw downward. "Tyler—"

"And the thing is, my mom *knew*. She *knew* they'd react like that, so she only told them after she'd packed two duffel bags. I mean, who knowingly makes their own kid homeless?"

I remember what May said about how he used his first paycheck to buy his parents their dream home. "And your dad's parents?" I ask. "Did they used to live here?"

He shakes his head. "Florida, I think. My dad called them from here to tell them about his engagement, and that was the last time they ever spoke. Well, until my first Oscar nomination," he adds with a scornful snort. "Our parents never kept the story a secret from us, but it's still weird as hell when your agent one day forwards you an email from someone claiming to be your grandfather."

"I . . . can't even imagine," I say, processing all of it. My grandparents are all dead (actually dead), but I was their only grandchild, and while they were alive, they loved me like nothing I'd ever seen. Each set would literally try to bribe my parents into letting them babysit.

"They do this on and off. Guilt me with 'blood is thicker than water' shit," Tyler says, rolling his eyes. "But truthfully, I feel like it's only a matter of time before they strike up some deal with a shady tabloid and 'spill' stories about my childhood, which they never even saw. Or about how—" His voice starts shaking. I squeeze his hand to remind him that he's okay, that whatever terrible memories he's reliving right now can't hurt him. He returns my squeeze, waits for his breath to stabilize, and continues, "—how I'm a terrible grandson who would turn his back on his own grandparents. How when they tried to instead reach out to my sister, *their* granddaughter, I told her to block them and had my lawyers threaten to take action for harassing a minor. How I told my parents that if they tried to bring their parents back into our lives, I would never speak to them again."

"Tyler," I say, not knowing what else to say. My own eyes start prickling.

"You know what the sad thing is?" he asks, biting down on his trembling lip as two new streams of tears race down his cheeks. I want to wipe them away, but I sense that what he needs—wants—the most right now is for me to just *listen*. "Sometimes, I still find myself thinking that it's *such* a shame that they did what they did because I could've, *would've*, really, really loved them."

And that is what breaks me, the final slash that splits me in half. On an autopilot mode I didn't even know was programmed into me, I retract my hand from Tyler's. I get to my feet and he looks up, dazed and eyes glimmering. "Wha—" he starts, then stops when I sit back down sideways on his lap. Taking him into my arms, I place my cheek on top of his head and run my hands up and down his back.

When he shifts, a jolt of embarrassment makes me lift my butt in the air a little. "Shit, am I too heavy? I can—" I begin to stand back up, hoping his tears will blur my mortified expression. Until I feel his arms lock on the small of my back and gently tug me back down.

"No, I just . . . wasn't expecting that," he says, resting his forehead into my collarbone. "You're perfect. I, on the other hand, am a certi-fied, clinical mess."

"Oh, come on now," I say, replacing my cheek on the crown of his head. "Why do you think we'd make the perfect Bonnie and Clyde? No fun having a partner in crime who's got their shit together."

"*You* do," he says.

I laugh louder and more harshly than I mean to. "Tyler, I'm a murderer."

"Self-defense."

"I am a thirty-year-old divorcée. My marriage didn't even last a year. Not even close. I went from a house with a green front lawn to a cold, empty apartment. I own precisely four mugs."

His snort lands as a sharp blast of air on my skin. "Didn't realize the number of mugs in one's kitchen was an indication of their general stability."

"Well, now you do," I reply. "One of these days, more than three people are going to visit me and ask for a hot beverage at the same time, and I'm going to be utterly screwed. Humiliated. Disgraced. Discredited."

"Okay, *Oxford English Thesaurus*. I knew journalism salaries were bad, but I didn't know they were 'can only afford four mugs' bad." I smile when I hear the teasing undercurrent start to return to his voice. It's muffled, but it's there.

Tyler pulls back and his eyes sweep across my face, his jaw flexing as he returns my smile. "Ugh," I groan. "We have *got* to stop doing this."

"Doing what?" he asks with a hesitant laugh.

"This!" I gesture between us with widened eyes. "Spilling our worst secrets and fears to each other! It's an emotional hazard! I *hate* crying in front of people, you know. Good lord, you conspire to cover up *one* murder with someone and then before you know it, you're—"

"Do you have any idea how much I want to kiss you right now?"

My mouth opens and closes without a sound. "Tyler," I croak out with the grace of a toddler saying their first word. "You can't just say shit like that. And to my *face*? Do you have no decency?"

His husky laugh makes me want to instantly cross my legs. "But it doesn't matter, right? Because we're not allowed to kiss."

"We're . . . not?" I ask, perplexed. The way this conversation is going—not to mention the way my body is spasming all over—I don't think even the earth splitting apart underneath our feet right now could stop me from shoving my face against his.

"No, we aren't, because it would be unethical," he reminds me, each syllable heaving out like he's being coerced into saying them. The way his hands are pressing into my back also tells me that his body and brain are, not unlike mine, waging World War III right now. "Because you're a journalist writing a story. On me."

I swallow as my brain conjures up an image of me *on* him. "Right," I say nonetheless. "We can't. But, just for the record, if we *could* . . ."

He chuckles. His eyes descend down my face, my neck, and start roaming across my upper torso. As though they've become sentient, my nipples pinch under my shirt. "If we could . . ." he repeats and trails off like I did. I can't stop staring at that mouth: delicious and daring and soft and rogue, even if he's not aware of it.

I have a vague memory of a whiteboard somewhere, of big block letters that I wrote down for myself specifically to avoid this exact scenario. Another one of May telling me something about all the reasons she refuses to get entangled with Tyler and me silently agreeing, because it all made sense. It *did* make sense. Back then.

Now, though? Now, the thought of *not* having him hurts so much I have to do something to alleviate this craving or else I'm going to die.

"Kiss me."

His fingertips dig into my shirt as though in reflex to what I just said, and I suddenly cannot think of anything other than that I wish they were making contact with my skin, heat on heat. I watch the reactions play across his face as if the latter were an Etch A Sketch. At last, the lines fade, and, I notice, spine already straightening to reach up, he asks, "Are you sure?"

I let out a short, impatient laugh, my own posture bending to meet him halfway. "I swear to god, Tyler, if you don't kiss me right this s—"

His lips are a few dry ridges rougher than I expected, but as soon as his mouth leans into mine, all I can think is, *Finally*. He doesn't take it slow; this is not like a first kiss at the end of a good first date, when you're both *pretty* sure the other person wants to kiss you just as much as you want to kiss them, but not sure enough to go for it. Because Tyler fucking goes for it. His tongue licks my bottom lip and I open my mouth and it's intense and heavy and *hot*. His touch slides down my spine, roaming until it finds the hem of my shirt. When I drag one hand into his hair so I can gently tug a fistful, he groans into my mouth.

"We have to stop," he whispers, although our lips are still touching, our torsos still converged across as much surface area as possible.

No, my brain protests immediately. Then, *More.* I want more. I want *all.*

"I know," I say, pulling away but not standing up, not just yet.

Our breathing is labored, like we actually went all the way instead of simply kissing for a minute—or was it twenty?

"You should go," he says. His eyes have this haziness to them now, and he's trying to maintain eye contact but failing as he keeps glancing at my lips, which must be as swollen as his are.

"Why?" I ask, and then want to fling myself out the window when I hear how whiny I sound.

"Because—" He shifts in his seat, the movement drawing my attention to the hardness under my thighs. Instinctively, I glance down. When I look back up, he's smiling. "Well, because of that," he says through a dark chuckle. "Because you drive me wild, and if you don't leave right now, if you, god forbid, stay the night—" He swallows, and the unyielding hunger in his voice and on his face makes me want to ignore everything he's saying and go in for another kiss. "I already know for a fact that nothing short of the apocalypse will get me out of bed come morning."

I can't resist. I trace his jaw from the bottom of his chin to his earlobe, lean in, and whisper, "And *I* already know something else that would've made you come in the morning." He lets out a guttural groan that sounds like it's barely tethered to his last shred of sensibleness, and I add, "Again."

Sixteen

I try to tell myself that I'm not thinking straight, that what I feel for Tyler is an inane crush. Sure, we kissed—but one, it was *just* kissing. And two, I've kissed dozens of guys.

Except it's the fucking cliché that I cannot overlook no matter how hard I try: Tyler isn't just another guy.

Because something's changed, and I don't know if it can be unchanged. It's fireworks: the difference between that first, singular, unassuming streak of orange that's shot upward, and the succeding brilliant, all-consuming, can't-take-your-eyes-off-of-it, visible-from-a-hundred-miles-away light show that paints the whole sky.

We don't talk about the kiss—don't even come close—but we don't have to. I know how that mouth tastes, the electric shudders it sends through my body when it presses into my own, and without him ever alluding to it, I can tell he keeps thinking about it, too.

It's the way his fingertips do a quick, delicate, inconspicuous jog across mine whenever we're standing next to each other. The fact that

I now notice how the instant Yasmin yells "Cut!" his eyes immediately jump over to me, as though his subconscious is always keeping track of my presence. How, on the days where I get to set first, I somehow find myself needing to answer just enough emails in my car until I see him pull in; how, on the days that *he's* there first, he's always having a conversation with Yan that wraps up right as I step out. It's him sitting at lunch with me and May one day and then, out of nowhere, squinting up at the craft services tent ceiling as though deep in thought before saying, oh-so-casually, "So I listened to all of *Red* last night, and wow, that album was absolutely robbed of a Grammy," and my this-is-the-hill-I-will-die-on instincts prompting me to yell, "Wasn't it?!" before realizing the full gravity of what he'd said.

How at the end of each day for the past week, he's found a way to steal us a few minutes alone so he can whisper "No news" with a quick reassuring hand squeeze that I know is meant to remind me that I'm still okay, and, more important, that he's still looking out for me. That he's *always* looking out for me. Just like he promised. Every day still feels like that crescendoing scene in the horror movie where you know the serial killer is going to pop out any second now, but knowing I have Tyler in my corner makes the fear manageable.

As the cameras start rolling on the last take of the last scene before we break for lunch, the additional coffee I'd had that morning makes its presence known in my bowels. And, of course, it is a very tense, high-stakes scene during which no crew member even dares exhale too loudly. Mra's ex-fiancé has shown up right as Nanda was about to profess his undying love for her, and he's asking her if she knows without a doubt which one of them she wants to be with because a part of *him* has known ever since she walked into the office five years ago that she was it for him, and she's crying, and I would be crying, too, if it weren't for the fact that I am now really wishing I hadn't worn a thong today of all days.

"You good?" Jason whispers when he catches me tiptoeing out.

"Yeah," I whisper back. "Bathroom."

Once I'm outside, I power walk to the ladies' bathroom, pleading my butt cheeks to stay squeezed for a few seconds longer.

I try the first door. "Occupied!" someone calls out, and the unturning latch confirms it.

"Sorry!" I say.

I rush over to the adjacent one, which is, yep, *also* occupied.

Stepping back to command my first place in queue, I try not to squirm too much, but the hideous gurgling sounds now coming from my gut make it clear that nature is about to call regardless of my ability to stay still. *Just one minute,* I plead with my body. *Please, please, please.* Once I hear the familiar sounds of digital candy being crushed in one of the stalls, I know two things: one, neither of them are going to be done in one minute, and two, *I* do not have more than one minute.

The only other place on set with a bathroom that I can access is Tyler's trailer, which I have a key to because that's where I leave my stuff. So that's where I sprint for, like a hurricane is on my tails and that trailer is my sole source of shelter.

I flush after a few minutes because while I might not be sleeping with Tyler, I still don't want him knowing what my shit smells like. Right as the water bowl refills, I hear the front trailer door click, and my ass cheeks inadvertently tighten once more, this time with trepidation and slight embarrassment.

Should I call out? What do I say? *Tyler? Hey, it's me, I'm taking a shit, FYI.* But it'd be weirder if I sat here and kept pooping covertly, right? Do I cough loudly?

"Sorry to cut into your lunch break, but I thought you guys should be looped in. I had a long call with Legal this morning."

Yasmin's voice screeches my train of thought to a complete stop. I definitely don't need *her* knowing I'm taking a shit. Guess we're going with covert pooping.

"About?" Tyler asks.

"Apparently, the police have been in touch."

"What? I thought that was over," May says. "They haven't been here since last week."

"Has there been a new development?" Tyler asks. Maybe it's because I can't see his face so my auditory senses are heightened, or maybe it's because I know him better now, but I can parse the tension in his voice.

"No," Yasmin answers. "Well, at least no developments in the sense of no new connections to us."

"So then why are they still contacting us?" Tyler asks. "We've answered all their questions."

Yasmin lets out a long exhale. There's pacing, and then the sound of someone (presumably her) settling down on the leather couch. "Look, I'm going to lay it out. The cops were *tactful* about this part, but from what Legal understands, the Australian embassy isn't going to let them close this case without finding the culprit. One of their citizens dies in Yangon and the police back off simply because it was near a film set? It'll look like they were lenient and lazy at best, and intentionally looked the other way at worst."

"But they have no evidence to prove it was any of us," May scoffs. "They're fishing in the middle of a desert. They can't arrest anyone."

"No, they can't," Yasmin agrees, but her voice doesn't make it sound anything close to good news. "But they *can* revoke visas and filming permits, and we've barely shot a quarter of the scenes we wanted to do here. It doesn't help that the Shwedagon Pagoda scene is both a key one *and* one that we can't do in a lot, and I don't want to jinx it and even start *thinking* about rewriting such a significant portion of the script, but if they put up enough red tape—"

Tyler barks out a laugh. "On what grounds? Those lawyers get paid literal thousands of dollars an hour and they can't even—"

"Obstruction of justice—"

"But it's *not* obstruction of justice—"

"They're not our only problem."

"What?" comes May's voice. "What else?"

"The studio is getting . . . antsy."

"Antsy?" Tyler echoes.

I imagine Yasmin nodding. "One of my friends who works there told me that there was a closed-door meeting. Rumor is they're considering pulling the funds."

"What?!" May yells.

At the same time, Tyler shouts, "Like fuck they are!"

"Okay," Yasmin's tone takes on one of a mediating parent, "it's still talks, but they are worried about what might happen if this leaks to the press. The authorities are doing a good job of keeping it a secret so far, and I know everyone on set has signed NDAs, but someone is going to talk at some point. And if I had to guess, the studio's drawing up a cost-benefit analysis right now to see if they should cut their losses early."

"You cannot—" comes Tyler's low grumble, but he's cut off by a phone's ringtone.

"Hello? Yeah, I can talk, one sec." Yasmin's voice drops. "I need to take this. I didn't want to worry you guys, but like I said, I thought you should know. We'll circle back later."

There's a long silence between the trailer door closing and May speaking. When she does, her words are wary but firm. "Ty," she's saying. "This is serious."

"They're fishing, getting desperate. Trying to scare us."

"Well, it's working." She sounds *just* as petrified as I was when I said those exact same words to him.

"It's fine. We only—"

"No, Tyler, it's *not* fine!" May snaps. "Khin has to come clean."

"How dare you even suggest that? Absolutely not." It's such a sharp reply that even I recoil in my porcelain seat.

"Tyler," May says. I can see her curled up on the couch like she was when she revealed that she knew, two fingers pinching the bridge of her nose. "I know she's scared and *I* would absolutely be, too, but we're going to get her the best lawyers. I'll help out. We're going to make sure she gets a fair—"

"She won't. It doesn't matter what we do, because it's not going to be fair, not for her," he says. Because he understands. He listens, and he remembers and knows and understands. "Besides, I thought you liked her. *You* were the one who came up with the cover story for her pen."

"I *do* like her," May says without missing a beat. I can tell she means it, but I also don't miss the underlying caution in her tone. "But I came up with that story because I thought I was helping you. I want to help *both* of you, but Ty . . . *you* are my priority. Khin is great, but she's not my best friend. She killed a man—"

"You know it was self-defense."

"Then she can tell that to the police."

"She's not going to the police."

"Tyler!" May says brusquely, losing her softness. "You heard Yasmin!"

"Khin could lose everything—"

"*We* could lose everything! How long do you think it'll be until either of us gets another job? How long do you think it'll be until *Yasmin* gets another job? She's an Asian woman director in Hollywood, and her first-ever feature film gets killed because of a murder scandal? Do you think Burberry won't rip up my contract if this gets out? And you can say goodbye to the Bond role—"

"I don't care about the Bond role—"

"Well, I do!" May's crying at this point. Her words sound like they're thrashing around on choppy seas. "I get that you care about Khin, but I care about you! And I know you're mad at me right now for saying all of this, but I have to because it's us. I have your back and you have mine—that's how this works. And Khin is amazing, she really is, but . . ." On instinct, something in my heart hardens, calcifies, prepares me for what is about to come. "What I'm trying to say is, Khin doesn't fit in here. She can't. This isn't a movie, Ty. She's not . . ."

"Not what?" Tyler scoffs, and I grit my teeth, uncertain if there is a single word out there in any language to encapsulate the emotion that's taken over me.

"She's not going to stay," May says quietly. "She can't. And neither can you. When we finish shooting here, you two are going to go your separate ways and live out the rest of your lives in opposite corners of the world, and that's it. Except, that won't be it, because I know you. You're too soft for this, too honest, too *good*. You are the best person I know, Ty. You're hiding it, but I know how anxious this must be making you, and telling the truth is the only thing that's going to make you feel better. Otherwise, this secret is going to haunt you for the rest of your life, and I'll be damned if I don't step in and at least try to stop that from happening. So please, for both of your sakes, please tell her to turn herself in."

After a considerable pause, Tyler replies, "She won't do it."

"She will if you ask her."

"I'm not doing that. I will do almost anything you ask me to, May, but not this. She's—" He takes a deep breath. "She's going to be alone in this if I turn my back on her. And I'm not doing that to her."

"Tyler." I've never heard May sound so desperate. So frightened. She's genuinely frightened. For herself, for Yasmin, for the movie. For him. "Do you think she'd do the same if the situation were reversed? Do you think she'd jeopardize her whole career for *you*?"

"I know she would," he replies instantly. My heart trips at the conviction in his voice. "Khin is a *good* person, loyal to the bone."

May's chuckle is so light that I'd have missed it if my ear were just two inches farther away from the door. "And you're in love with her," she says.

"That's—" He stops, and my mind plays an unprompted game of Mad Libs. *Ridiculous. Inaccurate. The absolute furthest from the truth.* "—irrelevant," he finishes.

Oh, I think, not even jumping at the knocks on the front door, followed by a muffled voice telling them that Yasmin said to eat lunch because shooting's going to resume soon and both May and Tyler yelling back, "Okay!"

I remain on the toilet for an additional ten minutes, partly to make sure that Tyler doesn't come back because he forgot something, and partly because it feels like my whole body has been anesthetized. At last, I hoist myself up, wash my hands, exit the bathroom, and, because I can't quite go out and face Tyler and May and Yasmin yet, not now that I know the pressure they're quietly bearing on everybody else's behalf, I drop down onto the couch.

Just then, I become acutely aware of a buzzing beside me. I'm so out of it that I stare at my phone for a solid three seconds before realizing *that's* what's buzzing, and that to stop said buzzing, I should answer it. "Hello?"

"Khin?"

"Yes?" I can't ascertain if I can't place the voice because I don't know whom it belongs to, or because it still feels like I'm processing the world from the other side of a dirty windshield.

"It's Dipar."

"Dipar? Hey! How . . . are you?" I ask, my brain going from blank to a hundred in a matter of seconds. Is this a trap? Are the police listening? Do I really watch too much *SVU*?

"I'm good, thanks. Just got back from holiday. After I found out about Jared, my girlfriends decided I needed to take some time off to process and they essentially kidnapped me to the beach," she says with a stifled laugh.

"That sounds . . . good," I say. I know it's such an incompetent adjective in this context, but the past twenty minutes are all collating into something so unmanageable that "good" is about as expansive as my vocabulary is at the current moment. "They sound like good friends."

"They are. I'm . . . calling to thank you," Dipar says after a pause. "You . . . you saved my life. And you don't even know it."

"What?" If this *is* a trap, I have to hand it to her, it's a good one. If the police are trying to disarm me, it's working.

"I know why he was stalking you."

The blood shoots to my head like a bullet. I instantly know what she means, but it's like there's a barrier that my brain has erected to protect me from the whole truth, even if it's precisely what I've been searching for this whole time. "He as in—"

Her voice sounds muffled through the thumping of my heart in my ears. "Jared," she says.

My fingers seize around my phone. "Why?"

"Because I was pregnant and he thought I got an abortion."

It feels like someone's turned on the windshield wipers to try to give me a clearer view, but not quite managing to. "Why would he think that?"

Dipar's rueful laugh gives me the answer first. "Because I did." I *feel* her dragged-out inhale and exhale more than I hear it. "I'd been wanting to leave him for a while," she says, voice lowering. Now I'm certain this call isn't being tapped, at least not to her knowledge, because she's talking with the solemnity of someone who was going to take this to the grave. "When I found out I was pregnant, I *knew* I couldn't have a child. Definitely not now, and absolutely not with him. I had the abortion and spent the night at my sister's, and when I came home the next day, he'd found the pregnancy test while taking out the trash. I lied and said I hadn't wanted to tell him until I could confirm at the doctor's, but when I went, it turned out I'd miscarried. And *then* I told him that the whole thing got me thinking, and I didn't see us having a future together, and that my sister was waiting downstairs, and I would be packing my bags and leaving. He must've sensed that something was up, hadn't believed that I had a miscarriage, and when he googled about abortions in Myanmar—"

"My article was the first hit."

"Yes," she confirms. "I would know because it's what saved my life. I emailed you under a fake name and fake email, and you connected me with your friend. That's how I got your number, by the way. I don't want you thinking *I'm* stalking you, too." We share a short, bitter laugh.

"Why . . . are you telling me all this now?" I'm scared to know the answer, but I'm more scared *not* to.

She draws in another long inhale. "The police talked to me the day after you found me, that night at the club. I had to remember to be shocked at hearing about Jared's death."

"Did you tell them—"

"No," she cuts me off. "Like I said, Jared was not a good person, and somehow, I knew I shouldn't be telling them that you'd been asking about him, too. But anyway, that's not why I called. I'm calling because—" Another inhale, another pause. "They came again yesterday. Or, more precisely, I went to see them. They called me while I was away, something about *new evidence*, so I explained my situation and told them I'd come in as soon as I was back in town. So I finally did, which was when they showed me . . . the phone."

"The photos," I say, blood pounding at a thousand decibels against my eardrums.

"Yes."

"They . . . didn't tell you about the phone before? Because that's how they found out his identity, which was how they must've tracked you down."

"I'm pretty sure I was also on their suspect list, so they didn't want to show me all of their cards."

"And . . . now?" Now she's no longer on their list. Which leaves—I can't even finish the thought.

"Now they must be getting desperate, because they showed me the photos," her voice slices through my anxiety. "And then they told me your name and what you did and asked if I knew you, or if Jared had known you, if there was any way your paths would've crossed, and as soon as I heard your full name, it all clicked. I knew what he'd done. I knew what . . ." She hesitates, but I already know how the sentence ends. "*You'd* done."

I'm already crying, and no matter how deeply or frequently I suck in air, it's not enough oxygen. "It was self-defense, I swear!"

Dipar's voice, however, remains level. "I know. I knew that must've been the case. Which is why I also told the cops that I had lied to them the first time, when they'd asked me if I knew anything about the fight that he'd gotten into before he died."

"Dipar," I say, ice spreading from my fingertips down to my toes. "You can't . . . What did you—"

"That he didn't take the combination of the miscarriage and breakup well. That he showed up at my sister's place that night. I knew she'd back me up if it came to it. But I told them he was drunk as always, which was true. And then I remembered them telling me about the marks on his face, and I explained that things got physical when I refused to get back together, and at one point he had me pinned against a wall and the only way I could make him let go was by grabbing the nearest sharp object, which was a pen, and stabbing him in the ear, which was why he had those injuries. Obviously, none of that was true, but it could've been. Anyone who knew Jared wouldn't have been surprised at that."

My breath shakes. "Didn't they get suspicious that you'd lied to them the first time around?"

"Yes, but I explained that I knew how it'd look. He's a white man, and we get into a physical fight on the same night that he shows up dead? I knew I'd immediately be their first suspect. But as luck would have it, I *did* have a solid alibi that night. My friends have been dead set on a mission to get me over this breakup, and now I'm actually *thankful* that they've been dragging me out to clubs every other night. I gave the cops the name of the club I was at on that particular night, explaining I'd gone out to clear my head and also to be around people in case he returned to the apartment. They could check the club's CCTV footage if they wanted. We might've gotten into an argument at my place, but he was alive when he left."

"Dipar." My voice is coarse. "You could've gotten into serious trouble. You *still* could."

"I know, but I would do it again in a heartbeat. Here's the thing—in that moment, I knew *I* had a solid alibi and that you didn't, and the choice was . . . clear." Her voice takes on a steeliness, the kind that you can't fake. "I stayed with him as long as I did, as long as I *could*, because despite it all, I did love him. But you know the first thing I felt that night that you told me he was dead?"

"What?"

"Relief. I was *relieved*. That's when I knew I'd made the right decision by leaving. You know—" She pauses. "I'd always wondered if I'd ever meet you in real life. You saved my life, Khin, without a doubt. I just returned the favor."

"Thank you," I say. It feels both not enough and yet all that needs to be said. "Just . . . thank you."

"You're welcome. But Khin?"

The caution in her voice makes my stomach roil in a new way. "Yeah?"

"I hope that what I did was enough, although I'm not sure it was. Maybe I'm reading too much into it, but those two detectives, they seemed to be really upset about your article. They kept circling back to it, showing me different photos of your face, repeatedly asking if I was *sure* I didn't know you. It was clear that they wanted me to turn on you, make me jealous, try to frame you as someone Jared was obsessed with more than he was with me or whatever."

Just like that, the wisps of hope and relief that I'd started to feel vanish. I bite down hard on my lip to hold back a sob. "Thanks for the heads-up," I say.

"Anytime. Again, thank *you*. I have to go, but . . . stay safe, okay?"

I nod, the tears practically gluing the screen to my cheek at this point. "Okay. You take care of yourself, too."

Outside, someone yells, "We're resuming shooting in twenty, people!"

"I'll see you on set," says Tyler over his back, closing the trailer door and already two steps in before he halts at the sight of me. "Oh my god, Khin," he says, rushing over. His hands reach out for my face but stop themselves in time, and, ever the boundary-respecting gentleman, he instead restrains himself to tilt up my chin with the back of his knuckles. "What's wrong? Did something happen? Is it the police? Did they call again? What can I do to help?"

"No, it's . . . stupid. I popped in to use the toilet."

He raises one brow to point out that that doesn't explain the crying part.

"I'm . . . PMS-ing, and I watched this video of this dog who got abandoned by her family and anyway—" I wave my phone in the air. "I'm okay, just need a minute."

"You're crying alone in my trailer because you watched a video of an abandoned dog," he deadpans.

I take a tissue from the coffee table and blow my nose. "Look, dude," I say, scraping together as much tenacity as possible. "I can show you my period tracker app if you want," I offer, realizing that my period seems to be my go-to excuse for any tricky situation.

For a beat, I worry that he'll challenge me on it. But then he raises his palms and moves backward. "Sorry. But still, is there anything I can do?"

"Yeah," I say, nodding. "Are you and May free today? After shooting? There are some things I want to go over. About the investigation. Strategize. And . . . stuff." I am a *wordsmith* today.

To my surprise, Tyler sits up and points a finger at me. "That sounds like a *great* idea. I was actually going to suggest the same thing." His voice has perked up, and his mouth is splitting into a smile that seems to want to grow larger already.

"You . . . were?" I ask, confused. Then it hits me—maybe he and May kept talking after they left the trailer, and she managed to convince him to convince me to go to the police. Maybe he's working overtime to put on an "everything's fine" air so as to ease me into the whole thing.

"Yeah. Your place okay?" There's a knock at the door. "Yes?"

"May's left her trailer," Tun yells from the other side.

"I'll be out in five!" Tyler yells back. He gets to his feet and I follow suit. We remain motionless, staring at each other in the foot of space between the coffee table and couch. At last, he grimaces and signals toward the bathroom. "Do you, um, mind leaving and meeting me at the set? Sorry, I feel weird peeing while I know you're on the other side of the door."

I suppress a rueful laugh. "See you on set."

Seventeen

In the carpool back to my place, something is way off. May and Tyler stick to strict work talk, neither of them making eye contact with me or letting me too deep into the conversation. It feels, frankly, like I'm third-wheeling while they're talking in secret best friend code that I'll never decipher. Eventually, I stop trying to. Whatever it is they're buying time to attempt to break to me, they're going to have to say it outright anyway when we arrive at mine.

Despite my fears, there's no crowd at my building, and we park and make our way up without any of the other residents spotting them. I fish out my keys, unlock my door, take a step inside, and, conscious of how quiet both of them have gone behind me, flick the light switch. *Let's get this out of the—*

"Surprise!" Nay and Thidar leap out of the storage closet a few feet away.

"Aaahh!" Eyes squeezing shut, I stumble back. I miss a step and get that sinking feeling when you know your butt is seconds away from making contact with the floor. Except it never does. Instead, my butt makes contact with Tyler's waist as one of his hands wraps around my stomach, and the other, my arm.

"I got you," he says.

"Thanks," I say, rapidly readjusting myself when I see the way Nay and Thidar are smiling at each other. "What the hell was that?!" I yell. When I glance back, May's and Tyler's faces are lit with giant grins.

"It's your surprise housewarming!" Thidar says with glee. She points over my shoulder. "I texted Tyler an invitation. And also to make sure you came straight home after work. And also to find out what *time* you'd be home from work."

I try to purse my lips in an incensed manner at Tyler and May, but I'm smiling too hard to even remotely succeed. "You guys are *such* liars!" I say.

"Hey, we're not Oscar-nominated actors for nothing," May says, opening a palm that Tyler, still grinning, slaps.

"But surprise!" Nay throws out her hands in a *ta-da!* gesture. "Do you like it?"

I step inside and motion at Tyler and May to join me. "Like wh—" I start, but a flash at the end of the hallway where it opens up into the living room catches my eye. Strung across the floor-to-ceiling glass windows is a banner with gold glitter letters that say I LIKE TO MOVE IN MOVE IN. Next to it, I count precisely four transparent helium balloons filled with confetti floating about. To be honest, the balloons look sad in the shadow of the giant glitter banner.

"You guys!" I laugh. "Why are there *four* balloons?"

Thidar chances a glance at Nay before widening her eyes at me to warn, *Don't get her started.*

With an exasperated sigh as though she's had to answer this exact question multiple times already, Nay explains, hands flinging about in frustration, "I told the store *forty* over the phone. However, it turns out the connection was spotty and they heard four. And when I got there, I was like, *Where's the other thirty-six?* And they're like, *What thirty-six? You said four* and gestured at these—" She points at the balloons bobbing around. "—like, *Duh. Can't you count to four?* And I asked, *Why would I want four balloons?* And the woman was like, *I dunno, maybe it's for a toddler's fourth birthday party,* and I asked, *Do I look like I'm dressed for a toddler's fourth birthday party?*" She stops to gesture theatrically at her lilac pantsuit. "So *then* I told them I specifically asked for forty and—"

"It's perfect," I say, seizing her by the shoulders.

"Really?" Nay asks with a small smile.

I nod. "Really. Three for each of us, and one for extra luck."

"Awwwwww." Thidar leaps forward and throws one arm around each of us. "So? Were you surprised?"

To be honest, part of my brain is still somewhat distracted by Dipar's call and what Yasmin revealed, but my friends' faces are so buoyant that it positively melts me. I push away everything else, because *this* is what I want to focus on right now. "Yes. Thank you. Just . . . thank you," I say, pulling them in closer to me, wanting to permanently print this moment, this feeling, on my heart forever.

"Mwah!" they say simultaneously, and the switch clicks in tandem with them placing a kiss on either side of my cheeks.

All this stressing and scheming and hiding is piling up like a giant mental Jenga tower, and as much as I'd like to keep pretending that I'm on top of things, I know I am a handful of moves away from the whole tower collapsing. My gaze catches on the pile of shoes by the door, and it occurs to me that I can't remember the last time I had so many shoes gathered there. I've missed all of this more than I'd let myself acknowledge—being with my friends, throwing parties, having *fun*. Not being on the run every minute of every day. Remembering how to just . . . *be*.

I want it back.

And there's only one way I can do that.

This secret of mine has cost me so much already, and it will only continue to drain me until I am a shell; I can see that now. But that's not all. If this tower *does* come crashing down, I'm not the only one who'll be buried underneath. It's already prompted Dipar to lie to the police. The whole movie—this movie that I know means *so much* to Tyler and May and Yasmin—is on the verge of being shut down. It feels wrong to keep any secret, but especially one this big, from Nay and Thidar, but if I tell them, I have no doubt they'll lie for me, too. *They* will put everything on the line, too. All for me. All *because* of me.

The sight of my office door out of the corner of my eye sparks a memory, and I immediately look over at Tyler, who's whispering something into May's ear, both of their faces still creased with glee. *You are a* good *person,* I think as I remember the whiteboard in that room—and now, I feel like a fool because I can't believe that I ever considered he could be anything *but* good. That at one point, I viewed him as just an actor whose secrets I could use as stepping stones to a glamorous *Vogue* job. I mentally wipe the whole board clean, all those little threads that I wanted to pull at and unravel to discover who Tyler Tun *really* was. I know who he is now. I'm not printing his secrets, which I also know means I'm not getting the *Vogue* job this time. In fact, I know with certainty that after tomorrow, I'm not *ever* getting this job—or probably any other full-time media job again, for that matter—but that's okay.

The epiphany doesn't feel like an epiphany, because epiphanies are meant to be sudden, unforeseen. I've seen this one coming for a long time in my peripheral vision; I just didn't want to acknowledge it. But I know how this movie ends now.

"Hey, are you . . . tearing up?" Thidar asks, a frown tugging her brows together.

"I'm PMS-ing." I dab my eyes before she can turn it into A Thing, and, remembering something, stretch my neck to look around. "Wait, where's Pa—"

"Out of the way, people, fresh lasagna coming through!" Patrick says, rounding the corner from the kitchen, *my* turquoise Le Creuset baking dish in hand, and we all part for him.

"Hi!" Nay bares her teeth at the two newcomers by my side. "I'm Nay! We haven't met!"

Tyler's face splits into another grin. "No, we haven't, but I've heard a lot about you. I'm Tyler."

"And I'm May." May waves at the two of them. "I haven't met either of you."

The beginnings of a squeal leave Thidar's mouth, and she covers it up with an un-coy cough. "Hi, May," she says. I can see her hands shaking. "We're big fans. My fiancé and I. Oh, that's him," she says, tipping her head over at Patrick, who is singlehandedly laying out the table like he's plating in a *MasterChef* finale.

"Hi," he calls as he straightens out the knives and forks against an invisible ruler. "I'd come over and say hi but I was put on food duty and told that if I fuck this up, I can find someone new to be engaged to, but the bad news is I'm hopelessly in love with my current fiancée so I can't afford to be distracted," he says in one rushed breath.

"Don't listen to him, he's always cracking weird jokes," Thidar adds with an embarrassed laugh. "None of us really get them. Shall we eat?"

"I'll get the beers," I say, starting for the fridge. "I'm sticking to water because I have to drive May and Tyler back. But is everyone else drinking?"

"Not me," Patrick says.

"Me neither," Nay says. "But *you* have to drink! It's your house-warming!"

"We can take them back!" Thidar says. "We'll take Tyler, and Nay can take May. Hey, that rhymes!"

"Khin, you're not going to be on designated driver duty at your own housewarming!" May says.

"Fine, fine," I relent, realizing May's actually just as pushy as Nay and Thidar.

While the rest of the group diverts toward the table, Tyler follows me into the kitchen. "I'll give you a hand," he says with a smile that feels more flirtatious than it should.

I crouch down in front of the fridge and reach in to wrap my hands around two bottles when my body tenses, a relaxed soldier instinctively snapping to attention. He's pushed the door a bit farther and now we're hidden by it. He bends over beside me so we're at eye level, our cheekbones barely skimming. "Hey," I say, already feeling my brain start to unravel and forget the entirety of the English language, or, really, any language.

"Hey," he says.

"Thanks for this."

"I played a very minor role. And anyway, I wouldn't have missed it for the world," he says, and somehow, *somehow*, I know he means it. That even if the Oscars or Grammys were happening right now, he would still choose to be here.

Because he stays.

I turn a mental dial and lower the sound of laughter from the other room so I can focus on this. Right here. And for a minute, I let myself dream, like a young, wide-eyed actress who's just landed in Hollywood with dreams bigger than anything she's ever known.

I bet, I catch myself thinking, *I would actually like hiking if we hiked through a forest that smelled like your cologne.*

I bet, I catch myself thinking, *if the timing had been slightly different, this would've been something so incredible, even we wouldn't believe it if it hadn't happened to us.*

And I bet, I think, breath shaky, eyes dangerously close to filling up with tears that I do not want him to see, a warmth whose intensity is so blistering it hurts as it surges through my body. *If I loved you any less, I could bring myself to be selfish enough to keep you.* Because I do, I realize. I love him already. Not that I would ever tell him.

I thought I would be mad at May for wanting to turn me in, or even for wanting to get me to turn myself in; I definitely tried to be— but I can't. Because I understand. All she wants to do is protect him, because if she doesn't, then who will? *Golden boy with an actual heart of gold,* I think ruefully.

"What is it?" Tyler asks, lips so close to mine I can smell the mint.

"Stay." I say it without hesitation, but also without regret.

He studies me, exactly the way he did at our first meal—like knowing me is the easiest thing in the world for him. Maybe it is.

"Okay" is all he says before grabbing another two beers.

———

Dinner is good. More than good, it's *fun.* Ben and I used to host dinner parties at our place all the time, and no matter how tired I was, it would be the highlight of my whole week. Ever since I moved here, dinnertime—or any meal, for that matter—has merely been a case of me shoving enough food into my mouth to keep myself alive. One plate, one spoon and fork, one cup: minimal food, minimal company, minimal dishwashing.

But tonight, I don't mind that I can already see the tower of cutlery and plateware in the sink from here. I don't care that more than one piece of food has been dropped on the ground, more than one drop of the boys' disgusting beer-and-champagne concoction spilled. I could burst with the joy that stems from remembering that I am not alone, that I have never been alone, that if all of these people—these people who are *the* best people I know—have shown up here because they love me and want to celebrate me, then I cannot be as big of a disappointment of a human being as I thought. And the *least* I can do is try to live up to this incredible version of myself that they see.

When the banana and chocolate roti are brought out for dessert, I stand up and clear my throat.

"Yessss, speech!" Thidar whoops.

"Only if you don't turn this into a thing," I warn. She and Nay make matching zipping motions across their mouths.

"So—" I try to begin, only to make the huge mistake of making eye contact with my friends, and then I feel the corners of my lips dragging downward.

"Are we still not allowed to make this a thing?" Thidar mumbles out of the corner of her mouth.

"I don't know," Nay mumbles back, voice high-pitched. She grabs two tissues, handing one to Thidar. "But I hope she does this quickly because my nose is already getting stuffy."

Despite my attempt at staying stern, I laugh at my ridiculous, wonderful, absolutely bonkers best friends. "I put off this housewarming because when I first moved here, I didn't want to accept that this was my home now," I say, this time embracing the stinging tears. "Living alone again wasn't part of the plan. I was embarrassed and bitter and, more than anything, lonely. I didn't *want* this place"—I gesture at the space—"to be warm or even a home, because I was like a petty child, adamant that this *wasn't* my home. But I also didn't have my *old* home anymore, so I thought of this merely as . . . a shelter. A shelter during a really terrible, shitty storm. Just a life raft to cling to while I waited for the shore to reappear." I swallow, not realizing how fully I'd feel the weight of my words.

"But you know what?" I shoot Nay and Thidar a wry smile. "It turns out that despite all of my pouting, you guys have *already* turned this place into my home. Because it's true what they say. A house is only a home because of the people in it, and how can I stand here and look at all of you and still insist that this *isn't* home? You *are* my home."

"Oh no, there I go," Nay whimpers right before a loud sob claws out of her. "Sorry," she says, sniffling as Thidar shoves another tissue at her. "Continue. We are *not* making this a thing, we promise."

"You *are*, though," I say as a wet laugh bubbles out of me. "Home, I mean. And making it a thing, but mainly home. And you're the best, sturdiest, safest, most loving, warmest home I've ever known. And no matter what happens, no matter where I go—" My voice breaks, but I don't bother to fix it. These are my people. My people who have seen me at my lowest, and still chose to remain my people. "You will *always* be my home. Always."

The rest of the night is a jumbled collage of drinking games and non-drinking games, of outdoing one another to see who can add the weirdest song to the playlist blasting on the speaker (thank god for soundproof walls), and, for some reason, trying to attempt the world's highest ice-cream sundae. Tyler and May suck the helium out of the balloons and have a Tina Turner–themed sing-off, and I'm accused of being biased when I crown Tyler the winner.

After my first beer, I inconspicuously keep topping up my champagne glass with soda water—an old college trick—because I want to remember everything about tonight.

"Hey," Nay says and lifts her head while in the middle of trying to plank on the back of my couch. "This isn't a *weird* song. Who ruined the vibe?"

At her comment, my ears perk up and my gaze lands on Tyler, who gets up, walks in a remarkably straight line for someone who has had *a lot* of alcohol, and extends a hand.

"Why?" is what my fuzzy brain and roti-stuffed mouth ask as I stare at his hand.

He steps closer, close enough so that to everyone else behind us, it looks like he's simply leaning in to brush my hair behind my shoulder. "Because," he whispers, voice holding a million watts of energy that make me shudder, "it sounds like falling in love."

He escorts me several feet away, and there, in front of the faraway Yangon skyline, under a giant gold glitter banner that says I LIKE TO MOVE IN MOVE IN, against the sound of fake retching and "Get a room" jeers from our friends, I have my first dance with Tyler Tun.

"Blame it on the alcohol tomorrow?" I ask as I sway in his arms, feeling safe and happy and free.

He nods. "Absolutely the alcohol."

No one asks twice when Tyler says he'll stay behind to "help with the cleanup," but no one leaves without shooting us sky-high, *Could you guys at least pretend to be subtle?* eyebrow raises either. Maybe it *is* because of the alcohol in their case, or maybe because I haven't been able to hide my splitting grin the whole evening, but even Thidar and Nay give me short, approving nods as we hug goodbye.

And then we're alone.

I spin around and flatten my back against the door. "Hi," I say. Heat circulates through me like I'm a closed-circuit loop, making me scared and exhilarated and sweaty and dizzy all at once.

Smiling like he has the whole night, smiling at *me* like he has the whole night, like I am just the most mesmerizing thing he's ever seen, Tyler approaches me with long, deliberate steps. "Hi," he says.

"You stayed," I say.

"I did." Then, "I said I would."

"Do you always keep your word?" I ask.

He closes the distance, and braces his hands against the door, around my shoulders, but doesn't touch me. "Yes," he says.

"Tyler—" I breathe.

At the same time, he asks, "What are we doing, Khin?"

I swallow. "What do you mean?"

"I thought we agreed that we can't do this."

"We did," I confirm.

"Then why—" He tilts his head and smiles, as though *now* he's got a better angle of my face. "Did you ask me to stay?"

"Why"—I lift a challenging brow—"did you agree to stay?"

He doesn't answer. He doesn't have to. I know why he stayed, just like he knows why I asked.

I bet, I think as he lifts my chin up with one finger so I have to look right into his eyes. *You would be the best sex I ever had.*

"Can we . . . go to bed?" I ask, not recognizing my own voice. When hesitation flickers across his eyes, I give him a reassuring smile. "I mean just . . . go to bed. Can we change into pajamas and crawl under the covers and maybe put on *SVU* and you . . . hold me until I fall asleep?"

Can we pretend for one night? is essentially what I'm asking.

And in spite of his obvious wariness, he nods with a gentleness that tells me he understands.

I don't bother with sexy lingerie, instead emerging from my wardrobe in a pair of gray silk sleep shorts and a giant white T-shirt with several toothpaste stains on the front. But the speed at which Tyler's mouth drops, and the visibly uncomfortable way in which he fidgets as he sits up and pulls back my side of the covers to motion at me to join in—it sets off a sharp yet delightful pain behind my solar plexus.

He's stripped down to his boxers, and as I place my cheek against his warm bare chest, hand grazing against his stomach when I reach for the remote, so many jolts zing through me that my mattress might as well be covered in electric fence netting.

"Hey," I say into his chest as I pick an episode. "Tell me a secret."

He considers it for a long time. "I cried at the end of *Moana*."

I bark out a surprised laugh and pull back so I can see his face. He's grinning, and when he grins like this with his full face, he looks nothing like the next 007 and everything like who May was talking about: the boy with the big, unrelentingly soft heart. "That is *not* a secret," I say. "*Everyone* cried at the end of *Moana*."

"Hmm," he says. His thumb slides under my shirt and makes a sideways swiping motion just above my waistband. "I . . . am worried you wanted to sleep with me tonight but then you changed your mind, but you'd already told me to stay so you felt bad about—"

"Tyler." I stop him by placing a finger on his lips. When he kisses it, I all but let out a moan. "None of that is true."

"You didn't want to sleep with me tonight?"

I mean to say *No*, but what comes out is "No?"

Of course, he catches the inflection at the end. "Liar," he says. Then, smile easing, "So why *did* you ask me to stay?"

Instead of answering, I trail my finger up and across his face. At one point, it's like it takes on a life of its own, achingly tracing every single one of his features before returning to his lips. "Isn't it obvious?" I ask, and his face scrunches up in a way that is so *cute* I want to grab it and kiss it.

His smile expands so wide, it looks like it's going to hook onto his ears. "Wanna play a game?" he asks.

"Always," I whisper deviously.

"If *this*—" He tilts his chin at me, and then tucks it back toward himself. "—*could* be possible, what kind of couple do you think we would be?"

"Oh, the kind that makes out literally everywhere. Have you seen us? We're *hot*."

He laughs, then asks, "In a booth, would we sit across or next to each other?"

"Across," I say immediately. "Tyler, we're not sociopaths."

"Would we . . . have nicknames?"

"No. I don't do nicknames. The occasional 'sweetheart' or 'honey' is fine, but no cutesy inside-joke nicknames. I don't like them. I'm not a toddler."

He nods like he's taking this seriously. "Noted."

"Where would we go on our first vacation?" I ask. I know we're way beyond playing with fire now; we're in the middle of a several-miles-long burning coal walk. And it should hurt, the pain should be making every single one of my nerve ends scream with delusion—but Tyler's still here beside me, and so it doesn't.

"Somewhere quiet," he says after a thoughtful pause. "Maybe a small village in Vietnam, by the mountains or—"

"Woah there, buddy." I shake my head, horrified at even the thought. "I don't do villages."

He flashes me the half smile. "You don't *do* villages?"

"Nope. No villages, nothing nature-y. And god, definitely no-where quiet. I like cities. The bigger, the better." I study him more closely. "Is this going to be a deal-breaker?"

"Khin," he says through a laugh. The hand on my back sprawls out so he can draw me closer to him. When I throw one leg across his, he makes a grunting sound. Recomposing himself, he says, "*Nothing* would be a deal-breaker. No villages."

"Is that what you want?"

"Huh?"

I hitch a shoulder. "Quiet. Is that what you want? Do you want to move somewhere quiet? Do quiet things?"

"Honestly?" His hand resumes drawing horizontal lines on my skin. "I . . . don't know. *Sometimes* I think it's what I want."

He doesn't know what he wants, May had said. Truthfully, a part of me is glad to see she was right. That makes this easier. I can't break his heart because no one, including me, can even have it in the first place.

"But my parents live here," Tyler goes on. "And I have to look after them, and after Jess, and then there's also May. I can't just unplug and go be a hermit for the rest of my life."

"Right," I say.

"Hey," he says, shifting in response to my own mood shift. "What *is* going on here? Not that I'm necessarily complaining," he hurries to clarify. "But . . . why are we doing this? Will this not . . ." He winces before he speaks again. "Make things worse in the end? Harder?"

I smile, the tears in my eyes thickening. "We can pretend for a night, can't we? Besides, we never know what's going to happen in life, right? So whenever you have something wonderful, you should make the most of your time with it. And you, Tyler Tun, as *exasperating* as you might be from time to time—" I twist my body and hold his face in both hands. "Also happen to be the most wonderful thing I've ever laid eyes on."

And I will keep you safe, I silently think, right before *I* kiss *him* first this time. Soft mouth that betrays far too quickly and easily just how soft his core also is. The same mouth that says things like, *Do you have any idea how much I want to kiss you right now?* and *I've got you* over and over until you believe it, and belongs to a good man who does way, way more than simply talk the talk.

Do you have any idea how much trouble your mouth could cause? I want to ask. *Do you have any idea how much trouble it's already caused?*

Because look at us now, touching and kissing like the other is the first and only person we've ever done this with. Then again, I suppose in some ways it is. Because it's never been like this, not for me. I don't think it has for him either. Everywhere his fingertips make contact with my skin melts me like a blowtorch melting sugar.

Our first kiss had been fast and hungry, like we didn't know whether we'd ever get to do that again, two kids quickly sneaking one in while no one was around. This one, though—this one feels like the rest of the world no longer exists outside of this apartment, and now we get to take our sweet, sweet time doing whatever we want for as long as we want. It's just us. It's just us, and god what I would give to have it be this way forever.

I ignore how hard he feels, how wet I already am. We pretend not to hear the moans that sneak out of our throats. I cannot have—will never have—all of him, but when it comes to Tyler, having even a specifically measured, delicious increment feels like having the world. *Maybe,* I think, *it's better that I can't have him wholly*; love that big could ruin me for the rest of my life.

I force myself to savor this moment, memorizing how even though he still smells like pine trees, he tastes like red bean and egg tart and chocolate—and also mint and deep laughter and making out late into the night and every single splendid thing I didn't even know I was looking for, which shouldn't make sense, but with him, it does. Of course with him, it does.

You, I think as I nip on his bottom lip, the act drawing a low groan out of him. *Always you.*

"I want to take you out on a date," he says after the most delicious kiss of my life.

I smile even though hearing that just makes it all hurt more. "Where? Going to whisk me away to Paris on your private jet?"

He rolls his eyes. "Okay, I get it, my private jet and I are single-handedly responsible for global warming."

"Glad to have it on the record."

Shaking his head, he buries a kiss into my hair. "There's this great Indian place around the corner from my parents' house," he says. Despite the innocuousness of the sentence, it's the way he says it, low into my ear like it's a promise he's intent on keeping, that makes a tremble zig and zag through me.

"And LA?" I ask, more tears filling the cracks in my voice.

"What about LA?"

"How—" I swallow. "How do we keep this going? What happens after this hypothetical date? When you go back to LA?"

His face is still buried in my hair, but I hear the way his exhale shakes. "We're pretending, remember? In this scenario, I don't go back to LA. Instead, I stay, and we have coffee together every morning out of one of those famed generic mugs of yours."

"Oh," I say, eyes prickling once more. "Okay."

"Okay," he repeats, like we could actually have this.

Eighteen

"How did your alarm go off before mine?" Tyler groans.

Because I turned off your phone and left it in between the couch cushions last night.

"Maybe your phone ran out of charge," I say, reaching to turn it off.

"Why is your alarm a duck quacking?"

"Because the sound of nature is the only thing that's annoying enough that I can't sleep through it."

"Ah, right, no nature," he says with a chuckle into the back of my head. When he increases the pressure of his palm on my bare stomach, every muscle in my gut tightens and my eyes fling open.

I take a deep breath. No distractions. I need to do this fast. "Breakfast?" I ask.

"You cook? Did I fall asleep next to the right Khin? Are you her secret domestic twin?" Tyler mumbles. "Kidding!" he says through a thick, sleepy laugh when I elbow him in the ribs. "Breakfast sounds great. What's on the menu, chef?"

It takes everything in me to maintain a smile as I look at him over my shoulder. I was already bracing myself for Disheveled Morning Tyler Tun, but my pulse jerks when I catch the actual sight of him, which is not so much disheveled as it is . . . rough, untouched, undone, naked (metaphorically, of course). His edges are round now and his curves, sharp. He looks, I suddenly realize, *exactly* like the kind of person who would talk to strangers on the plane.

"Why are you looking at me like that?" Tyler asks with a tentative smile.

"No reason," I say, allowing myself precisely three more seconds of staring before removing myself from his grasp and getting to my feet. I point across at my en suite. "And I'll see what I have in my fridge. You can use my bathroom if you need."

"I'm good," he says. He sits up and stretches through a yawn, forearms flexing on either side of his jaw. When he catches me looking, a smirk cracks. "Enjoying the show?"

I roll my eyes. "You are *so* full of it. I'll put on the kettle?"

"Yeah, thanks, I can't function without coffee in the morning."

"I know," I can't help but reply, although I ignore his questioning expression.

There's no point in trying to be subtle about it. As soon as I've stepped out and shut the door behind me, the *click* of the lock is loud and distinct.

"Khin?" Tyler calls out. I hear him scramble out of bed and walk over to the door, where he tries the handle before repeating, "Khin? What's going on?"

"Come on, Yale boy, what does it look like?" My sarcasm is swirled with tears. "I'm locking you in."

"What?" I can see him frowning despite the three inches of wood between us. "What?" he says again. "What do you mean you're locking me in?"

"I have to make things right," I say. I take a step forward, wishing that the door was at least made of glass so I could see his face.

"What the hell are you talking about?"

"You would've known something was up if I didn't come to work. And I know you would've locked *me* in a room if I told you what I was doing."

The handle jiggles again. "Khin, open the door."

"Sorry."

"You cannot be serious. You're going to leave me locked inside your bedroom?"

"Not forever!" I explain. "I'll text May in a couple of hours. Right before I—" The word won't come out, but even without saying it, the mere thought of it flips my gut upside down.

Tyler speaks slowly, softly, like he's approaching a person standing on a bridge's railing. "Right before you what?" I open my mouth, but my vocal cords are out of order. "Khin," he says in that goddamn way he says my name. "What are you doing?"

"Before I confess—" I get out in one breath.

"No, no way—"

"I heard you guys talking in your trailer. This isn't going away."

"But this isn't the solution!" The thud of his fist on the door makes me jump back. "It was both of us. If you're going to do this, I need to be there, too!"

"There's no point in both of us taking the fall for this. I'm the one who shoved that pen in his ear, who threw him over the bridge. All you did was stop *me* from falling over," I say, my voice stretched taut and thin. "I made a mistake. I have to own up to it. This person, the kind of person who recklessly jeopardizes the livelihoods of everyone around her because she refuses to own up to what she did—that's not who I am. That's not who I want to be."

I'm not expecting to hear the tears in his voice when he speaks. "Khin, please don't do this. We'll figure something else out."

"There's nothing else to figure out," I say calmly. "May was right. There's no way we could've kept this going—"

"No, you don't—"

"This is the only logical conclusion."

"What am I supposed to drink? You're going to let me starve to death in here?" It's a half-joke, half-desperate last-ditch attempt that, for a brief moment, cuts through the tension.

"My cup of water is still on my nightstand," I say with a miserable, unwanted laugh. "And I think I stashed a pack of Oreos in the drawer. They're vegan," I remember to add.

"What?"

"Oreos. Most people don't know it, but they're vegan."

"What if I'm allergic to Oreos?" he immediately counters.

That gets another laugh out of me. "You're not."

"How do you know?"

"Because." I start to back away. "I know you, Tyler."

I brush my teeth in the hallway guest bathroom with the spare toothbrush and paste I always keep in the cabinet, change into the set of clothes I left in my tumble dryer, and, as a last-minute and unconventionally sentimental gesture, I get one of my yellow mugs from the cabinet and place it in the middle of the otherwise empty dining table. Then, on the first piece of paper I can scrounge up—which just so happens to be a receipt at the bottom of my purse, because nothing screams "grand romantic gesture" like a scribbled note on the back of a receipt for one box of mints and a pack of bobby pins—I write: *I'm sorry I couldn't stay and have coffee together every morning.*

I'm not one for emotional goodbyes, but I can't help but stop at the door to survey the place one last time. I smile and nod to say, *Thanks for the memories.*

After coming at this from all angles, I've decided that I need to forget the police station and head for the Australian embassy. The detectives have made it clear that they have an agenda, but at least with Kira, I can be sure I'll get some semblance of a fair trial. And after doing a lot of research, I'm praying that I have this right, even if it is a technicality: if I confess in her office, it'll be on Australian soil, meaning she'll get primary jurisdiction over the case. One of the reasons Kira and I have always gotten along so well is because we're similar: hardworking, no-nonsense, blunt but fair. We might not be besties, but we *are* good friends, and I trust her as much as I can trust anyone in this situation.

The streets are still desolate at this hour, which cuts my travel time in half. I'm aware of my heart rate accelerating as the embassy gates come into view. You're not allowed to park in front of the building unless you're staff, so I find a place down the street.

"You got this," I whisper to myself as I take one last look in the rearview mirror.

Two bleary-eyed security guards are nursing tepid mugs of coffee when I walk up to the front shack. "Hi, do you have an appointment?" one of them leans down and asks through the small rectangular opening in the glass.

"I'm here to see Kira—" It takes me a second to recall her last name. "—Davis. Kira Davis."

The guard rubs the sleep out of his eyes, checks the time, and surveys me. "Do you have an appointment?" he asks. Beside him, the other guard swivels in his chair and grabs a clipboard—presumably a list of people who *do* have appointments.

"Not exactly. But we're good friends. Is she in? Can you please tell her Khin's here? Please, can you just call her?"

"I—"

I yank out my media accreditation card from my bag and place it against the glass. "I'm a journalist," I explain. "Kira knows me. Can you please call her and tell her Khin wants to speak to her?"

The guard leans in closer to study the card, and, deciding it's legit, holds up a finger as he picks up the phone. "Hi, Ms. Davis? There's a—" He peers back over at my badge. "Ma Khin Haymar here to see you. She says she's a journalist and . . . yes, will do."

I go through the usual proceedings: hand over my NRC card so they can take down my details, let them inspect my bag, go through the metal detector, and then one of them escorts me to Kira's office.

"Come in!" she yells out after the guard knocks on the door. She's behind a large wooden desk, mounds of paperwork outlining the edges. "Khin!" she says, face brightening when I close the door behind me; that should be a good sign. "Take a seat! It's been *forever!*"

"Busy morning?" I ask, nodding at the papers as I sit down opposite her.

She quickly types something on her laptop then pushes it to the side. "Do not get me started," she says, rolling her eyes.

I clock three separate empty mugs. She follows my gaze and gives a loud sigh. "Charlie says even my *hair* smells of caffeine these days and that it's like he's cuddling a coffeemaker in bed at night. But hey, it's either this or a concoction of highly illegal drugs, so—" She widens her eyes.

I snort out a laugh. "Things still good with Charlie?" I ask, aware that I'm stalling.

"I mean, it's been three years and I'm still not bored of him so I suppose that's a good sign. Anyway—" She steeples her fingers on the desk and shoots me a big smile. "What's up? What's brought you here at this godforsaken hour?"

Maintaining my own smile, I take in the deepest breath my lungs can contain. In a way, it feels *freeing* in this moment to know that whatever happens next is beyond my control. After weeks of always running, always trying to *figure things out*, to *stay ahead*, now I can let go. "It's . . . about that Australian man. The one that they found in the park." Kira lifts her head in an *ah* gesture. "Kira, I need to—"

"You sneaky little weasel, ambushing me without an appointment, asking about Charlie," she says. For a moment, my heart drops, thinking that somehow she already knows. Except, her mouth is still quirked upward. "Okay, okay, fine. Look, I can't give you an exclusive quote or interview, and I don't know who told you that we were releasing this today but—" she says, shoulders dropping in a surrendering sigh. "Since you got up this early and came all this way, I suppose you've earned the right to read the press release first."

I blink. "Wh—"

"But can you *please* tell whoever your editor is to not publish the story until we've officially released it to the public?" She's talking at her usual pace, which is approximately 150 miles a minute. "You can break it first, that's fine, but if a site publishes it before we've sent it out, then my boss and *their* bosses will be asking me what happened and I am already three coffees in at eight A.M. and I *really* do think I will explode if I drink more than five cups today, so just hold off on pressing the publish or submit button or whatever it is that you need to press to make a story live, yeah? I've just finished drafting it, hence the coffee, and Big Boss is going to look at it when she gets in in a few hours and then we'll send it out so you should be good to go by end of day."

"Good to—"

Before I can finish the question, Kira logs back into her laptop and hands it over to me. The first thing I catch is the official Australian embassy logo at the top center. Willing my brain to focus, I speed-read the whole statement. When I'm done, I read it another time, to make sure. Afterward, the only sentence I can form is "It was . . . a heart attack."

I lean back in my chair, fingers gripping the table's edge, but Kira doesn't notice because she's busy retrieving the laptop and putting it back to sleep.

"It was a heart attack?" I'm asking the question more for myself than her. "He wasn't . . . that's it? He died of a heart attack? There was no foul play?" I recall the exact phrasing in the letter. "I thought . . . the police were involved?"

"Don't you ever say I never do anything for you." Kira crosses her arms and gives me a devilish smile. "Basically, at first, the coroner said cause of death was blunt force trauma. But when the victim is a foreigner, it's usually protocol for the relevant embassy to hire their own separate coroner and perform another autopsy." I vaguely nod, feeling like I understand what she's saying, and also like I don't. "And *our* coroner determined that the cause of death was actually a heart attack. I mean, the dude's liver was absolutely wrecked from alcohol consumption and it's not like he was even close to being in the best physical condition, so it makes sense."

"But . . . the police," I point out.

"*That*," she says, widening her eyes, "is because at first, we were like, *Okay, well, that's too bad, but what can you do? Guess we'll start preparing the paperwork to fly him back home.* But *then* the authorities here were insulted that we'd said their coroner had fucked up. So then—" Her eyes look to the heavens for strength. "We had to get in a *third* coroner to determine who was correct. Because who cares about how much paperwork *that* requires, right? And who cares that *I* have to read through every single sheet of paper? But anyway, yesterday, we finally got that sorted and *that* coroner agreed that while there *was* blunt force trauma to his head due to the fall, which in turn was tragic but ultimately ruled an accident, especially given his post-mortem blood alcohol tests—but anyway, despite that, it *was* the heart attack that killed him. There was a small kerfuffle I think with some trauma in his ear as well, but they cleared that as having occurred in a separate incident. Honestly, it sounds like this guy was either always chasing down trouble, or trouble was chasing him. But now that's it. Case closed. The local police signed off on the closing paperwork last night. Praise Jesus or Buddha or Zeus or whatever entity you worship. I'm telling you, Khin, I am going to go to bed at eight tonight."

"That's . . . it?" I ask, my whole body trembling on this side of her massive table. "That's . . . the end?"

"Yep," Kira says, and reaches over to gulp down the last of the coffee in the mug closest to her. "I know it's not nearly as juicy as murder, but that's it. The. End."

Nineteen

I didn't kill him!" I yell as I slam my front door. Kicking off my shoes, I rush to make a right at the end of the hallway, then dig in my heels when I find Tyler sitting on my couch. I look over at my closed bedroom door, then back at him. "How did you—"

He holds up a bobby pin. "Found this in your bathroom."

"Oh, so you play *one* bodyguard role and now you're a master at picking locks?" I ask with a gentle mockery that freezes when he doesn't smile back. "Tyler?" I ask, stepping closer, although there's a part of my brain that warns me not to get *too* close.

"Hold up." He raises a hand, gaze widening. "You didn't kill him?" he asks, but it's like he's talking to me from the other side of a glass pane where I can see and hear him as usual, but it's *off*. "What happened then?" he prompts when I don't reply. And again, I can tell he's shocked and also relieved, but something is pulling him back from feeling the full extent of those emotions. It's like he's a muted, less expressive version of himself.

"It . . . was a heart attack." I'm still studying him for a clue as to the U-turn in his mood. Is he *that* upset that I tricked him and locked him in? "I went to the embassy, and my friend Kira showed me a press release that they're sending out today. The coroner ruled that the cause of death was actually a heart attack. Tyler," I say, attempting to infuse joy into the heavy air. "That's it. It's over."

He gives a short smile, nods, and the anchor in my gut drops lower. *Every* move he makes is making my senses tingle. "Good. That's . . . really good."

"Hey." With a few brisk steps, I sit down next to him and take his hand—except he stands up and walks away. "I'm really, really sorry about locking you in." I jump to my feet, knowing nothing good is going to happen after I ask this question. "How mad are you at me?"

You'd think that by now, I would have developed the ability to foresee huge life-shattering moments coming from a mile away. Except that's not how it works, is it? Because most of the time, life proceeds in a steady, unrecognizable blur, and you're unable to identify a big life-shattering moment until you are firmly in it. Sometimes it's sitting down for a dinner with your husband that starts with you asking "How'd your day go?" and ending with him saying "My lawyer will call you tomorrow" as he rolls out his pre-packed suitcase from behind the shoe cabinet. Another time, it starts out as a casual night stroll in the park and ends with you coming face-to-face with a stalker you didn't know you had.

And sometimes, it begins with you and the man you love, alone in your apartment, his brows furrowed, hands, you now notice, clenched into fists at his sides while he stands in front of the door opposite your bedroom. The door that you always keep closed but is now ajar, and suddenly you feel like those people on the beach who don't realize a tsunami has landed until it's too late.

"What's this room?" he asks.

"That's my office."

Another single nod. "I thought so. And the board? The one above the table? What's that?"

"The—" And I pause. Because I know. Because *he* knows.

"Sorry for invading your privacy," Tyler says as he opens the door, voice saturated with sarcasm. "But I was trying to contact your friends, you know, on account of you heading for jail and all, and thought maybe you hid my phone in here." He walks into the room, sunlight streaming through the windows and illuminating every corner and item, including the whiteboard.

I straggle in behind him, every step feeling like I'm trudging through quicksand. "I can explain. Please."

"Good," he says with a humorless voice that makes my pulse spike. "Because I have a few questions. First off, who's 'golden boy'?" I open my mouth, but nothing happens. "I'm assuming it's me, right?"

"Yes."

"And these are . . . what?" He waves around at the notes. "Ideas? Brainstorm sessions?"

My voice is thick. "Yes," I repeat.

I'm standing closer to him now and, for the first time, can see that his eyes are red. The thought of him crying alone in my apartment slashes deeper grooves across my heart. I want to reach out and hold his face, but I know that's the last thing *he* wants right now.

"For the *Vogue* story? Or for some deal you've made with a tabloid?"

"*Vogue.*"

"Really?" Tyler asks, already walking over and pointing at the two words I wish I could go back in time and stop my past self from writing down, even if it meant cutting off her fingers. "Why does that say 'abortion story'?" He stares me down for an answer, every one of his shields fully up. "Were you going to write about Jess?"

"No, of course not!" I blurt, finding my voice.

"Then why is it on the board?"

"Because—"

"How would *you* feel if I revealed a secret about *your* sister to the whole world?"

"My . . ." I trail off, confusion momentarily seizing me—until I remember. My lie at our first dinner. The lie that had felt inconsequential at the time but now feels like the thing that will do me in.

He stares at me for a long beat until realization hits. "You don't have a sister," he says through a dark chuckle.

I swallow. "No. I don't."

"Why did you say that you did?"

"Because—" My voice dies out, but I dredge it back up. "I needed to get close to you. Get you to trust me."

Tyler drags a hand down his face. He's trying to remain calm through the storm, but as always, his mouth gives him away; right now, it's twitching like mad, and I can only imagine everything he wants to yell at me. "What does—" He turns to the board, his jaw working as he emphasizes each syllable. "'Doesn't know what he wants. Not for you' mean?" His eyes flash back at me, and I cannot remember the last time I took a breath. If I take even half a step forward, I will collapse. "That's what you think of me? That I'm 'not for you'? And instead I'm, what? A project? One that you're simply laying out on a board and trying to reassemble for your article, grabbing as many pieces as you can even if it includes things I told you in confidence?"

"No, of course not. I was . . . Clarissa . . ."

At the mention of Clarissa's name, a new emotion splays across his face. It feels like the precise millisecond where the mug you dropped makes first contact with the ground, when it hasn't quite shattered yet, but you know the forthcoming damage is inevitable.

"What did Clarissa say?" he asks.

I take a deep breath and rip the Band-Aid off quickly. "I was trying to get a scoop on you, an exclusive. She said there were rumors—"

"Rumors?" he scoffs.

I give a stiff nod. "She said people are talking, saying that you've
been acting a little weird, clearing your schedule for something big.
That something's going on with you and that if I could find out what
it was . . ."

"What?" He takes one step in my direction, looking ready for bat-
tle. "What did she promise you if you could get a *scoop* on me? Was it
another cover story? The Oscars? Fashion week? Cannes? What—"
He places one palm against the wall, as if bracing himself for the answer. "—is my secret worth to you?"

What, I know he's asking, *is my trust worth to you?*

What am I worth to you?

Everything, is what I want to tell him.

"It doesn't matter, Tyler! Your secret was about Jess, and I *absolutely*
wasn't going to print that." I look over at the whiteboard, wanting to
scream at the stupid words I'd stupidly written and that now stare
back at me, taunting me in black and white. "And no, you weren't a
project—"

"Answer the question. You were offered something in exchange,"
he says in a voice of steel. I swallow, but it all tastes like bile. "What
was it?"

"A full-time position," I finally admit, emotion distorting my
voice. "She'd hire me as a full-time reporter."

"In Singapore," he clarifies. He can't blink back the tears anymore. Neither can I. He doesn't bother wiping them away. Neither
do I.

"Yes."

"I told you *everything*." His face is etched with uncontrollable rage, tears streaming down his cheeks, hair disheveled from how often he's grabbed at his roots. "Everything. I'm so stupid. So fucking stupid. This whole time, I thought we were a team, but I was some . . . some . . ." He stumbles over his words like a kid experiencing anger— real, unfiltered anger, the kind that makes your veins expand with boiling blood—for the very first time. There's no carefully crafted script that he's memorized. This is entirely him, raw and feeling the full depth of emotions that he's capable of. "Stupid . . . prized . . . farm animal. A . . . fucking golden ticket. Something that you . . . cash in at the end."

"No," I whisper. *Like he's a circus animal,* May's voice comes roaring back. "Tyler, none of that is—"

"You want your scoop?" He lets out a dark laugh. "Here it is. I'm retiring."

I jerk backward, like a dog on a pulled leash. "What?"

He gives a quick, small shrug. "This is the last movie I'm shooting. There you have it. Tyler Tun is retiring from acting. Put it in the headline, baby."

"But Bond," I stammer. "I heard you and May talking in the trailer. She said the offer was going to come in any day now."

"It did. Before I left LA. I turned it down."

"Oh my god. That call the other week. The—" *Studio stuff.*

"As you can imagine," he says in a monotone voice. "My team, as well as the studio, weren't—*aren't,*" he corrects himself, "thrilled that after years of careful deliberation, their first choice has said no. They keep roping me into calls to get me to reconsider, but I'm . . . not."

"Tyler," I breathe out. "You're . . . retiring? To do . . . what?"

"Come home. Figure out what *I* want to do with the rest of my life. Maybe eventually open up a drama school here? I don't know yet. All I know is that I'm done with acting. It was the Bond offer that made up my mind, actually. They said it'd be a minimum seven-year commitment, and instead of excitement, the first thing I felt was dread. There I was with an offer that actors spend their whole lives dreaming of, and the first thing I thought was, *Fuck, I have to do* this *for at least seven more years?* And that's when I knew I was done. I love acting, but it stopped being about acting a long time ago. I don't want to look back only once they've pushed me out and wish I could do things differently."

The information overload is overwhelming, dizzying—but also makes such perfect sense that I can't believe I missed it this whole time. Tyler saying he *wasn't making any plans.* Asking about adopting a dog. Why he'd fought so hard to get this movie funded, and how he had meant it when he said he'd *just wanted to shoot a fun movie with his best friend.* My chest squeezes when I remember him in bed last night, asking me about what kind of couple we'd be, throwing out ideas for a hypothetical first vacation. *Except,* I realize, and my chest is now constricting so hard it aches, *it wasn't hypothetical for him.* I remember his face, and now I can put a precise name to his expression then: hope. *In this scenario, I don't go back to LA.*

"But what will you do instead? In the meantime. Like . . . day-to-day-wise?" I ask.

"I don't know. That's the beauty of it," he says with a cautious joy that, despite the shock of all of this, still shines through. He sounds happy. Light. Free. "I have had my life planned out months, *years* in advance ever since . . . since a long time ago. Too long. And I don't know what I'm going to do after this movie, but I'm excited to have nothing on my calendar. I'll probably travel. Read a lot more. Maybe take up a sport. Every day that I've woken up here has felt increasingly *right.* I want to be able to see my parents and cousins whenever I want, go over to my parents' house for dinner, go on a family vacation for the first time in god knows how long. I want to be able to go to a restaurant *without* a baseball cap and sunglasses." And right when

I thought the pain couldn't feel any more acute, he adds, knowing *exactly* what he's doing, "For a minute there, I was even considering dating."

I want to tell him everything that's been going through my mind over the last few weeks, every single embarrassing, stupid, infatuated thought that I refused to let slip out because I thought we couldn't have it all. "Tyler," I say, knowing that this is irreparable, and nonetheless still wanting to fix it somehow, some way.

"I would've told you, you know, if you'd asked," he interrupts. "Fuck, it sounds so embarrassing, but one week by your side and I was a goner. And I know, I know that would've been foolish and reckless and it would've caused a hell of a shitstorm and I'm not someone who does reckless things, but that's what you do to me, Khin. When we're together, nothing makes sense except for you, and then you become everything and then it *all* makes sense. It's like the earth tilted on its axis the moment I met you, like my whole world as I knew it shifted, and I knew instantly that there was no turning back for me now.

"How could you of all people say that I don't know what I want? Has it not been humiliatingly clear by the fact that I would do anything, literally anything, including help cover up a murder, for *you*? I can't stop staring at you when we're in the same space, I think of your smile all the time. When I drop you off, it's all that I can do to not kiss you goodbye or ask if I can come over. Hell, I almost *did* tell you my secret last night. But—" His smile looks like it physically hurts. "—I thought it would've been more fun to surprise you," he says, each glass shard of a word slicing me to the bone. "If anything, I wish I was someone who didn't know what he wanted, because then I wouldn't care this much, and just like *I* am just another profile subject to you, you would simply be yet another reporter to me. I *wish* I didn't want you as much as I do."

My heart throbs with a pain that hearts weren't built to withstand. "I'm sorry," I whisper.

"I'm going to go now," he states, moving past me. Helpless, I turn and watch his back, shoulders low, gait heavy. Right as he takes one step across the threshold, though, he pauses and looks over his shoulder. "Can you do me one favor? I feel like you owe me at least that."

I nod feverishly. "Anything."

He swivels so he can look at me, and it aches to simultaneously have him so close and know that he's beyond my reach now. "Don't tell May about my retirement. I want to be the one to tell her."

The knowledge that not even May knows amplifies my shock tenfold. "She doesn't know?"

"No, I didn't want her to be sad the entire time we were filming. She doesn't even know we've already turned down Bond. But don't try to get a quote from her or anything, okay? Promise?"

The fact that he thinks that getting quotes for my article is at the forefront of my mind right now cuts deeper than I think even he intended. I rally for one last attempt. "Tyler, you . . . you *have to* believe me. I wasn't going to print anything that you told me in confidence. I would *never* do anything to hurt—"

"I don't think I *have to* believe that," he interrupts swiftly. "In fact, I don't think I have a *single* reason to believe that."

"Everything we said last night. Everything we've done for each other this past month. Isn't . . . isn't *that* enough reason?"

"What, that you pretended to like me so that I could be the next rung on your career ladder?" He shakes his head with a rueful snort. "Who would've thought that between the two of us, it'd turn out *you* were the better actor? By a fucking mile."

I am painfully aware of how a person's voice sounds when they've made up their mind about leaving you, that specific finality in their tone when they've decided that there isn't anything left to salvage. I drop my gaze to the floor as his footsteps recede. Several seconds later, the front door shuts.

As though his leaving has also sucked out all of the gravity in this apartment, I crumple down onto the floor, the waistband of my jeans digging into my flesh as I pull my knees to my face. Despite the sunlight warming my bare arms, a biting coldness settles in my bones.

With my marriage, we had been two tectonic plates gradually drifting apart until the gap became so wide that it was no longer unavoidable, no longer temporarily fixable by any amount of therapy or time apart or a succession of optimistic yet unfounded promises that *we'll be better tomorrow*. This, however, feels like a sinkhole—like one moment I was taking a photo of the view, and the next, the ground gave in and I'm still grappling for purchase even though I know there's no point. The ground is gone. My lungs scorch as I breathe in more sand.

Twenty

When I first met Tyler for that dinner in Chinatown, I thought he had been on his best behavior, a prime example of how to act and what to do and say, right out of the Universal Publicist's Handbook. I thought I'd been getting the Tyler Tun that every interviewer got.

I had been wrong.

It's been nineteen excruciating days since That Night, and now, every day that I show up on set, *now* I get the Tyler Tun that the rest of the world gets. "Morning, Khin," he says in the morning, mouth curving into a smile that, I swear, is the exact same length each time—wide enough to come across as convincingly genial, tame enough to be professional. He doesn't come find me in between takes; I try not to take it too personally—now that all the red tape has been cleared, we're shooting at rapid speed, everyone working even longer and harder than before, especially him. He's so exhausted, he barely speaks to *anyone* at the end of the day, I reason to myself. He still sits

with me at lunch, probably because it would look suspicious if we began eating separately and the last thing he wants is for more rumors
to spread, but makes the precise amount of small talk that you'd make
with a coworker whom you run into at the water cooler. May, on the
other hand, hasn't said a single word to me; I don't think he's told her
about his retirement, but he's certainly told her about the whiteboard.

Every night, I tell myself that it will hurt less in the morning, but
every morning, it turns out I was wrong. Instead, for the rest of our
time together, the pain is piercing and prolonged, easily the worst I've
ever felt; ignoring it doesn't work, but neither does giving in and letting the wave wash over me. By the last day of shooting, I'm so numb
that I don't feel an ounce of emotion as I say my goodbyes to everyone.

The wrap party for the Myanmar cast and crew takes place at
a rooftop Thai restaurant the following night. By the time I arrive,
everyone is already drinking, and most people are already drunk.

"Khin! Holy shit, you look gorgeous!" Jason engulfs me in a hug
from behind. He makes a twirling motion with a finger, and I oblige,
pulling off a 360-degree spin in my Alice + Olivia forest-green halter
dress with a cream-colored bow on the back. "Absolutely stunning,"
Jason says with a grin. His grin spills over when he notices something
behind me. Eyebrows waggling, he tips his chin toward the room.
"And clearly, I'm not the only one who thinks so."

I spin, and like a polarized magnet, latch onto Tyler, who stands
with May and two extras at one side of the bar. May is wearing a simple little black dress with two side cutouts, large gold hoops, strappy
black heels. He's wearing dark blue jeans with a black leather belt, a
light pink linen shirt tucked in, navy suede sneakers. They *look* like
people who were born to be famous. I expect Tyler to look away, but
he doesn't, and in response, my body stills as his gaze slowly travels
down to my feet until moving back up and fastening onto my eyes
once more. Whatever our separate reasons may be, we can't look

away. May tiptoes to say something into his ear, and he shakes his head. She follows his gaze to me and says something else, something that makes half of his mouth quirk into a smile this time.

Self-consciousness floods my body, but before I can stop the nearest passing waiter for some liquid courage, Tyler motions to the left with his eyes, at a hallway that rounds the corner. Handing his drink to May, he walks over and disappears down the hall. I count to three, and, ignoring May's scrutiny, follow.

At the end of the hall is a bright red fire escape door. When I near, Tyler pushes the horizontal metal bar and steps in, holding the door open until I cross over. I turn, he eases the door shut, the muted *thud* rings through the empty staircase, and then there's only the sound of us breathing.

"Hi," I say.

"Hi," he says with a small smile. Then, "You look good."

"Thanks. You too," I say, hoping he knows I mean it.

He inhales the way I've watched him do on set right before the cameras roll for a big emotional scene: deep, measured, deliberate, like he knows this breath has to last him a while. "I'm not going to keep you for long," he says, nodding around at the empty space.

"Well, we both know what happened the last time a guy tried to get me alone."

And then it happens. He laughs. It's small, throttled, a surprise. But he does it, and the grin that spreads on my face must look maniacal. Before I can add anything, he shakes his head as though scolding himself for making the mistake of sharing a laugh with me. "You know, May thinks *this*," he makes a wide circle in the air with one palm, "is a bad idea."

"What is? Talking to me?"

His nod is a gut punch. "She said to look at how much trouble talking to you has already gotten me into."

"Tyler," I try again—and again, the words don't come out, maybe because I'm scared I'll say the wrong thing, or maybe because I already know that there's no right thing to say here.

"I don't want to be mad at you, Khin." He looks up at me, *really* looks at me, in that way that makes me feel transparent in a matter of seconds. "I don't want us to end on a bad note. I don't want to go back to LA on Saturday and—"

"Saturday?" Somehow the silence around us has gotten louder, stiller. *But that's the day after tomorrow,* I want to point out. *Surely you're mistaken.*

"Yeah. I'm going to be here for a long time, so might as well get in as much of LA while I can. Plus it'll be nice to have a longer break before we shoot the rest of the movie there."

"Do you know when you're moving yet? Back here."

His forehead wrinkles with surprise at my question. Which, fair. Why does it matter to me? I'm about to let him off the hook when he answers, "After the movie comes out. Makes more sense for me to stay there until then. We'll finish filming, rest, do the press tours. And I'll need that extra time to ship all my stuff over."

I feel my head bob like, *Of course. That makes total sense. Of course it does. It's not like I was counting on an extra two weeks to—*

"But if you have any follow-up questions, you can always email me," he adds like we're wrapping up a meeting. "You were promised a full two months, so anything else you wanna know, just shoot me a message."

My heart buckles with a near-debilitating blow as I realize that this is what we've come to. Follow-up questions and shooting messages. "Okay," I croak out.

"Anyway, I—" He coughs into a fist that doesn't fully uncurl even once it returns to his side. "I wanted us to clear the air." He's taking his time considering each word before he speaks, and the realization that *this* is also what we've come to is a new, penetrating hurt. "I needed the time and space over the last few weeks to cool down, and now that I have, I want to apologize for . . . overreacting. Apart from, obviously, the note about Jess and the abortion story, the rest was you doing your job. I can't be mad at you for treating this article and our time together like a project when, well, that's what it was, right?" he asks with a chuckle. I think I smile back, but I can't be sure.

"But—" he continues, although I don't want him to. I want him to stop talking right now, to stop unraveling this messy, confusing, but also incredible thing we'd built together over the last month. "I know things got . . . intense for a while there. I was grateful for what you did for Jess, and you were grateful to me for keeping your secret, and after we were thrown into such a high-stakes situation, we mistook that for . . . you know . . . feelings. We were emotionally overwhelmed and crossed a professional line, and I'm also sorry for my part in that. I'm sorry I lost my objectivity and blew up at you. You didn't deserve that."

His words feel like one Alka-Seltzer tab after another, fizzing and dispersing in my head until I'm just trying to stay afloat in this sea of bubbles. "That . . . makes sense," I say, because at this point, it feels easier to let the wave of humiliation carry me forward and crash me into shore than to fight it. After all, what do you say when the man you love tells you he's *sorry* he developed feelings for you? What's the point of explaining that I've decided I'm not going to write this article *at all*, because if it comes down to him or any assignment, even *Vogue*, there's no competition? He'll just assume I'm doing it out of guilt. It's not going to bring him back. Nothing is going to bring him back to me.

"I'm sorry, too," I mumble.

A shadow drops across his face before instantly disappearing. He swallows, and says, voice so hoarse my first instinct is to ask if he needs a drink, "I'm glad we cleared that up."

A memory sparks in my head, an unexpected burst of flash. *And you're in love with her,* May had said in his trailer, when neither of them had known I was in the bathroom. He hadn't denied it.

But he hadn't confirmed it either.

"I'll miss you," I say before I lose the courage to say it.

The uncontrollable corner of his mouth twitches into a smile. I hold my breath, hoping he'll say it back. He doesn't. Instead, he says, "Perhaps our paths will cross again one day."

Our paths will cross again one day. It's so civil I want to hurl. "Maybe—" I get out. Then, "When are you announcing it?" He blinks. "Your retirement."

His brows lift almost imperceptibly. "Also probably once the movie comes out," he says, swallows, then adds, "but you can have the exclusive if you want. I can clear it with my publicist. I'm telling May on Saturday, on our flight home."

And then I understand. I want to clarify that that wasn't why I asked, that I'm genuinely curious—but why would he believe me? Nonetheless, I attempt, "No, Tyler, that wasn't—"

But he stops me with an open palm. "It's okay," he says, nodding resolutely like this is something he's had a lot of time to come to terms with. "I get it. Again, you're just doing your job. And hey, how could you turn down *Vogue*?"

I should leave. I should say something like, *Well, we should get back to the party,* or *I should return you before May starts getting worried,* but I don't. In fact, my jaw is aching because I'm gritting my teeth, because I have to physically clamp my mouth shut, because otherwise I'm going to cry, and it's not going to be a pretty, demure cry the way May cries on camera. No, it's going to be a full-on sobbing breakdown, and I don't want to do that. Not here. Not in front of him. It's already embarrassing enough to have him admit to my face that he regrets developing feelings for me; I don't want him to now awkwardly try to make me feel better as well when the only reason he pulled me aside for this conversation was to "clear the air" before he moved back and on with his life.

Tyler doesn't leave either. It feels like we're two cowboys in a standoff, except neither of us has any weapons, and there's not even something or someone that we're fighting over.

"Enjoy LA." Even before I've finished the sentence, my hand makes a beeline for my face, but it's not fast enough. The tear rolls down.

He presses his lips tight, looking increasingly uncomfortable. "Enjoy Singapore," he replies, granting me the grace of ignoring what just happened.

He does a half-turn to open the door, but before he can push the bar, I say, because he deserves it, "I *am* sorry. You don't have to believe me, but I was never going to use Jess's story. I wouldn't."

Glancing sideways, he nods. "Thank you" is all he says.

We go our separate ways once we rejoin the party. I don't eat anything, opting to nurse one watered-down Coke all night, because it's all I can stomach. At one point, Yasmin calls out, "Tyler! May! Speech!" and the room whoops.

I swear I try my damndest to stay, to look professional, look *happy*. But as I clock him sliding out of one of the velvet booths, bashful smile aimed at the floor as May fixes the collar of his shirt, something in me snaps, breaks clean in half. Maybe it's my heart, or maybe it's my dignity, or my tolerance. But suddenly, my throat starts closing up, and I move backward until I'm seeing the backs of everyone's heads and I can stride toward the door.

The coolness of the copper knob feels good against my skin, every inch of which feels like it's catching fire. I quietly turn it, step through, and, right before shutting it close, take one final look. And find Tyler watching me. Yasmin is talking, and May is laughing, and his mouth is smiling but his eyes are vacant, expressionless.

His brows furrow, discreetly asking, *What are you doing?*

I want to return a smile, but I can't. It's getting near impossible to breathe and to blink away the encroaching blurriness. So I do what I can, which is mouth *Goodbye*. And then, because it's my last chance, *I'm sorry.*

Twenty-one

My phone's incessant vibrations on the bedside console wake me up from my third (or is it fourth?) nap of the day. Then again, does it really count as a nap if I've only gotten out of bed to pee? Isn't it more of a prolonged sleep cycle?

I hesitate but ultimately pick up.

"Oh god, we thought you were dead. Didn't you get our texts?" comes Thidar's voice.

"What?" I grumble. "What time is it? I was asleep."

"Asleep? It's four." She sighs like a mother who's trying to wake up her child for school for the fifth time. "Just come and open the door."

"The d—"

"Now!" Nay yells. "We *will* camp out here if we have to!"

"I am confiscating your key cards," I groan as I clamber out of the bedroom.

Both of them physically recoil at the sight of me. "Have we . . ." Nay sniffs the air. "Showered recently?"

"Yes," I mumble with all the confidence of someone who is know-ingly deploying a liberal definition of "recently."

"Of course," she responds.

"What are you guys doing here?"

Thidar glances down at the phone in her hand, and my stomach sinks. "What?" I repeat.

"Did you know Tyler was leaving today?"

Oh. I nod. "He told me at the wrap party on Thursday."

"We saw the photos of him at the airport," Thidar says, motion-ing with her phone. "How are you?"

"Honestly?" They both nod. "I'm . . . I don't . . . We . . ." It doesn't come. I'd hoped that not talking to anyone for thirty-six hours would mean that I'd have recuperated enough to get my thoughts in order, but that clearly hasn't been the case.

"Can we come in?" Nay asks.

While they shut the door and remove their shoes, I pull my robe tighter around me. "So how—" Nay starts.

Detaching itself from my brain, my body lets out a sob, and then another, and another, and, no longer seeing the point in remaining upright, I'm sitting on the floor, knees pressed into my chest, rocking myself as tears that I was certain had dried up stream down my face. Two hands land on either side of my spine—not stroking, not rubbing soothing circles, just secured there, letting me know that it's okay, I can fall apart, they're here now.

I slouch sideways into a fetal position onto Thidar's lap. Nay lies down sideways, too, one hand propping up her head while the other tucks my hair behind my ear.

"I almost murdered someone," I blubber, figuring, hey, there's never going to be a *good* time to tell them.

They both freeze. Nay chews on her bottom lip, and, after a period of silence, asks, "Like . . . in a dream? Or metaphorically? With your words?"

I shake my head. "In the park. In the flesh."

"The park," Thidar states.

"On the first day of filming. And Tyler was involved and the police were looking into me and it turned out the guy had been stalking me for months but then it—"

"Woah there, halt, time out," Nay says, grabbing my face with both hands. "You're saying a lot of weird combinations of words right now, and frankly, the snot is making it difficult to understand you. I'm going to go and pee, and then I'm coming back with tissues and some water, and *then* you're going to walk us through the whole thing. Okay?" I nod.

Approximately five minutes later, she returns and plops back down on the floor in her initial position, but not before first placing the promised tissue box and mug of water between us. "Take a sip," she instructs, and I lift my head and obey. "Now blow," she says, giving me a piece of tissue. When I'm done, she says, "Now talk to us."

"Well . . . fuck," comes Thidar's voice from above when I'm done laying it all out. "You . . . and then . . . I mean . . . fuck."

I rotate so I'm on my back and I can look up at her, although from this angle, all I can see is her chin. "Are you guys mad I didn't tell you?"

"No, we're—" Thidar starts at the same time that Nay hits my shoulder and says, "Of course we're mad!"

Thidar tilts her head to glare at Nay. "We're not *mad.*"

"Yes, we are!" Nay snaps. "You were going to go to *prison* and not tell us? What the actual fuck? We're your best friends! I once fished a menstrual cup out of your vagina!"

I snort despite myself. "I'm sorry," I say. "I . . . I didn't want to implicate you, and also . . . I didn't . . ."

"What?" Thidar prompts when I trail off.

I inhale, no longer able to avoid what I know is the truth. "Also, I felt like *such* a huge disappointment. Every night, I would lie awake in bed and stare off into space, wondering what the fuck happened. I didn't have a marriage. I didn't have a house. And while Ben was so goddamn happy with his new sweet and talented photographer girlfriend, I was running around the city dodging the police after having murdered a man. Oh, and I was also head over heels in love with a guy who I *knew* I couldn't be in love with, but still I was, like a complete fool, and I couldn't do anything about it. It felt like I couldn't do *anything* right anymore. Do you know how humiliating it is for your husband to divorce you after less than a year of being married? It felt . . . it felt like he'd been right to leave me."

Nay snatches another tissue and dabs my cheeks. "No, but we *do* know how unhappy you were during those last months of your relationship."

I face her to make sure I heard right. "What?"

Her smile is kind. "You weren't happy anymore. We could all see it. *Of course* we were still rooting for you both, but . . . Ben made the right call, Khin."

"But I did everything right," I say bitterly.

"I know. And I know it *sucks* that it still didn't work out," Thidar says, pushing away wet strands of hair from my forehead. "But that's what happens in life sometimes. Things just . . . don't work out. Sometimes you fall out of love. And nothing you could've done or said would've stopped that." When she slants her head downward to look at me, I'm not expecting to find her eyes glistening with tears. "It hurt, you know, that you wouldn't talk to us about it. We saw what you were doing to cope."

"To—"

"Look around." Nay chuckles and makes a wide, open gesture

with one hand. "You bought the most expensive apartment your half of the house money would let you. And we know you like nice things, but this? This isn't merely a new apartment, this is a 'fuck my ex-husband, I'm doing better than I ever was' apartment. That, and the rug, and the wardrobe, and the nonstop freelance assignments you buried yourself under. We know you. You were trying to prove you were okay, and instead of admitting to us that you weren't, you distracted yourself."

Despite myself, I want to laugh. How did I ever think I was successfully lying to them? How did I ever convince myself that these women, my people, people who know me down to my blood and bones, would fall for the mirage? "I didn't know how," I say. "All I wanted to do every time I thought about it was cry."

"Then you could've just done that," Nay says, and when I look at her, *she's* crying, too.

"And what? Show weakness? Never. God, it's like you don't know me at all."

She doesn't accept the joke. "It's not weakness. Something terrible happened to you. You lost your marriage. Your relationship. Your partner. You could've called us up every night at two A.M., and we would've answered, and we never would've pitied you or thought you'd failed or whatever else you've been telling yourself this whole time, because that's not how our love works. But we needed you to talk to us, and you wouldn't—"

"Because that's not what you do when you fail," I say, aware how stubborn I sound. "When you fail at something, you don't sit and wallow. You get back up and make a plan and you try harder next time."

"Khin." Nay wiggles closer until our toes are touching. "Your *marriage* ended. *Of course* you sit and wallow. Not forever, but definitely for a fucking while. We love how determined and driven you are, you know that. We love your planning and your Post-its—"

"And your color coordination—" Thidar adds.

"So many colors!" Nay yells, and I chuckle. "But some things in life, you can't plan. And some losses, you can't just dust yourself off and immediately bounce back from. Despite what you've been trying to convince us, we're aware your spine isn't actually made of steel."

After a pause, Thidar clears her throat. "Are you really moving to Singapore?"

I consider before I answer. "If I get the job. But I have to deliver on the article first. And to be honest, I don't want to write it anymore. I don't have the words or the emotional capacity or, even on a practical level, the time. The draft is due in two weeks, and right now, I can't even write something that's good enough for an Intro to Journalism blog post."

"You *are* going to get this job." Thidar states it like a fact. "Because you're you, and I know it might not seem like it right now, but if you want this, if you really want this, you will rally and you will write a damn good article and you will get the job. That's not the question here."

"She's right," Nay says with a determined nod. "You *will* get the job. *If* you want it and you write this piece. But Khin, do you actually want to move to Singapore? Do you even . . ." She studies me with caution before finishing, "*Want* the job?"

"It's *Vogue*," I reply automatically.

"Yeah, and *Vogue* is impressive," she says, pursing her lips. "But is *Vogue* you? Is *Vogue* the career you want? This is your first celebrity profile, right?" I nod. "Do you like it? Do you want to do more of this?"

"What we're trying to ask," Thidar says, "is whether you want this job because you *want* this job, or because you don't want to be here. Because if it's the latter and you're simply running?" She smiles, seeing right through me in that way only the two of them ever do. "I hate to break it to you, but you might get to Singapore and realize you still want to run. You can't outrun this. Sometimes, no plan is better than a bad plan."

"So what do I do? Just sit around feeling shitty?"

"Pretty much," she says, throwing her hands in the air, her legs under my head jostling with the movement. "You sit there, and you feel shitty, because that's how people feel when they have to sit in a pile of shit. And then eventually, you realize you don't *want* to feel shitty anymore, and you work on it. And every day, there's a little less shit to deal with until one day, poof. No more shit. Or maybe a little shit."

"But not a giant football field of shit," Nay adds.

I snort. "You guys are making it sound *really* appealing."

"That's life," Nay says with a shrug. "One day, you're profiling the biggest movie star in the world, and the next, you're being forced to sit in a field of shit."

That night, sandwiched in my giant king-sized bed between my lightly snoring best friends, I stare out the window, watching the clouds move steadily as they play a game of hide-and-seek with the moon, whose light is bouncing off of the sliver of lake in the far distance.

I had once judged Tyler for not knowing what he wanted. But the truth was—is—he found me in the exact same situation. I'm thirty, divorced, and don't have full-time employment (aka overachieving teenage me's worst nightmare). I don't know what I want either. Do I want a full-time job at *Vogue*? Do I want to move to Singapore?

Do I want to be with Tyler?

It feels scary and ridiculous to even allow myself to think that last one because it implies that I might have a reasonable shot, which I don't. I take my mental eraser and scrub away that last question. The ones before that, though, stay. And no matter how hard I try to come up with answers, I can't.

I know what I *don't* want, though. I don't want to be mad at Ben anymore. Because Nay and Thidar were right, and so was he—by the time he asked for a divorce, we had stopped being in love for a very long time; the cracks had already started to show pre-wedding, but I figured that they were surface cracks, and besides, marriage would "solve" all of that; intentionally vowing to spend the rest of our lives together would bridge the increasing gap between us. I've been deliberate about never thinking about him, but tonight, I force myself to do just that. I miss him, it occurs to me, like you miss your childhood home. Nostalgia about something that was so familiar and yours for so long. Although, when you look at it objectively, you know that you should move on because you've outgrown it. The bed is too small. The color schemes that your parents picked and that you didn't think twice about when you were a kid aren't what you want in your own house now that you're older, different, someone new. It's not right for you anymore, but that doesn't erase the fact that it once was. You don't miss the home, you miss what it used to be.

He wasn't to blame for what happened.

Neither am I.

And I can't blame him for my own self-imposed shame either. This anger I've been harboring this entire time isn't because we got divorced, but because the divorce upended everything I'd known up to that point, like a tornado barging in and destroying my color-coordinated wardrobe, leaving behind a mess that I didn't even know where to begin to sort out. In a matter of months, I went from being someone who had it all figured out to someone who knew . . . nothing. *That* is the crux of it. I know less now about where my life is headed than I did when I was twenty-three. That's not how it's supposed to be.

I've always known what I wanted to do next, where I was going next, what the next goal was. *Next, next, next.* Will I never be able to know any of those things again? What's *next*? I become someone who doesn't have a daily alarm and "wakes up when she wakes up"? *This* is how society deteriorates into chaos. *These* are the people who die first when the apocalypse comes, or when the ship starts to sink—the ones without a plan.

Just then, Thidar rolls over and slaps me in the face. I gasp and my open mouth is ready to shout at her when I realize she's still asleep and not telepathically reading my thoughts. Gradually, her hand slides down my face and curls into the crook between my neck and shoulder.

I watch her and Nay continue to sleep, breaths steady, foreheads *not* peppered with beads of sweat, and it occurs to me that maybe it wouldn't hurt to at least try things their way for a little while. After all, *they're* not desperately fighting off panic attacks in the middle of the night.

Baby steps, I remind myself, and surprisingly, it gets easier to sleep once I *stop* thinking about sinking ships and the end of the world.

———

I n the morning, as we settle around the table with our own portions of caffeine, Nay snaps her fingers. "Mugs! *That's* what we should've gotten you!"

"What?" I ask, blowing on my coffee.

She widens her eyes down at her own. "We were trying to figure out what to get you as a housewarming gift. We should've each gotten you a new mug!"

"Yeah," Thidar says, eyes jumping between the three in our hands, as though noticing them for the first time. "No offense, but these are boring."

I give a small chuckle. "None taken. New mugs would be great."

"What should we have for br—"

"I changed my mind," I cut in. "I want to write this story."

They both turn to me, their mugs making a near-synchronized muted *thunk* as they place them down on the table. "What?" Thidar asks.

"The *Vogue* story. I want to write it. I don't know about the overall job yet, you know, assuming I even get it—" I look back and forth between their faces, and they both give me warm, sleepy smiles that say, *That's okay, keep going.* "But I definitely want to write this story. I've signed a contract, the photos have been shot, and the rest of the issue is already being planned around this article; if I take myself off of it, then Clarissa will have me blacklisted for the rest of my career, but more than that, she'll get someone else to do it. Someone who doesn't know Tyler like I do. Someone who wouldn't—" I think of May. "Be *fair*. And besides, I also kind of really . . . *want* to."

"Good," Nay says, beaming through her bedhead bangs. "Now that we've figured that out, let's tackle the next step. What are you going to give them?" When I look at her quizzically, she shrugs. "Do they get a, you know, scoop?"

That's the million-dollar question, isn't it? "This article is going to publish at the same time that the movie comes out. Which was when he was going to announce his retirement himself anyway," I say, speaking the thought bubbles aloud as they pop up in my head. "I would just . . . be the first person to have it in print. And this way, he'll at least get a heads-up about it instead of being blindsided by someone else. I know he hates me, but I'd like to think he'd still rather I break the story than, like, TMZ."

"That's a fair point," Nay says.

"And Clarissa is editing this herself. I file the draft, we work on it for a few months, and then it sits in her inbox until next year. We could easily keep this between the two of us until it publishes. Even for the layout, we could use placeholder text and change it at the last minute. A story this big, she would make sure this never leaked."

"Right," Nay says again. "But do you *want* to be the first one to print it?"

I open my mouth to say I need some more time to figure that out, but the words don't come. Because I know the real answer. "No," I answer truthfully. "I don't."

"Even if it means you don't get the *Vogue* job?"

I smile up at them, blinking through the wetness. "It was just a job. He's a person. A person that I . . . *really* care about. And maybe if I could ask him, he might say that from a purely publicity standpoint, he wants me to be the one to break it, but knowing that I was responsible for him not being able to do it entirely on his terms? I can't do that to him."

Thidar reaches over to squeeze my shoulder. "Okay, then."

"Hey, guys?" I say, and they both perk up in their seats.

With a low groan, Nay says, "*Please* don't tell us you snuck out last night and accidentally potentially murdered *another* man. I mean, of course we'll help you cover it up, but I have to start work in a few hours and—"

I let go of my mug so I can take both of their hands. "I wasn't running away from *you two*, you know that, right? Singapore, that was . . . I was chasing that because I'd wanted something solid. I figured that even if the rest of my life fell apart again, at least I would have a full-time job that was stable. Something reliable. Something that wouldn't snatch the rug out from under me on a random afternoon. A safety net."

"But you love freelancing," Thidar states in a matter-of-fact way.

I nod. "I do. You know what else I love?"

"What?" she asks, although the smile tugging her lips tells me she already knows the answer.

"You two," I confirm. "Your friendship, our love—that's the most stable, reliable thing I've ever had in my life. It's the one thing that has never, *ever* let me down. You guys are my safety net, the one constant that catches me every time I fall on my ass. I love you, promise me you'll never doubt that."

"We know," Nay says, squeezing my hand. "Forever."

"And ever," Thidar says.

Like the sun melting a Popsicle, the incontestable warmth of their love makes my grin unfurl to an uncontrollable length. "And ever," I say.

Twenty-two

'm having dinner with Clarissa tonight; she'd flown into town for four other meetings yesterday, and as someone who always prefers to do business in-person, had stayed an extra day because she'd rather we go over her notes face-to-face. I filed the story two weeks ago, and so far, all I've heard is the "Received. Thanks. C" that she'd sent back within an hour. I don't know if the silence is good or bad, if it means she has minimal edits and this is a celebratory dinner, or if there is such a long list of ways in which this is the worst celebrity profile she's ever read that she wants to take me somewhere with a good, expensive wine selection to soften the blow while she takes it apart line by line.

Despite my being fifteen minutes early, Clarissa is already there when I give her name to the maître d'. She's sipping on a glass of red with the fortitude of someone who is at the end of a ten-hour workday and can go on for another ten.

"Clarissa!" I say, extending a hand as I approach.

She stands up, white dress shirt staying perfectly tucked into her pine green wide-leg pantsuit even as she tuts away my hand and hugs me. "Drink?" she asks.

"Yes, I—" She raises a brow at someone behind me, and in seconds, someone is at my side, filling my wineglass. "Thank you," I say to the waiter.

"You did it, you filed a *Vogue* cover story!" Clarissa says, lifting her glass. I relax. This is a good start. With a bright smile, I clink my glass to hers. Right as the first few drops slip between my lips and onto my tongue, she states, "We can't print this."

I sputter red drops onto the white napkin on my lap. I hold up a hand and duck down, continuing to cough into the napkin until I regain myself. When I look back up, someone's filled a glass of water for me. "I'm sorry?" I wheeze.

Clarissa gives me a short smile. It's not a mean *This is where I fire you* smile, but also not a *I was just kidding!* one either. "The draft you filed," she confirms. "We can't print it. At least not in its current state. Good thing we have a lot of lead time with this one. I expect another draft in two weeks."

"What's . . . I . . ." I try to clear my throat as professionally as possible for someone who just spat out a mouthful of red wine. "Can you give me a bit more specific feedback?"

Clarissa opens her hands. "You didn't write a cover story."

"Oh," I say. That was not what I was expecting, and I don't know if that's better or worse than a straight-out *It was shit.* I don't know if this is standard *Vogue* feedback and I'm too ignorant to read between the lines, but I also need more than what she's giving me if I'm going to turn in a second draft that she *can* print. "As in, my tone wasn't exactly what you were looking for or . . . ?"

"Khin," she says with a short laugh. "You didn't write a cover story."

"I don't—"

"You wrote a love letter."

I had a feeling I shouldn't drink any more wine for the next ten minutes of this conversation, and once again, my gut was right. I mean to say *I'm sorry?* or *Can you elaborate on that?* or even a contemplative *I see*, but what comes out is a succinct "Huh?"

Clarissa laughs again at my expression. "Darling," she says, shaking her head. "You wrote a love letter in the third person and poorly disguised it as a profile. Don't get me wrong, it's a *great* letter. When I finished it, I was next to my boyfriend in bed, and I turned to him and said, 'I just read the most damn romantic thing I've ever read in my life. I hope someone turns this into a movie.'"

"Are you . . ." I swallow, cheeks flushed. "Did I email you the correct file?"

At that, she throws her head back and roars with laughter. I try to join her, but the best I can do is a frail "Heh."

"It's okay," she says, laughter subduing into a soft chuckle. "It stays between us, I promise. Although I *will* need an actual story for the next draft. Several of my editors are already asking to read it. Everyone's dying to get their hands on this one."

I feel like I'm standing in the middle of a room with a dozen different isolated tiny fires, and I don't know which one to address first. At last, I go for the most obvious one. "What do you mean it was a *love letter?*"

"Khin, did you read what you wrote?"

"Yes! Of course! Multiple times!"

"Did you read it as someone who—" She cocks a teasing brow. "—is *not* in denial about being in love?"

"Clarissa—" I laugh, but it doesn't sound funny. None of this is funny. This is my job, my career. And I cannot be sitting at a five-star French-Chinese fusion fine dining restaurant while my professional life falls apart before my eyes. "No offense, but do you think you read it through a biased lens? I know you weren't thrilled about the rumors after what happened at the dim sum place, and—"

Somehow, I know to stop talking when she picks up her wineglass. She swirls it around, sips, and puts it back down, never once taking her eyes off of my face. "I believed you back then when you said you weren't dating. And I don't believe that you ever were. Dating, I mean. You're too smart and too good of a journalist to let a man derail your assignment."

I nod, exhaling for what feels like the first time in twenty minutes. "Thank you. I am, and I didn't."

"But Khin, that's the stupid, infuriating, clichéd thing about love, isn't it? You don't get to choose who you fall for."

"I didn't—"

"I'm not going to press it," she says, raising her hands to stop me mid-protest. "I'm simply telling you *why* we can't print the draft you filed. By the way, I hope you don't mind," she continues breezily. "I went ahead and ordered us both the surf and turf. The steak and lobster here are *sublime*."

"The—" My brain stumbles on itself as it tries to keep up. "Steak and lobster?"

"Yes," she says, looking confused as to why *I'm* confused. "You're not allergic to shellfish, are you?"

That's not exactly why I'm stammering, but nonetheless, I say, "Uh, n-no."

"Good. Oh, another thing," Clarissa says, swilling her glass in the air once more. "The job's yours."

I do a double take, literally gripping the edge of the table to stop myself from falling forward. "What?" I breathe out. "The . . . full-time position?"

She nods once.

"But I . . . couldn't get you your scoop. I tried, but I . . . didn't do it."

"But you *did* do the best possible job anyone could. Look, I know I put *a bit* of pressure on you about getting me a nice, shiny scoop that I could put on the cover and frame for my office," she says, and I have to roll in my lips to stop myself from saying something along the lines of *That's putting it mildly.* "But despite this, frankly, *mess* of a first draft, it's clear that you've put in the work, and more importantly, that you cared about your subject. That's what I should've asked of you from the beginning. It's *all* I should've asked of you. Every single one of your previous pieces of writing, not to mention all of those stellar references, have proven again and again that you're the type of journalist who goes all in and cares about her subjects, and you did exactly that with this article, too.

"And the longer I sat with your draft, the more I realized *this* is the kind of story I want. Not a love letter," she clarifies. "But . . . *good* writing. Something that I'd be proud to print. And even though this first draft isn't quite what I was looking for, I admit, in retrospect, I let my personal desire to brag to everyone about securing a Tyler Tun scoop get in the way of, you know, good journalism." She shrugs, and I can't quite believe what's happening here. Clarissa doing a one-eighty and . . . admitting she made a mistake? "But I run *Vogue*, not some underhanded rumor mill. I want sharp, hardworking, trustworthy people with *integrity* in my office. Which is why you'll fit right in."

If I had felt earlier that my career was falling apart, now it feels like it's reassembled itself into some sort of super-charged version of its previous iteration. "Just so I have this right," I say, my chest squeezing tighter as the magnitude of the situation hits. "You're offering me a job at *Vogue*? A full-time job? At *Vogue*? As a reporter? Right now? Here?"

"Yes. To all of the above," Clarissa says with a wink. "How could I let a writer like you slip through my fingers?"

"Oh my god," I whisper, more to myself. My hands are still on the table edge, and I have to grasp it tighter to keep myself grounded. *This is it,* I think. I'd been petrified about where my life was going next, but here it is. I can see it. A job at *Vogue.* A *career* at *Vogue.* I could be in an editorial position in a couple of years. Hell, I could eventually be in Clarissa's position, I *know* I could. And beyond the job, I'm being offered a new life in Singapore. A fresh start. The fresh start I'd so desperately wanted.

I'm still lost in this weird hypnotic phase and only catch the last syllable of what Clarissa's just said. "Sorry?" I ask, sitting up. "Can you repeat that? Sorry, I'm a little overwhelmed right now."

She nods her head knowingly, as though this is everyone's reaction to getting a job offer from her. "I said, take the next two weeks to consider it."

Consider it? I open my mouth, ready to (politely) yell something along the lines of *I don't need to consider it! It's goddamn Vogue!*

But she speaks first. "While you're writing that second draft. Every time you're in front of your computer, think if you want to do more of this. There's no rush here, and I know it'd be a big next step for you. It'd be a change, and change can be good, but you need to make sure it's the right kind of change."

Three-months-ago me would've waved away her suggestion and requested she draw up a contract right now so I could sign it on the spot and we could wrap up the night by celebrating with champagne. But the words "think if you want to do more of this" flash in my brain like a dim warning siren. At this point, our food arrives, and even in my dazed state, the scent of freshly grilled lobster and steak arouses my hunger.

I pick up my knife and fork while Clarissa is already popping a piece of rib eye into her mouth. "Thank you," I say as I go to cut my own steak. And even though here is a next step, a plan that is bigger and full of more possibilities and more ambitious than anything *I'd* ever dared to dream for myself, handed to me on the most silver of platters, I hear myself say, "I *will* think about it."

That night, I light my favorite mahogany-and-lavender candle, wrap myself in my couch throw, sit down at my laptop, and open the draft—which I haven't so much as glanced at since sending it to Clarissa—and try to see it through her eyes.

"So what's he like?"

Those are the four words I've had thrown my way the most frequently over the past few months. Everyone wants to know what *he* is like.

"Who? Oh, you mean Tyler?" I sometimes reply casually.

When my editor first offered me this assignment, I was very aware that this was a once-in-a-lifetime opportunity; and while some things that initially feel like once-in-a-lifetime opportunities can turn out to be boring or regretful, shadowing Tyler Tun for two months has not been one of them.

Those two months were the first time he was back in Yangon after one and a half years away. He's here to shoot (part of) *Guns, Bars, and Getaway Cars* with his costar and real-life best friend May Diamond—which, if somehow you missed the million or so announcements about it, is the latest action-slash–romantic comedy film on his résumé. It is a movie that is big and fun and exciting and leaves you grinning as the cinema lights come back on and you brush stray popcorn kernels off of your jeans. In other words, it is the film equivalent of Tyler's personality.

Because the thing about Tyler Tun is, you get exactly the person you imagined, but also you don't, because you get *more*. He is the perfect casting choice for any action flick or romantic comedy, the actor that walks into the room and the casting agent immediately goes, "Yes. Him," before instructing their assistant to get rid of the other waiting hopefuls. Because there is no point in seeing who else will walk through the door.

I think that's it: "Yes. Him," is precisely what you think when he walks through a door, that door, or even this door, or any door. Yes. Him. Of course. Who else could it have been?

Yes.

Him.

Him, who is as handsome and charming and kind as he appears on your TV or laptop screen or whatever your streaming device of choice is, and also him who is sarcastic and silly and, frankly, easily tipsy. He is the diamond of every season, but he is also the friend who asks if you want to ditch the party and drives the two of you to the nearest McDonald's. He is soft with his emotions and hard in his convictions, generous with his time but careful with his trust.

Yes, naturally, him. Always him.

I get it now. It's been over two months since I last saw him, and all I can think about still is him.

Tyler is the kind of person that, when he looks you straight in the eye and tells you, "I've got you," the words imprint in your mind for hours that become days that become weeks that become months, because it feels like a lifetime promise, one that you can cash in anytime, anywhere.

To know Tyler Tun is to wonder how you ever moved through this world unaffected by his existence. To know him is to love him, love every single part of him, from the etched crow's-feet on his ridiculously perfect face, to the way his shoulders shake when he belts out a laugh, to the fact that his favorite song is Tina Turner's "The Best." Loving him is warm and slow, not in a stilted way, but sweet, warm honey taking its time melting and spreading; it is love that grows and grows, and just when you think you cannot be any more infatuated with a single person, grows some more when he does something that you thought only fictional men in romance novels did. I suspect he is the type of person who texts you "good morning" every day without fail because you once mentioned that you think it's cute when people do that. I suspect if you fall asleep on his shoulder in a taxi, he carefully holds your head steady so that you're not jostled awake by a speed bump. I suspect he picks you up at the airport and pulls you into him with a "There's my girl," regardless of how delayed your flight is. That if he has to leave town early in the morning, he unloads the dishwasher so that you have clean mugs ready for your morning coffee. I suspect he never lets you down, not once.

Perhaps this is a conversation I should have with my editor, but frankly, I don't know how to distill Tyler Tun, and specifically the Tyler that I now know, into a single article. I could have spent three more months to three decades with him, and it still would not be enough time, because every time I learned something new about him, I would once again be overwhelmed by the fact that a person like this exists. After all, scientists have spent centuries studying the sun and yet they are not done, they will probably never be done, never get to a point where they go, "Okay, we know all there is to know."

It is only fitting, then, that the world revolves around him, because that's what Tyler is: the sun. Warm and bright and beautiful, commanding attention wherever he goes. When he walks into a room and the whispers of "Is that—?" start, the only thing I now think is *Of course. Who else could it be?*

Yes. Him.

Twenty-three

I didn't think you'd pick up," I say, startled.

A beat. "I almost didn't."

"How are you?" I get up from the couch and power walk over to the window, then make a U-turn and head for the dining table. "How's LA?" I ask. In retrospect, I should've prepared for what to do if she *did* answer.

"What do you want, Khin?" May's tired sigh makes it clear that there's a timer on this conversation, and I'm guessing it's not very long.

"I need to talk to him," I say in a breathless rush.

She barks out a laugh. "Why? Because you need more gossip for your article?" I don't have a response. "Why are you calling *me* anyway?"

"Oh come on, that's the oldest test in the book. Thou shalt not reach out for reconciliation without first getting best friend approval."

There's another pause during which I want to say I can hear

her smile, but that could very well be wishful thinking. "This isn't up to me."

"But you know him better than anyone. If you don't think I'm good for him, then I'm not."

"How do you expect me to respond to that?" May scoffs. "That I'm still rooting for you two? That I've been waiting around for you to call me and ask me exactly this so I can orchestrate some big romantic reunion for you? You used him."

I watch my reflection blink back tears. "I know I messed up. When I took this assignment, when he met me, when *you* met me, I was in a bad place, although I didn't want to acknowledge it. And I'm not making excuses for myself. I kept telling myself that Tyler would understand because he was an actor, a celebrity, that this was his job. And I was a journalist, and this was *my* job."

"He's not *just* an actor, Khin," May snaps. "You think it was bad to have your friends and family judge you for your divorce? Try having the whole world judge you anytime you mess up, even just a little bit. And try doing that with the weight of *representation* on your shoulders. Actors like me and Tyler aren't allowed to say the wrong thing, or make one drunken mistake. Even on our worst day, we have to act like we're the happiest, most resilient people in the world. Every. Day," she says, sounding like she's talking through gritted teeth. "We have to act like we're *so* grateful for what these white producers and casting directors and magazine editors have given us."

"May—"

"He *trusted* you," she says with a quiet rage that gives me chills. "He'd tell me, *No, May, she's different. She understands.* Which I guess you did, right? You understood exactly what you needed to do to get a shiny magazine job. He risked everything he had and helped you cover up a *murder*—" She hisses out the last word. "—because he believed you were a good person. And even after *that*, you still kept up that cruel board of yours, still kept trying to find a malicious scoop so you'd get ahead in your career. So excuse me if I don't care that you felt like your job was all you had left. You're not some fresh-faced intern looking to break into the industry. If you were actually good at your job, you'd know that a good story doesn't come at the cost of exploiting someone's trust."

She sounds like she's started crying. I know I deserve every word that she's said, but that doesn't make the pain easier to bear. "You're right," I say. "Everything you just said is all true. I fucked up, okay? No one has fucked up harder in the history of fuck-ups. But all I'm begging for is a second chance. I'd decided a long time ago that I wasn't going to publish any of his secrets, *way* before he found that stupid whiteboard that I'd completely forgotten about. I'm telling the truth, I swear. I'm only asking for one more chance, please."

There's another long pause. Finally, she speaks one word: "Why?"

"Because," I say, dropping my forehead to the windowpane. "I have seen him at his best and his worst, and I can tell you right now that nobody will love him the way I do, as much as I do. I want *him*, May. I want him right now while he's at the top of his game and he's turning down Bond." May's scoff makes me flinch, but I continue, "And I would still want him if the whole world turned against him tomorrow, and I'll still want him when nobody remembers his name. I don't want *Tyler Tun*. I want just *him*."

I hold my breath. I don't have anything else left to say, no pleas left in me. And I meant what I'd said: I'm not calling Tyler until—*unless*— May forgives me first. If I really know him, if I truly care about him, then I should care about what May thinks, too.

"He's there."

I straighten so quickly that I lose my balance and stumble a few steps. "What do you mean he's . . . there? Or here? *Here* here?"

"He flew back a few days ago. Surprised Jess for her birthday."

After a beat, she says, having checked, "It's today, actually. Her birth-day. They're having a party at his apartment."

"What? He's been here this whole time?" I feel like someone pushed me onto a merry-go-round that's going a hundred miles an hour.

"Like I said, he wanted to surprise his sister for her birthday. But if I'm being honest." She hesitates for a few seconds. "I think it was also because he missed you." Another pause. "He showed me the draft."

I can't tell if my heart rate has accelerated or flatlined. "He . . . did? Wait . . . what? How? How did you—"

"Clarissa forwarded it."

"She . . . did?" I ask, unable to remember any words that contain more than one syllable. "Why?"

"Beats me. She just wrote something like, *Thought you should see this.*" Of course that's all Clarissa wrote. "You didn't include it. His retirement, I mean," May states as though she's testing my response to see if this is yet another one of my tricks.

"No." I swallow. "I couldn't. Even if I never saw him again, I needed him to know that I didn't print any of the things he told me in confidence. That he didn't mean *nothing* to me. Almost the complete opposite, really."

She lets out a frustrated sigh, the sound of someone accepting a reality they've tried to change at every point possible, but has chosen defeat. "He misses you. He's like a teenager who's fallen in love for the first time. Hard, fast, can't-eat, can't-sleep shit. It's honestly verging on pathetic. I've caught him staring at your name in his contacts list for several solid minutes. He listens to this one Taylor Swift song on repeat. That one you guys danced to," she clarifies, but she doesn't need to, because I already knew which one. My mouth stretches into a grin. "You know how I said Tyler doesn't know what he wants?"

I nod. Realizing she can't see me, I mumble a soft "Mm-hmm?"

"Well, he wants you, Khin. I've never been surer of anything when it comes to him. But I need to make sure that this idea of you, this idea of a relationship with you that he wants? It's actually who you are and what you can give him, and not just an idealistic dream that you've planted in his head so that he'll put his guard down."

"It's not," I promise. "I *do* love him. Please, I need to talk to him. *I* reread my own draft last night, and, well, it turns out it's pretty obvious that I'm kind of pathetically in love when it comes to him, too."

May chuckles. "Well, last time I checked, you had a car *and* his address."

"Should I . . . wait until the party's over?"

"If I know Tyler as well as I think I do," May says, and I *know* that she's smiling this time. "He's not going to want to wait another second to see you."

Tyler's doorman instantly recognizes me and gives me a wave.

"Here for the party?" he asks as I wait for the elevator.

"Yep," I respond with my biggest party-ready smile.

Even if I hadn't already known it was the last apartment on the left, the muffled sound of people and music would've given it away. I stride over, ring the doorbell once, and wait. And wait. I ring it again, twice this time. More waiting. Still no one. Finally, I press down on it for four seconds and, to make sure, knock on the door once, twice, thr—

It opens.

It's not Tyler at the door, but I place the face immediately. She's more muscular, and she's grown out her hair and has a full face of (stunning) makeup, but it's her. "Jess! Happy birthday!" I say, clocking the white-and-gold BIRTHDAY GIRL sash slung across her. "I don't know if you remem—"

"Oh my god, Khin!" Jess throws her arms around me. "It's been *ages*. What are—"

"Hey, who's at—" comes a voice from beside her, and the door opens slightly more.

And there he is. Blue jeans and a white polo shirt. Simple. Clean. Unadorned. So *him*.

Tyler's face cycles through joy to surprise to confusion before ending on an expression that's more serious than I'm comfortable with. The grin that he'd been approaching Jess with is gone. His brows are knitted, caution threading into his every vein.

"Hi," I say.

"Hi," Tyler says.

"I . . . heard you were in town."

The sight of his half smile makes my heart soar. "You *are* a good journalist," he says, then motions back behind him with his eyes. "I'm a little busy right now. If this is about the story, can you email—"

"It's not about the story," I blurt out.

"Oh."

"Can we please talk?"

"Yes," Jess cuts in. Before either of us knows what's happening, she takes Tyler's hand and drags him out into the hallway, closing the door with her other hand.

"Jess—" Tyler warns, but she waves him off.

"Thank *god* you're here," she says to me. "He has been absolutely *miserable* to be around, you have no idea. All he does is fucking mope. Between you and me, we've been saying that if this is how he's going to be all the time, then maybe he *shouldn't* move back home after retiring."

Tyler scoffs but, like me, a smile slips through. "Jess, I don't think this is the right time to be—"

"Jesus Christ, Ty!" She spins on her feet and snaps her fingers as though trying to snap him out of a trance. "I get it, Khin messed up. But good god, have *you* never made a single mistake ever in your whole entire life? Besides, you saw the draft. Khin didn't even mention your secrets! Any of them! Now can you please get off of your mopey high horse and listen to what she has to say?"

"I—"

"It's my birthday!"

Tyler cocks an eyebrow, but his demeanor makes it clear that he's going to give in because she has *always* had him wrapped around her finger. "You're pulling the birthday card right now?"

Jess points at the rectangular piece of white-and-gold satin draped across her. "I'm the one wearing the BIRTHDAY GIRL sash, aren't I? Now—" She points at the apartment door. "I'm going to go back in there, and we are cutting the cake in approximately half an hour, and you are going to stop being such a doofus." With a wave at me, she adds, "Hope you like red velvet, Khin!" before marching back toward the apartment and muttering under her breath, "Do I really have to do everything around here, even on my birthday?"

And then she's gone, and it's just the two of us in the middle of the long hall.

"So," I say, trying my hardest not to grin at what just transpired. "I see Jess is as . . . *independent* as always."

"Clearly," he says through a chuckle. He slides one hand inside the pocket of his trousers and the other through his hair, and, as embarrassing as it sounds, I'm not prepared for how my heart tries to thud its way out of my rib cage the second he looks up from the floor and locks eyes with me. "Hi" is all he says, except it's him, so it's enough to make me forget to breathe.

"Hey." He opens his mouth to respond, but I keep talking before I lose the nerve. "No, I need to speak first. I need to . . . say everything I have to say, and then *you* say what you have to say, okay?"

He nods, eyes burning with something I can't describe.

"When we first met, I was in . . . *not* a good place. Some might even say the *worst* place I've ever been in my life. My husband had left me, and it was like dominos—I lost my marriage, then my house, and then our mutual friends who would alternate between acting weird and being nosy and asking me *how I was,* and all I wanted to do was leave all of it behind. That's what Singapore was for me. It was a way out. A lifeline. And then right when I thought things couldn't get any worse, I went and killed someone. Everything was falling apart. Everything *had* fallen apart. When that thing at the park happened, I thought that that was it, that everything was done. But you—" I attempt a smile, shaky as it may be. "—kept me going. When I was down on my knees, you picked me up and carried the both of us on your back. And even though I was *so* scared—because what did I know about you apart from what I'd read in magazines?—I had no choice but to trust you. And the truth is, I kept waiting for you to let me down. I kept waiting for you to turn me in, or at the very least, wash your hands of me. I kept waiting for *you* to be just another thing in my life that didn't work out. Another domino that fell. But you weren't. You stayed and even when I tried to push you away, you still stayed. You *never* let me down."

"Of course I stayed, Khin," he says, voice just as ragged as mine. "We were on the same team. At least, *I* thought we were."

"We were, Tyler. I *am* on your team. I'm, like, the head cheer-leader!"

His laugh is a dazzling electrical storm. "I read your draft."

"And?"

"Why didn't you include the story? I gave you permission. That job would change your life. It would've been—" He swallows hard. "—your lifeline."

"If I can't write a good article without including a secret that you told me in confidence, then I'm not a good writer. I'm a journalist, not a paparazzo. Turns out, Clarissa agrees, and she offered me the job."

The smile that had been growing on his mouth halts. Then, remembering social protocol, he lets out a "Congratulations!"

The forced nature of his expression sparks something in me. I shake my head. "I'm not taking it."

"You're not taking the job?" he echoes, face raging with warring emotions.

"No."

"The *Vogue* job? Khin, if this is because of me, I don't—"

I take a step toward him. "I became a journalist because I wanted to write stories that matter. Don't get me wrong, they cover a lot of important stories. I'm not saying that fashion magazines like *Vogue* don't matter because we both know that's just misogynistic bullshit merely based on the fact that they have a primarily female fanbase."

"Of course," he agrees, smile returning.

"But they don't write the kind of stories that *I* want to write. I want to continue writing stuff like that abortion piece. You know, more stories about people that most mainstream media overlook but that readers need to know about. I don't want a career of hanging out with celebrities or backstage at fashion shows or, and no offense, more movie sets. Those things are so boring! God help me if I ever have to watch you run through a park one more fucking time. And there's so much waiting! My feet hurt and you don't have enough bathrooms and I don't get to drive my own car. And I have to watch each scene, like, fifteen times! I practically have the whole script memorized by this point!"

Tyler laughs at my pained expression. "So what're you going to do now?" he asks. "What do you want to do . . . next?"

I grimace. "Will it ruin the moment if I say, ideally, *you?*"

He lets out another unfettered laugh, and my god, if that isn't my favorite sound in the world. "It's the truth, you know," I say. "I want to make out with you and drive around with you and *be* with you. I want to cook with you and I want to take out the trash and pay taxes and slow dance to Taylor Swift songs with you. I love you, Tyler. I love you so much it's *embarrassing* for someone as hot and successful as myself."

He startles at my saying the word, but I don't; it's the easiest, most natural thing I've ever done. "You . . . love me," he says, voice petering out, like he can't quite believe it, which *I* can't believe. How could anyone *not* love him? Wonderful, brilliant, generous him.

"I love you," I repeat. "You are my favorite person in the whole world, and not just because you helped me try to get away with murder, although that did put you ahead of the pack."

He smiles faintly, but I can tell that he's distracted. He's turning over my words, coming at them from all angles. "I want to believe everything you're saying, Khin, I *really* do," he finally says, face torqued with anguish. "But I—" He takes a deep breath. "You hurt me. It hurt to know that every minute we'd spent together turned out to be just an opportunity for you to get something *from* me. Out of everyone who's ever turned their backs on me or used me, none of them hurt me like you did."

"I know," I say, because I do, because I can see it in every single line and dimple and scar on his face. "I meant every word of that article. You are the best person I've ever met, and you have this big, golden heart, and I know you trusted me and I'm sorry I broke that trust. I am so, so sorry. I can't go back in time and undo that, but I'm trying my best to show you that it's not going to happen again.

"Because here's the thing," I say, moving closer so that there's nothing separating us. I take it as a good sign that he doesn't move away. In fact, I observe his body start to relax like he's come home after a long trip, and realize that mine is doing the same, too. "I could tell you every single day just how much I love you, but ultimately, it won't matter if you don't trust me. And I know what it's like to love someone and still not have it work out in the end, but you know what, I have a *really* good gut feeling about us, and I want us to at least give it our all. This doesn't work if we don't trust that we will be right there by each other's side from morning to night and then all over again when we wake up the next day—which I will. Every. Single. Day. Through your highest highs and your shittiest lows. I *love* you, Tyler, and I will never, ever lie to you again." I raise a finger. "Well, unless if it's about, say, your birthday present. Then I'll probably lie my ass off, but only because I want to surprise you, because making you smile is one of my favorite things to do."

He grins, and in retrospect, my heart never stood a chance. Slowly, tenderly, he comes closer, his palms mold around my cheeks, thumb brushing away my tears before he leans down to press a kiss to my forehead. "You cannot imagine how much I've missed you," he says, and I am acutely aware that this scene feels like something you only get in the movies. He tilts my head upward so he can look me straight in the eye. "I love you, too. I wanted to call you so many times, but it seemed like you'd made up your mind about us, and that was that."

"You should've called. I would've answered," I whisper. "I'll always answer."

"I have spent the last few months searching for the back of your head in every crowd," he says before tipping farther down and closing his lips onto mine.

He tastes exactly how I remember, and when his hands slide down my shoulders and along my back before settling at the base of my spine, it sets off a thousand tiny explosions all through my body. It seems impossible that we've only ever kissed twice before because this feels so comfortable, like I've been doing it for years and years, like what *else* would we have been doing ever since we met?

"I love you," I say when we pull apart for air, and already, I want to repeat it to him over and over again, so that he never forgets. So that he never, not even for a second, has a reason to believe otherwise.

"I love you so much, you have no idea," he murmurs. "Even if you guilt-tripped me into selling my private jet."

I gasp. "You what?"

He rolls his eyes. "Apparently it *is* dreadful for the environment."

"Tyler Tun," I say, jutting out my bottom lip. "And here I thought I possibly couldn't love you any more."

"There I go, wrecking your plans again, huh?"

I snake my fingers through his hair and give him a soft tug closer. "That's my man," I whisper into his mouth.

I t was nearing 1 A.M. when all the parents and aunts and uncles and cousins and second cousins had left and we were completely, *finally*, alone.

"Dishes?" I ask, making for the kitchen.

"They can wait until the morning," Tyler says. I yelp in surprise at the feel of his arm snaking around my waist and pulling me back into his rib cage, although it only takes half a second for my body to fully settle into him. "I have a small surprise."

I shift my face to look up at his. "A surprise?"

He nods, and, moving his hand to the small of my back, directs both of us to his bedroom.

I do as I'm instructed, which is to sit in the middle of the bed and close my eyes. Right as my brain is about to have a *Fuck me, I'm in Tyler's bed* meltdown, I hear rustling, followed by slight grunting, followed by Tyler hurriedly reassuring me, "Don't worry, I'm fine, just keep those eyes closed," followed by a soft yet heavy thud on the spot on the duvet right in front of me.

"Okay, you can open them," he says, and when I do, he's standing at the foot of the bed, a giant cardboard box separating the two of us.

"Wha—" I begin, but he hands me a pair of scissors.

"It's all compostable, don't worry," he says. At my confused look, he motions at me to cut through the tape. I oblige as he keeps talking. "Obviously I didn't want them to break, but my now ex-jet and I both know how important sustainability is to you, so I made sure everything was recyclable, down to the tape."

"Didn't want what to break?" I ask. His playful half smirk is the only answer I receive. I lift open the top flaps, and am stunned—less in an *Awwww* manner and more in an *Uhhhh* manner—as a jumble of brown crinkled packing paper awaits me. "Tyler, you . . . got me packing paper?" I widen my eyes and jut my bottom lip out at him. "You shouldn't have!"

He rolls his eyes, but that delightful mouth of his has unfurled into something sincere and warm and uncontrollable, and I want to reach out and kiss it. "Take one out."

Upon closer inspection, the box is filled with an assortment of several items that have been neatly and very tightly wrapped in the paper. "Let me guess," I say, reaching for one in the middle and unraveling the wrapping. "You got me a selection of the finest vibrators money can buy."

He snorts in what is the most un-Hollywood gesture I've ever seen or heard him make. All he says, though, with a shake of his head is, "Woman."

"It's . . . a mug." A mug that is white and speckled with tiny natural black clay dots, and features large carved cherry blossoms and floating green leaves all around.

I grab another random tangle of packing paper and undo it to reveal another mug, this one black and glossy with a shiny navy sheen circling the rim. The next one is a speckled matte pistachio color with a ridged exterior. The fourth, another white one, has the words SEE YOU AT HOME carved into three lines.

"Tyler," I say as I trace the sand-colored words. I don't realize I'm crying until a gray spot lands on the *U* and trickles down. "What is this?" I ask, half laughing. "You . . . got me mugs?"

He crawls around to sit beside me. "It's cheesy, I know, but . . . you said you wanted mugs."

"So you . . . got me mugs?"

"Khin—" His thumb gently wipes away the wet trail on one of my cheeks, then the next. "That's how this works. You said you wanted mugs," he repeats simply.

"So you got me mugs." I state it this time, because I understand now.

"It would appear that way."

I will love you forever, I think.

"What if we'd never run into each other again?" I ask. "What would you have done with this, frankly, obscene number of mugs?" There must be at least fifteen here. *At least.*

"I would've still gotten them to you somehow," he says with a shrug. "They weren't about me anyway. They were about you. Then again, Khin, everything"—the sound of my name on his tongue reverberates through every corner of my brain, my lungs, my heart. He tucks my hair behind both my ears, and I close my eyes when he leans forward and kisses my forehead, and it's no longer that I can't believe that Tyler Tun is kissing me, but that I can't believe that Tyler, my absolute *favorite* person, is kissing me—"was always about you."

I grab his face in both hands and bring his mouth down to mine.

"It was always about you, too," I murmur, our lips still grazing, eyes mapping out our new homes in the other's. "You shook my hand in that wonton restaurant in Chinatown, and I was never the same."

"I don't think this was in the script."

I give his bottom lip a gentle tug before shooting him a conspiratorial smile. "Fuck the script."

Acknowledgments

This is the best job in the world, and my exceptional agent, Hayley Steed, will always be the person who made it all possible. When I first did a complete genre one-eighty and pitched her "a rom-com with murder," her immediate, unabashed enthusiasm gave me the courage to dive headfirst and just go for it. H—thank you for cheering me on through all the terrible first (and second, and third) drafts. I really lucked out in the agenting and friend departments.

This book has had the unusually delightful experience of having been in the hands of multiple editors, which is wild to me because for so long, I was certain not even *one* editor would want to publish a romance novel with Myanmar characters and set in my beloved hometown. So, thank you, thank you, thank you, Lisa Bonvissuto, Alexa Allen-Batifoulier, Amy Mae Baxter, and Christina Demosthenous, for loving this book and all the characters in it as much as I do. Thank you for being so meticulous with your edits, and for pushing me to make it funnier, sharper, swoonier, and just generally *better* (and, coincidentally, to use fewer italics).

Thank you to Vi-An Nguyen for a gorgeous cover that really captured my girl. Immense gratitude to everyone at St. Martin's Press who helped bring this book to life, especially Kerri Resnick, Meryl Levavi, Ciara Tomlinson, Marissa Sangiacomo, Ken Silver, Jeremy Haiting, and Sara Thwaite. And at Renegade, all my thanks to Sharmaine Lovegrove, Millie Seaward, Emily Moran, Sarah Pearson, Narges Nojoumi, Megan Phillips, Amy Patrick, Anne Goddard, Bryony Hall, Sasha Duszynska Lewis, Caitriona Row, Dominic Smith, Frances Doyle, Hannah Methuen, Lucy Hine, Toluwalope Ayo-Ajala, Kellie Barnfield, Millie Gibson, Sanjeev Braich, Andrew Smith, and Ellie Barry; I know Khin would be delighted that her story is being published by a young, bold imprint called "Renegade."

Thank you to my weird and hilarious family who cheers me on like no other. Mommy, most people *think* that they have the best mom, but I *know* that I have the best mom in the whole world. I love being your buddy.

It's so easy for me to give my main characters friends who demonstrate nothing short of unbounded, unconditional love, because that's what I've experienced my whole life. For responding to my texts/calls/emails with steadfast patience and kindness over the years, thank you: Hibba, Katie (and Babka), Noah, Cailey, Shoon Lei, Mra, Nanda, Christian, Marina, Jamie.

S, you know how much you mean to me. Thank you for always, *always* showing up, for having my back through any and everything. I can't wait to show you your book.

Corey, who changed everything when I least saw it coming. Thank you for knowing when (and how) to help me stay grounded and when to give me that small push, and for being so funny and hot and great with dogs. Love you so much you have no idea, pal.

And KHS, who lent me her name for this book, and her ear and heart for the entirety of our friendship. How lucky I am to have someone as generous and fearless as you as my best friend.

About the Author

Josh Sullivan

Pyae Moe Thet War is the author of the essay collection *You've Changed*. Born and raised in Yangon, Myanmar, she holds a BA from Bard College at Simon's Rock, and MAs from both the University College London and the University of East Anglia. She currently shares a home (and her food) with her dogs, Gus and Missy. *I Did Something Bad* is her debut novel.